The Forgotten Girls

BOOKS BY LIZZIE PAGE

The War Nurses
Daughters of War
When I Was Yours

Lizzie Page

The Forgotten Girls

Bookouture

Published by Bookouture in 2020

An imprint of Storyfire Ltd.
Carmelite House
50 Victoria Embankment
London EC4Y 0DZ

www.bookouture.com

ISBN: 978-1-83888-128-3
eBook ISBN: 978-1-83888-127-6

'The pictures are there, and you just take them.'
Robert Capa

PROLOGUE

NORFOLK, MAY 1950

The girls were behaving better than usual, which was a relief. Recently they had been arguing over what was black and what was white and if the moon was made of cheese. Elaine hadn't slept a wink. She didn't think she could handle it if they kicked off, not today.

She was hardly able to keep herself together, never mind them.

The girls laughed over breakfast. Barbara pretended her crumpet was a grizzly bear named Tony, who was afraid of jam. They giggled in the bathroom when Shirley got toothpaste down her Peter Pan collar, then they laughed all the way down the road.

They were under strict instructions to 'be good or else' but that never made much difference when they were in one of their moods: perhaps they were more chirpy than usual because they had been outdoors so much yesterday. Elaine knew she didn't take them outside enough. She remembered her mother used to say that children needed fresh air same as puppies. She did try, but so often life got in the way.

Not now though. They were on holiday, and the girls skipped, their long legs flashing under their simple smocks and their socks sparkling white. Shirley had insisted on plaits; helpfully, Barbara had obliged. Then Barbara had tied her own hair in a simple ponytail, but it was better than her usual efforts. Elaine approved. They looked clean, fresh and forgiving. It probably wouldn't last, it never did, but for now Elaine couldn't help but feel proud of them.

*

He was already there, waiting, at the agreed time and place. His camera was round his neck, his shirt was open at the throat, he was in casual clothes. Different but the same. Same but different.

They talked about the boat first. They just dived in, like they'd been talking about the damn boat every day for the last ten years. He had it for a few days, it belonged to a friend of a friend. He'd always had friends everywhere. It was one of his things. Effortlessly popular. They really were polar opposites, Elaine reminded herself.

The boat was called *Omaha Beach*.

The girls were thrilled to look inside, but Elaine stood apart on the bank. Although she had thought she was prepared for this – hadn't it been weeks in the planning? – it still felt like she was in shock. Emotionally she was right back in those years after the Blitz when everyone was neither here nor there.

Nothing had changed. This wouldn't change anything.

The girls came back out, clamouring to swim in the canal. Barbara went to the municipal pool with school – she had her 25-metres badge – and Shirley would go next year. It wasn't cheap, but Elaine thought it was just about worth it.

Elaine thought of all the bother a swim would entail, and she lied – she said it wasn't allowed.

He started to say, 'Oh, but it is—' but when he saw her expression, he agreed. 'You never know what's in there, girls.'

In a lower voice, he said to Elaine, 'They can dip their feet in though, can't they?'

'*Pur-lease*!' the girls begged like their lives depended on it. 'Can we, Mother?'

Elaine would normally say no, they knew that, she knew that. She couldn't say it now though, not in front of him, so she nodded just the once and they pulled off their shoes and peeled off their socks, rapidly, afraid she'd change her mind.

They paddled, got muddy, and Barbara's hair got messy, but Elaine refrained from saying anything. She wouldn't get wound up today.

*

They walked. The girls carried their shoes and socks and their feet got gritty. Elaine just about resisted saying, 'I told you so'.

While the girls stood ahead of them, he took a photograph of them. Elaine laughed. He couldn't just take a photo of them from the front like everyone else would.

'I'll send it to you,' he said.

'No, send it to Annie,' she replied, and he nodded. He understood.

He seemed very foreign here in Norfolk, more than he ever had in London. Maybe he was, or maybe she just hadn't noticed back then.

He showed them wispy dandelions and plump buttercups. 'Who likes butter?'

'Everyone in the world,' answered Barbara, making him laugh. Elaine blushed. Shirley shook her head, looking to Elaine for approval. 'Butter makes you fat.'

They were still on the ration, but he had packed bread, cheese and chocolate for the girls.

The girls started arguing over ladybugs and caterpillars and which were better. He told them to try to collect one of each and they ran off squealing.

'Stay where I can see you,' Elaine commanded, but they didn't know what she could see, or else they actually believed she had eyes in the back of her head – well, she'd told them that often enough.

Elaine was both petrified and delighted to be alone with him at last. Not until the girls were properly occupied collecting insects did she let him take her hand in his. It felt like a homecoming. Did he feel like that too?

Those dark eyes on her again after all this time. They were filled with tears. He always cried so easily, unlike her.

Did he know what she was thinking? Did she know what he was thinking?

'I miss Marty,' he said.

CHAPTER ONE

LONDON, SEPTEMBER 1943

'Robert Capa's in town.'

Despite the KEEP CALM AND CARRY ON poster right over their heads, Elaine's usually placid workmates were in a tizz. They were supposed to be typing up prisoner of war letters smuggled out from Asia, but Annie set down her papers and stalked between the desks making sure everyone had got the message.

'I thought he was in El Alamein?' said Felicity.

'Nope, he's definitely here,' said Annie.

'Really? NOW?'

'Yes, now. Well, tonight-now.'

'He'll be at the George?'

'Absolutely.'

Elaine stopped typing but left her fingers suspended over the keys, each one poised for activity. The E, the H and the N were fading fast due to overuse. As a young girl, Elaine had dreamed of playing the piano. Sometimes when she was in full flow, she imagined the typewriter keys were piano keys, the clatter, clatter was a symphony and the girls around her were the orchestra.

Listlessly, she poked the keys a few more times as Annie buzzed around the room, and then she too succumbed.

'What *is* Robert Capa then?'

Everyone laughed.

'What is Robert Capa?' repeated Annie incredulously. She stopped prowling and went back to her home-chair. Annie and Elaine's desks were so close, Elaine could swipe pencils from Annie's glass ashtray without her noticing. Annie rubbed her hands together, delighted at her best friend's naivety. 'Have you been living in a cave, Elaine? Robert Capa is the most agreeable man in all of London.'

The George was the public house on the corner of Wardour Street and everyone was going to meet there at five. Elaine demurred, 'I should get this letter done...' but her heart wasn't in work and it seemed like no one else's was either.

The thing was they hadn't *needed to get anything done* for months. During the Blitz, their vast office had found itself a headquarters for the war effort. The clerical girls were charged with marking on great maps where the bombs fell, and sometimes they didn't leave their positions until the sun was rising over the city, bleak, orange and shamefaced.

From six in the evening, the calls came from emergency centres across the city and the clerical girls started plotting them. Sometimes, you could hear the German planes coming over and the actual bombs going off. Sometimes you heard the name of an area where you knew someone lived or where someone's mother lived, and you just had to cross your fingers and hope they'd got down to the shelters in time.

There was nine months of that, nine long months of autumn through to summer 1941. Sometimes it felt like Elaine was holding her breath the whole while. It was a relentless time – and she would never say it aloud, but it was an exciting time too. Exciting and terrible. Straight out of secretarial college, thrust into that crazy new world, she wouldn't have believed it was possible if she hadn't been there.

Clerical girls catnapped in the day, ate on the move, and mostly talked about fires and numbers of casualties. It soon became horribly apparent that twenty dead was *not too bad a night.* On the way home – those early mornings – Elaine might see the fruits of the devastation that she had been assiduously logging: the shock of the newly homeless, the bravery of firemen still picking up burning timber, the unforgettable sight of a bewildered family dog.

Since the worst of the bombings was over, the girls had been moved up to the third floor, and they could stand outside the office in the open air. Yes, there were still doodlebugs to worry about – doodlebugs was the pretty name for the latest horror, the V-2 bomber. But with the doodlebugs, there was no escape, no warning, no logic and because it was so random, it bizarrely didn't affect morale quite so much. It was a different threat to the actual Blitz. Now, the clerical girls could smoke leisurely cigarettes in their own time. They could walk unfettered in the daytime, they could sleep (almost) untraumatised at night in their own beds, they could chat with friends in the street, but the trouble was: there was some slight uncertainty at work about what exactly they were all there *for*.

Correction: *great* uncertainty.

Every day, Elaine's uncertainty fattened up like a goose approaching Christmas. She'd worked so hard to get into clerical, they couldn't just let her go. It wouldn't be fair. The other clerical girls had come across to government from studying degrees in philosophy or English at Cambridge or Oxford. Even Annie had come from a great position managing a department at Selfridges. They had talents and successes, or three languages, they had places to go on to. Whatever way they went, they would advance. Elaine, by contrast, felt like she had crawled her way up out of the mud. And she didn't want to go back.

'C'mon, *you've got to* meet Robert Capa.'

Felicity, who usually made it her business to disagree with most things that came out of Annie's mouth, *and* had a bronze trophy for debating, surprisingly agreed.

'Oh, Elaine, I can't believe you haven't met him before.'

Before she could reply, Annie called out: 'She was ill when he was here, remember?'

Felicity didn't. Why would she keep tabs on Elaine's constitution? But two months after the Blitz, Elaine had gone down with a bout of appendicitis. It must have been around that time.

'You will love him, Elaine.'

'All the ladies love him.'

Felicity winked at Annie, who retorted, 'And the not-so-ladies.'

'Elaine's only got eyes for Justin,' said Myra gently. Elaine smiled at her. Myra was such a sweetheart (and proficient in English, French and Mandarin).

'No harm in making new friends, right, girls?' said Annie chirpily. Myra lowered her eyes, chastened.

'Mr Capa is actually a very agreeable man,' Mrs Dill joined in – this too was unnerving, for Mrs Dill (office manager and accomplished flautist) rarely had a good word to say about anyone. Indeed, 'agreeable' was a great compliment from her permanently pursed lips. However, all this anticipation about the prodigal mystery man, all this *insistence* was making Elaine less, rather than more, keen to meet him. She wasn't just being contrary – although that was maybe some of it. Everything about this Robert Capa felt over-egged: it reminded her of that film *Mrs. Miniver* – posters for it everywhere, yet when you saw it, you were left completely flat. And another thing, Annie had a history of introducing Elaine to people she was certain Elaine would love and she had a dubious track record.

'Will Marty be there?' asked Felicity.

'Robert Capa is never without Marty,' said Annie knowingly. 'You know that, Fee.'

'So, who's Marty then?' Elaine's interest was reluctantly piqued again. She had always been a fan of the underdog and she had a feeling this was what Marty was.

'Marty is Robert Capa's best friend. He's his loyal sidekick.'

Robert Capa got the accolades, yet Marty barely got a mention? It was a state of affairs Elaine felt familiar with.

'You make him sound like a puppy.'

'Marty is like a puppy, a greyhound maybe.'

'What does Mr Robert Capa *do* anyway?'

Other than send otherwise sane women into a tizzy.

'You don't know?'

'Nope!'

Elaine had always hated the emphasis on *what one does*. What does it tell us about the human heart? But she had learned a lot in her time in clerical. This was how society *ranked*. For the middle-class, it was the fastest way to establish who and who was not *people like us*. Anyway, she was intrigued. Most men had been conscripted by now.

Annie wore her incredulous expression again. 'He's a war photographer, Elaine… *the* war photographer. You *have* heard of him, surely?'

'Honestly, I never have,' Elaine protested, although come to think of it, a pea-sized bell was jangling in the back of her head.

'There isn't a conflict anywhere in the world he hasn't covered. The Spanish Civil War, the Japanese invasion of Manchuria… he was living in the Philippine jungles for a while.'

'Now you're making him sound like Tarzan.'

Tarzan hadn't been a disappointment. Elaine knew Johnny Weissmuller was one of Annie's crushes. Not her biggest, that honour was reserved for James Cagney, but he was top-five material.

'Funny you should say that, he *is* a bit like him.'

Elaine laughed, but Annie was being serious as she pencilled in her lips. 'But don't be getting ideas, Elaine.'

'Ideas?'

'You *know*.'

There was nothing you could say to Annie when she was like this, so Elaine got back to her letters.

*

The government office was three doors down from the building that hosted *Life* magazine, which was part of the bigger American company Life Corporation International. They were both tall, narrow red-brick buildings. The kind of building you would stand outside and think, wow.

The government office had a black double-fronted imposing door and once you were through there, you still had to get past the even more imposing Vera on reception. Vera pretended she couldn't hear anything and had an ear trumpet from the last century, but she also had an uncanny knack of overhearing anything controversial.

Everything in the government office was hush-hush, ask no questions, tell no lies. Best to creep in quietly, look around before you take off your coat, look around before you shake out your umbrella, but don't look around too much. Focus, focus. Clerical girls especially should be seen and not heard.

At Life Corporation International, by contrast, it was like they *wanted* people to know they were there. They even had a dark blue advertising sign out in the street, for heaven's sake. The journalists clipped up the steps two at a time, with worn-down shoes and wide-open mackintoshes, and sometimes a famous person would pull up in a chauffeured car while you stood there on the pavement trying to figure them out. Fact: famous people were all so much smaller than they seemed in the magazines or in the cinema. Annie always said she could fit Ginger Rogers in her handbag and President Eisenhower in her pocket. If necessary.

Elaine asked her when that would ever be necessary.

Annie said, *you never know*.

One time, Elaine and Annie came upon two worn copy-editors smoking cigars in the street. After they had whistled appreciatively, and done the obligatory 'Hello, ladies!', they said importantly, 'Do you want to know something really exciting? Churchill's just dropped by!'

Churchill wouldn't fit in anybody's pocket.

They told Annie and Elaine to go in, take a look, but sadly, Churchill had already hotfooted it out the back door by the time the girls got up to the news room.

At Life Corp. everything was out there, offered up to you like a fancy dessert on a fancy plate. *This must be what America is like*, Elaine imagined longingly: Freedom. Openness. Fish tanks in the hall. A meritocracy. A discussion where all voices were welcomed, no one shunned because they had the wrong accent, the wrong address, or the wrong kind of figure.

Life Corp. had revolving doors. You could keep going round like a three-year-old for ages and ages and no one would even stop you.

Elaine and Annie had done it. (Sixteen times, if you want to know. They only stopped because Annie thought she might be sick.)

Every corner of the George was strung with cobwebs like paper chains. It had boarded-up windows and on one of the outside walls was a daubed 'Fascists Out' from the Mosley days.

The reason it was popular was simple. It was the last pub standing. Most of the pubs in Soho had closed: either the drinkers had been conscripted, or they had been blown up. During the Blitz, most of the George's windows had been blown in, but it was the neighbouring King's Arms that took the brunt of it. Elaine remembered, the morning after a particularly heavy night's bombing, seeing Bessie, the landlady of the George, trying to console Bertha, the landlady of the King's Arms. Both were sitting amid the rubble, drinking tea out of bone china cups on saucers.

As always on a Friday evening, there were lots of people from Life Corp. and lots of people from the government offices at the George, but there was no sign of this guy Annie and the girls were making such a song and dance about.

Annie and the girls looked around them disappointedly. They were all polished up, eking out their make-up rations.

'Tarzan stood you up then?' Elaine whispered. Annie's face fell, but she refused to believe it.

'He wouldn't.'

'He's far too agreeable,' said Elaine sarcastically.

But then he was spied, helping Bessie with the barrels. He was lugging them up from the cellar for her; he'd built up a sweat in that white shirt, brown leather flying jacket and the high-waisted trousers that all the civilian fellas wore now.

Annie and the girls clapped when they saw him and called out. He unloaded the barrels on his back, went down to hump up another, then slumped into the space they'd saved for him on the velvet banquette. He grinned around at everyone delightedly, mopping his forehead with a handkerchief that Elaine, who had an eye for detail, saw was pale pink and monogrammed.

'Either those barrels are getting heavier or I'm getting weaker.'

To Elaine's surprise, Annie plumped fat kisses on his cheeks. 'Weaker? You? Never!'

Usually Annie was an advocate of the treat-them-mean, keep-them-keen school. Shocking to see her capitulate like this.

Robert Capa gave out compliments freely – the rare sort, the *noticing* sort. Oh, he *was* an agreeable man, that was obvious.

He observed the heels on Myra's shoes.

'What do they call those? Kitten heels?'

'Blister heels,' Myra retorted shyly.

'Brilliant!' He roared like he'd never heard anything funnier. Shy Myra, who no one ever joked with, gave him an appreciative smile.

He enquired about Mrs Dill's stepchildren, who had been evacuated to Wales.

She said, 'I can't understand them… Their accents are so strong now.'

'*Dim rhaid i chi ddweud caws ond mae'n helpu*,' he said.

'What's that?' Everyone leaned forward.

'You don't have to say cheese, but it helps.' He laughed. 'It's the only Welsh I know!'

He asked about Felicity's younger sister. 'Still learning the violin?'

'For my sins, yes.'

'Better than the recorder, no?'

'Every night it sounds like a cat being strangled… I reckon if the Jerrys heard, they'd turn their planes back.'

Elaine watched her colleagues having fun and it was like she was watching from somewhere far away. She felt that she was learning more about them in those few minutes than she had in all the years they'd been working together. *She* hadn't known anything about Felicity's sister's violin, or Mrs Dill's stepchildren's accents. She didn't know that trembling Myra had a sense of humour. She thought suddenly that she should ask them more questions, but whenever she tried, everyone seemed to think she was prying.

Everyone opened up to Robert Capa like blooming oysters.

A quarter of an hour passed, and Elaine found that, try as she might, she simply *couldn't* dislike him. She would have just been cutting off her nose to spite her face. But also he really was exceedingly nice and Elaine was never good at being haughty.

He had a slight accent: what was it? Austrian, Bulgarian, Italian, American, Canadian, French? He had a winning smile, just as Annie had said, and now Annie was nudging her triumphantly.

'Close your mouth, there's a double-decker coming.'

'Don't be silly.'

'I told you he was darling, didn't I?' she said knowingly.

Always had to have the last word, that was Annie all over.

'Well done, Leon. Still a full head of hair, I see…' Robert Capa said to old Leon Harper, their postman.

'I'm hanging onto it gamely – unlike you, Mr Capa!'

'With a face like this?' Robert Capa grinned broadly, part self-effacingly, part glowing with confidence – 'who needs hair?!'

'I don't think we've met before,' Elaine said when it was her turn to take his attention. She held out her gloved hand and as she did so, she felt what a peculiarly old-fashioned and English gesture it was, while he was so fresh and exotic.

'I'd definitely recall if we had.' His hand was warm and hung onto hers for longer than necessary.

Elaine laughed. His eyes were dark, long-lashed and compelling, even in the smoke-fug. She had to force herself to look away.

He said he liked her gloves.

'They're beautiful quality.'

Of all the things he could have said! Elaine blushed. Looking expensive was a preoccupation of hers. She didn't shout it from the rooftops but another of the joys of being clerical – apart from the contribution to the war effort, of course – was dressing for the job. Even through the Blitz – when clothes were supposed to be the last things on your mind – she had kept up appearances: Elaine Parker always looked the part. It was more important to her than it was to the other girls, but then they had all those other things going for them too.

'They suit you.'

Clive had got them for her. There was no need to tell Robert Capa that carefully stitched inside the gloves was the name of their previous owner: 'Mildred Cousins'.

Here he came, Marty the faithful greyhound. He arrived by Robert Capa's side, with a tray of glasses filled to the brim with gin, and they all had to shove up. Older, blonder, paler, smaller… no, he wasn't smaller, he just *seemed* smaller. Definitely narrower in the shoulder department, but actually way taller. Six foot two or even three. Deceptively built. Rectangular wire glasses. Fragile-looking. Less energy. More Cheetah than Tarzan. Wouldn't hurt a fly. No wonder he rarely got a mention.

More and more people gathered around their banquette. Girls – pretty girls from Life Corp., all coming to have a look. Elaine was introduced to some of them: *Hello Faye and Merry*. Elaine didn't like the way Merry looked at Robert Capa with those eyes. And what on earth was the girl using for blusher? She felt strangely protective of her new friend.

'We're going dancing,' Robert Capa said. 'Won't you join us?'

He looked directly at Elaine as he said it. She gazed back at the twin peaks of his tanned, slightly shiny forehead. He wasn't typically attractive – he certainly wasn't her type – and yet… The big smile, the twinkle in the eyes, it all added up to something.

She shouldn't go. *Absolutely* not.

'Come on, Elaine, you know you love a party,' said Annie, nudging her.

Gazing at her, Robert Capa seemed to be asking even bigger questions with his puppy eyes. 'It won't be a party without you,' he said finally.

Unfortunately, her brother Clive was outside the pub as they left. Elaine tried to sneak by, but you could never sneak by Clive, especially when he was calling out, 'Elaine, over here, ELAINE!' She and Annie exchanged looks. She'd told Clive a hundred times not to come here, and definitely not to speak to her if he did.

Now Clive sat kerbside, still in his fish-stained overalls, his club foot stretched out into the road, plaintively asking people to bring him out a pint. Most ignored him, but as he often said, *you only needed one sucker to feel sorry for you.* (He'd inherited that piece of wisdom from their dad.)

'What *are* you doing here?' Elaine tried not to sound as accusing as she felt. Not because Clive didn't deserve it – he was generally up to no good – but because no one likes a woman who scolds. Everyone had left the pub now and was crowded in the street, debating whether to go on or not. Robert Capa was looking over at her curiously, more than curiously. She couldn't help knowing he was interested, even though she'd deny it to Felicity and Myra. *That's what you do, if you don't want to be arrogant.*

People talked about Elaine's body as though it were a thing separate from her– the way you might admire a cute kitten in the street. 'Curvaceous,' they said, or 'should be in the films'. It was a body that sent out a message, apparently – a veritable postal service – but it was mainly men between the ages of sixteen and sixty who felt obliged to reply. The fuss was silly. It was amusing while at the same time it could be repulsive. Sometimes, though, it had its uses. Robert Capa hadn't taken his eyes off her and it felt good. Hands on hips, Elaine turned back to her co-workers. 'Go ahead. I'll join you in a minute.'

'Don't worry, Elaine always manages to catch us up,' Annie called out.

Elaine couldn't help but think, *one day, I mightn't be able to.*

Clive was only eighteen but he had the cunning of a gangland boss twice his age, and looks many women bizarrely seemed to find appealing. *He'll go far or to jail,* their mother used to say. His club foot didn't stop him doing anything – he was so adept with a stick that he played goal for Tooting football club when they were desperate and had only missed three Charlton Athletic home matches in his life, but it had stopped him getting called up. Now, he was reaping the benefits of the lack of male competition not just for sports, or for women, but for everything.

While the Blitz was in full swing, Clive's foot didn't hold him back from breaking into houses, riffling through jewellery boxes, trampling through allotments, then 'comforting' anxious women in the underground. It was Clive who got their family the wireless and a gramophone during the Blitz and even a garden bench for Mrs Perry to sit out on downstairs, which was taken from the Devonshire pub's gardens and which the police had put up signs about.

'Where's Justin?' Curiously, Clive liked Justin, despite Justin never giving him the time of day.

Why did he have to have such a loud voice?

'Not here,' whispered Elaine. 'What is it you want?'

'Got any dosh?'

'I'll give you some later, at home.'

'I need it *now*, Elaine.'

If Elaine asked Clive for a saucepan, there would be four on the stove within the hour. Ask him for the moon and he would find you a ladder. He was very generous. Clive kept them going after Dad left. If it weren't for him there would have been no *The Quick Brown Fox Jumped Over the Lazy Dog* books, there would have been no secretarial college. There would certainly have been no clerical work in a government department – there'd have been no future for her at all. Elaine owed him. She handed over a shilling, but he looked so despondent that she dug in her purse for a second.

'I'll pay you back,' he said.

He never did.

Annie was right. Elaine never could resist a party, even on a work night, *especially* on a work night. And somehow, in a way that seemed too easy, too filmic, she was through the doors, and in a basement room, and there was Robert Capa. He was waiting for her. He was surrounded by women, all preening and smiling at him, but he had eyes only for her. She found herself next to him and they started dancing. The only thing that wasn't like being in a film was that Robert Capa turned out to be a truly terrible dancer! Who would have thought it? He was verging on the diabolical. Somehow, Elaine found herself teaching him moves. It was a mystery how he got them so wrong. It was like he found it hard to connect the music with his body, like he had no idea that *that* was the point.

'All right, put your arm round me here.'

'Here?'

'No.'

At first, she thought he couldn't possibly be that clumsy and that he was just pretending – and then she realised that, yes, actually, he *was* that clumsy.

It wasn't that Elaine was a different person when she was dancing, it was just that she felt as if she had been sleeping and then suddenly she was awake. All her senses were suddenly alive, alert and aware. Elaine lost herself to the music, the moves. If she had only known adult life could be like this, she was sure she could have had a better childhood. She would certainly have had something to look forward to and having something to look forward to would have made all the difference in the world. When she danced, she felt energised, plugged in, switched on, alight.

In a world that was dreary with sudden deaths, rationings, bad news on the wireless, dancing was the perfect antidote.

'Are you American?' It wasn't the first question she wanted to ask Robert Capa, but it was a start.

'Not quite.' He smiled back. Elaine didn't know what that meant. 'Would you prefer it if I was?'

She shrugged. *It has nothing to do with me what he is*, she told herself.

He was watching her all the time and it was as if they knew each other well; she had to remind herself that they'd only just met. She stared back, drinking him in. His eyebrows were too dark, the classic beetle baddy's brows from a children's story. His nose was too strong – was it Roman? Inherited from an emperor, quite possibly. His skin was brown, yellow, olive, white, green.

He had too many teeth for his mouth but then, look who was talking! On first impression, Elaine's teeth were excellent – indeed Annie and Myra claimed to be jealous of their straightness –but secretly, shamefully, they were like those uninhabitable houses in Whitechapel they kept talking about on the wireless: they might look all right but they could crumble at any moment. Elaine tried to remember to cover her mouth when she smiled, but she often forgot. They would be the first thing she would fix if she ever came into any money. They were a big clue to her background; she had been quick enough to work that out.

She and Robert Capa danced some more. He apologised for not being nimble enough, but it was fine, she could fill in his spaces with more movements. Twirling, whirling, obliterating this silly, silly, never-ending war.

And the thing was, she was having a better time dancing with him and his two left feet than with all the good dancers she had ever danced with put together.

It wasn't until gone midnight that she realised that the others had disappeared; even Annie had faded away some time earlier. It was too late for the underground, so Robert Capa offered to walk her home. It was with a start that she realised she was still wearing her work clothes. Usually dancing this wildly was reserved for Friday and Saturday nights, not Thursdays.

'Where is Marty?' she asked, although she didn't much care. 'I was told you two were inseparable.'

'Marty knows when he's needed and when he isn't.'

'And he's not needed now?'

He smiled, raising his beetle baddy brows at her.

Robert Capa negotiated the blackout darkness well. Elaine even let him take her hand, although it was something she usually disliked. Down and along, up and down; she only stubbed her toe twice on the kerbs and he only brushed against her a few times, apologising each time. She told him he was like a cat. He said if he had nine lives, he'd already used ten of them. He asked her if she liked cats, so she told him about Bettie Page, her tabby with unfeasibly long whiskers. He said he'd love to meet her one day.

Elaine paused, wondering whether inviting a man to see her cat was a line that was sensible to cross.

They came across some nervy police officers, who told them to watch themselves. Heard a whistle blow, but nothing came of it. Occasionally a car with no headlights would purr slowly down the street. A man wobbled by on a squeaky bicycle.

Robert Capa said that in the pub his first impression of her was that she had ginger hair.

Ginger? 'At least I'm not going bald like you,' Elaine snapped, '…anyway, I don't!'

He laughed loudly. 'Your hair *is* kind of pink.'

'No, it isn't.' Self-consciously, Elaine swiped her hand through the blonde, carefully waved hair of which she was so proud… *maybe it was?* 'Are you colour-blind?'

'A little,' he said unexpectedly. The blackout was a good thing now – he couldn't see how much she was blushing.

He didn't seem to mind though. 'Green and red. They wouldn't let me in the air force.'

'You wanted to?'

'Fly planes?' He laughed again. 'Who doesn't?'

She didn't want to talk about the air force because – no getting away from it – it reminded her of Justin, who was giving his all for the country, possibly right this moment even. There was no other way of interpreting her behaviour, cat invitation or no. Dancing in a club, walking home with another man, was disloyal. As disloyal as a person could be. Even with the best intentions (and Elaine wasn't sure she had those), it looked bad. Justin and Elaine had been courting since July the year before. They were not engaged, but Justin constantly dangled the prospect of a ring over her, like she was a dog and he had all the biscuits.

Disloyal though it was, Elaine couldn't stop imagining the man alongside her in a flying uniform right now, every girl's favourite uniform (although Annie was coming round to the sailor's kit). He was bulky and strong, a rectangle to her figure of eight; he would fill it out nicely. She shook herself.

What a lack of self-control!

She tried to concentrate.

'So – so… doesn't being colour-blind affect the photos you take?'

He shrugged. 'No, why?'

She didn't know. She felt this strange compulsion to niggle him. Different from how it was with Justin, whose skin was so wafer-thin that she had to apologise for aggravating him daily. He liked to spend his leave at his mother's. Justin liked his home comforts.

She remembered some of the conversations she had overhead about Robert Capa in the office and at the George. 'Is it true you're frightened of the sea?'

Robert Capa laughed again. *He laughs too much*, decided Elaine. There, she knew she'd find something wrong with him eventually.

'Everyone should be frightened of the sea. You have to show it proper respect.'

She liked his answer though. She couldn't help liking him, could she? There was nothing *inherently* wrong with that. He went on, 'Sadly, I am not the greatest swimmer in the world. I hold my head up like this.' He imitated an old lady. 'I keep my hair dry.'

'What hair?'

'Very funny.' He locked his arm in hers and said something in a low voice; she wasn't sure what it was, but it might have been: 'You're lovely.'

They had reached Balham station. Elaine suddenly didn't want Robert Capa to know exactly where she and Clive lived, which was directly opposite the underground exit and two storeys above the WHSmith bookstore. She felt she had given enough away already. She tried to focus on Justin. Her beau. Her pilot. England's hero.

'Here is fine,' she said. *This is where it stops*, she told herself. Willpower was never more important. She tried to think of some of the patriotic posters at work: SELF-DENIAL IS HOW THE WAR WILL BE WON. Which was fair enough when dealing with a butter-less baked potato. Less easy when dealing with a man like this.

'Just here?'

'Yes.'

He pointed to where you could just make out a large crater in the ground in front of the station.

'You live right here?' One beetle-brow was raised quizzically. It was annoyingly attractive.

'I *said*, here is fine,' Elaine snapped.

During the Blitz, the statue of Andrew Bonar Law had collapsed, taking down with him Mrs Holcombe in her wheelchair. Elaine had spent all day long trying to calm down Mrs Holcombe's daughters, waiting for an aunty to collect them from Nottingham. It had been horrendous. *And* she had got a written warning from work for unauthorised lateness the next evening.

'It looks a nice area.'

She couldn't tell if he was joking or not.

'It's all right.'

'A bookshop for a neighbour? Could be worse.'

Elaine nodded.

When she rose up from the tube after a long session at work and caught sight of that sign: 'Blacked-out evenings – Take home some books', it meant she was safe and dry. And Elaine often did as instructed and took home books, because Mrs Marriot, who ran the WHSmith now that her brother and his son were away fighting, was unfailingly generous. Mrs Marriot was salt of the earth. She had been there for the Parker siblings not only when Elaine's mother was killed, but also when their father had left. Elaine didn't know what she'd do without her.

And Mrs Marriot understood, whereas so many others didn't, that even though Elaine nowadays looked all clerical, and all professional, spruced up in her finery, she still struggled with the rent. And the utilities. Mrs Marriot suggested that if Elaine read the books and magazines carefully and didn't break any spines, and didn't make any coffee drips in them, then she could bring the books back the next morning and no one would be any the wiser. Elaine did read carefully and rapidly and she managed to avoid breaking spines by wearing her expensive-looking gloves from Clive even indoors and she avoided coffee drips by never drinking while reading.

Mrs Marriot was the perfect person to have downstairs… unlike their landlady Mrs Perry, who lived up on the third and made everything her business. Mrs Perry was a classic busybody, as officious as Mrs Dill was at work but without the education, the empathy, the good manners or the important duties.

There was a couple under some coats in a nearby doorway. Elaine hoped Robert Capa didn't notice them, hoped he wouldn't comment, but who could fail to see one pair of lady's heels and another pair of shiny men's boots? They were lucky Clive the magpie wasn't about.

Robert Capa, war photographer, smiled with all his teeth. *What big teeth you have, Mr Wolf,* Elaine thought nervously. Each one was like an ivory piano key ready to play.

'Who were you speaking to outside the pub?'

She raised an eyebrow. '*That* is none of your beeswax.'

'He looked like you.'

'Well spotted.'

'So, he's not your boyfriend then?'

'He's my younger brother,' she said. 'I have two: Clive and Alan,' she added, although the word 'Alan' stuck in her throat.

'Good.'

Elaine felt she might come undone under Robert Capa's stare. She couldn't do silence, never could (with two younger brothers she'd hardly needed to).

'Why is that good?'

Her silly traitorous heart was beating nineteen to the dozen.

'Because I'd like to take you out some time, Miss Elaine who lives somewhere around this crater.'

Inhaling from her cigarette gave Elaine back some control, the illusion of control at least. 'I don't think so. Clive is not my boyfriend but um, actually I do… I do have someone on the go.'

Elaine couldn't believe she had actually said 'on the go'. It was the sort of old-fashioned thing Mrs Dill might say.

She thought of Justin, squirrelled up in his cramped bed at the barracks (Elaine hadn't been there, but a girl can imagine). She recalled his peak-caps, his toothpaste breath. His devotion to his mother. His family had made a fortune from cigarette machines and Justin wanted to make something of her too. As soon as the war was over, he'd see to it that Elaine never had to struggle again. Possibly, they'd move out of south London. Probably he'd even see to her teeth.

'Thank you for walking me home though and dancing with me,' she said finally with the self-control and willpower that everyone said would surely win Great Britain the war.

Robert Capa seemed surprised, but he reined in his expression as though adjusting notches on a belt. Elaine thought of all the women in the pub drinking their pink gin and pinning their hopes and their eyes on him.

'You'll have no problem finding other dancing girls.'

'Very well.' His lips went tight for a microsecond, then he smiled his warm smile again. 'You look like a woman who knows what she wants.'

This was an observation that had never been made about Elaine before; nevertheless she liked it.

'I am.'

'I won't try to make you change your mind.'

'Good!'

'Although I would love to meet your Bettie Page—'

'GOODBYE.'

He turned to go. She couldn't make out if he was still smiling or not. Elaine wanted to cry out. She had turned him down when she wanted nothing more than to get under a coat with him in some shopfront or other.

CHAPTER TWO

SPAIN

JUNE 2016, DAY ONE

It's the heat that hits you first. The unmistakable foreignness of it. I used to love this dry, dusty Mediterranean heat. Now I know I need to slap lotion on my perimenopausal face just to get from plane to luggage carousel without breaking out into a pink sweat.

I'm still trembling from the flight. It wasn't too terrible; I'm just an anxious flier, that's all: I'm anxious about pretty much everything at the moment. The steward squealing 'Screw this for a game of soldiers!' during turbulence did nothing to allay my fears.

Crowds of people are waiting at Arrivals. A delighted grandad ducks the barrier to uproariously greet two girls. Picks them up, long skinny legs all over the place. Teenagers, much like my Harry, mooch through. Headphone wires dangling, their support systems. Holidaymakers trudge through with their trolleys, wondering about onward transport. The white, the pasty, the sandalled and the bum-bagged. When I used to walk out to the Arrivals lounge twenty years ago, I used to pretend I was Olivia Newton-John. Now I wish I were the Invisible Woman.

There's a scribbled 'JENNIFER's taxi service' on a sheet of cardboard and behind it, two small elderly ladies are cracking up with laughter: Mum and Aunty Barbara.

It's nice to be met at an airport as though I'm an important person and it's a relief that I don't have to go on the hunt for a taxi or bus. I hurry over and kiss them, almost stomping on Mum's raspberry-painted toes in the process.

'Mind!' she yelps.

Mum says she wanted to hold up a 'welcome out of the loony bin' sign but Aunty Barbara wouldn't have it. Mum always paints Aunty Barbara as a killjoy. She's not at all – she's just more of a deep thinker than Mum and she drinks less. I've always adored my aunty. A woman's liberator in the seventies, she also spent two years at Greenham Common until her knees gave way from all the sit-ins. She was a destabilising, unsteadying influence on my early life – thank goodness for her!

'You look wonderful,' she says, 'look at that terrific hat.'

I knew Aunty Barbara would like it. I bought it half with her in mind. It's large, straw and it feels like a disguise. I hope to become a different person wearing it. Someone good in hot weather, maybe. Who doesn't look better in a hat where you can hardly see any of your face?

They both look me up and down and don't mention the obvious: my weight gain; although Mum will comment later. Mum is whippet thin – if she isn't naturally, she makes sure she works at it. I look them up and down in return, and think, *they really are shrinking*. It's as though someone's put them on too high a wash.

Mum's hand is on my elbow, her infamous steer move. 'Come on then, Matthew is in the car.'

'He didn't want to pay for parking?'

'Well, it *is* such a rip-off,' says Mum, defensive of the golden boy as ever.

We trot past book stalls and coffee stands. Women in cute uniforms directing people to car-hire, men smoking cigarettes indoors and holding dollhouse-sized cups. On the rotating stands, the English newspapers are outnumbered by the Spanish and German, but they are still holding their own.

Matthew has always wanted me to visit, but over the past few months he has grown more insistent, even offering to pay my airfare (I did not accept). Gisela is away teaching yoga – she does this every few months or so – and he said I should come then, while she's tied up in knots. Why not? Mum, Derek and Aunty Barbara would come to stay too. All of us together. A relaxing family holiday. This is not typical of our family or Matthew – togetherness is not our usual way – so as we walk out of the air conditioning into the heat again, I ask Mum what's really going on.

Mum doesn't know anything. Matthew and Gisela are doing just fine, the girls are fine, Matthew doesn't have a new job or anything... she doesn't know what it is. It crosses my mind that he could be ill, but when the car pulls up, and I see him for the first time in four years, I dismiss that outright: mirrored sunglasses, white shirt, tanned neck, bobbly silver hair; my brother is the very picture of middle-aged health.

Matthew waits in the car while our seventy-one-year-old mother and I struggle to open the back.

'What took you so long?' he asks, and I don't know whether he means today or in general.

Mum gets in next to Aunty Barbara. I protest, 'Take the passenger seat, Mum, please,' but she says, 'We all know you get carsick.'

My brother looks at me sideways. I may not have seen this face for some time, but it's utterly and disconcertingly familiar to me. It's like looking into a crazy mirror at the fairground. His face is browner, leaner, longer and hairier, but otherwise it's mine.

'You're looking well.'

'You mean fat?'

As he reaches over to kiss me on the cheek, his eyes are twinkling. 'You said it, not me. Now, what's this ridiculous thing on your head?'

*

Matthew's house is perched up on the top of a mountain like a fort. A place for seeing off marauding invaders. He tells me that he and Gisela have been here two years now and they couldn't be happier.

'Smell that?'

Money? I think. 'Lavender,' I say.

'Uh-huh. You've always liked it, right?' Matthew claims to remember everything about our childhood. I say he's got false memory syndrome.

It's a large red stone bungalow. No, not large, *enormous*. 'No stairs,' he says proudly.

There's a pool here, a long glistening rectangle of blue like in a Hollywood film. Of course, I didn't bring a swimsuit. I didn't bring the right clothes at all. In England, it was grey-skied and miserable. When I packed, I lacked the imagination or the foresight to realise things might be different here.

'Olympic-size,' he says.

'Because you are an Olympic swimmer?' I say sarcastically.

He lightly punches my arm. 'Never change.'

'Is the water warm?'

'Gisela and I don't swim much,' Matthew says, stroking back his bouffant hair, and I suspect the expensive blow-dry is the reason. 'It's for visitors really. And the girls,' he adds.

Matthew has two girls: the older one, Kate, is at university in Madrid: English and German literature. Alyssia is somewhere here. As we go inside, Matthew calls for her and she emerges from one of the eleven-teen doors off the long corridor.

'Hello,' she says reluctantly.

I say, 'Hi Alyssia,' enthusiastically. I like other people's teenagers. She's a small, thin dark-haired girl, her nose in her iPad. I try to be aunt-like and ask her about school. Friends. Books. Sports? School again. She says 'fine' a lot. She's shyer than she used to be, but that's normal with that age, at least it's how it is with my Harry. They do a kind of reverse tortoise at high school – going back into the shell. I decide I will try to bring her out this week.

Matthew leads me away by the elbow in the same way Mum does. My feet flip-flop loudly on the stone floor.

'I'll show you the gym.'

'I'm okay.'

'You may want to use it.'

I hear: *you should use it.* My turn to punch his arm. 'Thanks.'

Matthew goes off to check something for work. Mum has disappeared behind one of the walnut doors. Aunty Barbara is in the kitchen making tea. There is a massive industrial coffee-maker that she confides is too complicated for her to use. 'The cold drinks are in there,' she says, nodding towards another identical walnut door. She holds something up to me: little grains in a pale net.

'There are coffee *bags* now, Jen. Can you believe it?'

'Shocking!' I say. 'I would never have thought it of Matthew. He's changed.'

We laugh companionably. With her, it's like no time at all since we were last together. Our relationship has always been easy and unforced. When I used to go to concerts or events in London, I slept over at hers. She had a tiny flat in a tall apartment block with colourful shawls draped over the windows and on the pull-out sofa.

'How are you *really* doing?'

Such kindness in her voice, it nearly breaks me. *Don't be nice, don't be kind. I can't bear it.*

'Not too bad,' I say. 'You?'

She lunges at me, holds me close. I am almost a head taller than she is. I'm sure I didn't used to be. I smell the sun lotion in her sparse hair.

It's been months of utter agony. But before that, there were months of bewilderment and confusion. So, if you add them up, it's probably fair to say I have been miserable for quite a long time.

'How's Harry?'

'He's doing okay.'

'Any chance of you and Paul reconciling?'

'Don't know… don't think so,' I say into her hair.

In February, Harry found the texts on Paul's phone. Agonised over them for three days, then told me. All hell broke loose and, well, here we are.

'It must be hard.'

It is, and what I'm struggling with now is that it doesn't seem to be getting any easier. Paul and I haven't resolved anything. We seem – no, *I seem* – no further on from where I was in February. I have this profound sense of shame that I should be moving on, everyone thinks I should be over it by now, but I'm not. Not nearly. I still love Paul. I still want him back. He is, *was*, the love of my life.

He says he doesn't know what he wants.

Who. He doesn't know *who* he wants.

He goes to see a counsellor once or – when he is in crisis – twice a week. It's sixty pounds a pop. Sophie the counsellor seems broadly on my side, from what Paul says, but other times, she is resolutely pro-Paul. I suppose *he who pays the piper* and all that. I used to joke that there are now three people in our marriage – him, me and Sophie – but actually there are far more than the three of us. There are all the women he texts for a start.

Aunty Barbara pours the hot water and I stir the teabags. We can't find any rubbish bins in this pristine place, so my aunty rebelliously deposits them in an abandoned saucer.

'Harry didn't want to come?'

'No,' I say, thinking, *why would he?*

'Who's he with?'

'Paul's staying with him at the house.'

She looks surprised. 'You and Paul are still close then?'

'Yes,' I say, chin up in the air, 'closer than ever.'

My aunty looks at me sceptically. 'For Harry's sake,' I add. Sophie the counsellor is very fond of keeping things amicable.

I admire the hydrangeas and clematis in the garden. Aunty Barbara talks me through the plants, like she's introducing me to old friends. Everything here looks lush and well-tended, and Aunty Barbara is in her element. I remember the little spider plants she had in her old flat and the row of dry cacti on her windowsill. She says Matthew has a man who comes twice a week. I think, *of course he does.*

Out in the back, there on the decking, is Derek, my stepdad: floral shirt and florid skin, cooking meat on the barbecue. Is this the time to remind him I'm vegetarian? I have told Mum several times, but each time I could feel she wasn't really listening. Bracing myself, I go over to him.

He is examining the blackened outsides of the chicken legs with the precision of a heart surgeon. He has an extraordinarily large set of tongs.

'Well, well, well,' he says, 'who do we have here?'

'Ha,' I say.

'Thought it was about time you visited, did you?'

Here we go. 'You could always come and visit Harry and me, you know.'

He drops a chicken leg on the floor, then puts it back on the grill. 'Five-second rule?' I say.

'You didn't see that,' he says at the same time.

Mum and Derek live in Spain too, in one of the towns dotted around the valley; they live in a small apartment and their pool is shared. Derek is in property management. He makes deals for retired British pensioners. Matthew began by working for Derek, only he is more on the development side of things now, whatever that means. For this week though, Mum and Derek are staying here so we can all be together and, most importantly, so we can all have a drink. If you can't have a drink, what can you do?

There's so much room here, after all. The six of us don't even touch the sides. The house has eight bedrooms – eight! It seems Gisela loves entertaining lots of people, just not Matthew's family.

'I wish Paul could see this place,' Mum says. 'It's wonderful, isn't it?'

'It's beautiful.'

'He would have loved it here. He's missing out.'

'That's his problem,' I say.

When Paul first moved out to find himself, I lost it completely. I couldn't work, I couldn't sleep, I couldn't do anything. I called up Mum and begged her to come to stay with us. I had never felt so alone in my life.

'Matthew needs help too, Jen,' she had told me. 'Gisela is away again, you see. What do they call it? Retreats, is it? She's always retreating to one place or another.'

'Just for a weekend, Mum. Just to spend an hour or two with Harry maybe?'

And with me?

'We'll see.'

We never did see.

Aunty Barbara has been out here since Friday. She left London some years ago and lives in Scotland with her partner Nelson. Nelson is fifteen years younger than her and for two years she and Mum didn't talk over it. Now they just don't talk about him.

Barbara is keen to visit Granada, but no one else seems to want to go.

'You'll come with me, won't you, Jen?'

'Arab city,' says Derek. 'Get enough of them trying to get in from there.' He points at the vast Mediterranean glistening in the far distance. It looks like someone has stuck a zillion diamond shapes on a blue page.

'Sure,' I say to Aunty Barbara, more to wind up Derek than from any burning desire to go. 'Let's make a plan.'

*

I tell them I'm going to my room to unpack, but really, I need to get away from them already. *Five-second rule.* I feel claustrophobic and hemmed in. I am eight years old again, feeling sullen towards Derek the interloper and ambivalent towards Mum.

I call home, but no one answers. I leave a message saying I'm worried about Pushkin: *has he been fed?* I'm far more worried about Harry, obviously, but Harry hates it when I'm – what he calls – overprotective. 'I'm *seventeen*, Mum!'

Harry and Paul are both terrible at replying, but the landline makes such an infuriating ring that if you're there, you kind of *have* to pick up.

They don't pick up.

I text Harry. 'Please answer or I'll worry.'

Nada.

I wish Harry had agreed to come out here with me, but I also wanted him to spend more time with Paul – they need to bond. Sophie the counsellor thought so too.

I watch my mother and Derek and know that Sophie would probably advise me I needed to spend time with my parents as well. We're not at all bonded.

For years I have been floating away from my family. If I was an astronaut untethered from earth, then Mum would be Ground Control, chatting to her friend about a fantastic cocktail she and Matthew had discovered in Costa del Mar, Pineapple and lemon. 'You wouldn't think they'd go together but they do!' she'd be saying as I ran out of oxygen.

Well, this week is as good a time as any to get Ground Control's attention.

It's the kind of sticky heat that sucks the will to live out of you. It's the kind of sticky heat where you can't imagine anything else but this.

Derek grills me a corn on the cob, which I have with Spanish-brand crisps with a chirpy little bear on the packaging. The bear is having a great time. Derek said he didn't know I'd 'turned' vegetarian. Alyssia has as well apparently.

'Is that since… the Paul thing?' he asks.

'Um, it's six years this summer,' I say, and he nods like I've confirmed what he's thinking.

After lunch, my mother keeps getting up and down, rearranging her sunlounger to escape the shadows. She likes the sun on her face. She is wearing white trousers and a white shirt, pretty daring for a barbecue. She is good-looking for her age – for any age. Attractive gold-red hair, attractive golden skin. People says she's got good bones. She and Derek have been together for years. He was my dad's best friend.

Mum has a fan – a flamenco dancer fan with a lacy stretchy bit. I know in my hands it would only last five minutes. Mum, by contrast, is very careful with things. Always has been.

Alyssia is in the pool, on her rubber armchair – Matthew calls it her throne – swiping at her phone. Her feet glow white in the water. I wave at her and she smiles back, indulging me. She's a sweet-natured girl. Also in the pool is a blow-up dolphin – no, it's a shark – and two beach balls that seem to lie on the surface as listlessly as the rest of us. Mum and Derek have taken over the sunloungers and there are towels, towels everywhere, but not one for me to sit on.

Derek is lying on his front reading the newspaper and Mum is ineffectually fanning his vast red neck. She says he is as sticky as flypaper.

Matthew comes out, glass in hand. I smile at my little brother. *This is going to be fine*. I needed a holiday away from Paul and from trying to get him to choose me. I feel like I've been a performing monkey for the past few months, doing my best to be the wife he wanted: I can relax now and be myself for a bit. I can do this.

'It's idyllic here, Matthew, really it is,' I say.

Carefully, he places down his beer. 'So, I have news.'

CHAPTER THREE

LONDON, SEPTEMBER 1943

Mrs Dill was not impressed by the pinks wrapped in newspaper and lying on Elaine's desk like a swaddled baby the next morning.

'Is someone dead, Miss Parker?'

'Huh?' Elaine picked up the bouquet and examined it.

'What is the need for flowers?' Mrs Dill continued.

In the centre of each flower was a dark round like the pupil of an eye, like *his* eyes, and each of the surrounding petals went from light to dark, overlapping and soft. There was a ribbon attached to them with a handwritten note that said nothing but: 'Pinkys for the girl with pinky hair.'

The words sloped to the right: clear, bold and beautiful. Elaine dropped the bouquet back onto her desk.

'No need at all, Mrs Dill.'

'I wonder who sent you those?' Annie said, chewing her pencil. Elaine told her she'd get lead poisoning if she didn't stop. 'They don't seem Justin's style...'

And die a slow and lingering death.

Elaine grinned at her. It wasn't a question, so it didn't demand an answer. And anyway, anyone who managed to get these past Vera the dragon and her ear trumpet on the front desk deserved a medal.

The clerical girls were supposed to be looking for clues in the POW letters that had been smuggled out. But there were never any clues. Elaine felt – and she did feel guilty about this, maybe she was massively underestimating the captured British soldiers – that most of them were just desperately trying to stay alive.

Elaine tried to transcribe the letters as quickly as she could so she could wave them on their way: they could go on their excruciating journey from the railways of Japanese occupation to the wives and mothers in Hampshire or Devon.

The conditions were dreadful – you could tell that sometimes from what they didn't say. You had to read between the lines as the boys – as she called the prisoners of war – tried their best to keep their chins up. Sometimes she and the others couldn't face thinking about what they were reading and did it mechanically, unconcernedly, and sometimes they couldn't read them for 'getting specks in their eyes'.

But you soldiered on.

Elaine was in the middle of one from a poor soul, William, to his mother. William was a descriptive writer and built up quite a picture: bamboo sticks. Building bridges. The death marches. Dropping dead like flies. Squatting for the toilet, shot in the back of the head. They were supposed to be looking for locations, plans, pockets of resistance. Elaine was looking for signs they would get through.

That evening, Mrs Marriot in the shop downstairs also assumed the pinks were from Justin.

'Pretty,' she conceded. She couldn't resist adding, 'Although I am not Justin's number one fan.'

Justin, a self-confessed bibliophobe, had told Mrs Marriot that in twenty years' time no one would read books or newspapers any more: all information would come via tiny speakers in the ear.

'Are you in the top ten of Justin's fans?' Elaine joked.

Mrs Marriot could have an icy stare when she wanted. 'I doubt whether I am in the top one hundred, dear.'

Elaine watched the shop while Mrs Marriot went to do her business. The stress of the war had given her a permanently dicky tummy. The first time Elaine had been left alone – face of WHSmith, Balham – was intimidating, but now she rather liked sitting pertly at the counter and wiping the smears on the glass with the rag. She knew she probably fitted in a lot better here, playing shop-girl, than she did in the tippy-tappy world of clerical girls.

Some people came for their orders. Others perused the magazines and newspapers. In the ten minutes Mrs Marriot was away, Elaine gave out four copies of the *Daily Express* (*Allies attack Milan and Turin*), two of the *Daily Mirror*, two of *The Times* and a naughty magazine.

There were comics for children too, where dogs with bared teeth were routinely defeated by mice, posh boys were flattened by urchins and many a villain was caught on the toilet with his pants down. It was a brilliant world of comeuppance where everyone got what they deserved.

Could you believe: there were hardly any WHSmiths left now. Three years earlier, Mrs Marriot had heard their store in Paris had been taken over by Nazis; 'overrun' she said, 'like rats,' and she had wept in Elaine's arms. Elaine understood. It was one of those horribly symbolic moments when it felt like nothing was sacred any more. Mrs Marriot said if the Nazis did invade, she would set fire to the shop herself, *oh yes, she would*, she would rather see WHSmith Balham burned down than have it ransacked or their *Alice in Wonderland*s or their *War and Peace*s ripped up to wipe Nazi bottoms.

In preparation for the dreadful day, Mrs Marriot kept her Swan Vestas in the till alongside the breadknife she would use for the hand-to-hand combat.

Every ten minutes or so, a stream of workers came up from the underground, blinking like moles tunnelling into sunlight. Before the war, the commuters were mostly male; now it was probably equal numbers of men and women, all held together like parcels in their overcoats and scarves. There were men in uniforms now too. The homeward-bound ones smiling, readying for a welcome, the outward-bound ones more reflective, less friendly.

Mrs Marriot returned from her ablutions and recommended a romance novel – *The Vicar and the Choir Mistress* – about, strangely enough, a reverend and one of his parishioners in a Suffolk village. It was lovely when she got a recommendation right: like being matchmade; however, Mrs Marriot and Elaine's taste in books did not entirely coalesce. This one looked harmless enough though, so Elaine took it home for the night.

The communal phone in the hall was ringing just as Elaine walked in. Bad timing. She wanted to leave it: she had a feeling it would be Justin. It wouldn't be Alan, would it? But it might well be Robert Capa and she needed to thank him for the flowers. She mustn't be rude. What would her mother have said? She picked up.

'I have two days off, Elaine,' said Justin after Elaine had breathed the long Balham number.

Elaine couldn't help it; her heart really did seem to helter-skelter downwards fast on a rattan mat. Bouquet of flowers still in hand, she felt indecent, like she had been caught with a weapon.

'Thought we could meet.'

Elaine thought about all the conversations she had had with Justin about his hair or about his mother. She thought of all the conversations she was yet to have with Robert Capa and might never get to have.

'I have work.'

'After work, obviously.'

'I've been tired recently.'

'Everyone wants to see you.'

Justin yearned for the approval of others. He preferred to be with a crowd rather than on his own with her. He was gregarious when he was with his pals. Alone with Elaine, he was like a train that had run out of steam. *Sorry, sorry, next time?* He always needed to sleep, or to eat, he needed to stretch – anything rather than do what the vicar and his church-ringing parishioner were so very desperate to do.

'I want to show you off…'

He always said that like she was a fancy brooch or a new automobile. Today it left Elaine feeling like she was not a nice thing at all. She could not have been behaving any worse.

'It will do you good to have some fun, Elaine.' Justin tried a different tack. 'You work so hard.'

Not that hard, Elaine thought despairingly. She was only tired today because she had spent last night on the razzle.

'I'll pay.'

Justin wasn't put off that Elaine was, as he euphemistically called her, 'a normal girl' (Justin was too delicate for the phrase 'working class'). He liked that she was eager to learn, to improve herself. 'You're Eliza to my Doctor Dolittle,' he often said.

It worked. At least, it *had*.

'We'll see.' Elaine wanted to get off the line. The exhaustion coming over her wasn't just due to work or lack of sleep. There was trouble ahead whichever way she turned. Wasn't there always? She thought of poor William from the letter suffering in his prisoner of war camp. Really, she had no right to complain about anything.

'Elaine, is everything all right?'

All right? The way Robert Capa had looked at her! Elaine could hardly breathe for thinking about it. She remembered his hands placed firmly round his glass of beer. *Oh, how would it feel to be that glass of beer!* Even the writing on his note had her enthralled. The loops of the Ys felt like a sexual innuendo. The dots on the Is felt like she was being thrown over his shoulder…

Good grief. Had she been put under a spell? She couldn't explain it to poor Justin. She could hardly explain it to herself. She breathed in the flowery scent. She got so close that the petals tickled her nose.

'Everything is fine, thank you, Justin.'

She felt grubby and guilty, but not quite grubby or guilty enough to arrange to see him. *Next time*, she resolved, *she just wouldn't answer the phone.*

That evening, Clive was in an excellent mood. On the way back from his job at the fishmongers, he had acquired both a whole chicken and a new girlfriend. While he efficiently de-feathered the former, he told Elaine about the girl with the unlikely name of Maisie May Mahoney. She worked in a municipal canteen, she was twenty-three years old and she blew the socks off everyone left in London (a feat probably not quite so difficult as it once was).

'I suppose you *told* her you were twenty-five.'

Clive did his enigmatic shrug as he coated the chicken in lard.

'She is going to bring us some stale cake.'

'Excellent.'

While the other clerical girls complained daily about rationing, Elaine didn't join in. She was one of those rare beings who found food was *improved* under rationing. Coupons, work canteen, plus Clive's ingenuity meant they were eating better than ever before.

'She looks exactly like a German,' Clive added, slamming the bird in the oven. While he would happily strangle Nazis with his bare hands, ever since he had started chasing women – from the age of thirteen and a half (an early developer) – he had had a distinctive type. He liked women blonde and sturdy, long-legged and broad-shouldered. If it weren't for the blasted war, Clive would almost certainly have brought home and married a full-blown Fräulein. He'd admit that to your face as well.

The weekend dragged horribly. Punishment, Elaine felt, for being disloyal to Justin. There was only a light rain, but it spoiled the washing and there was no hope of getting it dry for Monday. A cat, or maybe a fox, got into the cold safe – Bettie Page was quite the useless guard – and although the animal got nothing but a half-pat of butter, the door needed reinforcing with hammer and nails, which proved a dull task.

Elaine had a letter from her brother Alan – he wrote every three weeks or so, and he addressed them only to her, never to Clive. He didn't sound right at all. Hard to put a finger on it, though. She thought about calling to speak to his superior, but who knew where to begin with that?

And what to say? 'Excuse me, our Alan is very… sensitive'?

That was the word Mum had used, and that was before he stepped up his 'sensitivity' to a whole new level.

She quickly wrote him a postcard, went and sent it, then thought the brevity might upset him, so sat down to write something longer. Such a dreary Saturday. It was hard to find anything to say: Robert Capa was taking up most of her thoughts. Elaine regretted turning him down, but she also regretted turning down Justin. She regretted just about everything she'd ever said or done.

Annie called late afternoon, wanting to go out, but Elaine explained she was not feeling up to it. In truth, she would have gone but had realised she had no money left. Clive was out with her last shillings, looking for empty train carriages – to which to take his new sweetheart for a warm beer picnic, no doubt.

The best thing about the weekend was the chicken she finished with basil from the backyard and grated cheese, and the book Mrs Marriot had lent her. Elaine fell quite in love with the vicar and the ever-loving parishioner. Whatever obstacles the vicar threw at her, the parishioner only loved him more. It was remarkable.

Thank heavens for weekdays. Elaine couldn't be the only young woman in the country who craved the routine of work on a Monday morning, could she?

She waited patiently at the front desk for Vera to sign her in, and to scold her about her shoes – girls these days wore them far too high, apparently – then clattered up to her office, intrigued as to the day's offering from Robert Capa.

There was nothing there. No flowers, nothing. Never had a desk seemed so unwelcoming. Disappointment dropped on her like an object from the sky. She could guess exactly what had happened: she had taken too long to make up her mind. He was probably in bed with a Merry or a Faye right now. Damn it.

Well, that would serve her right. Elaine told herself she would be mad not to stick with Justin. There was something wrong with her for trying to twist again. As if she deserved better than a pilot in the Royal bloody Air Force! A pilot with clean breath and good hair. She was not only looking a gift horse in the mouth, she was arrogant too. Justin was the stuff dreams were made of. *Come on! Know your place, Elaine Parker*, she scolded herself. *Be humble. Don't get ideas above your station.*

But then, just as Elaine had reconciled herself to Robert Capa's disappearance and gone down a regretful litany of her own stupidity, she opened her desk drawer and found there a beached bottle of whisky. And a note:

> *Miss Parker, if you won't come out with me for a drink, shall we stay in for a drink sometime? Sending love to Miss Bettie Page.*

Elaine wanted to press the note to her heart, so thrilled was she to see it there.

Very little escaped Annie, and she whispered now, 'What's that you've got there, Elaine?'

'A… bottle of Scotch.'

'Justin again?' One eyebrow raised to the sky; Annie clearly didn't believe a word of it.

'Uh-huh.'

Annie stuck out her tongue.

'Scotch? He's even better connected than I thought.'

In the dimly lit canteen in the basement, dinner-ladies Dolly and Joyce slopped what passed for lunch onto chipped china plates. Spam pie, spam stew, curried spam. Provisions were getting worse and worse. Very little produce was getting across the Channel. You couldn't help but worry. People didn't talk about it much, but Elaine remembered her mother telling her that when she was young, people were dying in the streets of south London from hunger.

Annie sat opposite Elaine. Spam was her favourite, and she was oblivious to the discontent around her: Felicity was pretending to faint with horror and Myra was pretending to fan her awake.

'Were the whisky and flowers really from Justin?'

Even Annie would admit her mouth often ran away with her. 'Loose talk costs lives'. It was there, right there, on the poster above her. Next to 'What to do if you're in an automobile when the sirens go off'.

Still, Annie was Elaine's best friend, and they shared many dark secrets. Annie didn't want children, ever, and neither did Elaine. Both of them were ambitious and wanted to be independent. Annie loved working; Elaine loved the money. And now Elaine was desperate to talk.

'Not exactly.'

Annie shook her head. She knew. 'They weren't from Robert Capa, were they?'

Elaine shovelled spam stew into her mouth to avoid answering.

'Oh, Elaine!' said Annie. 'Really?'

Elaine chewed on the stubbornly tasteless meat, then nodded. She regretted having said anything. Sometimes when things are out in the open, they lose their appeal. There, they should have put *that* on the government posters.

'You won't get serious about him though, will you?'

'About Robert Capa? No,' Elaine replied confidently. Then after a few moments, she couldn't resist asking, 'Why not?'

Wasn't Annie the one who had raved about him only last Thursday?

Annie flew her fork over Elaine's plate, landed it on the spam pie. 'I'll finish it if you're not going to…'

Elaine nodded. She hoped Annie hadn't forgotten the question. She prompted her.

'What's wrong with Robert Capa then?'

'Oh, nothing's wrong with him. He's adorable, but he's no good for a boyfriend.'

'Why not?'

Chew, crunch, munch; for goodness' sake, Annie was making a right meal out of this spam.

'Because he's a fly-by-night, that's why.'

'Really? He's a… he's a playboy?'

'Yes, really. Of course, he's fun, handsome and personable. We all adore him, you know that. Just… don't get attached. He's not reliable.'

'I won't.'

Annie eyed her disapprovingly. 'Anyway, I thought you and Justin were going all the way.'

'I don't know which way we're going.' Elaine felt helpless suddenly. The situation seemed silly. Here they were in the middle of the war and she was mooning over a virtual stranger. She should be ashamed of herself. For the last year or so, she had begun to see Justin as a passport to somewhere better. But Robert Capa had suddenly come along, with a prospect of a different destination altogether.

'You know he's Hungarian? And…' Annie looked around as though checking no one was listening. 'His mother is Jewish?'

'I don't care where he's from,' Elaine said truthfully. But in another way, she cared about anything and *everything* to do with Robert Capa.

She wanted nothing more than to talk about his loopy Ys, his love of cats *and* his receding hairline endlessly.

'He has very nice teeth,' she said finally and Annie, who also had an eye for such things, couldn't resist.

'He's definitely got a bit of Rock Hudson about him.'

'Doesn't he?'

'And Bogart around the hairline.' Annie sniggered. 'But what are you going to do about Justin though?'

'Don't know.'

Annie leaned forward, cabbage between her teeth, and whispered, 'I suppose what Justin doesn't know won't hurt him.'

'Oh, Annie,' Elaine said. This seemed spectacularly bad advice even for Annie. Disloyal. Unkind. Treacherous even.

And yet.

Lunchtime the next day, Elaine and Annie snuck off to sit in a corner far away from the others, where they could dissect Robert Capa's eyes – hazel brown or nut brown? – and the stirring way he said 'resistance', with the flourishing roll of the 'r', in peace. They had just laughingly decided on 'rabbit-stew brown' when Leon came in, saying that Larry Hubbard, who worked at Life Corp., wanted Elaine to come up and see their latest photos. The clerical girls often got a sneak preview before the magazine went to press, but Elaine felt embarrassed that Annie hadn't been included – the invitation seemed to have been extended to her and her alone. But Annie laughed, said she knew where she wasn't wanted.

'Go,' she urged, 'I've got to write to Billy anyway.'

Annie's cousin Billy was on the HMS *Belfast*. Annie was blessed with a large cheerful family to whom she sent jolly letters and received jolly letters in return. Elaine tried her best not to be envious.

Leon was still waiting for a reply.

'Um, okay… Annie, if you really don't mind?'

Annie was already immersed in her letter; she waved a hand of dismissal at them both.

Larry the darkroom man was waiting for Elaine on the outside stairs of Life Corp. During the Blitz, Larry was blasted out of the third floor of a building. Damaged his own legs and broke the arm of the man he landed on. Everyone said he was lucky it wasn't worse. He still volunteered nights as a fireman. He lived near her, had the same background as her. They got along well.

'Here's my favourite girl!' he called as she approached.

Small dark room. Smell of wet and mercury. A flickering lightbulb and two circling bluebottles.

'These are the ones,' said Larry, steering her gently to one side.

Elaine looked at them as they dried. Previously, heinously, she had thought the photos were one of the least interesting parts of *Life* magazine. She liked reading. She liked words. Not just words, everything about words – like fonts and typefaces. The way writing looked on a page. The difference between a poem or prose, a letter or a postcard, a cartoon or a book about a clergyman. When she had gone, or rather, when Justin had dragged her, to the art gallery in Dulwich, she had spent half the time reading the side-notes explaining the pictures, the where, the when, the how.

Not now. These photos didn't need side-notes. They told whole fantastic stories of their own. They didn't need explanations. There were acres of story in each one. Now she could see.

She knew who they were by, she didn't have to ask, it all made perfect sense.

They were pictures of boats, pictures at sea. The convoy he'd come to London on. The captain leaning across the side. The sailors gathered listening to the news on the wireless. A telephone operator with tears in his eyes. A man vomiting into a bucket in a cube of sickbay. Shadows of sea creatures under the ocean surface. Gulls flying in formation. First glimpses of a port. For a man who was nervous of water, he'd sure done a lot of criss-crossing the Atlantic. What a journey – and each moment of it was encapsulated here.

It was like a door had suddenly opened to another world. A world of waves and storms and sailors under pressure and she was lost in it too.

Everyone should be frightened of the sea. You have to show it proper respect.

'There are some older ones here you might want to look at,' said Larry when she finally pulled herself away. Standing over her, his breath smelled of pickles. 'His Blitz pictures.'

This was surprising, though. Elaine had assumed Robert Capa was fresh off the boat – the boat in the picture. She had forgotten he had been in London during the Blitz. She realised there was probably lots about him she had simply assumed.

'He was here?'

Larry explained, 'Robert Capa is wherever the action is.'

Actually, the Blitz pictures appealed even more to Elaine for their *lack of* action, not mundanity exactly, but the way they had captured everyday life as it was now. He had captured the moment when a mother reads a letter from her son, the relief embedded in every facial feature. The woman by her side – sister? Or neighbour? – her face wreathed in pleasure. Elaine knew that probably would sound dull and many a more thrill-seeking photographer wouldn't have sat around to take it. But he had.

He had photographed a girl hesitantly – from her body language – learning to milk a cow. The size of the udders, the determination on her freckly face! He had photographed a bright-eyed young woman proud as she kneaded some dough, a smattering of flour on her nose, the white hands in the foreground made huge and essential.

There was as much drama in these as in the photos of the men in uniform.

Then another, a woman stirring a large pot at a stove, with a dog, a Cocker Spaniel maybe, who was looking up at the woman, his eyes beseeching for snacks to come his way.

Elaine couldn't help it, she couldn't help feeling tender towards the person who had seen these things and recognised them as important. Other photographers mightn't have built up the relationships, others mightn't have waited for the revealing shot, others mightn't have seen the deep emotions at play here. These pictures indicated a sensitive heart. Other photographers, other *people*, would have ignored the trials and tribulations of these forgotten women behind the scenes. This was someone who saw. This was someone who understood. This was someone humane.

Elaine quickly put them down.

The last thing she needed was for Robert Capa to know that she was admiring his work.

'What shall I tell him?' Larry always had a playful expression, but it was more pronounced than usual now.

'How do you mean?'

'Mr Capa wants to know what you think of them.'

So just as she suspected, this *was* a set-up and Larry was a part of it. Robert Capa had sent flowers, he had sent contraband alcohol, and now he thought he could win her over with his photography? It was all some elaborate seduction dance. And it had the whiff of the practised seducer all over it.

'Tell him, I thought they were very...' Elaine tried to think of the right words, 'moving. But...' The truth was, she was enjoying this: '*I'm* not moved by him.'

Larry looked so disappointed that she felt bad. Maybe she had been too harsh.

'Tell him, I wish him all the very best.' She hesitated. 'And to enjoy recording these remarkable sights.'

The walk out of the Life Corp. building felt different from the walk in. Elaine felt enlightened and informed but also decisive. She did an extra rotate in the revolving doors just for the heck of it – and because it reminded her of dancing, with him.

Down the street Elaine went, a spring in her step. The power of the snub. The game of cat and the mouse. He still liked her. The thrill of the chase. The *inevitability* of it. Then curiosity got the better of her. She gazed up at the window of Life Corp. Someone was standing there, staring out from the second-floor window. It must be him.

Whoever it was waved down at her. Whoever it was blew her a kiss.

Justin called again that evening. How had she not noticed how reedy his voice was? His agitation with her was growing. *Well, why wouldn't he be agitated?* Elaine rationalised. She was turning down all his invitations. Other girls would do just about anything to be invited out by a handsome pilot and he'd spelled out as much. All he wanted was to show her off to his colleagues. What was the harm in that? That's what any boyfriend was within his rights to want to do, especially these days when you didn't know if jackboots would be stomping down the Mall tomorrow and if you'd have to set light to your favourite Penguin Classics to avoid them getting into Nazi gloves.

And the thing with Justin was: he accepted her, warts and all. Well, he certainly didn't know *all* her warts – especially not her brother-sized warts – but those that Justin was aware of, he seemed quite prepared to overlook.

Two days later, there were chocolates on her desk. Dark and hard: the real thing. Someone was still getting sugar. And someone hadn't given up on her yet.

'How on earth did these get here?' Mrs Dill, whip-smart. 'If they're black-market I'm going to have to report you.'

'They're not.' It was unlikely Mrs Dill understood what Elaine was saying, because Elaine had shoved them in her mouth so fast.

'Belgium. Justin,' she lied, keeping her fingers crossed under the desk. *Good grief, what was she becoming?*

Then two days after that, propped up against her typewriter, as though it were always meant to be there, a tiny photograph of a cat. A cat in the street with watchful eyes, its tail held high, alert but friendly, if you can imagine such a thing, cautiously rash.

The note with that lovely alphabet of curves:

Do you know how hard it is to get a good picture of a cat?

Elaine did not. She read on.

Elusive little buggers. Anyway, this marmalade beauty reminds me of you.

Only two ys, two delicious loops.

With more kisses. *Too many kisses for a stranger*, thought Elaine gleefully. But Robert Capa didn't feel like a stranger any more.

He was a smooth operator and no mistake. It finished:

Off tomorrow. Might not make it back, darling girl. Farewell, adieu, goodbye.

Elaine suddenly felt sick to her stomach. The phoney war was over, she realised. Now, now, was the time to act.

CHAPTER FOUR

LONDON, SEPTEMBER 1943

The Friday night crowd were already gathering at the George. Elaine had to push through to the bar with sharp elbows and all the '*dreadfully* sorrys' and the 'do excuse me, thank yous'. Fortunately, the mood was good, the atmosphere was light. Another working week had been survived – the Nazis hadn't yet invaded; Churchill remained their prime minister – it was time for celebration. People were getting sloshed. One of the editors from Life Corp., Peter Barnet, pulled out of retirement by the war, was already at the piano doing a stirring if out-of-tune rendition of 'Daisy, Daisy, Give Me Your Answer Do.'

'I'm half-crazy all for the love of you!'

If *that* wasn't a sign, Elaine didn't know what was!

Marty was at the bar, rising above everyone else, that lanky lamp-post of a man, a human streetlight, pushing his glasses towards the rim of his bony nose. Marty but not his sidekick, Robert Capa.

Oh God, was she too late?

He saw Elaine and smiled slowly. He mimed getting a drink. She mouthed, 'I'm fine, thank you.'

Please don't let him think I'm here for him!

'Where's Robert Capa?'

'And how are you, Marty?' He put on a funny voice to remind her of her manners. He had wispy hair on his upper lip, not enough to be called a moustache. Elaine found him obnoxious and felt certain the feeling was mutual.

'Sorry. How are you, Marty?'

'Fine, thank you.' He drank his rum slowly, blinked at her with his opaque eyes. She couldn't for the life of her understand how he and Robert Capa were best buddies.

'Do you know where Robert Capa is?'

'Away on a job.'

Damn it.

'I… I thought he wasn't going until tomorrow.'

Marty shrugged.

The Larry photos had showed her how dangerous his work was. Robert Capa could be anywhere: shot at, exploded, blasted into, lost at sea. Anything could happen. Why hadn't she considered this before?

'Where is he going?'

Now Marty laughed. 'I can't possibly tell you. It's hush-hush.'

Elaine's stomach clenched. She'd blown it now. She should have just asked Clive. Clive would have been able to find out in a jiffy. He did that for people sometimes: spying, she called it. He preferred 'investigating'. *Private investigator for our boys.* They loved him. They didn't love him when he tried to seduce their wives, but to be fair, he had only succeeded the once. But although she had written to Alan about Robert Capa – Alan was always someone she had felt free to bare her soul to – she wasn't ready to mention Robert Capa to Clive. He was a big fan of Justin, for one thing. He wanted Elaine to marry a rich man with big rich houses (that he'd look after for a fee).

'Is it dangerous?' Elaine could contain her fears no longer.

Marty blew smoke before replying. It probably wasn't meant for her face, but it went that way and she coughed.

'Do you know Robert Capa at all?'

'I don't know him very well,' she admitted. 'But… I'd like to.'

He stared down from his great height. He couldn't help but be intimidating, but she would not be intimidated. 'Robert Capa *only* does dangerous work. You'd do well to remember that.'

As Marty walked over to the bar, Elaine noticed his limp. She supposed she would have noticed it the first time they met if she hadn't been so dazzled by the brilliance of his best friend. She wondered what happened to him – she guessed that, unlike Clive's limp, it was from a wound, maybe from the Great War. He was just about old enough.

He got her a gin and she swallowed it back in one because it felt like a test.

'It's just, he asked my opinion on something.' A half-truth and Marty knew it. 'I… thought I should let him know it before he went.'

'You're not the first girl who thinks her opinion is important.'

'I know that,' Elaine said curtly.

He must have taken pity on her. In a strangled voice he said: 'I suppose I *could* tell you where he is leaving from tonight.'

Elaine brightened. All was not lost. 'Please. Oh, thank you, Marty. I really appreciate it.'

She reached over to kiss his cheek. It was light, moist and slightly stubbly. He flushed salmon pink. First, he wrote down the name of a station, then he wrote down the time of Robert Capa's train, which he underlined twice.

In the taxi to Euston, the elderly driver apologised: the car smelled of vomit. 'Soldier didn't want to go back,' he said. 'Parents sat either side of him, holding him down.'

Elaine thought of how Alan hadn't wanted to enlist either. She thought, *don't judge*, but she couldn't bring herself to say anything.

She imagined she would find Robert Capa in the railway bar surrounded by people.

He *was* in the railway bar, but fortunately he was alone. She watched him for a moment; he was making notes in something like a school exercise book. The clock over his head said ten to eight but if it was, he would have missed his train. She checked her watch: it was only half past seven. The clock was fast.

Pulling her coat tightly around her, she walked in, then stood over his table, aware of the shadow she cast over the wall. Now, hopefully, she would find out if he really wanted her, or if she was just another playboy's conquest.

When he looked up, he didn't seem surprised she was there. Delighted, yes, but as though he had been waiting for her all along. It was an incredible feeling.

'Mr Robert Capa? War photographer?'

'Miss Elaine Parker, Clerical girl, cat owner and crazy dancer.'

Elaine felt suddenly woozy, like the time she had drunk too much gin and Alan had to carry her home while the sirens were going off.

'What brings my favourite girl here?'

Her excuses were lined up and at the ready. 'You wanted to know what I thought of your photographs, didn't you?'

'Couldn't it wait?' he asked with his flinty black eyes: how could she have thought they were brown?

It was not just his bared teeth; he was like the big bad wolf. Only at that moment, she wanted nothing more than for him to eat her all up.

'No, I thought you ought to know before you went… away.'

Her hands had somehow found their way into his. This was no time for pretending or hiding anything. There was no time for playing hard to get. He had a train to catch to somewhere dangerous. She might never see him again.

She had a peculiar sensation of wanting to lie down very close to him in some dark, warm place and have his body on hers. It made it difficult to find the words.

'I thought they were incredible. *You* are incredible.'

There, she had gone and done it now.

He laughed. 'Thank you.'

'And you're going off to do more incredible work now?'

He shrugged. 'It's my job… I go where they send me.' Again, the shy glance seemed almost boyish. Suddenly vulnerable. 'So that's really why you made this dash to Euston? In response to the pictures?'

'I decided it was an emergency.' Forget the clock, she was the one who was fast.

They grinned boldly at each other. Everything felt out in the open now. No secrets. No shame.

'Can I call you Pinky?'

'Why?'

'It suits you.'

She showed him her little finger. 'In English, *that's* a pinky.'

He seemed to have taken that as an excuse or a reason to put his arm right round her. Perhaps it was a sign of where he was from – public demonstrations of affection were not the done thing here. His arm felt heavy, cloying, clogging. Wonderful.

'But to this foolish Hungarian, Pinky suits you more.'

'Okay.' Elaine felt as though she would never want to say no to him about anything, ever. 'Only if I can call you…' She pretended to think, although in fact she had already whispered it to her pillow – 'Bobby.'

He laughed, squeezing her shoulder tighter. 'You can call me anything you like.'

'Don't you dare get killed,' she mumbled into his jacket collar. *Oh, it smelled of him.*

'I'll do my best,' he said. He stroked her hair from the roots to the tips. He didn't miss a bit.

'And you, my darling Pinky, don't run off with any other guys.'

Guys? Plural? She was going to joke, *so I can run off with just one then?* But as she looked up at him, his face was deadly serious.

'As if I would. I hate to think of you going into danger.'

He pulled back, gazed at her. 'I think the danger is all here actually… I find you irresistible.'

And then he kissed her.

CHAPTER FIVE

SPAIN

JUNE 2016, DAY ONE

Matthew goes into the house, then comes back holding a picture in a dirty gold frame.

'Remember this, Jen?'

Black and white. It's a photograph of two girls, two little girls, but they're not facing the camera, they're looking the other way over a stretch of water. Most people would have done the old 'look this way!' but then they wouldn't have caught the cold whiteness of their legs, the pretty lines of their dresses or the smooth surface of the water.

I know it's Mum and Aunty Barbara, but I don't think I would have known it unless I'd always known it somehow.

In the photo, Mum looks smaller, more vulnerable. It's Aunty Barbara who looks the one in charge, for once. She's got Mum firmly by the hand. Maybe she thinks that if she doesn't, Mum might jump in or something.

It's not only the positioning, or the angle of the shot, it's the lighting that makes it special. Whoever took it knew what they were doing – that, or they got lucky. It does happen. I know.

I used to take photos professionally. Well, when I say *professionally*, I mean I was paid for it. There was nothing professional about it. There were twenty, twenty-five clubs in Ibiza, and I would go around and spend time at each of them. My subject matter: happy girls in triangular bikinis and boys going, 'Yeah!' with bottles of beer. Sometimes, girl on boy's shoulders (going 'Yeah!' with a bottle of beer), sometimes a triangular-bikini girl having a snog in the corner. Double points if it was with another triangular-bikini girl. No one got tired of it. It's odd to think about it now, from the distance of twenty years, but my club photos were regarded as some of the best on the island – and once I had that reputation, it seemed to stick and everything I did was good simply because it was me who had done it. It was something I could never quite believe at the time, even less now. People talk about a golden time in their lives – I suppose you could say, without me having realised it then, that was mine. It's a time I was proud of, yes, but at the same time, I find it painful to think about now.

I examine the picture again. Mum and Aunty Barbara look like best friends here, even from behind; they look united and full of fun.

I suppose the camera does lie, sometimes. Or maybe not lie exactly, it just doesn't tell the whole story. It can't. It's just a moment from a life, a single currant from a fruit cake.

This photo used to be kept on the mantlepiece, above the electric fire in Mum's old house in Croydon and next to a school photo of Matthew and a football trophy: 'Ramblers Most Improved Player of the Year 1996/7'.

I wonder how this is 'news'.

Meanwhile, Matthew is staring at me expectantly.

'How come you've got it?' I ask.

Matthew wipes his forehead. This, I realise, was the wrong question.

'Mum gave it to me.'

Of course she did.

'Right. So?'

'Look at the back.'

I turn it over. Bottom left-hand corner. Small squiggled letters, private or secretive maybe. It says *B and P forever.*

'What's that supposed to mean?'

'Exactly,' Matthew says triumphantly. 'So – and this was Gisela's idea…'

Gisela always comes up with the ideas.

'She got me a meeting at an auction house in Malaga.'

'Right?'

He looks at us all dramatically. 'And I found out it was taken by the war photographer Robert Capa. You've all heard of him, right?'

'No,' says Mum firmly, as Aunty Barbara shakes her head.

'Don't think so, Matty, sorry.'

I have. Paul used to have a print of one of his photographs on the wall over his bed. I remember going round to his flat in the early days and seeing it, admiring it – not because I liked the image, more that I liked Paul. *The Falling Soldier* was the photo of a man who'd been shot – that very instant. Those were his dying moments. He had a rifle in hand, his arm slung back and bullet cartridges round his neck. He was still standing, but about to go down, and his chest seemed to be puffed out, proudly embracing his fate but also rebelling against it. I can't remember much else about it, but it was hung next to the famous print of a young Che Guevara in a military beret. Paul had quite the thing about revolutionaries back then. We both did.

Later, when I did an evening course in photography after Ibiza, when I still had dreams about making a living out of photography, the tutor showed us a picture and told us Robert Capa's philosophy was 'get closer'.

'But if it were taken by Robert Capa, wouldn't it say R.C.?' I suggest, stating the obvious. 'Not *B or P* and certainly not *forever…*'

Matthew shrugs.

'And if it was him who took the picture, wouldn't Mum and Aunty Barbara remember him?'

'I don't remember anything about it at all,' says Mum with finality. 'Where was it taken?'

Matthew doesn't know.

'Must be worth a few bob?' offers Derek.

'Bingo!' Matthew points at Derek. 'I've been offered a couple of grand for it... but Gisela thinks I should wait till next year.' He licks his lips.

Mum looks thrilled. 'Well done, Matthew!'

I sit back in my chair, thinking, *what's going to happen between now and next year?*

'But the thing is, guys, there's more. You're not going to believe this... the auction house did a bit of digging and it turns out not only did Nana know Robert Capa' – Matthew grins at us – 'it turns out that she very likely had some sort of relationship with him too, during the war.'

I don't remember Nana Elaine very well. I remember her sitting in the corner of the room of her home eating sugared almonds. She had tree-trunk legs and wore bandages wrapped round them. The talc she used made me sneeze. One time, I locked myself in the loo at hers and she broke me out – she was astonishingly proficient with a coin in the lock – and when she did, she hugged me close and whispered, 'You were frightened. I remember being frightened,' which even then I thought was an odd thing to say.

She paid for Matthew's and my piano lessons too, but used to get gloomy when we didn't practise our scales for her. I remember her shaking her head at me. 'You can lead a horse to water, but you can't make it drink,' she'd say, which I erroneously thought meant that I could have the riding lessons I would have preferred. She had shelves full of books and always said, 'Take one, Jen. What lives! What stories!' which I had always interpreted as her not having much of a story of her own.

I remember going to school the morning after she died. I hoped the teachers would treat me differently for my suffering – and they did, for a day or so. They said I could stay in at break if I wanted to. They were so nice, I shamefully wished I could tell them the news every few weeks or so.

'Did you know any of this?' I ask Aunty Barbara.

She makes a face. 'Sorry.'

'I had no idea,' says my mum. *Fan, fan, fan. She'll get repetitive strain injury.*

A tiny lizard whips under the sunlounger. It seems to scratch itself ostentatiously – *look how flexible my limbs are* – then runs off. I squeal at the sight of it, but no one else remarks on it. I guess they're a common sight out here.

Matthew continues. 'Apparently, they were like the *it* couple of their time. He even wrote about it.'

'It couple?' asks Barbara.

'Like Kanye and Kim,' says Mum. A surprising example and I'm not surprised that Barbara looks none the wiser. 'You know... Astaire and Rogers?'

'What about Grandad?' I ask. I have no memories of him – he died when Mum was pregnant with me. There were a couple of photos, I think, formal ones, but that was it. He had fought in the war apparently, but no one knew much about it.

'I'm not sure if—'

'Anyway,' interrupts Matthew, 'there's this production company who are making a documentary: *Robert Capa – A Retrospective.* There's been loads about him already of course, but this is going to be the definitive one.'

'Which production company?'

'Oh, one in London,' he says vaguely. 'They've done loads of big shows.'

'And now they want to do: *Boyfriends of Nana...*?'

'Uh huh.'

Even Alyssia is moved enough by this information to turn her face forty-five degrees away from the phone screen.

'What exactly are they planning to do, Dad?'

'They want to include us in the documentary.'

'How?'

'Just… we'll talk about Nana. They'll record us and maybe take some photos,' Matthew says vaguely.

'Oh,' says Aunty Barbara. 'Will this Kim and Kanye be in it too?'

Matthew rolls onto his stomach. There's a fine lattice indentation on his back from the sunlounger. It looks like honeycomb.

'It's up to you, guys,' he says impatiently. 'We don't have to get involved, but I thought it could be fun.'

He covers his face with a towel. Mum paws at his shoulder.

'It does sound fabulous, darling. Well done.'

Alyssia squidges up her pretty face. 'I'm not doing it.' *She's hilarious*, I think. *Completely uncooperative.*

Aunty Barbara muses, 'I wonder if Mum would have wanted us to take part?'

I feel sorry for Matthew. His big announcement has not gone down as well as he had anticipated. But I am feeling confused. Our nana had a famous boyfriend? And what about Grandad? I wonder if they split up, or if he died, or what? Then I wonder what Paul would say about all this.

'When do they want to do it?'

Dramatically, Matthew throws off the towel, looks at his watch, then poufs up his hair.

'They'll be here any minute now.'

CHAPTER SIX

LONDON, SEPTEMBER 1943

'I'm sorry, my heart is no longer in this,' Elaine told Justin. 'In *us*,' she added, just to be clear. She had borrowed the words from *The Vicar and the Choir Mistress*. She had to tell him. Even though it was three days since the goodbye kiss with Robert Capa, she still felt like she was on fire.

'Mine is,' Justin said flatly, which was not what the hero in the book had said at all.

'It takes two to tango.'

'I suppose it does.'

She could hear other men laughing in the background at his end. His phone was in the mess room. How excruciating this must be for him. Jilted in front of an audience of pilots. She wondered idly what the word for a group of pilots might be. A *drone*?

Please, don't ask me if I've met anyone else, Elaine thought. And, as though he were reading her mind, the next thing he said was, 'Have you met anyone else to tango with?'

Elaine sighed; she couldn't help it. And he understood the meaning of that sigh, for very stiffly, he continued: 'Oh, I see! So now I have to fly my plane over Germany and fight for my country knowing that my girl is in love with another man.'

'I'm sorry, Justin.' Elaine hated herself, but at the same time she couldn't help wondering about the relevance of that comment. After all, it was neither her idea nor her fault that he was a pilot.

'They told me you weren't good enough for me,' he added. Elaine swallowed. Whoever the mysterious 'they' was, she bet they had. She had suspected it all along. It was obvious that she was not the right kind of girl for Justin. She didn't have the right accent, the right name, the right figure. All she had was the right kind of gloves and coat and the right kind of profession and these were temporary window-dressings that could be taken away at the slightest nudge.

'I wish I had listened.'

The problem, Elaine now realised, was she didn't even know where she stood with Robert Capa. Was she his girl or not?

Monday lunchtime was fried fish and there was quite a buzz, for they'd not had fish for a while. Elaine was unimpressed – even less when it turned out to be breaded skate fingers.

Over their trays, she continued to pick Annie's brains. She wanted to know everything about Robert Capa.

'What did you hear about his last girlfriend?'

'Oh, Robert Capa had all the girlfriends…'

Elaine shivered. 'But no one serious?'

'Oh yes,' said Annie imperviously. 'One very serious.'

Elaine froze. She should have anticipated this, but she hadn't. 'And?'

'She was a revolutionary,' said Annie, chewing vigorously, for she had notoriously low standards when it came to food. 'Mmm, this is so good.'

Justin's previous girlfriend was a ballerina and that had been bad enough. For weeks, Elaine had fretted about this girl who did the *pas de deux* and the splits at the Lyceum. Then they had met, by pure coincidence, in a basement bar under Tottenham Court Road and Elaine realised she was just a normal girl, albeit with exceptionally big eyes and quite muscular calves.

'A revolutionary?' Elaine's heart sank. While she found 'clerical girl' prestigious, revolutionary was, of course, glamour on an unprecedented scale. 'How do you mean?'

'You know – like an agitator, a protestor, a freedom fighter – and an amazing photographer too by all accounts.'

'Oh,' said Elaine, for this was far from what she had hoped to hear. 'What happened?'

'She was killed,' said Annie. 'A terrible accident. A tank. I've never tasted anything like this.'

'I see,' said Elaine, not seeing anything at all. She had once been worried about a dancer in a tutu, now she had a legend to contend with.

'But you're not seriously serious about Robert Capa, are you, Elaine?' continued Annie. 'I mean, he's very agreeable but don't you remember what we discussed?'

Elaine did remember what Annie had discussed, at length. She remembered it so well, the words kept her awake at night.

'I'm not seriously serious,' Elaine lied. 'It's just a wartime romance, you know how it is.'

'Phew,' Annie said, 'because much as I adore him, he's not sensible, he's not reliable, and he's not a good bet for you. I'd hate to think you'd split up with Justin for him.'

That afternoon, it was a relief to finish transcribing dear William's letter to his mum. As she did so, Elaine reminded herself of what Mrs Dill called the first rule of letter transcribing: *Don't get too attached.*

Perhaps it would be good to apply that to her personal life too.

Autumn was definitely biting. The leaves were changing colour and sometimes it looked like the whole street was bathed in gold and orange. *You notice these things even more in times of war*, thought

Elaine. One minute the branches were trembling under the weight of the leaves, another moment they were stark naked. How could you not notice how transitory everything was with this as your backdrop?

The next Friday after work, it started drizzling as soon as they left the office. Typical! Elaine, Annie, Leon and Mrs Dill hurried over to the George, Myra hobbled after them a short while later. They were just celebrating having made it through another week when Mrs Dill nudged Elaine and pointed excitedly at the pub door.

'Look who's here to see you!'

He's back, he's back. Elaine's heartbeat went wild. Only it wasn't Robert Capa, war photographer, returned from his travels, it was Justin, and quite out of sorts he looked too. His face was bright scarlet and sweaty. Even the smart uniform couldn't counter it. You could cook an egg on each cheek, he was that hot and red. Surveying the room with blurry eyes, it took him a while to focus on her, but then he stumbled over. Elaine saw that Bessie, the eagle-eyed landlady, was already registering him as a steaming drunk. Bessie would prefer to throw out fifty innocent men than have a fight in her precious bar.

'Is that him, then?' Justin pointed at Leon with a sneer.

'What? Who?'

'Your new fella.'

'That's *Leon* from the post room… you know Leon, you've met him before.'

The table Justin was leaning heavily against began to tip. The glasses slid and only with some dexterity did Elaine manage to save them from slipping to the floor. Great, she thought, not only did she have to contend with Justin, but now she smelled of beer as well as skate fingers.

'So where is your young beau?'

'He's not young,' Elaine countered lamely, as though this constituted the problem. She rearranged the glasses in the middle of the table. Anything to keep busy. 'And he's not here.'

Thank goodness.

'He's the famous photographer chap, isn't he? Robert Capa?'

Elaine froze. How could he possibly know?

'Word gets around. He's not even English, is he? Is he a Nazi scumbag?'

'A Nazi? Don't be ridiculous, Justin!'

'He's a Kraut though, isn't he?'

'No, he was Hungarian originally. He left there a long time ago… anyway, this is nothing to do with you.'

'I can tell you this: he's gone. Finished. Kaput.'

Elaine couldn't help it. She let out a horrified squeal. She covered her mouth with her hands, then whispered, 'Dead?'

'No, not dead.' Justin looked as surprised as she was by her outburst. He proceeded contemptuously. 'Not *yet* anyway. I mean, whatever's going on with you and him, there's *no way* it's going to last. It's impossible.'

Elaine gripped the tabletop, found it drenched, took away her hands in disgust.

'I should have known what a girl like you was like,' he continued. 'You've got no class.' His fist was very close to her face and for a moment, Elaine thought he was going to hit her. She closed her eyes and waited for the blow. It didn't come. When she opened her eyes, Annie had inserted herself between them. There was nothing about her that wasn't clear and strong, like a headmistress dealing with a particularly incalcitrant pupil.

'Look here, Justin,' Annie said. 'You need to back off.'

But Elaine wanted to know more before he went. 'How do *you* know whether it will last or not, Justin?'

'Exactly what I said. Everyone knows Robert Capa.' Justin spat out the words. 'He's not just famous for his photos. He has a girl in every port. Someone to keep the bed warm everywhere. You are nothing special, Elaine Parker. Never were.'

Annie sighed. 'Do we have to do this?'

But Elaine's temper was up now. Who was Justin to talk to her like this?

'Jealousy doesn't become you.'

'Doesn't it?' He wobbled. 'And to think, I was considering marrying you.'

Elaine flushed.

'Don't come crawling back to me when it doesn't work out with your foreign playboy.'

'I wouldn't dream of it.'

Annie was the only one Justin would listen to. She pulled him outside, leaving Elaine alone and ashamed. This wasn't supposed to happen. Mrs Dill and Myra left quietly under a cloud of umbrellas and anxious looks. The rain was really coming down now. After about ten minutes, Annie came back in, sopping wet and shaking her head resignedly. Everyone was looking at her. Droplets fell onto her shoulders and her make-up had smeared, giving her panda eyes and faint tramlines down her cheeks. She even smelled damp.

'Thank you,' Elaine said several times. She got Annie a drink and a tea towel to dry off with. 'I owe you.'

Annie was still miffed. 'I really like Robert Capa,' she said.

'But?'

'But… I'm not sure you've made the right decision there, Elaine.'

It was another slow weekend, but Elaine helped Mrs Marriot in the shop on Saturday, which passed the time. She read the contents of *Life* magazine from cover to cover because it made her feel closer to Robert Capa. He didn't have a photo in that edition, but there was a tiny photo of him in the contributors' section. Studying it, she decided he looked much older in it than he did in real life. He wasn't smiling and he looked like a man who worked in an office. There was something funny about that somehow. She saw that Marty, photo-less, was also credited as an executive, which she decided was a title as enigmatic and confused as the man himself.

There was no letter from her brother Alan, which was worrying because that made it one whole month without news. She wrote to him anyway, a hearty missive full of skate, spam and what Bettie Page had brought in (a half-dead mouse) and wasn't she a clever girl? Alan loved Bettie Page more than life itself, so the ten lines Elaine devoted to her was not entirely excessive. Elaine also told Alan a little more about Robert Capa, but reassured him that nothing would come between them. Alan did need reassurance about such things. Always had. When he was living at home, Elaine had been confident she could keep him calm. Now he was away, she was not so sure.

She tried to keep her tone light. 'I don't suppose you've met any nice girls, have you?' she wrote, then crossed it out and started again. She didn't want him to feel pressured. And the most surprising things could do that.

Best return to the neutral subject of Bettie Page.

All weekend, Annie and Justin's words went round in her mind like a revolving door. And Marty's too, for hadn't he insinuated the same? *Robert Capa is a playboy, unreliable, impossible.*

She didn't quite believe it, but she wouldn't, would she? That was part of it. The girl in every port thing: they all thought they were the only one – that was the charm.

On Sunday afternoon Clive's new girl, Maisie May Mahoney, came round for a formal introduction. She had brought iced buns in brown paper from work *and* a slice of corned beef for Bettie Page. How thoughtful this was, how kind! Elaine liked the pretty young woman immediately. She hoped Clive would work at keeping this relationship – but at the same time, secretly thought Maisie could probably do better than her brother. Especially if she continued at the municipal canteen. This was a coveted job in a time of food shortages.

The buns were stale, as Maisie had warned, but they were better than a kick in the teeth and Elaine knew she would get several sentences out of them in her next letter to Alan.

CHAPTER SEVEN

LONDON, OCTOBER 1943

On Monday morning, leaves were piled high in the streets outside the office, filling some of the craters in the road and sticking to the soles of Myra's ill-fitting shoes.

Elaine arrived to find there was a note on her desk. Annie leaned over, desperate to know what was going on.

'That's from Robert Capa, isn't it?'

'No,' Elaine lied, for Mrs Dill and Felicity had big waggling ears. She made a face at Annie. 'Shhhh.'

Only when they were sharing a cigarette outside, sheltering from the wind that had struck up from nowhere, did Elaine finally come clean.

'He's invited me to dinner tonight.' She paused. 'At the Savoy.' There had been no way to reply. He must have been that certain that she was coming. The cheeky so-and-so. And the Savoy! Whoever went on a first date to the Savoy? Even Justin, who was posher than Neville Chamberlain, had only taken her to Browns in Covent Garden.

The Savoy!

'What if you couldn't make it?' Annie asked disapprovingly again. How she could switch so seamlessly from *he's the most agreeable man in London* to *you've not made the right decision* was anyone's guess.

'Thing is, I can,' said Elaine, giggling. 'I guess he just knew.'

*

Robert Capa, her Bobby, was waiting in the bar. He was a fish out of water in the Savoy, but – if you can say this – in a good way. In an interesting way. He looked just as sturdy as the mahogany counter he was propped against. But he was not uptight, not rigidly formal like most of the men, and he gave her the biggest, unashamed, lusty grin. Here was someone easy with himself, easy with the world. She mustn't think of the moments their bodies had made contact when dancing, although she couldn't get them out of her silly head. And the moment he had kissed her and stroked her hair. Is that what he did when he was away? With other women too?

She looked around and she could see that there were couples, some in uniform, wartime romances all over the place. That's what Annie and Justin thought she was having, obviously. And maybe she was. She just had to concentrate on the now.

He's back. At last.

She never wanted him to go away again.

People liked Robert Capa. Men and women liked him. You could see that. The elderly waitress fluttered at him; the cook limped out to say hello. They were down to their last, even at the Savoy, but they had saved one of everything for Robert Capa and his lady friend, of course they had. He wouldn't struggle keeping a woman in every port, that was obvious.

He ate his steak rare, naturally; she had the pork medallions, which he recommended. She'd never had them before. They were excellent and she thought, *if this doesn't work out – which it probably won't– I'll have always had the pork medallions.*

'And your brother – Alan, is it?'

'Conscripted,' she said. 'Army…'

'France?'

'Still in England. At least, he was when I last heard.'

She lit a cigarette with the match between her teeth to cover the awkwardness she always felt when Alan was the subject.

'Good trick.' He smiled.

'Do you have any?'

'None whatsoever.'

She was sure he was lying. He seemed like a man full of tricks. He asked her to guess his hobby. How would she know? She couldn't possibly. She could hardly think straight around him, it was that bad.

'Tennis, golf, drawing, dice?'

He laughed. *Was it something rude?*

It wasn't. 'Stamp collecting. I've got albums of them. My mother took them with her to New York. One day, I'll show you them.'

'But they're in America?'

He nodded. 'I'll have to take you there, then.'

Don't smile, Elaine told herself, *don't let him know how much this means to you.*

In the street outside, darkness was descending fast. A swaying Navy man looked up at Elaine and pointed. 'There's the girl I want to marry.'

Bobby laughed; he helped the unsteady fellow to his feet. 'Too late, my friend, she's taken.'

The men shook hands. 'Lucky bugger,' said the other. 'What I'd do for a woman like that!'

Elaine felt thrilled and insulted at the same time. As they walked along, coyly she asked, '*Am* I taken?'

'I'm working on it,' Bobby said.

Elaine could tell he was smiling to himself. He looked down suddenly at the camera slung round his neck. She felt a sudden worry that she might be taking him away from something important.

'You can take photos if you like.'

He smiled at her in that way he had.

'It's fine; when I take photos, I like to give it all my attention. So now, I want to give *you* all my attention.'

He didn't kiss her *properly* that night though, and she wasn't sure why he didn't. Their parting was all a bit rushed, the hailing of a cab, the unexpected arrival of one almost immediately, the jumping in, the goodbye… but still. They had kissed deeply at the train station before, had he forgotten? It felt like a step back and yet…

As he stroked her hastily on the cheek he whispered, 'You're dangerous, Pinky,' and even that made her shiver.

For their next date, they went dancing with Annie and Marty. It was a wild and sweaty Saturday night and the band didn't let up for a moment. This time, Elaine and Bobby didn't just brush past each other, like ships on the Atlantic, but gripped each other tightly and with intent. His leg was between hers, his hands on her waist; he might not be able to dance well, but he knew about getting closer.

In the bathroom, Elaine told Annie that it would be perfect if Annie got together with Marty. But Annie said not unless Marty were the last man left in England, and even then, no, thank you.

Fortunately, although Annie didn't like Marty *like that*, she was still content to boogaloo with him. Marty was surprisingly light on his feet, leaving Elaine and Bobby to wriggle in peace – or in mad abandon, whatever the music dictated. And then, before too long, it was 2 a.m. and Bobby was saying to her, 'I'll put you in a taxi.'

'The men are off to play poker,' Annie told her, eyebrows raised. 'They always do.'

Elaine didn't like this. She felt offended, not only that they were off for cards, but that Annie knew and she didn't. This wasn't as she'd pictured it. Yes, it was only their second date, but it was *kind* of their fourth if you counted the evening they first met and the meeting at the train station. She was so attached to him she had written to her brother about him twice already! And why wouldn't you? She wasn't sixteen any more.

Bobby held her close, but less in a seductive way, more as if she were a prop in a theatrical performance.

'I want to get under the coats with you,' she murmured hotly in his ear.

She felt him having some unspoken conversation with Marty over her head.

'Let's stay at the Savoy, please, Bobby,' she blurted out.

He stroked her hair, smiled at her tenderly. 'You've had a lot of champagne, sweetheart. I think maybe it's best to get you home.'

He came in the taxi with her and accompanied her to her front door. For once, she was too single-minded to be ashamed of where she lived. Trying to kiss, they ended up wrapped around each other against the door frame and inadvertently ringing the bell. Footsteps down the hall and then the mighty Mrs Perry stood before them, full of scornful fury. She, who wasn't scared by the Luftwaffe, wasn't going to be fazed by doorbell-ringing at half past two.

Was Elaine seeing things or was she actually wielding a rolling pin like a landlady in a cartoon?

'Is she drunk?' She pointed at Elaine.

'She's got food poisoning.' Bobby winked at Elaine, putting his fingers on her lips.

'There's not enough food in London for poisoning,' Mrs Perry stated flatly.

'A bit of an exaggeration,' Elaine tried to point out, but it came out as 'Sh'not true.' She continued, 'The Savoy have these incredible pork medallions—'

Bobby felt in his pocket. 'I have these cigarettes, Mrs Perry, and not a home for them to go to. Would you do me the honour?'

Elaine's flat felt five times smaller than it had that morning. Bobby was talking approvingly though about how tidy it was and how it was on the safest floor. He was always talking about fast exits and being alert to the enemy, keep your friends close, your enemies closer; most of which went over her head.

What a comedown after the Savoy, thought Elaine, looking around at her simple home. She was sobering up with a rapidity she wouldn't have thought possible. How she wished she hadn't asked him back here. She realised he didn't want to make love with her and now, she had decided, he would hate her. He would see the dirty working-class roots of her. He would know what lay behind the clerical girl – not much – and he wouldn't like it. What was she thinking, cooing over him like some wanton woman, letting him come back here to know more of her? What a fool she was. She was full of drunken regret.

'I have to go,' Bobby said predictably.

'You don't have to.' She felt like she was drowning.

He looked around. 'Your Mrs Perry won't like it.'

'I'd like it,' she said, although she was not sure what she wanted now. She held out her arms for him and he cuddled her, but he was still holding back.

'Not like this, sweetheart.'

In the morning, she woke up alone to cold black tea, a paracetamol, a thumping headache and a taste in her mouth beating a pulse: *He didn't want her. He didn't like her. He would leave her.*

CHAPTER EIGHT

LONDON, OCTOBER 1943

The war still wasn't going their way and it sometimes felt like there was a time limit on everything good. The clock was ticking. They were running out of days. Soon, the Nazis would be here, rampaging through the streets, and everything would be over.

If that happened, best to see to it that you were dead before they got to you.

Some people said rat poison would do it. Clive had brought home a large knife from the fishmongers and said he would sort her and Maisie May Mahoney. What a way to go, though. And what would happen to Alan if the Nazis came? Elaine couldn't imagine the Nazis having more patience with 'the sensitive' than the English did.

Some people said duty, perseverance, patriotism and forbearance were the only way. Other people said *we must make hay while the sun shines*. Elaine thought maybe it was a little bit of both.

Robert Capa called Elaine the night after the party, and the next night, and the night after that they went out dancing and they went out to dinner again at the Savoy and the pork medallions were just as good the second time. Just him and her, no Marty, no Annie and no plans for poker games after midnight. They talked and talked about his photographs, his love of Europe, his hatred of fascism, and Hitler and Mussolini, his regard for America. They even talked a little about Marty.

'Why do you like him so much?' Elaine ventured.

'Marty saved me,' he said, ordering more champagne. (Goodness knows where it came from.)

She pictured Marty saving Bobby. Perhaps abseiling down a cliff-face. She thought he might have jumped over to cover him, taken a bullet… or perhaps that was the cause of the bad leg?

They were on the dessert course – apple and fig crumble, his, suet pudding, hers – when Elaine dared to bring up the other subject that had been occupying her mind.

'Have you had lots of… relationships, Bobby?'

He made an unreadable face. 'One or two.'

'Will you tell me about your last girlfriend?'

Elaine had been mulling this over constantly since Annie told her. She had to trust Bobby was no longer a playboy. She had to trust he wasn't going to chase Merry or Faye. But the past? The past was a different kind of rival. *A revolutionary? And dead?* In a horrendous heart-breaking accident. How does one get over that? How does one *compete* with that?

'All right,' he said simply. 'You know I will always be honest with you.' Big brown puppy eyes. 'What is it you want to know, Pinky?'

'How do you feel about her now?'

He didn't even try to cover it up. He said, 'Gerda Taro was the greatest, bravest, sweetest girl I ever knew. Had she lived, she would have been more genius, more productive, more than anyone. She shouldn't have died. I wish she hadn't.' He hesitated. 'I told her not to go that day. She wouldn't listen.'

Elaine felt a chill run through her. *What was she even doing here?* She remembered her coat had been taken off her by a wizened old man at a counter. He'd taken it to some far-away room. That's what posh people were like: they could afford to give up their coats to complete strangers. She grabbed her clutch handbag and her gloves. She hadn't been fool enough to give those up too.

'Pinky?'

I will go back home, eat bread on the turn on my own in the dark kitchen. Clive will still be out with Maisie May Mahoney.

Perhaps she would call Justin and apologise. Beg him to take her back. Say she'd been afflicted by *a moment of madness*. He might even understand. But the thought of lying underneath Justin again, so shy and awkward and unenthusiastic, when she could be spending time with Bobby, repulsed her. He had spoiled her for all other men.

'What are you doing? Where are you off to?'

'You don't want me,' Elaine said in a tiny voice she barely recognised. She stood over him. She wanted him to stop her, but she was not sure he could. 'You want *her*.'

'Don't tell me what I want,' he said, and although his voice was as light as it always was, there was a hint of menace there too. 'She's not here, Pinky.' He touched her wrist; he did not pull at it, he didn't have to. 'She's not a threat to you, Pinky. Please stay. I am ready for you. Let me show you how devoted I am.'

He hailed a taxi and they went back to his flat in Belgravia.

My goodness.

My word.

Golly gosh.

Elaine couldn't believe it. Now *she* felt like a character from one of Mrs Marriot's cartoons with stars in her eyes or a lightbulb over her head. Or being hit over the head with a rolling pin.

Everywhere she went, on the tram, the train, on the stairs to the office, she couldn't stop smiling. 'Morning, Mrs Dill!' she sang out. 'Hello Vera, wonderful day!' 'Mrs Marriot, let me help you unload those books!' How did people go about their business after such a thing?

Annie said, 'Oh dear!' She could see Elaine was properly smitten. Elaine couldn't deny it and didn't even try. She had a swing in her step, a swagger in her walk. When men whistled at her in Piccadilly Circus, she beamed back. *Spread a little happiness*, she thought, *and be kind. Not everyone has got what Bobby and I have.*

In the canteen on Wednesday, over the dreaded lentils, when the high from the weekend was just about beginning to fade and the old anxieties were creeping in, Elaine asked, her voice thick with fear, 'Do you think Robert Capa is using me? Is it just a wartime thing?'

'How would I know?' Annie responded, which was no help at all.

Elaine scowled.

'Why not just enjoy the moment for what it is?' advised Annie, scraping her plate.

'Yes,' said Elaine uncertainly. Much as she liked to think that was an excellent philosophy, especially for these fraught, future-less times, that wasn't what she was about. She liked parties, she liked passion, but yes, she liked predictability and security too.

Over the next few weeks, Elaine and Bobby saw each other as often as they could. Elaine loved her late evenings at Bobby's apartment in Belgravia or at the Savoy, and she loved dancing at the underground clubs that only he seemed to know about. They sent each other little notes. She would slide hers into his overcoat pocket so he wouldn't forget about her, and he would send postcards through the post that would make her cheeks burn and meant she could never meet the postman's eyes again.

By early November, Elaine was feeling confident enough to invite Bobby over to her home in Balham. She didn't really want to, but then of course he had already been there once. She knew he was curious to see how she lived – this was his nature – and she knew that being honest with him was better than not. Still, it was with some trepidation that she wiped and dusted all day, put away Clive's things in the cupboard – they had a tendency to wander – and told Clive he had to stay out with Maisie May until midnight at least (which was what he did most Saturday nights anyway).

Elaine had her own room, which used to be hers, Clive and Alan's when they were little, and Clive had the larger room, which used to be their parents'. Their dad had left almost six months to the day after Mum had died, and once they accepted he wasn't coming back, they'd swapped the rooms around, although Elaine couldn't exactly remember why.

She diced potatoes, cauliflowers, swede, carrots and turnip and made a gravy her mum would have been proud of.

Bobby came round with his camera hanging off his neck as usual. She said it was like an extra limb, he said it was his third eye. He was delighted: on the way, he had seen some men fighting in Elephant and Castle. 'Classic shots,' he said with a wink, 'nosebleeds and everything.' He was always taking photos of things no one else would think to. He quickly recognised where a story was.

He had brought with him some flowers – pink, of course – and a bottle of rum. He looked around the kitchen, beaming from ear to ear.

'This reminds me of my home in Budapest,' he said and proceeded to tell Elaine about his ramshackle apartment block next to a train line, with a permanent saucepan in the bedroom to catch the rain, and about the brambles along the line where he went foraging for berries. With that, Elaine grew more at ease and after he had kissed and cuddled her some more, she thought it wasn't going to be too bad after all.

'So,' she said, holding out the casserole dish, 'my first attempt at a steak and ale pie.' She laughed nervously. There was worse to come. 'Which I proudly present to you, without the steak and ale.'

'Aha,' said Bobby knowledgeably. 'Woolton pie.'

'Yes!' Elaine was surprised. She thought this was the provenance only of housewives.

'I know it. I photographed Lord Woolton once.'

Of course he did. There was hardly a gentleman or lady in England who Robert Capa hadn't captured on his camera.

Bobby was in raptures over the pie. Every mouthful was delicious; he held up his fork, surveyed the pie, like a scientist examining cells.

'I haven't eaten like this in years.'

'Too much, Bobby!' Elaine laughed.

But he told her it wasn't too much, he loved home cooking and bless her, his own dear mother was a genius at so many things, but the kitchen brought her out in hives.

Elaine felt reassured. She had nothing to be ashamed of, nothing to be worried about. He made everything so easy.

He had brought some photos to show her. He was always reticent about showing her his pictures: 'I don't want to bore you,' he said. 'I know it's my stamp collection that you're after, really.' But she had asked and he had obliged. There was something about knowing what he saw, knowing what had been in his head that made Elaine feel she understood him more.

They sat there, flicking through an album of photos he had taken in North Africa. Men throwing stones, a woman in a veil staring at the camera, a child ecstatically holding a new pair of shoes. What he could do with his box Kodak was nothing short of amazing. She could have been there standing next to him. She could have shaken these people by their hands. She felt she knew them better than she knew the people in her life. She looked at Bobby, awestruck again. He was a genius, and yet *he* said he was crazy about her. Her, yes, little old Elaine Parker, from a family of ne'er-do-wells.

Elaine couldn't help it. She thought her heart would burst with happiness.

'If you had to give one piece of advice on how to take a good photo, what would it be?' she asked, although she had no intention of trying it herself. She had never been good at art. She didn't have an eye for a picture, she was better with an ear for a word.

'Hmm,' he said, and stroked his chin. 'Get closer.'

'All right,' she said, putting her arms round him. 'Now tell me.'

He couldn't speak for laughing. Took him a good couple of minutes before he could say, 'That was it, Pinky! That was my advice!'

About ten thirty, she heard the rattle of the key in the lock and jumped up, unnerved. She feared it was Mrs Perry with her talk of tawdry girls, but it was Clive. As he came in, a dark expression on his face, Elaine told herself, *don't react, don't. It'll be fine* and Bobby stood up. His hand was outstretched, ready to defuse.

'Oh, I see. Where's Justin?' asked Clive, his voice flat.

'This is Robert Capa, Clive,' Elaine said meekly. *This was embarrassing.* 'There's left-over Woolton pie if you'd like.'

'I thought Justin was going to be here.'

Elaine knew Clive was saying that to cause a stir. She saw Robert Capa stay virtually immobile, except for the small bite his teeth made on his lip.

Clive eyed Bobby up and down. 'Civilian, huh?'

Bobby nodded. 'And you?'

Clive pointed at his foot by way of explanation. 'I just came back for some stuff.'

'Fine,' said Elaine non-sensibly. If he couldn't be nice, the least he could do was to clear off.

Clive scowled some more. Then he went over to the cupboard and rifled through it. The ironing board fell out and he pushed it back in like he was having a fight. He left, slamming the front door behind him.

Elaine felt a great lump in her throat. This wasn't how she'd planned it. She looked at the empty plates and the glasses, the vase with the pinks now in, the pretty cloth, all the small efforts she'd made, all ruined. Clive had no reason to be nasty, it was just how he was sometimes. He had liked Justin, yes, but he could hardly pretend to be devastated that she had moved on, could he? Why couldn't things ever be easy?

'Hey, Pinky,' Bobby said gently. 'Come over here.' He patted his thighs. Elaine was going to start cleaning up, but instead, blushing, she went over and balanced precariously on his knee. He wrapped his arms round her.

'Families, eh?' he said, with such understanding that suddenly things didn't seem to feel as bad as they had.

'So now you've met my brother Clive…' she said.

'Perhaps I'll get on better with your brother Alan?'

She could tell he was smiling. Elaine made like she didn't hear and buried her face in his collar. He smelled of Woolton pie. Sans steak. Sans ale. She squeezed herself against him.

If he *was* using her, if this was just a wartime fling, he was very good at pretending that it wasn't.

CHAPTER NINE

LONDON, NOVEMBER 1943

Before too long, everyone at work seemed to know about Elaine's 'friendship' with Robert Capa. There was a buzzing in the office, a chatter in the canteen. His glory was rubbing off on her. At first, Elaine thought she must be mistaken – it couldn't be that, surely – but then she realised it must be. What else was there? Both Dolly and Joyce, on separate days, asked her if she wanted extra crumble. Joyce said she could do some vegetable gravy for her to take home if she liked. And Vera started complimenting her on her hairstyle.

The cartographers worked on the fifth floor – apart from the clanging of the lifts, you usually barely heard a squeak out of them.

'I hear you know Robert Capa,' one of them – the others had sent him over – said in the canteen.

Very little impressed the cartographers but they were impressed now.

'Tell him to keep up the good work,' one said.

'I love his photos,' said another. 'His Chinese ones are amazing.'

Elaine, who didn't know Bobby had been to China, nodded slowly. Was there anywhere he hadn't been? It was impossible to keep up.

'I didn't know he was *that* famous,' Elaine whispered to Annie later, thinking *how could a photographer be as famous as his subjects?*

'Oh, Elaine, just be careful, that's all.'

'You still think he's unreliable?'

Annie smiled secretively. 'Jury's out on that.'

*

Patter, patter, like raindrops on windows, their fingers were tippy-tappy on the typewriter keys. Elaine loved the sounds of everyone in the office working in unison. Everyone typing immense letters of love and loss from the other side of the world. Sometimes, it was a huge privilege. What greater task could there be than to transcribe one person's love to another, whether it was to a parent, a child, a sibling, a friend, or even, as is the case with Cyril Marshall, a note for his dog, Fletcher?

And Elaine was in love too. She was in love! She had always doubted she ever would be, doubted she was capable of it: she had not trained in it, had not witnessed it, but now she knew.

Every day, her fingers danced across the keys with vigour and excitement. She didn't have to look for the exact key to know it was there. And love was the same. It was there, bouncing off her fingers and at the end of every line, the ting was like a church bell chiming out in celebration.

Bobby arranged to meet her one lunchtime. When she arrived outside, he kissed her smack-bang-chop on the lips in a way Justin never had, in a way that Justin would never have dreamed of. This was in the street! In public! Elaine drew herself closer to him. She felt hugely happy every time she saw him. This was it. *Now* she understood why all the songs, the poems, and all the books were about it. It was blooming brilliant, that's why! Now, she consumed the romantic books Mrs Marriot selected for her with a new fervour. *The Ringmaster and the Tightrope Walker. Forbidden Nights in the Kasbah.* Now, she didn't shake her head at the yearning within, but empathised and identified with every sigh or pout.

'Where are we going?'

'You'll see.'

Elaine laughed. She liked this game, silly to pretend otherwise. The smokers outside the office were staring at him – no, they were staring at *them*.

They headed off towards Trafalgar Square, so grand with its statues of lions and Nelson's Column. Elaine was reminded of Alan chasing pigeons here when he was very little, then of herself comforting him when he got poop on his collar.

The National Gallery sat at the top of the square and there were crowds of people dotting the front.

Bobby took her hand and walked her past all the people.

'Press,' he murmured whenever anyone scowled at them. His camera was round his neck as usual, the way other men wore ties, and he couldn't have looked more like the professional photographer. It was almost a costume, like if you were playing an artist you might wear a smock and a beret. Elaine nodded, also trying to look like someone who knew what she was doing, sure she was failing. She felt people were murmuring, 'That's Robert Capa, that is,' and it shouldn't have, but it gave her a thrill.

They had emptied the galleries out on day two of the war. All the paintings had gone. Taken to safe-houses and underground bunkers all over the country and beyond. No setting light to the classics here. Elaine knew all this, but what she hadn't known was that they still wanted to provide culture for the miserable people of London, so an orchestra played to the public every day.

'Really?' asked Elaine when Bobby told her this. This was *such* a different world.

'Even during the Blitz,' he said. 'And that's one of the many reasons I love this city.'

He kissed her again. 'And that it gave me you, of course.'

When the music began, Elaine closed her eyes and let it wash over her. Her hand in his, safe, like she was sheltering from a storm in a forest with a companionable bear.

And then a German woman sang. A German woman, here in London, during the war? Could it be? Elaine looked around, but no one was reacting, so she wouldn't either. The voice was high-pitched, like notes you'd never dream of, and Elaine thought of the piano she never learned and it was so exalting, so exciting, that she wanted to do something with her hands, but ended up clasping them in front of her chest, then grabbing Bobby's and squeezing them tightly. Each squeeze was trying to say, *thank you, thank you for sharing this with me.*

She felt like weeping. She might have wept when it was over – *how dared they finish?* – it should go on for ever.

Bobby whispered that he wanted to introduce her to someone. Elaine wanted to say no – she still felt in a dreamlike trance from the music – but he was already waving at the woman seated in front of the grand piano and there was no way she wouldn't notice him. The woman did see, she got up, and she was actually calling out across the vast room, 'Well, if it isn't my man, Robert Capa!' And everyone turned to stare.

The two of them hugged and hugged some more. They *were* pleased to see each other. Elaine waited. She felt like a spare part. She didn't used to get this with Justin; he mightn't have been that interested in her, but at least other women didn't interest him either.

Bobby introduced the woman as the brains behind the whole performance: Myra Hess. 'My hero,' he added, somewhat unnecessarily, Elaine thought, because it was clear how smitten he was. The woman had cool black eyes like coal. There was something of an exotic bird about her. She had shiny red earrings that matched her red straight skirt and jacket.

Myra Hess surveyed her.

'Mr Capa, you told me you'd sworn off women!'

'Only singers,' he joked. 'The rest of them are fine.'

Elaine thought Myra Hess was going to say something about her to Bobby; that's what people usually did. Instead she leaned into Elaine and whispered in her ear.

'Take care of this one,' she said. 'He's more fragile than he looks.'

*

Bobby pulled her up onto a bronze lion in the sunshine, south of the square. Some soldiers had gathered around another one, and clerical assistants picking at sandwiches were on the others. You could see the travelling WHSmith bookstore over by the tube station, busier than the one at Balham. And the buildings that had been bombed. *So arbitrary. So random.* Here, a stubborn clothes shop, next to it, a nothing. She could remember when it was rubble, but hard to remember what it was before. Was it the post office or was that further along? Was it another bookshop, maybe?

Elaine thought – *God only knows how I'm going to get down.* The lions were higher than they looked. She would just have to trust in Bobby. She stroked its mane, even though it was cold and unresponsive.

Then Marty came along too. As he clambered up to join them, Elaine tried not to be annoyed, or to notice how ungainly he was. Bobby was delighted to see him. Elaine wondered how he had known they were here. Well, Bobby must have told him where they were going, she supposed, although she didn't know why he would have.

They got to talking about the outbreak of the war in 1939 – *gosh, four years ago already, the Phoney War, before anything of remark had happened* – and then Marty, smoking and dropping his ash far to the ground, said, 'Heard you were in London during the Blitz, Elaine?'

'Uh-huh.' She tucked into the chocolate bar Bobby had bought her. He was watching her, smiling. Between bites, she explained. 'I had only been at the office for a month when the first bombs fell.'

'You didn't want to get out of the city?' Bobby asked.

Elaine laughed.

'I had work. Anyway, where would I go? I didn't have anyone I could go to.'

'No relatives? No kindly benefactors in the country? Grandparents? Cousins?'

Elaine blushed. 'No one.'

It felt personal, as though she'd got rid of them all deliberately. *It wasn't my fault*, she wanted to say. *This is how it is to be normal* – you just don't know people in the countryside. You don't know people with spare rooms.

This was something Justin never seemed to understand about her. Bobby seemed to get it, though. He was looking at her not with revulsion or disbelief but with admiring eyes. Marty picked at his fingernails.

'So, you kept your family together? You and your two younger brothers?'

'And my cat, Bettie Page,' Elaine said defiantly.

Bobby laughed. 'Never forget Bettie Page.' He paused. 'It sounds like a fairy tale.'

'It was a nightmare most of the time.'

'I know,' he said. He squeezed her arm. 'I was there. I wish I'd known you back then.'

Elaine remembered one night when the city was under constant bombardment. It must have been a weekend, else she'd have been at the office. She was playing gin rummy in a shelter with trembling hands. Alan was scrunched up, humming to himself. Clive was trying his luck with a skinny blonde. Elaine sensed the girl's family's displeasure. She told Clive quietly, 'She's way out of your league.' The girl had big brothers, large guys, who were looking over at them angrily, loudly deciding what to do about this idiot.

Clive decided, abruptly, that they had to go. Whatever he did, he didn't like being beaten up for it. He wasn't a fool.

They ran out of the shelter to the wail of the sirens – her pulling Alan, chasing Clive. Elaine was furious with him. 'If we get bloody killed, it'll be your bloody fault.'

But it didn't happen like that.

After they'd gone the length of the street just as she and Alan were arguing to go back, the bomb fell. They threw themselves into a doorway, Clive gripped her, she gripped Alan – the Parker siblings were wrapped around each other. She could smell their sweat, or maybe it was hers. When the worst was over, they stood up, shook off the masonry, smashed glass, unidentifiable bits and blinked and stared.

The shelter they had just left had completely collapsed.

The people inside had been buried alive.

They tried to excavate it as fast as they could. Others appeared from nowhere, clawing at the rocks, and that was before the rescue workers and the fire engines came with their spades, torches and whistles and their proper equipment. Elaine, Clive and Alan were on their knees, their bloodied hands scraping at rocks – calling, then shushing and hoping to hear signs of life.

She can still see them all clear as day, clear as the moment they'd left them: The family of the girl Clive had been pursuing, the large brothers with the menacing eyes, the little boy who had lent them the playing cards. The mother who was breastfeeding a friend's baby as well as her own. The old people in a circle repeating the old theory 'if it's got your name on it' like an incantation. All of them. Entombed under filthy cement beams and lime. But not them – the mad, bad Parker siblings. They were the lucky ones. They were the free.

It made you never want to be vulnerable again.

'Elaine?' Bobby was talking to her. Elaine realised where she was. She was on a lion in Trafalgar Square with her love and his best friend. The war wasn't over, not by a long shot, but she was no longer alone. She picked up the chocolate. She tried to put the girl and her threatening brothers behind her. There had to be a reason for these things.

'Sorry.'

There was no reason for these things.

She smiled up at him anyway. Robert Capa, famous war photographer, was looking at her with those hazel-brown or nut-brown – who cares what colour they were – eyes full of affection.

'Time to go,' Marty said.

She and Bobby continued to see each other at least two or three evenings after work and much of the weekend. The size of her home, her love of champagne and a pork medallion, her wantonness, hadn't managed to put him off her yet. She blushed to think of it. No, if anything, the more Bobby got to know her, the more he seemed to like her! It seemed impossible, it seemed everything she would have expected in reverse, but it was true. They were terribly, sickeningly in love.

He was passionate about politics and she learned, listening to him pontificate in the George. He had been involved in demonstrations and resistance to the regime in Hungary, had been beaten up in a prison cell – by the police – before he escaped. In the George, he and Bessie talked a lot about Hungary and also Poland, where she was from. To Elaine, it seemed as though their conversations went round and round.

Bessie would say, 'We get the leaders we deserve.'

'No,' Bobby would insist, 'we get the leaders we tolerate.' And 'The normal people in Nazi Germany did not understand what it was they were supporting.'

But Bessie would say, 'They did, or they didn't fight it enough when they could.'

'It's the leaders to blame, not the people.'

'The people are to blame too,' Bessie always insisted, exasperated. 'We *all* suffer for their naivety.'

Elaine read the newspapers now, the bigger ones with the longer words, and she was pleased that the Allies had set up a commission at Nuremberg to investigate war crimes once the war was done. Bobby said this was 'a good thing' and Elaine respected Bobby's opinions more than anyone's. The Americans were making gains in the Pacific and German U-boats were being sunk in the Atlantic, but she knew nothing was settled when it came to the Nazis, nothing.

What would her mother have said about Bobby? Elaine wondered. She would have liked him, she was sure, but she probably would have expressed caution. That was her nature after all.

But where did caution ever get you?

Elaine only got glimpses of Marty, the best friend; he was like an extra in a movie, playing many parts. He often got up and bought the drinks so Bobby didn't have to. Elaine imagined that this must be what having a butler would be like. An unwinding, never-endingly long, narrow figure, a beige unobtrusive man of service. When she said this to Bobby, he laughed. 'A butler? Good grief, no, he's a friend!'

If he were in a photograph, you mightn't see him at first, then you would notice something not quite right, like one of those ghosts in the Victorian pictures. *Flower fairies. Now you see them, now you don't. Were they real?* That's not the important question.

'He is a bit spooky,' Elaine confided in Annie as she helped her change her typewriter ribbon. 'He's always there, in the shadows.'

'Even when you're… you-know-what?' Annie loved a bit of bawdy talk.

'Don't be daft,' said Elaine, blushing. But, she thought to herself, that was probably the only time he wasn't.

They were lying in bed at his rooms and Elaine had just told Bobby that she thought Marty was posh. Bobby did his throaty laugh. 'Posh? Marty? Whatever makes you think that?'

'He… he's so tall,' she said lamely. 'And thin… and aristocratic.'

'He carries himself well, I'll give you that.' Bobby laughed. 'Marty is hard-working, shrewd, but his family have no money, never have. He's a working-class boy at heart. Those are the kind of people I like best.' He kissed her neck, leaving her in no doubt that he was talking about her. Everything led back to her and she liked that.

'So how did he save your life then?'

Bobby looked confused. 'You remember that?'

'I remember everything you say.'

Bobby flushed. He did not easily admit weakness, but he would if he had to.

'Okay, well… after Gerda, I wanted to die. You could say I was killing myself. Oh, not directly – slowly drinking, you know. I was in Spain, America, China, all over the place. I was in a funk. Marty got me out of it. He took me off to a cottage in Scotland, and we argued. A lot. But Marty persuaded me to stick around for a bit longer. He fought in the Great War. He knows what it is to be blue. I picked up my camera again. He got me some contacts, got me some freelance work with *Life*. The rest is history… Don't look so serious, Pinky.'

He brushed her cheek.

'It was Marty who got me back on the straight and narrow.'

Elaine laughed: he was naked, drinking neat liquor. She squeezed herself closer to him. 'Is this the straight and narrow then?'

His glass met hers. He gave her a wink. 'It is for me, baby.'

CHAPTER TEN

SPAIN

JUNE 2016, DAY ONE

A car sweeps up the long drive, its tyres spitting dust in the gravel. Matthew jumps up, delighted.

'And they're here!' And dazed though we are, we all get up, sarong and sandal on, and troop obediently to the front of the house like children on a school trip.

As we watch their approach, Matthew grins conspiratorially at me. 'You'll see – this was worth making the trip for.'

The director of *Robert Capa – A Retrospective* is Nick Linfield. Around my age, I'd guess, but aging better than me. He is wearing tan leather gladiator sandals as though he is about to slay lions. I am relieved he is not some young smooth buck, but I wish I'd had time to go inside to freshen up. I'm wearing a vest top and shorts – perhaps not the greatest look with my legs. Paul used to say my legs would be the envy of any football player.

Nick Linfield has more kit than a soldier, and he manoeuvres it slowly out of the car. It would be intimidating but he has a friendly, open face.

My hands are heat-clammy. I wipe them on my top, then shake his.

'I'm Jen, Matthew's sister.'

'Lovely to meet you. This is so fascinating.'

Fascinating? Two minutes ago, I was a nobody, and now I'm fascinating? Because of Nana Elaine? Because of her thing with Robert Capa?

Then from the passenger seat, a beautiful ingénue – a model or a celebrity – arises. I don't know why, but my stomach drops. Nick introduces her as Stella, his brilliant researcher. It was Stella who was in touch with the auction house around the same time as Matthew was. A perfect coincidence. She is probably early twenties, improbably thin, neat and pretty. Tiny ear lobes with tiny diamond studs. Long legs in skinny jeans. T-shirt flattering her skinny arms. Another posh girl, of course. There can't be much money in this documentary film-making – you have to bring your own sandwiches to the picnic.

Nick shakes hands with Derek. Derek believes in handshake personality analysis the way the Victorians believed in bumps in the head. Nick's was pretty firm, so I think he may have passed Derek's test – *just*. He kisses Mum and Aunty Barbara. Barbara says she'll introduce him to the plants – 'there are prickly pears here, lemons there, tomatoes…' and he tells her, 'There is nothing I love more than a woman with green fingers.'

I don't know what motivates me to say it, but I do. 'Shame. I can't keep a plant alive.'

'To every rule there's an exception.' He grins at me.

'Where are you staying?' Mum asks.

They're not staying here, thank goodness. They're in a hotel in the town, down the valley.

'It's perfect,' says Nick. 'Lovely restaurant, verandah for drinks, couldn't be happier.' Stella nods enthusiastically, and I wonder if they're together-together. Stranger things have happened. Some women like an enormous age gap. I should know this.

He gazes around him. 'Not a patch on this though, Matthew, I have to say.'

Matthew offers to show them round.

'Oh, it's wonderful,' encourages Mum. 'You won't have seen anything like this, Stella!'

I sincerely doubt that.

'No stairs,' Matthew explains proudly, 'and there's a gym.'

'Are they here for a documentary, or to buy the house?' I say, but no one is paying any attention. In the hullaballoo, Barbara is already planning which cuttings Nick can take away, and Mum is telling Stella about Derek's terrific barbecues and how vegetarians are catered for, because you've got to these days, it's almost normal.

Back in my room, I try to contact Harry again. He's still not answering the phone and I am losing my mind, for what good it will do me. I call Paul's mobile. After he moved out, I was going to change his name in my phone to *Prat* but I couldn't. He's still Paul to me, although I managed to change his picture from one of him smiling to one of him that is little more than a dark shadow in the distance. He's so far away, he could be anyone.

I don't like calling Paul any more because of the cold businesslike voice he puts on with me now. It's like he's pretending we hardly know each other. But today, unexpectedly, not only does he pick up promptly but he sounds warm and friendly, as though nothing has happened between us. Before I can get a word in, he asks about my trip, the flight, Mum and Derek. Matthew and Barbara. He even asks after Alyssia, although he says, 'What is she now? Ten?' Maybe he's thawing. Maybe he misses me. It must be strange to be back in the family home without me there. I *hope* it's strange. I picture him at the cupboards, at the hob, making up one of his breakfasts. He always did a fantastic breakfast.

I don't tell him about the documentary. Although I like the idea of impressing him – a rare thing these days – and he *would* be impressed, I prefer the idea of keeping a secret from him. For once, let him be the one in the dark.

When I can trust my voice, I ask, 'So how's Harry then?'

Paul continues to sound jolly, which is a relief. 'We had a fantastic time yesterday. Went to a gallery, then out for dinner.' My heart yearns to be with them both, to be tripping alongside the river, embracing the city. This is how it used to be. The three of us, exploring the second-hand book stalls under Waterloo Bridge, choosing between pizza or Mexican food. I can picture the two of them together. Harry, taller than his dad now, laughing at him, with him, stopping to listen to a busker. Paul saying, 'If you hadn't given up the piano, this could have been you…'

God, I love these two.

'And today?' I ask, smiling.

'Ah…' Paul goes, and my heartbeat changes its rhythm. 'Harry is staying at his mate's house. Finn, is it?'

This wasn't the plan. I like Finn and I especially like Finn's mum and dad, who are brilliant parents without being know-it-alls, but we can't be offloading our parenting responsibilities on them (however much I'd like to). This was supposed to be Paul and Harry's bonding time. I hadn't forced him – Paul had agreed to it. And it wasn't the plan because ever since we split up, Paul's been coming and going like a man on a bungee elastic and Harry's been low. He's had to take time off from school – he never used to – and his grades have tumbled.

'Why?'

It feels like a long time before Paul says, 'I decided to go away too.'

For a second I wonder if that means he's decided to come here, here, to chase after me, to beg my forgiveness. I picture him running to catch the next plane like a tortured soul in a romcom… I picture him here, in the pool, cajoling me to get in, wrapping himself around me in the cool sheets of the bedroom.

'You're leaving Harry?'

'I'm not *leaving* him,' he says, the dial firmly switched to 'chilly'. 'He's seventeen, he's got his own things going on.'

'But… but you were supposed to be spending time with him.'

What does Sophie the counsellor say about this? I think. I'm willing to bet he hasn't told her.

Paul laughs. 'Harry doesn't want to spend time with me. Believe me, he's happier with Finn.'

'Where are you going then?'

'Ibiza.'

And breathe.

He doesn't want me any more. He's abandoned Harry – okay, he's left him in the safest hands in town – but still, he's abandoned Harry and not to make it up with me, but to… who knows what he's going to do in Ibiza?

I feel terrible. *Why do I let myself build up hope again and again and again?*

'Does Sophie know?'

'I've stopped seeing Sophie,' he says. 'It was all getting too pricey.'

And a holiday in Ibiza isn't?

I should have known it. Paul was hardly likely to experience an epiphany in my absence. My trip was hardly likely to bring him to his senses – he wasn't going to realise what he was throwing away, because he was throwing it all away deliberately and ruthlessly.

'I see.' I say. *Now who's cold and businesslike?* I am the coldest and most businesslike I have ever been. I am the cold and businesslike self I should have been six months ago. 'And what have you done about Pushkin?'

The pause tells me Paul hasn't thought this through. He never does. The cat he got us while he was doing all his sexting – *God only knows what he was thinking.*

I can almost hear him squirming. 'I'll sort it.'

'You had better.'

I have to ask. I have to. 'Who are you going with then?'

He pauses. I know the answer. For God's sake, I should understand it by now. How have I been so naive?

'Her name is Eva.' In a much lower voice, he says, 'But Jen, it's not like that. You're still my—'

I hang up, fumbling, then change his name in my phone to *Paul the Loser*. It should be satisfying but it isn't. It just hurts. Oh, it hurts.

I text Harry saying that I'm sorry Dad had to go away and is everything okay at Finn's? and please tell Finn's parents a massive thank-you from me.

That moment when Harry was born and placed in my arms and I had never seen anything so amazing in all my days, and Paul was just as besotted and he said, 'I'll never let you two down, never.'

Harry replies, *It's cool, Mum. Having a good time. Speak soon.*

Now I have to go out and be sociable and level-headed with the visitors and pretend I care about my nana's love life (which was clearly and depressingly far racier than mine).

I think about putting on jeans – my legs prefer an air of mystery – but since it is far too hot, I fear it will look silly, not enigmatic. I do put on my large sun hat though, regretting that I wasn't wearing it when Nick and Stella arrived and that it doesn't hide my red eyes.

I needn't worry. Stella is so beautiful it is like we belong to entirely different species.

Derek is firing up the barbecue. Again? Is this a second lunch or an early dinner? Whatever it is, it isn't going to help my leg issues.

There's a lovely breeze that makes the seashell wind chimes make a pleasing clickety-click sound. Everyone (except Alyssia) is standing by the pool. Gin and tonics in hand. Mine is waiting for me on a tray. Nick smiles at me when I emerge.

'I love that hat,' he says, and I wonder if he's gay.

Stella is telling my mum that she has a boyfriend back home (she and Nick aren't together then, presumably), who loves barbecues so much he has them in the rain. Mum says Derek would be the same, only it never rains in Spain.

'Only in the plain,' says Derek, which makes Mum squeal with laughter. I envy her sometimes – that she finds him that hilarious.

Derek is going to grill a couple of peppers for any vegetarians – fortunately that's only Alyssia and me. 'There is still some baguette,' he says, 'from breakfast. It's not too hard.'

'Ooh,' shrieks Mum. 'Naughty!'

'Are you sure that meat is done, Derek?' Matthew asks in a low voice, so Nick and Stella can't hear. Derek slaps him on the shoulder, complains loudly that he's a snowflake. Matthew had warned me that 'snowflake' was Derek's new favourite word and it fits him – Derek, that is – beautifully.

When Aunty Barbara comes out, I quickly tell her that Paul is on his way to Ibiza with his… pause… 'lady friend'.

Her face falls. 'What about Harry?'

'Oh, he…' I think about his text – 'he seems fine. But still, I can't believe Paul would just leave him like that.'

She squeezes my hand. 'And what about you, my darling?'

I shake my head and mouth, 'Fine, fine,' because if I don't, I'll cry and anyway, Nick has set up the recording equipment and is waiting for us to pipe down. He nods at me gratefully. Then he tells us that today he's just building a picture of Nana Elaine. He smiles. 'So, act natural.'

'I'm not sure we can do that,' jokes Matthew. Mum raps him on the knuckles with her fan. 'Speak for yourself, darling.'

I think of Paul and this Eva checking in, kissing in the departure lounge. Getting drunk and relaxed before the flight. Paul making lame jokes about the mile-high club (what if they really do that?) or boasting about all the times he's been upgraded.

Upgraded. I hate that word.

I try to focus on my nana, not bloody businesslike Paul. I've already wasted months – no, years – on him. *Concentrate*. Perhaps there was more to Nana than met my eye as an unmusical seven-year-old? In a way, it *is* exciting to draw back the curtain on my family history.

As I watch Nick prepare I realise, shamefully, that I have never given my nana much thought. Somehow, I've only ever pictured her as someone in her late seventies who never had much going on before.

I suddenly wish that Harry had had the chance to meet her. What a pity he didn't. Nana Elaine might have been a more involved grandmother than my mum ever was. It wouldn't have taken much.

Nick twiddles some more with his laptop. He's got a quiet authority about him as he puts on glasses. 'Shall we begin?'

My mum goes first. Aunty Barbara is again away with the plants. 'She was very ordinary, really,' she says. She looks over at Derek for confirmation. He nods.

'A very ordinary person.'

'Did she ever talk about Robert Capa?'

'Never.'

'Nope,' agrees Derek.

'How about the war years, did she ever talk about them?'

Mum shrugs. 'She didn't mention them really. But you have to realise, people didn't in those days, no one did. They didn't talk about the hardships of the past. They just got on with things.'

Derek chortles. A sound that makes the small birds in the nearest hedge fly away. 'Not like now. I mean, you can't imagine the youngsters of today being able to deal with what they went through.'

Or you, Derek, I think. *It's not like you flew a Lancaster.*

'It was a different time.' Mum nods and fans, fans and nods. 'Very.'

Is she looking at me? Is this about me and Paul? Is she saying I'm a snowflake?

When I told Mum that Paul was texting other women, she said, 'Just texting?' and 'It happens to a lot of couples, it doesn't have to be the end.'

I don't think Mum will be charging sixty pounds an hour for her advice any time soon.

I put my arm round Alyssia, who stands next to me wrapped in a Scooby-Doo towel. She snuggles into me gratefully. I know she'd rather be floating about on her inflatable armchair, but I'm glad she is here. I feel stronger when it's the two of us, the uncooperative ones, and I think she might feel the same.

Nick smiles at us all, tells us we're doing well and it must be difficult but bear in mind, this is just a try-out, not the real thing. Smiling, he turns to Aunty Barbara. 'What can you tell us about Elaine?'

She sits down dramatically. 'Well…'

I hold my breath. I have a feeling my Aunty Barbara, always the more emotionally intuitive sister, will have the good stuff. I find myself hoping she does. I'd love to hear something exciting about Nana Elaine. I'd love to hear that she lived well, was loved passionately or left her mark in some small way…

'She was just a normal woman,' says Barbara finally, fiddling with plant cuttings in her lap. She sneezes, then blows her nose. 'I mean that in a good way. Mum was lovely, nice.' She pauses. 'If unremarkable.'

I sigh. I can't see how this is going to work in a documentary. It's too uneventful, surely? If Nick is also disappointed, he doesn't show it. He does his shy smile, rubs his eyes and continues.

'Okay, so what did she do for work?' He looks up. 'Do you know?'

My mum pulls a face. 'Nothing, I don't think?' She fans herself some more. 'Did she?'

'How about during the war?' prompts Nick.

'She might have been a typist…' suggests Aunty Barbara eventually. 'I think she said that once.'

'Really? I'd be surprised if she could type,' says Mum. She looks at me again, then fans herself. 'She had such sausage fingers, didn't she? Towards the end.'

I look down at mine. They're still finger-shaped. She can't get me on that.

'Hobbies? Interests?'

Aunty Barbara says, 'Oh, I know. She loved reading!'

Nick looks up, suddenly interested. Aunty Barbara hesitates. 'Romances mostly.'

'Good, good.'

'She always had her nose in a book, and a sweet in her mouth,' adds my mum.

Matthew raises his eyebrows at me. Mum notices.

'Well, she did, darling, I'm not being funny. That's why she was so… It was the rationing, you see. A lot of people put on weight after the war.'

Nick says that's fine, this is all great. 'Don't worry,' he repeats. 'This is just to get a picture.'

Derek says, 'Come on, everyone, food's up!'

Stella goes over to him first and politely requests a burger in a bun. As he hands it over, Derek relates how he can drink eight pints a night in Spain and feel no ill effects the next morning. And do you know why? It's because you eat too! Lots of small dishes. They call it *Tapas*, he repeats. *Ta-pas*, Stella. You've got to try it.

Stella's expression does not waver. You'd have more chance of reading the mind of the Mona Lisa. She sits back down and eats her burger with relish. Her eyes never leave the plate. She is so thin; you could fit another Stella on the chair and they wouldn't touch each other. Her handbag at her feet, by contrast, is enormous. I wonder if she is missing her boyfriend. It can't be much fun being stuck out here with all us old people going on about the past, surely?

'And what about her relationship with your dad?' Nick asks.

'They were happy,' my mum says firmly. 'They were in love.'

'Well, we don't actually know that,' Aunty Barbara interjects. 'Do we?'

'Well, they stayed together,' Mum says. She doesn't meet my eye. Was this another message for me about Paul? *It happens to a lot of couples, it doesn't have to be the end.* I'd tried that approach though, and it still didn't seem to have got him home. 'What other measure is there?'

I grab a rock-solid baguette and plain rice. This is going to be a carbohydrate-heavy few days. I wonder if Harry is eating enough. *Finn's parents are good like that*, I tell myself. They're definitely *from scratch* types.

I lower myself gingerly into the garden chair next to Aunty Barbara and she reaches over to me, pats my wrist and I drop my fork.

'Oops, sorry, but isn't this fantastic?'

I'm not sure if she means the second barbecue or the whole Robert Capa thing, but I nod. *Yup, yes, it is.*

'And what kind of mother was she?' Nick asks as he squirts sauce on his burger.

I stare between Mum and Aunty Barbara. It's a question I would have never dreamed to ask. It's not really something you can sum up in words, can you? I certainly couldn't.

They both gaze back at him. They are not used to interrogation. I can almost hear my mother's thoughts: *Can't we talk about the weather now?*

I wonder if Nick is going to remind them: *Don't worry, this is just to build a picture.*

'Good?' says Mum in a high-pitched voice.

'That's right,' says Derek supportively. His face is changing to red, not from the sun but the wine. You can see it charging up his cheeks and his nose almost as clearly as if he were a jug that wine was being decanted into.

'Well, actually, I'm not sure she was… cut out for it,' says Aunty Barbara slowly. 'Put it this way, we're not all maternal.'

'Oh, Barbara,' says Mum, 'how could you? That's not true.'

Alyssia is spellbound. I think, *Mum, please don't row with Aunty Barbara in front of her, she's only young. And impressionable.* And shivering in her towel.

'You were her favourite, though,' says Aunty Barbara. 'You would say that.'

Mum flushes. 'I do not believe in favourites. Never have.' She stands up abruptly and squeezes her fan shut. The flamenco dancer collapses in a thin black line. 'Do you want me to do the dishes now, Matthew?'

CHAPTER ELEVEN

LONDON, DECEMBER 1943

Elaine planned her and Bobby's first Christmas together with an attention to detail Field Marshal Montgomery would have been proud of. They would go to the Savoy for Christmas Eve and there would be a band and she would continue teaching Bobby how to rumba. There would be drinking gin and lovemaking of course, at his flat in Belgravia. And she would make a pudding with the raisins she had been saving all year. It would surpass even her Woolton pie. When she was in the canteen, she knitted scarves for him, Clive and Marty. For the rest of them, she had chosen books: for Annie, an instruction manual for 'career women' and for Maisie, who was interested in cooking, a ration recipe book. Alan was the hardest one to get presents for – nothing seemed to excite him – but she chose a volume of Great War poetry that she thought might warm his heart. She wanted him to know that whatever he went through, he wasn't alone.

She had never had a picture-book Christmas, the kind she read about in her novels. Dad was always too skint, Mum was too exhausted. And then after Mum had died and Dad had gone, she and the boys had agreed a Christmas truce: no more presents, although Elaine made sure her brothers had a single chocolate square or a tangerine and Clive had wangled home a salmon from work in recent years.

Felicity was returning to her family pile in Twickenham, Myra was taking her elderly mother to even more elderly relatives in Cheshire.

Mrs Dill was visiting the stepchildren in Wales. Vera mysteriously refused to say. Annie was off to cousins in Hove. Only Elaine would be left in London.

She put all her hopes in this one. Bobby deserved it, she thought, and truth be told, so did she. They might be in the middle of a bloody world war, there might be no end in sight, there might be hardly anything to eat, but Elaine couldn't wait.

'Ah,' said Bobby when she told him the plans, 'Pinky, here's the thing.'

He was going away for Christmas. Work was calling. *How the troops were celebrating overseas.*

'It's a big topic,' he said lamely. 'I thought you knew. Everyone wants to see how their sons and brothers are coping away from home.'

Elaine wanted to cry. 'I didn't know, no. You didn't say.'

'I won't be away for too long. Three, maybe four weeks.'

Three or four weeks!

'Perhaps you could come?'

But Elaine knew it wasn't a real invitation – it was a lie-invitation. Bobby did that sometimes rather than be brutal, and he knew she knew it too, for very swiftly it became: 'I'll make it up to you, sweetheart. I promise.'

She was working until Christmas Eve anyway, and she knew she should spend the day with Clive and his sweet Maisie who she'd grown so fond of, and maybe Alan might be able to take some leave, which would be glorious. The days would probably fly by, but still, she had wanted so much to spend it with him.

She suddenly had an insight that this was what she had signed up for – if she had signed up at all – and she was not entirely thrilled.

Throughout December, she listened closely to the news and his plans. The RAF were now bombing Berlin to smithereens and the fighting in Sicily was more brutal than ever, but what exactly would Bobby do on the continent and with whom? At Christmas? With the whisky? With the girls? They sent entertainers out to the troops over the holidays, not just the big names like Vera Lynn but performing girls, dancers with peacock feathers and super-high heels to cheer up the fellas so far away from home. He would surely like to 'photograph' them too? He was London's most agreeable man. *For agreeable, read eligible. For man, read bachelor.*

The relationship wasn't going to work, went through her head sixty, seventy, times a day before Christmas. It *can't* work. I'm just asking for trouble.

He will abandon me like everyone does. Why wouldn't he?

CHAPTER TWELVE

LONDON, JANUARY AND FEBRUARY 1944

Bobby's Christmas photos came back long before he did and they were widely fêted. Mrs Marriot wept at the spread in the magazine. 'It's like being there,' she explained. 'He brings the boys home to us. It's as good as a letter or a hug.' She said the entire country loved Robert Capa now. That felt too much and it made Elaine feel ten times less important than she had only moments earlier.

If she was only one of millions, it meant she was dispensable.

At eleven thirty on 31 December 1943, Elaine sat alone in her flat, a half-composed letter to Alan in front of her. She didn't know what to write any more. Somehow, their once-close connection was weakening. Mum would have been annoyed if she knew. 'Family first, Elaine,' she would have reminded her, but Elaine could only chew at her pencil and think enviously of Annie and her large complicated family or Mrs Marriot and her small uncomplicated one.

Even Bettie Page was out. Clive was hardly ever home, and Maisie rarely came over any more. No doubt Bobby would be at a party using the very dance skills she had taught him to impress other women. *Please don't fall in love with anyone else*, Elaine told the kettle and the stove. *Please remember the girl in this particular port, keeping the bed warm.*

Just after midnight, she sloped off to her cold bed.

Happy 1944 to me.

*

In January Leipzig was devastated, while in London children were begging in the frozen streets. She gave them some chewy liquorice as she passed. She saw some children pretending to be parachutists – getting tangled in the strings, getting shot dramatically on the ground or screeching about a bullet to the head. Another time, Elaine came across two little girls who seemed to be having a darling tea-party on a doorstep with pretend sandwiches and buns. When she went by, she heard one say to the other, 'You drink the blood of Adolf Hitler,' as she poured from her pretty teapot.

Damn war, it had to end soon. For the sake of everyone's state of mind if nothing else.

Painfully, horribly, for a few days that new year, Annie too was chilly with Elaine. Elaine couldn't work out what she had done wrong. During the working day, Annie kept her head down and said, 'I'm busy,' or 'Don't you have letters to type?' if Elaine so much as looked in her direction. At lunchtime, she marched her tray self-righteously to the other side of the canteen against the propaganda posters. (This must have been quite the sacrifice, for Annie loved to pick at the leftovers on Elaine's plate.)

One morning, a major came in and gave a pompous speech about 'V for Victory', the new campaign from the BBC, and he showed everyone the two-fingered sign that was supposed to give you hope and confidence. He talked about the importance of their work and, in particular, their code-cracking. He was a terribly high-falutin' person, with the medals to prove it, but he had very prominent teeth and Elaine couldn't help thinking he looked like a beaver. This was quite off-putting. The beaver major said the clerical girls were to study the letters with greater attention than ever, for they might be an essential resource.

Felicity put her hand up incredulously. 'You really think those poor prisoners might have information for us?'

'We really do,' the beaver major's teeth said. 'I want you to be alert to strange patterns, strange phrasings.'

'He's never met me when I've had a few too many,' whispered Annie.

'Lucky him,' smirked back Elaine.

Annie must have forgotten she was in a mood, for she threw back her head and laughed until a hairgrip fell out. At the canteen that lunchtime, Annie asked if Elaine minded if she sat with her, and then she carefully placed down her knife and fork next to her ham and told her what was wrong.

'The thing is, Elaine, you can't just pick me up when Robert Capa is out of town and then drop me when he isn't.'

'I'm so sorry.' Elaine was shocked. She had certainly never meant to do that. She had no idea she *had* done that. Didn't she always invite Annie along? Yes, she did, but she had to admit, more often than not, it was to make up a four with the ubiquitous Marty. This wasn't the behaviour of a good friend, she knew that. It felt like she was failing all round.

'No matter,' said Annie stiffly. 'I suppose it was mostly my fault for introducing you two lovebirds.'

'Yes, it was,' said Elaine, trying to introduce some levity. *Lovebirds*, eh? She quite liked that. 'You said, "he's the most agreeable man in the war". And you were absolutely right.'

'I also said that you should be careful, didn't I?' Annie sniped back but then she lost her frosty demeanour and smiled at her old friend. 'Oh, Elaine, it's impossible to have the hump with you...'

Yet still Bobby didn't come back. He wasn't home the entire month of January. What the hell was he doing? How long did taking photographs take? These were supposed to be Christmas shots – since when did Christmas run into February? And what was he doing for travel documents? For travel documents were the bane of Robert

Capa's life. He said his work was 5 per cent perspiration, 95 per cent bureaucracy.

A small distraction from her worries about Bobby was provided when Alan unexpectedly came home for one day's leave. It was a foggy Saturday afternoon and there were queues outside the bookshop below. Spick-spot and unsmiling in his uniform, Alan stood at the front door. Even after Elaine had opened it, his hand was still poised from where he had been knocking.

'You look like a proper soldier!' Elaine couldn't believe he was back. She rushed to hug him, but he was even more reticent than usual, and wouldn't hug her but let his arms hang uselessly at his sides. 'Oh, Alan, you should have told me. I would have got out the fancy china!'

Alan said anything would do for him, a trough or a saddlebag.

He was nineteen now and had to shave once a day, sometimes twice. He still had his boyish good looks, but under his eyes were blue shadows and his brow seemed heavier than ever. Elaine loved him dearly. He was such a stoic when Mum died, and he was the most relieved of them all when Dad had left. He really didn't get on with Dad, even though he looked like him the most of the three of them.

'You going to let me in then? Your Robert Capa's not here today, is he?'

Elaine trembled slightly. You never knew where you stood with Alan. One day he was the life and soul of the party – he could rival Robert Capa with his storytelling – the next he was sullen and withdrawn. At least with Clive, you could always expect the worst.

Alan said his job was running assault courses for new conscripts. He had always been a burly, able lad. 'Under the nets,' he said, 'over the hurdles.' He showed her in the kitchen, leaping over the chairs and then squatting under the kitchen table, then grabbing the kitchen poker and shouting, 'Fire, fire, fire!'

'That's enough, Alan!' said Elaine firmly, for they really didn't have the room for those shenanigans. Mrs Perry would surely come up with her rolling pin, screaming about male visitations, and even poor Bettie Page, who usually adored Alan, was petrified. She had leapt to the windowsill and wouldn't be coaxed down for ages.

Then Alan surprised her. He slumped into the armchair, put his fists over his eyes. 'I hate it, Elaine. I hate, hate, hate it.'

'Oh, Alan, I'm sorry,' Elaine said, feeling quite desperate for her brother. 'Is there anything I can do? Will they move you very soon?'

She felt like the Alan she had waved away at King's Cross station had disappeared. This person who had replaced him didn't seem to remember himself at all.

Seconds later, Alan had sat himself up straight and started singing some song she didn't recognise in a silly high-pitched voice. She didn't like to keep asking him to keep the noise down, but this was ridiculous.

The tea stopped him singing on, *thank goodness*. And then Elaine produced the macaroon biscuits that she had been saving for Bobby's return, but oh well... Alan chomped them down one by one, then asked her if she had ever seen a real-life swastika.

'I don't think so,' Elaine said cautiously. She had seen them enough times in Bobby's photographs, but she didn't think Alan meant that.

'It was an Indian peace symbol,' he said cryptically. 'You knew that, right, Elaine?'

'Well, it isn't now,' she said.

'Isn't it?'

For the first time that month, she was suddenly glad Bobby wasn't there.

Clive managed to avoid Alan, so Elaine couldn't compare notes with him, but she definitely found her middle brother more towards the sensitive end of things than ever before. *Strange patterns, strange phrasing*, thought Elaine, remembering the Major's talk.

Oh dear.

When it was time to go, Elaine had walked Alan out to say hello to Mrs Marriot, but he shot such an angry look at the newspapers that if they'd been people, Elaine would have been afraid for them.

If he had his way, he would rip up each and every one of them and start a whacking great bonfire. Journalists were all in cahoots with the government, and they were, without exception, filthy propagandising bastards. This he shouted at the top of his voice.

Elaine wondered if he was making a dig about Robert Capa, but Alan wasn't snide, he had probably just forgotten Bobby's job. However, it was another uncomfortable moment in an uncomfortable day. She remembered her mum dying on the cobblestones not fifty yards from their home. 'I will take care of the boys,' Elaine had promised in those bewildering and frantic last minutes. 'Of course I will, don't worry.'

Well, how was she to know how things would turn out?

Elaine missed Maisie May too. After she hadn't seen her for what felt like ages but was probably only about two months, she said to Clive, 'Where's Maisie? I miss her cakes.'

Clive was polishing his boot. He looked up at her furiously like he wanted to sink it into her face.

'You miss her *cakes*?'

'It was a joke,' she added quickly. Gosh, he was quick to flare up nowadays. 'I miss her too. Very much. She's a nice girl.'

'She's working,' he said flatly, scrubbing harder than before. 'And so am I.'

Still, that weekend he brought Maisie home to say hello, so something must have gone in. Elaine was elated. She and Maisie May chatted and laughed. Maisie May, bright-eyed as ever, told Elaine she had moved departments and was now stuck in laundry. Delousing stinky men's uniforms all day long, she still managed to smile. So, there were no more cakes. As she left, Elaine hugged her warmly and promised to get her some stockings. Bobby had better bring some home. It was lovely to have another female in the family. Bettie Page was sweet, but a potential sister-in-law was sweeter.

'Don't leave it so long, Maisie,' she insisted. And before she could stop it, the words were out of her mouth. 'We love you.'

Clive shot her one of his looks, then walked Maisie home.

Elaine was shaken awake after midnight. Clive's panicky face was over her. 'My knife, it's gone. What the hell have you done with it?'

Elaine didn't understand what he was saying at first. 'What's gone? Where?'

'I bet it was that bastard Capa,' Clive said darkly.

'Don't be ridiculous!' she said. 'Why would he do that?' but Clive had already wandered off.

It took Elaine ages to get back to sleep.

Bobby was on his way back to London, apparently, but then he stopped overnight in Dover – and one overnight turned into four days, and then, last-minute plan, if you can believe it, he was sent to an airfield, Stow Maries in Essex, and then onwards to an American base in Norfolk, where he would spend just over a week.

Elaine grew more despondent. She didn't see why Bobby couldn't come straight back to her. Weren't there enough things to photograph here in the city, for goodness' sake? Not enough children crying or not enough damage from the evil V-2s?

Finally, a telegram arrived at work on Wednesday afternoon, just after lunch.

> Come quickly, Pinky! Savoy? Dinner? I need to see that beautiful smile.

It was the kind of cold winter evening when the mist clings to you like a cloak and your hair wraps onto your cheeks. Elaine didn't have time for make-up – frankly, she didn't have much left anyway.

Still, she knew she looked grand with her shining eyes and mouth curving upwards. Love, impatience, anticipation and relief that he was home made her sparkly, inside and out. Bobby didn't mind about make-up anyway. He grabbed her in the foyer, said he was elated to be with her, to be home again and that she was the most gorgeous thing he'd ever seen.

We're lovebirds, thought Elaine to herself. *We really are.*

They drank too much and cooed too much, gazing into each other's eyes over some food; for once, she hardly knew what she was eating. He had missed her terribly, achingly, heartbreakingly. He had missed her bright pink hair – hah! – her Woolton pie and the way she liked the bath too hot, which made her thighs go red.

He said he loved Norfolk. 'It's what you imagine life in England is like – if you don't know England at all.' And when Elaine told him, shyly, that she'd never left the city, except one unsuccessful day trip to Brighton many moons ago, he said, 'We must go to Norfolk one day. Definitely. Put it on your calendar, sweetheart.'

He had bought her cigarettes, lipstick, a blouse and enough stockings to share with Maisie May too. No one had ever bought her such nice things before. 'Oh, I nearly got you gloves,' he said, 'but none I saw were as good as the ones you have now… I know it's late but Happy Christmas, darling. May we spend all our future ones together.' They clinked their glasses to that.

The following morning Bobby asked Elaine to go into Life Corp. with him before she went to her office, to see how the airbase photos had turned out.

Just being with him in the underground made it feel less grimy. She let him take her hand for once and he smiled at her like it was a victory of sorts. Above ground, they crunched through the frosty London streets together and the newspapermen were shouting about

Hitler's terrible new victories and Japan's terrible new plans and each time they did, Bobby's nostrils flared, and his lips went tighter.

'We're not winning then?'

'Not yet,' he said, then squeezed her closer. 'We will, Pinky. We have to.'

Everyone at Life Corp. greeted her cheerfully with a 'Morning, Miss Parker,' or Hello, Pinky'. *Journalists are a familiar bunch*, she thought, the American ones especially. It was like they had become best friends without her quite being aware of it. They couldn't have been more different from the government crowd, or the cartographers, who seemed to think that asking 'How was your weekend?' was verging on the indiscreet.

Larry called his hello from the darkroom, then came out, drying his hands.

'Terrific work, Mr Capa, sir,' he said, pumping Bobby's hand up and down, up and down. He took off his cap to Elaine. 'And how's my favourite girl?'

'All the better for seeing my favourite fella.'

'Boss is going to love these.'

'Thank you, Larry,' said Bobby, handing him a pack of Camel cigarettes. 'I'd be nowhere without you.'

That was another thing about Robert Capa. He was always chatting with a doorman, or a porter, or sorting out a tip for a cleaner or a maid. He seemed happy to associate with everyone. He treated everyone with the same respect and charm. Elaine had never seen this in action before she had met him and it delighted her.

These photographs were of the American pilots at their base. Flat and eerie, it was different; it was modern, efficient-looking, even without the machines in the background. The straight lines made it look quite utilitarian.

And the pilots. Of course, Robert Capa's photos captured them. With their caps, with their stripes, with their trousers pulled high, with their hair smoothed and twisted into quiffs. (Amazing what you could do with an inch if you were so minded.) The prints were stunning.

You could feel everything from their faces, the intensity, their listening. Elaine felt emotional as she looked through them. You couldn't help it. In one, a pilot was making a two-fingered salute, another was writing a letter, a love letter maybe, but he was looking up, winking at the camera. You felt like you were a conspirator with him. You felt like you and he were having a private moment.

Here on his plane. You could see everything. The wings. The codes. *My goodness, the details, the details.* They'll be front cover of *Life* magazine. Forty thousand copies, easy.

You couldn't look at these massive machines and these bread-and-honey boys without feeling hopeful. You couldn't look at them without feeling, *we're in safe hands.*

'They're so good, Bobby. I almost feel like I'm there, with them.'

That was his power: he unlocked the window to real people's lives and let the rest of them peer inside. Sometimes, Elaine felt as though he was unlocking their heads.

Bobby shook his head. 'They're the brave ones. They know. They know… they might not come back.'

That was why this work, these photos, were so important: he gave everyone a look *behind* the newspaper headlines and the announcements on the wireless. He made it real.

She swallowed. She remembered that Bobby had once wanted to be a pilot.

'Did you wish you were flying?' she asked, softly. If Larry heard, he pretended not to.

'Not any more, Pinky,' Bobby said, gripping her hand, 'I've got other things to do.'

That evening, on a wobbly table in the George, pressed against the boarded-up windows, Elaine helped him write captions for each one of the photos.

'They have to be catchy,' Bobby kept saying. 'I just can't find the right phrases in English.'

'Won't the journalists help?'

'It's my job –' he said, biting his lip – 'and it's my weakness. I can't do words at all.'

'Course you can,' Elaine told him, for often she forgot Bobby wasn't a native speaker, forgot he spoke three other languages. Yes, there were tell-tale traces of an accent but he knew every bit of slang, every slogan, every swear-word in the book (and certainly some that wouldn't be in any book).

He had said he'd get one of the women at Life Corp. to help him if Elaine preferred, but she knew both Merry and Faye were sweet on Bobby and the last thing she needed was for him to be indebted to an attractive blonde girl. She didn't particularly want to do the captions when they had so much to catch up on, and when she didn't really know what she was doing, but she'd be damned if anyone else would get the chance.

So, Elaine laboured over them, determined to get them right. They had to be authentic, to work with the photo, to elaborate on the photo, if that was possible, and to draw you in but not mislead you.

Elaine concentrated. Her brow furrowed; she chewed her lip. Around her, workers poured in, looking for some relief in a bottle of alcohol.

'You look pretty like that,' he said. Bobby was certainly doing his best to distract her.

'I like this one best,' she said. She picked up a shot of one of the pilots sitting in his seat, saluting. It was hard to know what exactly it was that made that one stand out. Probably the expression on his face, a mixture of fizzy excitement, nerves and pride, the youth of him coupled with the maturity of the task ahead, or the size of him compared to the plane; he was dwarfed by it. There was something of Alan about him too, around the gills.

'Ah...' Bobby surveyed it. 'Nice, shy guy, I remember him well.'

'Did he... make it back from the raid?' Elaine said, trying to sound indifferent. He had told her that he watched the return of the planes from the ground, six hours later, and they were counting them back in. Twenty-four went out. One... two... three... eighteen in total came back.

'I don't know.' He grimaced. 'I never ask.'

As expected, *Life* magazine loved this set of photos and they agreed to use Elaine's 'excellent captions' too. They were going to be used on several pages of the European *and* the American editions and, in a tribute to Elaine's discernment, they had chosen her favourite one for the front cover. Bobby was very pleased. Larry was pleased. Boss was indeed pleased. Everyone was pleased.

And then Elaine got a lovely letter back from Alan – he was bright and breezy, full of sweet anecdotes about getting people's names wrong, wearing odd socks, larks with Sergeant Major and a trip into town and meeting a girl called Suzy with plaits who was the spit of the sexy GI Jane from the cartoons. Elaine doubted that, but she was relieved, so relieved. Happy Alan was back. There, she didn't have anything to worry about after all! The Parkers were moving forward, moving on. *It's all right, Mum. We're coming good after all.*

*

On the Friday evening, they went out to celebrate Bobby's latest successes with three journalists from Life Corp., plus Annie, Marty and a novelist friend of Bobby's called Ernest and his glamorous girlfriend, who was in town for once. The girlfriend, Martha, was a fantastic-looking woman, although Elaine thought it a shame that she was so very tall and angular. She made all the men – except for Marty – look either weeny or stout.

That evening, Annie had put her reservations about Elaine's relationship to one side. As they crossed over to the George, she said, 'Robert Capa's a transformed man, Elaine. Honestly, I've never seen him so happy.'

'Really?'

'Yes, darling.' Annie squeezed her friend. 'I'll have to get a new hat.'

Elaine laughed. 'We're not that serious, Annie. Not yet, not yet.'

But increasingly, Elaine was. She couldn't help it. She stroked the front of her blouse. She looked pretty, she knew she did.

That night, they stayed out indecently late and smoked all the cigarettes. Ernest's girlfriend Martha was, like Bobby, a photographer, although her specialty was not only war; as she said in her drawl, 'just about everything is up for grabs really.' Bobby explained to Elaine that Martha was quite the bigwig in the world of journalism, and he listened even more carefully than he usually did to everything she said.

Elaine tried to chat with Martha, but it was clear Martha was not really interested in Elaine. Elaine got the impression – she might have been wrong – that Martha made it her policy not to bother with Robert Capa's girlfriends, perhaps because she didn't think they'd be around by the time she was next in London. It was nothing she said, exactly, it was just the way she was. Elaine was a flea, Martha was interested only in the dog.

Elaine was beginning to realise that with the journalists and the more creative crowd she now mixed with, her clerical job wasn't all that interesting. They saw her as a dull typewriting girl. They didn't know that it wasn't just transcribing letters, it was searching for clues and hints, trying to piece together strange patterns, strange phrasing; but even if they had known that, Elaine had a feeling they still wouldn't have given a damn.

Clerical work and housework were second class – even if it was mostly the only work women were allowed to do. A coincidence? Elaine didn't think so. She might have hoped for a more sympathetic hearing from Martha, but when she asked Elaine what she did and Elaine brightly declared herself, 'clerical girl', Martha simply screwed up her long handsome nose and said, 'Was there nothing else you could have done?'

Once again, Bobby, Ernest and the journalists were talking passionately about their favourite subjects: the birth and death of fascism, how nationalism was a sickness across Europe, and they were sharing their various solutions – which, depending on how much had been drunk, were: education, love, books, strong leadership, a revitalised League of Nations, international sports, free trade and love again.

Elaine was pleased to see Annie was also chatting sincerely with one of the journalists. It was a potential romance, she decided, alert to any possibility. She was keen to pair Annie off, even though Annie protested that at thirty-five she was past it and the best she could expect was an old impoverished farmer. She claimed this was a joke, but Elaine wasn't sure it was funny.

Martha spent a lot of time huddled up with Marty. There wasn't much room in the banquettes but even so, Elaine thought, they needn't be that close. You'd think it was those two who were the couple, not Martha and Ernest. Elaine tried to listen in on their impassioned talk: it seemed to be about some place in South America where all the Nazis were planning to go, if or when they lost.

It was decided they would go on to a party. Elaine was pleased – she much preferred dancing to talking. It was a far superior way of putting the world to rights – and if sometimes she worried that people would wonder what Robert Capa had ever seen in her, when she was on the dancefloor she had no such doubts. On the dancefloor she was 100 per cent everything. People liked watching her. She made them feel better about their lives. Bobby teased that her dancing was her patriotic duty.

While they were waiting for the cabs, Ernest sidled up beside Elaine. His whisky breath made her recoil slightly, but she smiled at him anyway. He had paid scant attention to her in the pub, but now she felt him surveying her figure closely. He was a very different character to Bobby. Bobby's charm was in his lightness and his kindness; Ernest seemed the opposite: he came across as cynical and brusque. He nodded towards Martha, who was still talking animatedly to Marty. She looked long, rangy and glamorous as she leaned into Marty, who clearly was more dog than flea.

'Never get in a relationship with a photographer, honey. They're always outside looking in and they always disappear when times get rough.'

Not Bobby, Elaine thought, not *her* photographer. He was more 'in' than anyone she'd ever met before.

A taxi finally pulled up. Two older couples got out and Annie and the three journalists replaced them, calling out, 'Later, alligator!' One of the women who had just left the cab was staring intently at Elaine and Ernest, and then, after saying a word to her companions, she bustled over to them. She was a bosomy, self-righteous woman and full of rage. Elaine backed away immediately. Her first thought was that Ernest must somehow have upset her. He was the type to disturb or provoke. But the woman was glaring at Elaine, not Ernest.

'You there. Yes, you! Those gloves. They were my mother's.'

Elaine froze. The woman was in front of her, blocking her like a chess piece.

'I don't know what you mean…'

The woman was now standing over her, menacingly. Checkmated, Elaine could feel everyone's eyes on her.

Bobby put his hand reassuringly on Elaine's elbow and then opened his arms to the woman: 'Steady,' he said reassuringly, commandingly. 'I can see you're upset. Let's talk. She hasn't done anything wrong.'

But for once his diplomacy didn't work.

'She has!' The woman had climbed down a notch or two, but still every part of her was riddled with anger. 'Our house was bombed during the Blitz but worse than that: it was ransacked.'

'My good woman, this is very unlikely!' said Bobby, yet Elaine knew that despite his sincere attempts at placating her, he was also very much amused. He did love a scene. 'How on earth do you know they're yours? They're gloves, not the Crown Jewels.'

'I know because they were handmade for her by Ray Costello and they are one of a kind.'

Elaine tried to think quickly but couldn't. This was dreadful, dreadful.

'One of a kind?' repeated Bobby. 'I don't—'

'My name is inside the gloves. Check them, I tell you.'

Rapidly, Elaine peeled off her beloved gloves. *Oh God, so this was Mildred Cousins' daughter.*

'This is crazy. How could you know? They're gloves, for Christ's sake.'

But Elaine handed the woman the gloves wordlessly, shamefacedly. Bobby's eyes were on her.

'There, you have them now, madam,' he said to the woman. 'I hope you're happy.'

She tutted loudly and turned away.

'Enjoy yourself, lady!' he called after her. He suddenly sounded very American, very cocky.

Marty was watching it all too. Elaine could feel the disapproval pouring off him. He tried to hail a passing taxi, but the driver just ignored him and powered away. This only added to his annoyance.

Elaine felt like a naughty little girl again. Exposed and vulnerable.

'Your brother Clive, I presume?' Bobby said quietly.

'Um, maybe.' She stared at a scrunched-up newspaper blocking a drain.

'Where did he get them?'

'I don't know.'

She didn't know, but she *deliberately* didn't know.

She was criminal. She was rotten. Her family weren't even as desperate as some. They had a roof over their heads and shirts on their backs. Elaine looked up at Bobby, expecting revulsion in his eyes too.

He was smiling at her so sympathetically that she could have wept from embarrassment and shame. That he should have seen! That he should know this about her! She wanted to bury herself in rubble.

He leaned towards her and whispered, 'I should have got you new ones, Pinky. Next time.' Then he too stepped into the road and this time the taxi stopped immediately like it had no alternative but to stop right there and then. Marty was still scowling.

Ernest nudged Elaine's arm. 'This would make a fascinating short story.'

'Thanks, Ernest, I'd really rather you didn't.'

Elaine stuffed her hands in her pockets. It was one of those February nights when you could really feel the cold.

CHAPTER THIRTEEN

SPAIN

JUNE 2016, DAY ONE

That evening, Matthew and I sit out on the patio and share a bottle of wine.

Alyssia is still up, watching TV game shows inside, but the others have gone to bed.

The moon hangs high in the sky and the stars twinkle as if, in a place with less electricity, they're restored and renewed. I wish I was restored and renewed too. I suddenly feel wiped out but I'm too weary even to get up and go to bed.

'It's exciting, right, this project?' says Matthew. 'I knew you'd enjoy it.'

'I don't know,' I say truthfully. 'It's all a bit… unexpected. One minute, I'm coming to see my family. The next, we're making a show.'

'A documentary,' he corrects me.

'Same thing.' I grin.

'I thought it would be good for you.'

'Yeah, yeah.'

Although I love Matthew and Matthew loves me, I doubt my well-being is number one on his list of priorities.

'It's true!' he persists. 'Really. I think it will be good for us all, finding out more about Nana Elaine. Gisela thinks it will help us find out more about each other… and ourselves.'

Then why isn't she here? I think.

We've been sitting out for over an hour, chatting about how undignified getting into a hammock is, and how expensive running a swimming pool is, before Matthew can bring himself to ask what exactly is going on with Paul, 'my' Paul.

'How do you mean?' I'm still reeling from the Abandoning Harry for Ibiza with Eva news and not sure I can yet talk about it, especially not to my brother, without crying.

'Well, has he come back?' Matthew drains his glass. His lips are stained dark red.

'He's been and gone, he's gone and he's been… I don't know what he's doing any more.'

'Well…' Matthew looks concerned. He's always been a straightforward fella. Gisela was his first girlfriend, they married at twenty-one. He doesn't really do dramas or existential angst. 'Is he staying this time?'

'It's looking less likely now that he's gone off to Ibiza with his girlfriend.'

'Shit.'

'He says it's a "midlife crisis",' I say, 'like that's an excuse.'

Matthew looks at me sympathetically. I hate that. I prefer it when he's teasing me. I remember how we used to fight. He once took my beloved Slinky toy from my room and when I found he had broken it, I peeled his beloved *Back to the Future* poster from the wall and held it ransom for a week.

'So, he's in love with this woman?'

'I don't know. He says he loves me, but he isn't *in love* with me.' It feels clichéd, saying it aloud. It *is* clichéd but when he's saying it, sitting in the kitchen, drinking coffee, it seems to make sense.

I look down at my thighs, expansive on the chair.

'I feel so frumpy.'

'You could never be frumpy,' Matthew says affectionately before spoiling it with a 'But a tan, and a bit of make-up, would probably help.'

'Thanks. Perhaps if you hadn't stolen my Slinky, I'd like you more.'

'I swear I didn't. Mum said I could have it.'

'But it was mine!'

We laugh. It's good to be here with Matthew. No one knows me like he does. There's something very comforting in that.

'I should have come over when it first happened,' he says darkly. 'Paul would have listened to me.'

'Paul doesn't listen to anyone.'

'He'd listen to Mum.'

I laugh. 'She'd probably take his side.'

'Give her a chance,' Matthew says, as he always does.

I think of her face, the slight shake of her head she does at me when she doesn't know I'm looking.

'I've been giving her a chance for years.'

Matthew pours another glass for himself and for me. 'I think we ought to brace ourselves for more revelations tomorrow…'

CHAPTER FOURTEEN

LONDON, FEBRUARY 1944

The celebrations about the photos proved premature. *Epically premature*, Larry said. The next morning, Bobby announced that every single copy of *Life* magazine had to be destroyed. Incinerated. Obliterated. Forty thousand of them. The American edition *and* the European edition.

'But why?'

Bobby had intercepted Elaine on her way to work. Crunching on frost, her nose pink and her lips blue. Her joy at seeing him was quickly replaced by fear. Was he going away again? Did he want to break up?

'I have to meet with a panel this afternoon.'

'Wha-at happened?'

'They think there was a security breach. I've photographed classified material. Of course, I didn't do it on purpose,' he added. 'But whatever the reason, it seems I've done it.'

Elaine stared at him in amazement.

'It gets worse.'

'How could it be worse?'

Bobby sucked in his teeth. 'They could throw me out of the country.'

Elaine felt sick and clammy. 'Why?'

He made a sound like a laugh, but it didn't extend to his face.

'I'm not British. No visa, no stay. This is the way it is. If they take away my visa, I can't work. I'm finished.'

'Where would you go?'

Looking pained, he grabbed her fingers. 'Pinky, you know I've always wanted to be in America. That was my first choice. Maybe this is a kind of sign that I should be there now?'

Control yourself, Elaine told herself firmly. *Don't let him know how much this hurts. Don't let him know the agony. Be cool.*

'But they might not?'

He looked relieved that she hadn't caused a scene.

'They might not.'

'So?' She shrugged. 'Let's not worry about it before it happens, Bobby.'

He'll leave me though, won't he? They all abandon me in the end. Mother, Father, now Bobby. I shouldn't have let him into my heart.

The newspaper seller shouted, 'Stalin's Big Offensive!' As the clock across the road struck eight, the latecomers at Life Corp. galloped up the stairs.

'You'd better go. Now listen, if anything happens, know this.' He leaned forward and whispered hotly in her cold ear.

'I know you do,' said Elaine, trying to be brave. 'I know.'

Elaine typed letters all morning. Myra was working on the ones from Germany and at one point, she ran out, weeping. Felicity was wearing plasters on her fingers – she was prone to blisters, but she was also a hypochondriac, was Felicity. Bless her.

There were no strange patterns. There was no strange phrasing.

Elaine had two letters from a darling chap called John; there were shades of Alan about him. *Will I never not worry about Alan?* Letters from a Geoffrey who was unrelentingly cheery. You'd think he was at Clacton in a holiday camp. Only someone good at reading between the lines would understand what it meant, and Elaine was getting good at that. *Will his family understand?* Maybe.

Bobby was in his meeting now. He was there and they were probably telling him to get out. And he would leave her and she would be back where she started, back to square one, although everything would be five hundred times worse than where she started. He had spoiled her for everyone and everything else for he was so damn lovely.

Blast those photos and this stupid security breach.

Lunchtime, Elaine didn't go to the canteen, she raced out to the George to find Marty. If anyone knew anything, Marty would.

'Have you heard?'

Marty peered back at her, expressionless. She couldn't tell if it was good or bad news. Sometimes she wanted to shake him.

'There was a tribunal. In came Bomber Fisher and explained: he had let down the aircraft hatch two minutes early.'

'So?'

'The breach wasn't Robert's fault.'

'Well, that's brilliant, isn't it?'

'It means he's not being sent away this time. It's fine. They'll extend his visa. Hopefully. He'll get a few more months.'

He turned away from her and ordered himself another drink.

At the lounge in the Savoy that evening, Bobby threw Elaine over his shoulder in a celebratory fireman's lift and carted her up two flights of stairs, past all the military men, the aristocrats, businessmen and politicians as though she were a sack of potatoes.

'That's the war photographer, Robert Capa,' Elaine heard among the peals of laughter.

'Well, he's got himself a nice model there!'

Bobby dropped her on the hotel bed, his face glowing, catching his breath.

'Blimey, you're a dead weight, Pinky!'

'Worse than Bessie's beer barrels?'

'Much!'

She rolled over, laughing. 'I take it you're not being thrown out of the country?'

'Not yet. Anyway, if I were, would you come with me?'

This was joking, but it was also testing the waters, Elaine knew that. Here was a sign. Bobby. And America. Who said dreams can't come true?

'Would I get to see your stamp albums?'

'Definitely.'

'Then yes.'

He jumped on the bed next to her and for a short while, they forgot all about stamps, visas and wars.

CHAPTER FIFTEEN

LONDON, MARCH 1944

Surely it *had* to be over soon. But it didn't feel like that to Elaine: it probably didn't feel like that to anyone. They'd had five hateful years of it and everyone had had enough.

Was your glass half-empty or half-full? they used to say and they'd tell you if you were an optimist or a pessimist. Now you asked someone, and they'd say, *What bloody drink? What bloody glass?* It felt like things had been stolen from you. Time and freedom, your youth. Things had been pulled away from underneath them all. It felt like you were missing your footing, like losing your keys but on a national scale – and the consequences? The consequences didn't bear thinking about. You went to sleep thinking about Hitler's attack plans. He was such a confident little bugger. The Russians had seen the Nazis out of Leningrad but only barely. Anything could happen. And yet at the same time, they were bored of it. Come on then. Let it be over, one way or another. Let it be done.

In the canteen, Annie whispered that one of the cartographers was sweet on Elaine. Julian was the same age as Elaine, yet seemed much younger with his acne-stained cheeks and his embarrassed grins. But Elaine had eyes, ears and everythings for only one man: Robert Capa. She hadn't even noticed this Julian before Annie pointed him out. A couple of weeks later, she learned that he and Felicity were dating and Felicity had even taken off her plasters in the hope of a ring. When Annie asked about it, Felicity was furious. She said it had nothing to do with a ring, but everyone was sure it was true.

See Bobby's photos in the magazine, show them off in the office. Look at Mrs Marriot's face light up when they come in. Watch an old man poring over an old *Life* magazine in the underground. See him wipe his teary eyes at *that* photo, the one of the woman reading a letter from overseas.

My boyfriend took that.

Elaine, who had never had family to be proud of, was filled up with happiness at the connection. My boyfriend. My Robert Capa. *Get closer?* They couldn't get any closer if they tried.

Elaine was typing out letters from POWs in Burma and reminding herself that she would not cry. Poor Geoff doubted whether he would ever see his children again. 'Tell them they mean the world to me.' *Come on, Geoff.* Elaine wanted to reach out into the letter, hold his hand or chide him. *Hang on in there.* If only he knew that they were reading, they were listening, they were holding him. But Geoff was running out of steam, you could feel that. The weariness jumped, no, it staggered off every letter, every word on the crumpled page. She didn't understand how this letter got past the censors. It was impossible. But it did. It wasn't patterns or phrasing that made it strange, it was the fact that he wrote nothing but the truth.

'*It's a cult,*' he wrote, in an analysis befitting the fact that he used to be a professor of anthropology. '*These people have been brainwashed to believe we are lesser than them, and they treat us like you would an insect, a fly, a mosquito, a wasp…*'

'I can't do this any more, Mrs Dill,' Elaine suddenly said. She surprised herself that she had said it aloud. She had been so keen to shut down any emotional reaction to the letters. She had been careful to try to analyse the content with that searching eye just as the major beaver had advised.

Maybe it was because Geoff was so tender towards his two sons, maybe it was because he was so compassionate about everyone he met, even the prison guard who whacked him over the head three times when he bent down to see if his best friend was dead (he was), maybe it was because he was trying to keep going.

Maybe it was because, before she knew Bobby, to be parted from your loved ones was just a terrible nuisance, but now it had become Elaine's greatest fear. Now she understood what love was, she understood what suffering was, and it was agony. It was too awful for words.

Mrs Dill took her to a small cupboard/office. There was a bottle of whisky and a collection of mugs that Annie claimed harboured all sorts of nasties.

She poured Elaine a large cup as Elaine told her about Geoff's letter. About his friend beaten to death in front of him for no reason, no reason at all. Like a fly, a mosquito or a wasp.

'We keep calm and carry on,' interrupted Mrs Dill and Elaine nodded wordlessly. *Of course we do.* What else was there? She felt quite resolved as she drained the cup. The fire in her throat did the trick. It came as a shock to her, then, when Mrs Dill suddenly burst into hot racking sobs.

'Those poor, poor men…'

CHAPTER SIXTEEN

LONDON, APRIL 1944

Alan's letters grew erratic again. Elaine despaired for her little brother. After she had received that lovely card from him, she had thought things were going better. Now she realised they weren't. It was painful to deal with sad letters all day long at work, and then to open up Alan's. But maybe he just needed her as an outlet and once he'd written down all his woes he felt better? Elaine hoped so. She couldn't confide in Clive about it. They barely saw each other, and he hated talking about his brother anyway. He said someone owed him money for the disappeared knife, then scowled at her menacingly.

In the George, Elaine asked Bobby about it.

'Missing?' Bobby repeated. He seemed to take it a lot more seriously than she or even Clive had. 'Knives don't just go missing, Pinky. When did it disappear? Who saw it last?'

Immediately, Elaine regretted bringing it up. She hated spoiling the nice time they were having together.

'It's just a… Clive wondered where it was, that's all.'

Bobby looked mystified.

'Forget it.' She decided she would give Clive a few shillings and just hope he would shut up about it.

Despite Elaine's worries, the spring of 1944 was also a time of passion, dancing and fierce friendships. She loved going out with Annie, Felicity, Myra and even Mrs Dill. They could always make each other laugh. Mrs Dill's stepchildren came back from Wales with bags of vegetables, which she shared out freely. Felicity's sister did a violin recital that they all attended. Myra thought she had broken an ankle, Annie took her to the clinic, but mercifully, it turned out to be just a sprain. Myra's mother paid for them all to go to the movies and Leon won second prize at his amateur art group for his painting, *London under Attack*.

There were Americans and Canadians in uniforms everywhere. You didn't talk about it, you didn't draw attention to it, but you couldn't not notice them. They were chewing gum on every street in London. They were blowing kisses from the windows of the trams. A group of ten or twelve of them even took up two banquettes at the George most Fridays.

Something was going on. Annie told Elaine not to tell a blooming soul but she'd heard something about a planned invasion of Calais. 'We're going to get France back,' she said. Elaine nodded. She didn't swear her to secrecy but Annie knew Elaine told Bobby most things anyway.

Terrible things were happening, more terrible things were probably about to happen, but who knew days and nights could be so sweet? Elaine was having the time of her life. She was ashamed at this but at the same time, she couldn't help herself. This was what it was to be in love with Robert Capa during a time of war.

Elaine and Bobby were splashing in the magnificent bath at the Savoy. Elaine joked that the bath was bigger than her bedroom. (It was probably about the same size.) She was used to an old tin tub dragged in from the shed once a week. She knew she would never tire of this one. The size! The taps!

Bobby was tentatively telling her about his next job. A big one in Europe. The big push. Elaine's exuberance waned. So, Annie *was* right.

'I didn't realise it would be so soon.'

'Well, now you know.'

'And you think it will be the end of the war?'

Elaine thought of sugar, bacon and soap and petrol and the trips they'd go on when all this was over. She would be out of a job, probably, but how could she complain? Imagine being with Bobby and not wondering if he was going off to die at every minute! *It could be amazing.*

Bobby traced a line along her cheek. 'I think, I hope, this one will be the beginning of the end.'

'And what will you do?' She knew, she just knew he would be in the thick of it somehow. Even though the bathwater was warm, she felt herself shiver.

'I'll photograph it,' he said lightly. 'What else?'

'You're not actually going with them, are you?' Elaine began. 'With the soldiers? To free France?'

She remembered what he had said about the sea. He couldn't swim well. And he was colour-blind too, for goodness' sake. *You can't go,* she wanted to say. *You're too vulnerable. Plus, you're supposed to be mine.*

'I'll do what's necessary. But frankly, I can't wait. We have to take Europe back from the fascists, we have to win this.'

Elaine felt a fearful howl inside her.

'I don't want you to die.'

'I don't want to die either.' He splashed his face. 'But if I have to die, there are worse times to die than setting Europe free.'

'Don't die,' she repeated helplessly.

'I won't if you promise you won't leave me,' he said. 'That's the thing I fear most in the world.'

'I never would… I just, I get so lonely without you,' she admitted.

'I'll get Marty to take you out.'

Marty, she thought, *what on earth use is Marty?*

'But… but it still might not happen?' she asked. 'Maybe there won't be an invasion.'

'It has to happen, Pinky. There's no other way.' He smiled at her. 'Now didn't you say you'd go at the tap end?'

CHAPTER SEVENTEEN

SPAIN

JUNE 2016, DAY TWO

Aunty Barbara is the only one of us who swims, properly swims. She glides through the water effortlessly, doing her forty lengths' breaststroke. 'Not bad for an old lady,' she says. And she wears a massive bodysuit too. She calls it a burkini. My guilty pleasure is to watch the disdain on Derek's face as she powers through the water in it.

Harry has called, and what an amazing mood-enhancer speaking to him is. Finn's parents have taken them go-karting and for noodles and they are having a brilliant time.

'I'm worried about you,' I say.

'I'm an adult,' he says, which secretly makes me want to snort.

Naturally, there are no messages from Paul the Loser, which is probably a good thing. Who wants to hear how much better Ibiza is with a brand-new Eva than the mountains of southern Spain with the stale ex-wife?

Nick and Stella arrive at midday in a flurry of cameras and microphones. After a veggie sausage-in-roll lunch – thank you, Barbecue Derek – we go into the living room, where the sound will be better for the recordings. Huge sofas and a glass table dominate this room. There are four carved wooden Buddhas. Gisela's sky-blue yoga mats are rolled in the corner. It's dark in here even in the day. It's the cool room. Alyssia troops in reluctantly. I pat the place next to me and we smile at each other, ready for more nonsense.

Bouncing around, Matthew is really enjoying this. He offers to light some incense. I am pleased when Nick says, *sorry, mate.* It makes him cough.

I've decided I quite like Nick. I helped him bring his equipment from the car and he talked easily with me. I've learned he is single, no kids and from London. He used to work in the City but was made redundant ten years ago, so he decided to pursue his dreams. I tell him I googled his previous films: one about an obscure First World War artist, Olive Mudie-Cooke, and another about the poet Mary Borden, and they both look great.

'They're an acquired taste,' he says, but he looks pleased I've done some research. He says he loves doing what he does and I say, 'Well, that's the… the thing, isn't it?'

The heat is making me forget my words.

It's been a long time since I've enjoyed what I do. I work in marketing in a college. That alone tells you what kind of college it is: it's the kind of college that spends money on five of us doing marketing rather than the teaching. I shouldn't look a gift horse in the mouth, I know that. When I started, it was that combination of things I enjoy: education, young people, being creative with words and images, but there is less and less of that every term.

Barbara sits the other side of me. Alyssia whispers, 'This is boring,' and I can't think of a reply that will appeal to her yet won't annoy Nick, Stella or Matthew if they overhear, so I just squeeze her hand in agreement.

Nick is saying we should just relax when Derek interrupts, 'Lie back and think of England, eh!' Mum yelps with laughter. 'Oy yoy!'

'So, we know Elaine's mother died when she was young…' Nick begins.

I think, *I did not know this. How did I not know this?*

Mum looks up. She seems surprised. 'Yes,' she says begrudgingly. 'There was an accident.'

'That's awful,' I say, and Aunty Barbara nods sympathetically at me.

'A car accident,' Mum adds.

I feel a new and painful empathy for my Nana Elaine. *Why didn't anyone tell us?*

'It was awful,' Mum agrees. 'She was walking with her mother at the time, close to home. They were holding hands in the street, then suddenly… she didn't have anyone in her hand.'

Everyone sucks in their breath, picturing the dreadfulness of this.

'And what about her dad?' I prompt.

'I don't know,' says Barbara.

'I presume he was knocked down as well?' says Mum, examining her perfect nails.

Poor Nana, I think, *she didn't have much chance.*

'Now, did she have any brothers or sisters?' continues Nick.

Neither Mum nor Aunty Barbara reply.

I try to be of some help. 'Not that we know of.'

'That's not right.' Mum's voice interrupts my reverie. 'There were… two brothers.'

'What?' I hear Matthew say it a split second before I do.

'Mum had two brothers. Younger, I think.'

'What?' Matthew asks again, his jaw slack. 'Why didn't you tell us?'

'I didn't think it was important.'

In the muddle, I can hear Aunty Barbara saying, 'I warned you this would open a can of worms, Shirley.'

'So, let me get this straight…' Matthew's voice is incredulous. 'There are uncles and maybe cousins and God knows how many relatives out there? And you knew all about this, but didn't tell us?'

'I suppose so, Matthew,' says Mum. 'Since you put it like that.'

After Nick and Stella leave and after we finish dinner (Derek's special barbecue), Matthew wheels out the karaoke machine and we all applaud and drink faster. It will be good to focus on something that is not the Uncle-elephants in the room. Strangely, Mum's secrecy doesn't annoy me as much as it surprises me. I suppose I have always seen her as a bit shallow or conventional maybe, and this revelation has revealed hidden, darker depths. Matthew isn't happy about it at all though. He kept making little digs at her.

'What else have you been hiding, Mum?' he insists, while she fans herself.

'Nothing, darling, honestly. And I wasn't *hiding* it, I just didn't see the point of mentioning it.'

I've always thought Matthew was spoiled by Mum, and I suppose I've always been jealous of their relationship too. I am forty-four and I know these are the woes of a four-year-old and I should have got used to them by now. The fact that I haven't is what annoys me most. I haven't got over it. I'll *never* get over it. I'm jealous of my brother and it will always be a point of shame for me.

Matthew carries on needling Mum. 'How many children have you got then? Are you sure?'

She laughs. Matthew can talk to Mum like that without getting her back up. If it were me, she would throw a fit.

Aunty Barbara goes first on the karaoke with an Abba song. She has a sweet voice, but more than that, she is an incredibly mesmerising dancer; she really loses herself in the music. Even Alyssia nudges me to say, 'Wow, she's great, isn't she?'

Matthew is up next. He pouts and performs like Elvis. He's not too bad either, but Alyssia covers her eyes and whispers that it's *cringe*.

If Paul were here, he would sing the Clash or the Sex Pistols. We weren't brilliant singers, either of us, but we made up for that with our enthusiasm. Many an end of an evening at a bar, Paul has sung me a love song. My favourite was Depeche Mode's 'Enjoy the Silence'.

He's probably singing that to Eva right now in Ibiza.

I can't bear to think about it.

Derek and Mum sing 'I Got You Babe' by Sonny and Cher. They sound surprisingly harmonious. Laughing, Alyssia and I put the torches on our mobile phones, hold them up and sway from side to side.

Then Mum insists I sing. She goes on and on about it. It's hard to resist when she's like this. I say only if she helps me out and she agrees. We sing 'We'll Meet Again' by Vera Lynn, one of her favourites, and to be honest, it's not as bad as I expected. Everyone claps. And Mum even hugs me and says how delighted she is I came out to Spain. After all this time.

I manage to tell her I'm happy to be here.

I want to say something about the revelation about her uncles, but I can't, I daren't. I'll leave that to Matthew.

Barbara, Alyssia and I do some Abba songs and I just about manage not to cry during 'Slipping Through My Fingers' – *Oh, Harry!* – then Matthew and Derek get up to sing a Tom Jones. Mum throws her shawl at Derek, and he drapes it round his waist, faux-sexy. I cover Alyssia's eyes and Barbara shrieks, 'Off, off, off!'

Later as I head to bed, I realise I am getting along without Paul. I *can* do this. I haven't fallen apart, or if I have, I'm putting myself back together again. It's been a good night, even Alyssia said so, and I am looking forward to the next day. I'm not sure what I'm looking forward to most: finding out more about my Nana Elaine or seeing Nick Linfield again, but whatever it is, it's delightful to feel enthused about *something* again.

CHAPTER EIGHTEEN

LONDON, MAY 1944

Larry was dead. Larry the Life Corp. darkroom man who was always so kind to Elaine, his favourite girl, was dead.

Bloody waste. Bloody, bloody war. Sometimes you let down your guard. You let yourself forget how terrible war was, and then the war came back with a vengeance to remind you.

Elaine was so angry, she forgot herself and where she was; she wanted to smash something up. She wanted to throw her typewriter to the office floor. She wanted to rip papers with her teeth. She had liked Darkroom Larry very much. He was generous with his time and with his praise. A widower, who had fought in the Great War, he had hated everything about that war too.

There was no way a sixty-year-old with poor health like Larry should have been gallivanting around the city in the fire service. No way. Elaine didn't want to know the details, but Leon told her them anyway. Leon was in shock. He'd only had a drink with Larry at the George two days ago. Larry owed Leon a round apparently. At this, Leon broke into sobs: 'Bastard just died to get out of paying.'

Larry had been killed in a house fire after a V-2 attack. Damn unpredictable doodlebugs. At least with the other bombs, there was some kind of warning, but there was no escaping these. Just a random rushing, creaking and crashing from the sky. Noise of hell. 'If it has your name on it, it has your name on it,' everyone said.

Some consolation. Larry had run inside the house on fire, apparently, with no thought for himself. He thought there were kids trapped inside a burning building. Smoke inhalation had got him. He was too old to be doing it. The worst thing – or was it the best? – was that the kids were already safe outside. He needn't even have been there in the first place.

In the pub, Bobby, who had turned quite green on hearing the news, raised a glass with a trembling hand: 'Poor Larry, he didn't deserve that.'

And Marty said, 'Terrible timing too.' When no one said anything, he added, 'It's going to be a right chaff to get the invasion photos developed now.'

Everyone said, 'Shut up, Marty.' Even Bobby for once spoke sharply: 'Now is not the time.'

Marty said, in a bewildered tone, 'What? I'm just being practical, you know how important these next few weeks are.' He poured his beer into his ugly mug, sulking.

Elaine disliked him more than ever then. Marty had no compassion. Sometimes the war brought out the best in a person but sometimes it brought out the worst.

'Is it Calais?' she later asked Bobby. 'Are we attacking the Nazis there?'

He pulled her to one side. 'Where did you hear that?'

'Everyone's whispering it,' Elaine said. Bobby had a tiny smile playing on his lips before he kissed her.

'You mean Annie is?'

'Uh-huh. Has she got it right?'

'Maybe, baby. Either way, nothing for you to worry about.'

When Elaine came home and told Clive about Larry, she could hardly speak for the tears prickling in her eyes but she wouldn't cry, she wouldn't. She had got through long mad years of war without blubbing; she had made it through the devastation of the Blitz, reading heart-breaking letters daily, she had survived her own mother's death, she wasn't going to let poor old Larry be the straw that broke the camel's back. There was no straw in the world that she would allow to do it.

Clive was smoking a cigarette over the oven. Smoking made him less hungry. His face looked lined and drawn in the shadows. She couldn't help thinking he looked like one of the villains in Mrs Marriot's books.

There was nothing in the bread bin but some mouldy crust. She got out some potatoes to peel. They were green and had enough eyes to need glasses. She was going to say that aloud, cheer them both up, but Clive was standing still and had on his 'thinking' face. It didn't suit him.

'So, does that mean *Life* magazine will need someone to do the darkroom?'

Elaine cottoned on immediately. She knew Clive. 'No way!'

'But, Elaine, you know how I love being in the dark. I'm a natural.'

'Huh! Clive, it's not about being in the dark. You've got to know about developing and about mercury and… all that stuff.'

'I know my planets,' he said.

Elaine ignored him. Well, she took a cigarette from him and then ignored him. She gave up on the potatoes. She would just make herself an egg, an old-fashioned boiled egg, and Clive could fend for himself. She wanted a moment to remember Larry.

Not Clive and his stupid ideas.

But early the next morning, in the kitchen, there Clive was, wearing Dad's old black suit, the only one Dad had, the one he wore for funerals. The trousers were far too big for Clive at the waist, even his braces couldn't disguise it, yet at the same time they were too short at the ankle, revealing one black sock.

'I'm going to Life Corp. now.'

'You can't replace Larry, Clive.' Elaine tried to think quickly of reasons. Reasons that would deter him were few. 'You're too young for a start.'

'They'll not find anyone better than me,' he said confidently.

'You're inexperienced.'

'I'm a quick learner.'

'What about your foot?'

'What's that got to do with it?'

'I don't think you should, Clive.'

'What could possibly go wrong?'

He laced up his boot like he was closing the opposition and he was, she supposed. 'I'll just go in and ask, that's all. We really need the money.'

Had he lost his job at the fishmongers? It wouldn't be the first time. But surely not, for he still came home reeking of fish.

'What for?'

'Stuff… you don't know what it's like. You've got your rich boyfriends.'

Boyfriend. Singular. And he's not rich.

'No one is going to help me, Elaine.'

'I will—'

She held out a note – it was a bribe really.

'Don't go, Clive. It's not your place.'

He stuck the note in his pocket without even looking at it.

'All right. I can't tell you about it now,' he said cryptically. 'But I need to be making more money. I need to do *something*, Elaine. Do you understand?'

*

That was the night the police knocked at the door.

Her brother was sitting on a bench in Catford High Street, ranting and raging. He was very distressed. He had a knife. He had *the* knife.

Alan, not Clive. God knew where Clive was. Never there when he was needed, that was for sure.

Elaine rode in the back of the police car, slip-sliding on the leather bench. She was probably in shock, she told herself. She felt strangely calm though. She asked the back of the officers' heads questions, but they knew little more than they'd already said. Alan had told them the address, apparently – which Elaine, grasping at straws, thought surely meant he couldn't be in that bad a way?

'He won't hurt anyone,' she told them, three, maybe four times. 'Not Alan, he's a good boy.'

'We know that,' the police officer said, although she wasn't convinced that he did. 'But he might hurt himself.'

A small crowd had gathered around him – kids, elderly folk – a police officer was keeping them back. 'Let him breathe, folks.' Alan sat there, digging the knife – Clive's knife – into his sleeve, into his skin. There was blood on both arms. His shirt was speckled red. His face was white as chalk and his eyes were huge.

'Ally,' Elaine murmured, taking her brother's bloody hand. 'It's okay, love. I'm here.'

Does he recognise her?

Yes, he does. 'Elaine. You're the only one.'

'You're my sunshine, Alan.'

'I don't know what to do,' he repeated. 'I don't know what to do.'

They took him and Elaine to the police station in the car. It was only five minutes away. They told her he'd spend the night there and the next day, they'd take him to a special hospital.

'Military hospital?' Elaine asked.

The police officer looked at her sympathetically. 'They want him in the asylum.'

Oh God, not that place. Elaine knew it from the news clips and the articles. Everyone did. Asylums were hell on earth. They weren't the place for Alan. He'd rather die. 'You can't put him there!'

'They're not as bad as they were,' the police officer said, but this was salty comfort. Elaine knew what they were like. Only last month, she had read a novel about a woman who was murdered by a runaway from the asylum. Her fiancé never got over it.

'You don't want to go there, do you, Alan?' She tugged at his sleeve, but he didn't say anything, just hung his head low. Elaine felt like she had lost the battle before it had even started.

'There's one in Dartford. We'll take him first thing.'

'I'll stay here with him,' she said. This was the least she could do if her brother was going to an asylum.

'No,' the police officer said firmly. 'This is no place for a girl. Come back tomorrow.'

And Elaine couldn't help but agree. She told Alan she was going back home.

'I don't know what to do,' he said again, wringing his hands, but he wouldn't meet her eye and when she next whispered, 'Al,' he mechanically answered, 'Private Parker.'

The hall phone was ringing. Elaine, who had barely slept, sprang out of bed. *Oh God, Alan.* What now?

'I've got the call, darling,' the voice whispered. It was Bobby. Usually, speaking to him filled her with hope. Not now. It was six thirty on Saturday morning.

'The call? What call?'

Elaine didn't cotton on straight away like she normally would have. He wasn't talking about Alan and the asylum or the trip to

Dartford, he was talking about the plan to recapture France. The Calais invasion.

'They want me to go tonight. Can you come here today?'

'I don't know if I can…'

Elaine leaned against the wall, sank down on the floor. The skirting board had tiny holes and paint slurping upwards towards the wallpaper. *Steady*, she told herself. *She could do this.*

A pause before he asked, 'What is it, Pinky?'

Could she tell him? Tell him about her lunatic brother? Yes, she could, but not now, of course, not now. *He doesn't need this now. He needs to focus. He must go with no distractions, with no silliness. He doesn't want to go away with her disastrous family on his mind. This was his moment. Not hers.*

'I'm not feeling great, Bobby.'

'Sweetheart, what is it?' He sounded so concerned.

'Look, I… It could be…' She wanted to say something contagious. Ran through illnesses in her head. *Rabies? Where did that come from? Malaria? Fool. Measles? He'll worry too much. Chicken pox. He'll probably laugh.* Blast. Where was the right illness when you wanted it?

Appendicitis of course.

'Pinky, I'm so sorry. I'll bring a doctor.'

That wasn't the idea.

'No, no, it's not too bad. I'll be fine.'

'Well, is it or not?'

'It is and it's not,' she said, trying weakly to make him laugh. 'I'll live, but whatever it is, I don't want you to get it. You need to be strong.'

'I wanted to say goodbye to you properly.' He sounded tired. No, he sounded scared. Elaine had worked the difference out by now.

He breathed down the line. There was nothing more she wanted than to be in bed or bath with him. Shut the wicked world out. Just the two of them. Tap end.

'I know you do,' she whispered.

'I might not make it, Pinky.'

Elaine didn't think she could bear it. She needed to be at the police station when it opened.

'Do you have to go?'

'I have to get involved. It's my work. And…' He paused. 'I want to.'

'I will try to get there as soon as… as soon as… as soon as I'm given the all-clear.'

'The all-clear?' he repeated. He didn't believe her.

'Yes, darling. What time are you leaving?'

'Eighteen hundred hours.' His voice was flat.

'Say it in English,' she said. This was one of their old jokes but he didn't laugh.

'Six o'clock this evening.' He sounded more annoyed with her than she'd ever heard him before. It was a shock somehow. She poured all she could muster into her words. 'I promise, darling, I'll be there. Hold on for me.'

'Do you have to handcuff him?' Elaine asked the police officer, back at the station later that morning.

Apparently, they did. They pulled Alan into the car and they rode down to the place in Dartford. In the car, Alan gazed at her docilely. They had given him something to calm him down, she knew it. He kept saying, 'Private Parker' over and over, until one of the police officers said gruffly, 'We've got the idea, son.'

On the doorstep, an elderly nurse told them, 'I don't know what you're doing here. We don't admit at the weekend.'

The police officers looked at each other.

'We'll have to take him back to the station for another night,' one said.

'Not my concern,' she said, closing the door on them.

Elaine threw herself forward. She beseeched the woman. Alan couldn't last another night at the station, he couldn't, and neither could she, *please.* Eventually the nurse took pity on her. She went and fetched a man – a doctor maybe? – who tried to flirt with her. 'Well, for a pretty lady like you, let's see what we can do…'

Before they left, one of the police officers leaned forward, squeezed her shoulder and said, 'He's a lucky boy to have you on his side.'

Alan obediently let the staff lead him away. Elaine remembered that day when she had to tell him and Clive that Mum wasn't going to be back, ever, and how he had just carried on skinning dead mud off his shoes. He was thirteen, Clive was twelve. She had sworn to keep them all together. Family first.

There was a mountain of paperwork to sign. *Alan Joseph Parker. Son of Shirley and Alan Parker deceased.* 'Both?' asked the flirty doctor sympathetically.

'Yes,' she said. *Deceased, run away, same thing.*

Age, address, occupation, symptoms. Time was slipping away and *Bobby, Bobby was off to Calais tonight.*

She made it through the questions, Alan slumped beside her like a ragdoll.

'I have to go.' But Alan, who had been docile for so long, now began to act up. He grew distressed. He whimpered. He was racked with great tears. His shoulders shook. He gripped her hand and whispered, 'Private Parker.' When the doctor tried to peel him away, he kicked out.

'Don't go.'

No one seemed to know what to do so Elaine agreed. 'I'll stay till he's calmed down.'

He needed a long time to calm down.

Elaine took a cab to Belgravia from the train station. She could barely afford it, but there was hardly any time and she knew it was her only hope of getting to Bobby's. Unfortunately, luck was not on her side. A funeral procession was clogging up the roads. It seemed like a bad sign. Elaine threw her money at the driver and ran the last mile or so.

She rang Bobby's doorbell. It was five past six. Eighteen hundred hours had been and gone. There was no reply. She rang and rang but there was nothing. Just the clanging of the bell, like an echo in a deep, dark cavern, and then silence.

Elaine crouched on Bobby's doorstep. She was exhausted, but she wouldn't cry. She had a terrible premonition of him dead in some foreign field. Her darling, catapulted into the air, different languages shouting commands. Her Bobby. Oh, the unfairness of it all – to be so in love now, in such a rotten time as this.

She thought of all the things she wanted to say to him. She hadn't got the chance to tell him she loved him. She hadn't got to say goodbye. Alan may have been lucky to have her by his side; Robert Capa hadn't been. And now it was too late. This was such a blow; on top of everything else, she didn't know if she could bear it.

She walked to the bus stop, waited for one hour, and then walked across London. It took two hours and all her resolve.

CHAPTER NINETEEN

SPAIN

JUNE 2016, DAY THREE

Matthew says I should get in the pool and have a go on Alyssia's armchair, but she looks up at him moodily. I call out, 'You're all right, Alyssia,' and she waves, half-sulky, half-relieved.

'I didn't bring my swimsuit,' I say to no one in particular.

I sit by the side, and swoon in the heat. How the birds can sing in this, I don't know. I can't remember ever being this hot. Kicking my legs in the water, I'm reminded of the photo that started all this off: the photo of the two darling girls. *Poor Nana*, I think. *There is so much I never knew, so much I never even imagined about her.*

Aunty Barbara comes out. She is wearing a drab grey dressing gown and looks very sorry for herself. I ask her if she drank too much at the karaoke last night, and she scowls; she thinks she has food poisoning. She thinks Derek's chicken drumsticks have done her in.

Mum ignores her. She is lovingly applying oil to an oblivious Derek's back.

Matthew whispers to me, 'Do you think she'll sling him on the barbecue next?'

'She wants to have the same skin colour as the migrants she dislikes so much.' Matthew's laugh is like a barking dog. 'Gisela always says that about her too.'

*

We are sitting under the sun-umbrellas when the car crunches up on the gravel. I am thrilled to see Nick and Stella again: it's not just me, I think the others are too. They dilute us. We need them to show off our better sides.

Nick bounces out. Stella looks tired but more beautiful than ever in that fragile way she has. I go inside to get drinks, crisps and olives. Matthew always prides himself on his 'delegating skills'. Nick comes into the kitchen and offers to help. He smiles brightly at me, tearing open the crisp packets with the little bear.

'No hat today?'

Damn, I think, *why did I forget to put it on?*

He tells me about his evening: he went and saw the sunset and it was amazing. I tell him about our karaoke. He says, 'Next time I'll join you guys.'

'I'd like that,' I say, then blush. 'Can you sing?'

'Not at all.' He laughs and I say, 'You'll fit right in.'

We place the glasses on a tray and he says, 'Matthew told me you used to take photos, is that right?'

'Yeah,' I say, a bit taken aback.

'I thought... See, the thing is – I've got this spare camera here. I thought if you didn't have one with you, maybe...' His voice trails away. He lifts the camera strap over his head and hands the camera to me.

It's a Nikon D3500. 'It's a good one,' I say, flustered.

'It's just a loan.' He laughs again. 'But, you know, it's a good loan.'

'Thanks, Nick,' I say, cradling it in my hands. 'That's really thoughtful.'

He carries the tray outside and I stand in the kitchen for a moment, thinking, *well this is nice.*

*

Nick says they actually want to film us today, looking over the notes and photos. But only if we're up for that.

'We're up for that,' shouts Derek. Then he and Mum look at each other. 'Fame at last!'

'You know the kind of thing,' Nick says, although I'm not sure we do. 'Leafing through photo albums, checking out the notes, that's all, nothing too…' He pauses, 'ambitious.'

'Film us?' I squeak. 'Wouldn't it be better doing that in London?'

I'm thinking, *London – where the rest of my clothes are?* Everything I have here shouts out 'tourist' as surely as if I wrapped myself in a Union Jack and wore socks with my sandals. Plus, I'd love Harry to be involved in this. He *should* be involved. I wish I'd fought more to bring him out here. Until six months ago, Paul had been a committed father. He'd rush back from work to get to parents' evenings and football matches. He always made time for both of us. How was I to know that the new Paul would feck off to Ibiza instead of bonding?

But everyone has agreed, the camera is set up and we are, three, two, one, recording.

Today, Nick and Stella have brought a folder of letters to show off. They're not the originals, but photocopies. 'They are pretty illuminating though,' Nick says.

'Ooh goody, love letters,' says Matthew. I look up, surprised at his reaction, but he seems genuinely enthused. I try to ignore the camera but it's very hard.

Nick says, 'You can see that Elaine calls Robert Capa "Bobby" and refers to herself as "Pinky".'

'Aww,' says Mum as though it's not aww at all. 'Young love, eh?'

> *My Darling, Thank God you're home safe. Don't ever frighten me like that again!* says one.

Stop sending flowers, Bobby, or I will get in trouble with Mrs Dill! Mrs Perry will be eternally grateful if you can get more cigarettes. Can you think of any ways I could make it up to you!?!?!

Don't forget to sign a copy of last week's Life *for Mrs Marriot's sister-in-law, Judy? She's your biggest fan, apart from yours truly, of course!*

The affection is not a surprise. The lightness – or is it the normalcy? – is. I suppose I thought it would be more elevated, more poetic. These seem to be the writings of people who know each other very well. People who are honest, unpretentious and loving with each other.

Nick watches us reading them, then says, 'I think they're beautiful.' I look up at him and our eyes meet.

'He kept them,' I say, forgetting the recording. 'That's really… something.'

'He did. I wouldn't say he was a hoarder in general, but everything to do with Elaine, he did keep. He went out with some high-profile women but nothing from any of them has been retained. It's all her.'

'Wow.'

Unfortunately, there are not many photos of our grandmother. This prompts us to speculate. Maybe they were destroyed, intentionally or otherwise? Maybe she didn't like being photographed (my suggestion) or maybe Robert Capa didn't like photographing her?

'Maybe he just liked to keep his work and private life very separate?' Nick suggests.

'That's the way,' says Matthew approvingly.

But there is one of her, and Nick has brought along a print wrapped in tissue. The first thing you see, though, are the flat white buttocks of a middle-aged man and only when you force your eyes away from those do you see the pretty young woman laughing fit to burst by his side. Nana Elaine had hair like my mum and a very sexy figure, yet a wholesome, pretty face. She has lovely teeth. I try to reconcile that with the sugared-almond addict nana who smelled of talc. There is nothing here of the guarded woman I knew.

'This was taken in 1944, some of the darkest days of the war.'

It doesn't look like a dark day for Elaine. It looks like she is having the time of her life.

'She was visiting Hemingway in hospital.'

'Um… *the* Hemingway?'

'Uh-huh,' says Nick. I notice suddenly how attractive his wrists are. They are paler than the rest of him, and black hairs curl over them as though they are in rapture too. 'They ran with quite the interesting crowd.'

Matthew lets out a low whistle. 'Go, Nana.'

'This feature will segue well into Robert's famed attraction to Spain,' Nick says. He switches off the camera, tells us we've done great. 'You know he was here during the Civil War – in the 1930s? His most famous photo was taken here.'

He holds up the print of the falling man.

I think, *what must that do to a person to capture someone's death? What cost to their humanity? How do you live with it, justify it? Does it not screw them up just a little bit?*

'He also became engaged to Gerda Taro in Spain. His connections with this area are legendary.'

'This is not just a jolly for you then, being out here?' asks Mum. She can come across as quite mean-spirited sometimes. She would say she was 'just honest'.

'Not at all,' says Nick smoothly.

'There's a reason for everything,' says Aunty Barbara philosophically.

Stella pipes up. She doesn't often speak, so everyone listens hard when she does. 'By filming here, it's a good way to demonstrate how the attraction to Spain was passed down the generations…'

Everyone gazes at her. There is a silence except for the tinny noise from Alyssia's phone.

It is Aunty Barbara who speaks first. 'Um, but we're not actually Robert Capa's family.'

My mum actually laughs. 'You do realise that, don't you, Stella?'

Stella flushes pink. 'I didn't mean…' She loses her professional *froideur*. She looks up at Nick pleadingly as though to say, *help me deal with these people.*

'I hope you've not wasted your time,' says Mum. She's lying. She looks absolutely thrilled. 'We're all very boring here.'

'Very boring,' echoes Derek. He is wearing a white chef's hat, the tip of which has toppled over.

Nick bites his lip. He looks at Stella, then looks at all of us, a nervous smile playing on his lips. 'Well, here's the thing… This is what we've started wondering.'

We all stare at him. Matthew stands, gripping his gin and tonic, his shorts flapping slightly.

'I mean, that's another thing we were going to talk to you about. We've got our suspicions about… Robert Capa and Elaine.'

'Suspicions?'

'We think maybe… You know the timings. He was back in London from 1943 to 1945 and you were born 1944 and 1945.'

Mum and Barbara stare at each other.

'Oh my God.'

'To be clear, it's early days, it's just an idea…'

So, this is why the interest in us. Of course! There had to be more to it, I knew it.

'Who?' I ask, my voice trembling, 'which one of them do you think is Robert Capa's daughter?'

Nick gazes awkwardly at me. He shrugs. 'We're still…'

My mum stares at Barbara. 'I bloody knew it!'

'I don't think so…' says Aunty Barbara. She tries to put on her jumper, but it gets caught up with her sunglasses.

'You were always so different from the rest of us,' Mum says. 'Dad always said so.' She puts her drink down and the ice clinks. You can hear a pin drop now. She addresses Nick: 'I think it's more likely to be Barbara. Definitely. I mean, look at her.'

We all look at her. They are different, Mum and her, that's true. Now that we are talking about it, I can see that, yes. Barbara's arms, the moles, Barbara with her wiry, untamed grey hair, but with the laser-sharp cheekbones, Mum with the control-blonde look, the neat versus the fuzz, the smooth versus the bumpy. But there are similarities too: the way they both sit forward very straight, the way they walk, the way they pronounce *Majorca* and *Malaga.*

I stare at them both. I feel like I'm looking at them for the first time.

Like a psychologist in an American film, Nick continues, 'We're *really* not sure of anything yet. Barbara, how would you feel about that?'

But Aunty Barbara is sitting in the chair, shaking her head and squinting into the sun.

'I don't think so, Shirley.'

And my mum, smug as a bug in a rug, carries on. 'It does though, it makes perfect sense. You're dark, I'm blonde.'

'But that doesn't mean anything, and anyway, both your children are dark.'

Grey, more like.

'And look at Jen. She worked as a photographer, didn't you, Jen?'

'It's not quite the same—'

'It *is* the same,' she snaps back.

'I don't think there's a gene for that,' I say.

'It's quite a shock, I imagine,' Nick says soothingly. He keeps glancing at me.

'Yes,' says Aunty Barbara.

'No,' says my mum. 'It all makes perfect sense.'

I pipe up again. 'Or both? It could be both of them, right?'

Nick meets my eyes. He nods just slightly.

'It could be, but as I say, it's early days.'

I can feel my heart leap and I don't know if it's him or this idea. I can feel the camera heavy in my hands, and this… I can only describe it as a dawning – Mum's right. *This makes perfect sense*, I think. *It really does.*

Mum shakes her head at Aunty Barbara. 'But it's not me, it's you. You always were a little cuckoo in the nest, I knew it.'

The look on Aunty Barbara's face is priceless. It is a pure Robert Capa shot. Unadulterated drama. She stands up, re-knots her dressing gown and glares into my mum's face.

'I would stay and discuss this further, Shirley, if your husband hadn't poisoned me.'

She turns on her espadrille heels and shuffles out of the sun.

Nick and Stella leave pretty soon after. There is some discussion about how we proceed from here and it is Matthew's idea, which I think might have been Nick's idea originally, to do DNA tests. But because it is Matthew's idea, my mum thinks it is absolute genius.

'Won't it take ages?' I ask.

No, it won't, because Stella knows someone who knows someone who can do it really quickly. Stella knows *everyone.*

'What kind of test is it?'

It's a simple swab. They take a saliva sample, send it to the lab, and Bob's your uncle. Or, as in this case, Bob's your grandad.

'Will Barbara agree to do it though?' Nick is looking more and more uneasy.

'I'll make sure she does,' Matthew promises. I scowl at him. *She might not want to*, I try to say with my eyes, but he is pouring another gin for my mum, who is fanning herself like a crazy thing.

I walk them out to the car, where Stella air-kisses me, her eyes fixed on the distant Sierra de Tejeda mountains. She says, 'I hope your mum isn't too upset at the idea,' but I don't get the sense she is that worried.

'Oh, she's always upset at something or other,' I say disloyally. 'She'll be fine.'

Nick smiles ruefully at me. He waits until Stella has shut the passenger door before saying in a low voice, 'That wasn't meant to happen like that. It's all a bit of a bombshell, I imagine.'

'Not at all,' I lie, 'it's good to put the pigeons out with the… cats.'

He nods politely, as if I am making sense.

'And thanks for the camera,' I say, then correct myself, 'the loan of the camera.' I weigh its lovely heaviness in my hands. 'I'll work on it.'

I crunch my way back poolside. Aunty Barbara still hasn't returned, and Matthew is teasing Mum. 'You'll be Jewish, Mum. You'll have to go to the synagogue.'

My mum brushes imaginary crumbs off her trousers. 'Well, I always liked Neil Diamond.'

This is the kind of thing Paul would have been brilliant to chat about to. At that moment, I suddenly miss him fiercely. I had been getting on so well without him, but Paul would have said the right things about this, he would have known what to do. He was good in a crisis. I remember him taking Harry to the hospital when he had broken his elbow; Paul knew exactly what to do. When the chips were down, he was brilliant.

But, I remind myself, *the chips aren't down. This might actually be something really exciting. For all of us.*

Robert Capa. War photographer. My mum's dad? My grandad?

Alyssia looks up from her iPad, suddenly. Like Stella, she doesn't speak often, but when she does, she has a nice authority, or at least an earnest way about her. 'I learned at school that the Jewish religion passes down through the mother, so I don't think you would count.'

'I don't think Grandma was actually thinking of doing anything about it, were you?' Matthew says.

'No,' Mum says defiantly. 'It wouldn't change anything even if it was true.' Her voice trails away. 'And it isn't.'

'It's against the Trade Descriptions Act,' says Derek.

Matthew laughs. Mum looks annoyed.

'How do you mean?'

'If I bought a car, I'd be angry if it wasn't the make I had specified, that's all.'

'Are you comparing me to a car?' Mum asks haughtily. It's a tone I recognise, but not one I've seen her use on Derek before.

'Just saying.'

I'm not going to let Mum off the hook that easily. 'Still, all that foreign blood… Well, well, well…' The thing my mother dislikes, she might well be. It has the most beautiful symmetry. In a way it *is* too good to be true.

'Don't,' she says. 'It's Aunty Barbara, not me. I feel it in my bones.'

I am still feeling buoyant. 'Shall we do some karaoke later?'

Mum flicks her fan towards me. 'Bit tired tonight.' She pauses. 'That is, unless Matthew wants to. Matthew?'

Eventually, Matthew looks up from his phone. 'No thanks, Mum.'

CHAPTER TWENTY

LONDON, JUNE 1944

Annie leaned over Elaine's desk as she did most Mondays. 'How was your weekend?'

Elaine pointed to the new poster above her: LOOSE TALK COSTS LIVES. Fortunately, Annie realised what she meant and didn't pursue it further, although they went for their eleven o'clock cigarette at ten forty-five. Mrs Dill was too busy to notice.

Elaine had decided that she didn't want Annie to know about Alan and the asylum. She knew Annie wouldn't tell anyone, but it was uncomfortable having one person know so much about her. Secrets were like eggs; best not have too many in one basket. One loose-cannon brother is a misfortune, but two looks like carelessness... And anyway, wasn't there quite enough sadness for one breaktime with the departure of Robert Capa?

'Bobby's gone,' she told Annie miserably. 'And I didn't even get to say goodbye.'

'Oh, Elaine...' Annie went to put her arm round her, but Elaine shook her off. No crying. 'I'll be fine, Annie, you know me.'

There was cheese on toast for Monday lunch, but Dotty told them there would be 'Welsh Rabbit' tomorrow.

'Isn't that the same thing?' Elaine asked Dotty, who frowned and insisted it wasn't.

*

Clive turned up that evening. Goodness knows where he'd been over the weekend. *He's like an alley cat,* thought Elaine disdainfully, so much worse than Bettie Page, who sat on her blanket, taking in everything and saying nothing. Poor Maisie.

She told Clive about Alan while he washed his hands. He used the last bit of soap; said he'd find some more tomorrow.

'So, Alan was the one took my knife then?'

'I guess,' Elaine said. Honestly, was that all he was worried about? 'Look, we can visit next Sunday. You'll come with me?'

The horror on his face! He pushed back his hair and surveyed her dispassionately.

'I don't really care.'

'How can you not care about your own brother?'

'I'll come on one condition,' Clive said shortly.

Elaine's heart sank.

Lunch break next day, Elaine slipped out to meet Clive. For once, he was on time – a sign perhaps of how much this meant to him.

'What about the fishmongers?' she asked.

'This is important too. Thanks, Elaine.'

'I'm not getting involved *properly*,' she said. 'I'll just do the introduction and that's all. And you'll come and visit Alan?' Elaine thought of her mother. What would she have done? *Blood is thicker than water, Elaine. You'll take care of your brothers for me?*

Clive, who never touched her, who would do anything to avoid being close to her, squeezed her shoulder. 'Absolutely. You're the best,' he said. But as she chatted to Faye and Merry at the desk, a picture editor who she had met briefly one time, a Mr Bell, invited them into his room. He insisted they had tea with him. He even found an ancient custard cream for them both. Mr Bell was a huge admirer of Robert Capa's photography and wanted to talk all about it.

'It's extraordinary, the way he captures the ordinary,' he said. 'In his hands, the normal becomes special, and the special becomes exceptional…'

Clive was coming out with all the right words too.

'He does something few others can, few others have tried. What a privilege it would be to take his photos on the final stage of their journey.'

Elaine stared at him. She hardly recognised this sincere, serious Clive.

'You've got the job, son,' said Mr Bell cheerfully. 'When Robert Capa recommends someone, we listen.'

Elaine flushed. 'Robert didn't exactly—'

But Clive was speaking at the same time and he drowned her out. 'I won't let you down, sir, I will absolutely do my best,' he said, shaking Mr Bell's hand and giving Elaine his triumphant grin.

American and British planes were flying over London in formation. They were not as noisy as some but boy, you knew they were there. The attack must be happening soon. The invasion was steaming ahead. And somewhere out there, Robert Capa was getting ready to take photos for the people back home. Getting closer all the time.

Keep him safe, please.

As it became clearer that yes, the 'push' was under way, Elaine felt increasingly nauseous. She worried about Alan constantly, yes, but there was something in her that must have been prepared for bad news with Alan for a long time – this fear she had now for Bobby was newer and it was off the scale. Now, she understood how it felt to be one of those people desperately waiting for their husbands, boyfriends and sons, unable to even think of anything else, let alone do anything.

Please let him have changed his mind. Don't let him have gone. But she knew he had gone.

Everyone said, 'No news was good news', and 'bad news travels fast', but she would have done anything for any news, fast or slow, *any* word from him. *Let him be alive.*

'Anyone heard from Robert Capa?' she asked in the street of the *Life* staff, who were running in or running out of the office. (They never walked anywhere any more. Everyone was far too busy.)

They shook their heads.

'The war photographer?' she added.

'We know as much as you do, doll.'

'Which means we know precisely nothing,' said the man next to him, tipping his hat.

Those nights, Elaine was haunted by horrible dreams. The nightmare of Bobby's death was so vivid, so real, that it woke her up. She couldn't shake it out of her head, and she didn't want to fall back to sleep and see it again. She saw his death as in a series of his photos:

The first, he was teetering on the edge of something. Then came a fall from a height, sailing in the sky. Next, flat, his body was face-down on the ground. Finally, a panicking crowd was running towards him. Headlines: Robert Capa is dead.

She swung between, 'I'm just being anxious and ridiculous' and 'I could put bloody money on it'.

She could hear Mrs Marriot open the shutters of WHSmith downstairs, and she picked up her torch and her book *The Heartbroken Nurse Who is Cured by the Sailor* to escape from this world for a little longer. Bettie Page crept up on her bed and kindly allowed herself to be petted.

Everyone was waiting for news. Mothers, sisters, wives. Elaine knew she was no one special in that. In fact, she was worse. She hadn't even got to say goodbye to him… What kind of sweetheart did that make her? A rubbish one, that's what.

And still, in between worrying that he was dead, she wondered, *What if he meets someone else? What if he meets someone better?*

In the George, there was Marty, propped against the bar, and Elaine flew over to him, she flew. When Marty was worried, his eyes crossed over; Bobby had told her this. Now each eye was transfixed by his pinkening nose. Before Elaine could say anything, he had shaken his head several times: *nothing*.

'You must know *something*, Marty.' What she meant was that he knew everything.

He poured a glass of gin for her, told her to drink it up. She hated being told what to do, refused.

'Marty, what have you heard?'

'Nothing.'

She didn't believe him. He eased himself away from the counter, stooped down to her level.

'Okay, it wasn't Calais.'

'What?'

'The attack. They let everyone think it was Calais but it wasn't. Clever, eh? It was nowhere near there – it was Normandy instead. Can you believe it?'

'I see… but… but Bobby?'

'I heard he may have gone in with the men.'

'In? Where in? What do you mean?'

'Into the sea.'

'But, Marty, he hates the bloody sea.'

He is afraid of the sea.

'I know that,' Marty agreed. His eyes were properly crossed.

She drank her gin and the one he bought her next. Their legs brushed on the chairs. Their thighs touched. *It's all right, he is Bobby's best friend. He wouldn't overreach.* She remembered kissing him on the cheek that time and she tried to forget that glimpse of something tiny, something haunted, she caught in his eyes. *She was being silly. Arrogant.*

'In the actual water? The Channel?'

She thinks of Bobby and the way, laughing, he showed her how he swam: with his face upwards, keeping his hair dry. She thinks of him swirling among the fishes. Stuck between a fish and a bullet.

What a stupid idea.

Work was just a waiting game. She could hardly bring herself to look at her POW letters. Oh, what was the point of it all? Will they have heard about the attack out there in Singapore and Borneo? Will it give them heart, those trapped in the ghettos and camps in eastern Europe? Or those hiding in the attics and basements of the resistance? Will they think: *It will be over soon*?

Elaine couldn't face the enforced jollity of the canteen: she went outside to the street to smoke instead, where she watched a bird peck a worm to death. She felt even worse: she had just stood by and watched it. Shouldn't she have chased it away? What was the matter with her? She felt suddenly weak and hungry. She hadn't had breakfast, she remembered. She had to remind herself to eat.

Reports were coming in that there were thousands of casualties. The men had slipped off the landing crafts and walked into German gunfire on the ground and from German planes above. But they had not given up. They had never given up. She and Clive listened to the wireless together. They were quite companionable until she asked him again to go and see Alan. 'Mum would have wanted you to,' she added awkwardly.

'Don't,' he said. The look in his eyes was vicious. 'I'm not Mum and neither are you.'

Elaine slept fitfully again that night and just about got through another day of typing letters. There was not a single clue to speak of. Recently, she had been thinking what a joke it was, this interminable searching. It was just a way of keeping the clerical girls out of trouble; of course it was, she knew that now. Then, other times, she hated herself for thinking that, *of course it was important.* It was essential, whether they found strange patterns and strange phrasing or not. She was another one bearing witness to all the atrocities that were going on. *When people forget all this, that's when we would be in trouble.* And when she thought not knowing whether Robert Capa was dead or alive was torture, she could remind herself, *it was difficult, yes. Torture? No. She knew what torture was, it was in the prison camps of the Far East.*

At lunch, Dolly and Joyce put on a wireless the cartographers had brought down to the canteen. The message was muddled, but generally the same: a great many brave, brave men had been lost, but small buds of hope were flowering. The Nazis were being driven back. Not Calais, but Normandy. Northern France might soon be free.

In the George, Elaine headed for Marty like a homing pigeon. He might have been waiting for her. Maybe not; hard to tell. What was easier to tell was that something had changed. Something was different. *Good news?* He watched her quick-step over to him, then pulled her into the most awkward, most unlike-Marty hug ever. His brass buttons banged against her wool jumper.

'I'm picking him up from the south coast tomorrow.'

She couldn't speak. *Bobby was alive, he was alive. He'd made it.*

And all of a sudden it felt like: *Of course he had made it.* How had she ever doubted it, doubted him? This was Robert Capa they were talking about. Not some amateur! Not some kid. He was the best photographer in the world. More than that, he was a survivor.

'I'm leaving at five tomorrow to pick him up,' Marty continued. 'Do you want to come?'

He looked surprised at himself, as though he hadn't meant to say it.

Elaine was surprised too. She couldn't think fast enough.

'Yes or no?' he persisted.

'Yes!' she said, before either of them could change their minds.

'It's early,' he said, 'but I could do with the company.'

Elaine swallowed.

I was not thinking of you, she thought.

She went back home, told Mrs Marriot the good news and helped her tidy her display in the shop. Mrs Marriot had heard from her nephew too that morning, so they were both in fine fettle.

They sold out of newspapers and magazines. Everybody was hungry for the invasion stories but it was too soon, very little detail had come through yet.

'Our boys will be back soon,' Elaine told Mrs Marriot. She couldn't stop smiling.

'And your fella with all his photographs,' Mrs Marriot said admiringly. 'Oh, Elaine, Robert Capa is a good man – making a difference.'

It was another of those moments when it was hard not to cry.

Back at the flat, Clive was ducking in front of the shaving mirror, trying to see his reflection. His chin and cheeks were foamed up white like Father Christmas.

'*Life* want me to start,' he said, his chest puffed up and defiant.

'So soon?'

'Yup.'

Elaine couldn't care less about anything at that moment but that Bobby was alive. Still, she said, 'Well done,' and 'You'll be great.' But then she looked at her brother's stubborn worried face as he drew the razor down the side of his cheek. He nicked a tiny bit and a spot of blood appeared. He tsked himself and continued.

'Do you really think you can do this, Clive?'

'Yes.' He looked hesitant. And for a moment, a river of doubt spilled through her, breaking her good mood.

'Are you absolutely sure, Clive? You know how important these photos will be.'

He dunked his face in the sink, then stuck a small piece of newspaper on the wound.

'Have I ever let you down?'

She didn't say anything. She found him intimidating lately. It was so unfair – he could shut her up with a look or a word and she had no tools to use against him. But he softened suddenly, and feeling his chin, he said, 'Thank you, Elaine. I mean it. If it weren't for you—'

'You're fine,' she said. 'It's what Mum would have wanted. Family first, right?'

That night, Elaine slept more easily than she had done all week. Not a single black dream disturbed her rest.

Bobby was coming home, and that was all that mattered.

Marty drove with great precision, which was a relief. He was sober and careful and although he cursed every other driver, it seemed to be more from a sense of habit than real annoyance. *Just get us there in one piece*, thought Elaine. Wouldn't it be dreadful if they died in a road accident? After all the soldiers had gone through for them!

'Does Bobby drive?' The question suddenly occurred to her. She imagined the two of them, whipping along some open road, her hair flying all over the place.

Marty looked over at her, his lips curved into a half-smile. He kept his hand on the gearstick. His fingers were clean and his nails were trimmed, but the hand was also only three inches from her knee. Elaine didn't know if you had to leave it there or not to drive. She knew she would look ridiculous if she said anything about it.

'Why do you always call him Bobby?'

Elaine paled. *It was going to be like this, was it?* 'I just find calling him Robert Capa is a bit… formal?'

'You know, Robert Capa is not his real name.'

'Oh.' It was painful, humiliating, to be told this by Marty. It was one-upmanship. She wanted to say that she knew things about Bobby that he didn't know, could never know. Things between a man and woman and the night.

'It's a name he and Gerda Taro conjured up together,' continued Marty.

But does she rub it in his face? No, she doesn't.

'His real name is Endre Friedmann. And yes, of course he can drive.'

He has so many names. Does this mean there is something insubstantial at the core of him, Elaine wondered. *Something fickle or disloyal?* She had always been simple Elaine Parker – Pinky was her first and only nickname – should she trust someone who hadn't told her his real name?

Marty smiled suddenly. 'You knew he was from Hungary, right?'

'Yes,' said Elaine cautiously. She supposed he was going to say actually he was from Timbuktu or something. 'I knew that.'

'Course you did.'

Why was Marty so edgy with her? They were similar, Bobby had said. Same background, same ambition. Same chip on their shoulders. Same baggage. He had his leg. She had her brothers. You'd think they'd get on.

A small insect was flattened on the windscreen. Marty took hold of the hand wiper and vigorously turned it. Elaine watched as the insect was moved all around the windscreen until finally, after several false promises, it fell off.

After an hour or so, the driving motion began to lull Elaine's concerns away. She closed her eyes and thought of Alan sedated at the asylum, Clive at his new job (!) and Bobby on his journey home, and she thought, with some satisfaction, *well, at least everyone is safe, for now anyway.*

The next thing she knew, Marty had stopped the car and was saying, in that impatient tone he had, 'Elaine, we're here. Get up.'

*

They were outside a guesthouse in Eastbourne. It was a tall, absurdly pink building called See Views. Yes, they spelled it with a double E. Bobby would love that. They rang the bell and a child – probably no more than eleven or twelve, maybe a daughter of the house – told them Robert Capa was in room six. Three storeys up and no lift (Bobby would be less keen on that). They knocked at the door of number six, Elaine's excitement mounting, but there was no answer for a long time.

Then finally he was there, apologising; he said he had been in the deepest sleep known to mankind, a hibernation, he said. He could sleep all winter, summer, year, for ever. Then he clutched Elaine first – good – but not for very long, then he clutched Marty into a bear hug too. Elaine tried to relax.

He said he had slept for thirty-six hours straight. Marty looked relieved. He pushed his glasses up and rubbed his eyes.

If Marty hadn't been there, she would have jumped straight into bed with him, no question about it, but Marty wasn't going away now. Bobby was wearing thin blue pyjamas; he looked more like an inpatient than Alan did. He was adorable and the way he looked at her said nothing had changed for him either.

Nothing has changed. Remember that.

'Where are your clothes?' she asked uncertainly.

He said his clothes were so rank that the landlady had insisted on putting everything in the wash. The pyjamas brought out the purple shadows under his eyes – he looked utterly and completely done in.

He had gone in with Company E in the first wave. The ship unloaded boats into the water and the boats unloaded the men up onto Omaha Beach, Normandy. That's where he'd got in.

Elaine didn't quite know what this meant, but she could see from the shock on Marty's face that it meant something big. Marty shook his head, a mixture of admiration and envy.

'Elaine,' he instructed, 'can you go and find Robert Capa something to wear? We can't possibly wait for his clothes to dry.' She was going to protest but guessed there was something they wanted to talk about and they didn't want her there.

I should have brought him clean clothes, she thought. *I'm an idiot.*

In the back of the car – Bobby was sitting in the passenger seat where she had been – she felt like an interloper. She felt like she was being smuggled somewhere by people who didn't want her there. Bobby was constantly turning round, checking she was all right, but still she had the feeling that she had made a mistake coming here. Bobby wanted Marty – he wanted men-time. Small talk with people who understood. Bobby was passing her bonbons, asking about Annie, Mrs Dill, Myra, even Bessie, getting their names right, but still, she felt she shouldn't have come. *His name is Endre. Endre Friedmann.* If she hadn't even known that, what other secrets were there?

She thought they were going back to the Belgravia flat but first, they went to Life Corp., where Marty bounded up the front stairs to deposit Bobby's four rolls of film. Bobby had taken two cameras with him. He said it was a miracle that they'd both come back in full working order.

Elaine remembered suddenly that Clive was there now, not Larry, and she wondered if Marty knew of it or if he would mention anything. She guessed he would lean over the front desk to Merry or Faye and tell them to take the films up to the darkroom. Now, please. Perhaps he would give them a wink and a promise that Robert Capa would come in to thank them later.

With Marty out of the car, Elaine and Bobby were free to smooch. This was a language Elaine was better at. And wasn't this so much easier than speaking? Elaine leaned forward, and Bobby leaned back. He still wanted her, that was clear as day. Far more meaning in their bodies and their kisses than in their words. Elaine wanted nothing more than to be alone with him, show him how much she'd missed him, but all too quickly Marty had thrown himself back into the driver's seat. 'Come on, Casanova. Let's celebrate the wanderer's return.'

The George was even more packed than usual. People – some Elaine recognised, some she didn't – gathered around to welcome the great Robert Capa back. He was offered drinks and slapped on the shoulders. Peter played 'Pack Up Your Troubles'. Even Bessie came out from behind the bar to listen to his stories. Bobby always said he was better with images than words, with photos than speeches – but that wasn't true. He was as mesmerising a raconteur as a photographer.

'I thought I was fish food. I thought they'd put me in as bait.'

'Are the pictures any good?'

'If your pictures aren't good enough, it's because you aren't close enough. I got pretty close.' He grinned.

'Can't wait to see them,' Bessie said.

'It'll be just like being there,' Peter added.

Everyone went silent for just a second.

Then the girls from Life Corp. came in and the celebrations grew more and more frenetic. Pink gin was flowing, and Merry and Faye were putting their arms round Bobby and whispering things in his ear.

'We knew there was going to be an attack on Calais!' Merry said triumphantly. Bobby winked reassuringly at Elaine.

Six o'clock and they were still at it. Elaine noted they'd been drinking for nearly six hours.

'I'm so glad you're okay,' Annie told him fervently. Myra could only nod at him, her face wreathed in compassion. Marty too was elated, he grew louder and louder the more he drank.

'These photos are going to be really big.'

'He's already big,' Annie reminded him.

That was true. It was not like Bobby's reputation was waning. He was at the peak of his powers. He ruled the photography world. Students lined up with their box cameras, wanting tips and hints. 'The pictures are there,' he always said. 'You just take them.'

Bobby nudged her. 'We'll be able to dine and stay at the Savoy for months.'

Elaine laughed, looking around the George. 'But I like it here.'

Bobby was already whispering in her ear. 'It might change things for us, are you ready for that?'

Elaine stared at him. She wasn't sure what he meant. And still, she remembered, she had to tell him about Alan. But something was pulling at her, saying this wasn't the time. This was Bobby's moment. Let him have it.

Everyone wanted more. 'Speech!' they called out. 'Come on, Mr Capa! We want the scoop.'

'For one moment, I hesitated,' he began, 'but I was kicked up the rear end into the sea!'

Everyone whooped. 'I held my camera high as I could. I shot the pictures, non-stop, taking it in, drinking it in. Ninety-five shots, five rolls of film. I didn't look, I just clicked the shutter.'

'Yes!' said Marty emphatically. 'You've done it!' He pushed his glass onto Bobby's. 'Cheers!'

'The war will be over soon,' Bobby said softly. 'The Nazis were weaker than we expected. They've had enough, you can just… feel it. It's palpable. We suffered a lot of losses, terrible losses, but the tide is turning.'

He paused before shouting again. 'It was good to be there. A privilege. It was worth it. Show what heroes our boys are, and we triumphed, and we will triumph, again and again and again!' He grinned proudly. 'Always, because we are on the right side!' and now they all clumsily 'cheersed', and the beer nearly slopped over the sides of the glasses, but no one was quite that clumsy not these days, now that beer was so scarce.

As soon as they were back at the flat, Elaine decided, she would tell him about Alan. She found she could hardly wait to let it out. Secrets were bombs. You could think you were safe, protected, but then they'd go off. There was nothing to be ashamed of. Alan could no more help his situation than those men floating in the English Channel could help theirs.

Towards closing time, Bessie went to her metal safe and got out her infamous autograph book. The regulars cheered. They knew what this meant: Robert Capa had made it.

'I thought you'd never ask,' Bobby sighed melodramatically, and Bessie put her hands on both his cheeks like she did when she was properly emotional and kissed him four, five times. They spoke some strange language together. Then Bobby took the book. He pushed through the pages of tissue paper of proud names. At the signature of Johnny Weissmuller, Annie gasped. 'Tarzan came here?'

'Always!' said Bessie. Overwhelmed, Annie clutched Elaine's shoulders. 'How come we missed him?'

'Here.' Bessie pointed. 'And write a message… a personalised message, please. None of that "Roses are red, violets are blue" rubbish, I've got too much of that.'

Bessie never did mince her words.

'By hook or by crook,' started Bobby, while Bessie pretended to swat him about the ears.

'Here,' he said, reading aloud. 'To the George and Bessie, the loves of my life…'

Everyone cheered. Marty laughed the loudest. Bobby whispered something to him. Marty's eyes flickered towards Elaine, then away.

Elaine was scarlet as a pillar box. She was wondering if she would ever get him alone. Hadn't she waited and waited like some biblical wife, like some pillar of bloody salt, for his prodigal return?

Even when they were leaving the pub at midnight, people were still wanting to slap him on the back euphorically. He was like a mascot. The Americans. The Canadians. The British. 'We did it. We did it. We're winning. Can't wait to see all the photos. Brilliant.'

Bobby walked towards Marty. They were laughing, making triumphant plans. Elaine caught up with him. 'You're not playing poker tonight!'

A swift sideways glance at Marty. 'Course not,' he said. 'Just saying goodbye.'

Elaine would rather have gone to the Savoy – his rooms were basic, not unlike hers – but he wanted to go home. Of course he did. Back in Belgravia, he grabbed her in his arms passionately. Elaine thought he was going to kiss her, but instead he burst into hot tears. He was sobbing so much; her blouse grew wet and her arms began to ache from the effort of holding him upright.

'My darling, it was terrible.'

Elaine hadn't expected this. All that exuberance in the George and now this? She had never seen him like this. She has never seen *anyone* like this, ever.

Poor Bobby. She hadn't realised. He had told her what he'd been through, yes, but she hadn't realised what it had done to him. She was struck with a powerful awe and sympathy, an overwhelming need to make it right.

He talked of a sea turned red with blood. Of young men obliterated in front of him. They were talking to him one minute, showing him photos of their girlfriends; the next, they were face-down in that deadly sea. 'They drowned…' He could hardly get the words out quick enough. 'I couldn't do anything. I tried, but they were just tangled, limbs in my arms. I tried, Pinky, I tried so hard, but the guns… We were walking into gunfire. Lambs to the slaughter. It was relentless. They were massacred.'

She didn't like him talking about it, talking like this, but she couldn't stop him. He needed to tell his story.

He went to the outside lav. After ten minutes or so had passed and there was no sign of him, she tiptoed down. She found him cradling the toilet bowl.

'They died, Pinky,' he said from the floor and retched. 'All those young men. Dead. Before they had a chance to live.'

Elaine put a damp flannel on his forehead. He begged to drink vodka in bed, and she gave him some, but watered down. If he noticed, he didn't say anything. He told her he loved her. He would take care of everything. He clutched her to him and then he fell asleep. She watched the rise and fall of his chest. She watched his eyelids settle. His despair had thrown her. She hadn't foreseen that, but they were together, and she knew he would get over this, and even if he didn't, she would do everything in her power to help him.

Bobby was safe. Bobby – Robert, Endre, whoever he was – was back. And he loved her deeply. Not Marty, not the George, not the girls, not Gerda. Not Martha. She was his number one. Nothing and nobody could take that away.

At about seven the next morning, Elaine scribbled Bobby a note, then crept away. She went home to meet Clive and take him to see Alan, as was the arrangement. As she sat in the kitchen, trying to get Bettie Page to pay attention to her, she wished she was still with Bobby.

By nine, Clive had still not turned up. By ten, Elaine realised he must have lied to her and probably had no intention of ever seeing Alan again. She had fallen hook, line and sinker for yet another of his scams. *Would she never learn?*

She stroked Bettie Page, who allowed a moment of friendliness, then went to see Alan on her own. There he was, in the grounds, banging his head against a tree.

'How are you, my dear Al?' Elaine asked hesitantly.

'I'm Private Parker,' he insisted. She led him to a bench, where he rested his head on her shoulder for the entire two hours while she patted his hand.

CHAPTER TWENTY-ONE

LONDON, JUNE 1944

Clive was standing at the bedroom door, whispering her name. Elaine woke, head aching, body clammy. It was Monday morning. She'd slept but could do with more, always could recently.

She could hear Mrs Marriot calling out the news from the street. 'Normandy! Invasion!'

Bobby's photos would be in *Life* magazine tomorrow. It was going to be a special issue edition: Normandy Landings. The Longest Day, they called it. It would make America head office sit up. It would make *everyone* sit up. Churchill would call a meeting. The King would splutter into his tea. Even Mr Hitler – could you imagine that? *They say Mr Hitler gets sent* Life *magazine to his bunker in Berlin!*

Mrs Marriot would congratulate her. Mrs Pepper would remark on how agreeable he was. Joyce would give her extra gravy.

Clive didn't come in straight away. He was afraid of something, she knew that much. *Had the Nazis come?*

'It's about the pictures.'

No, it wasn't the Nazis.

'Great,' she said, sitting up too quickly and feeling dizzy. 'Are they any good?'

He didn't say anything. Elaine looked at him expectantly. She was hot in her nightie. It was boiling for June. *What time was it?* She pulled the blackout curtains up. Sunlight shafted the room. She squinted at her brother.

Clive sat on the end of her bed, something he had never done before. Long legs kicked the china jug kept under the frame. He took off his cap, wrung it between his hands as though it was soaking.

'I screwed up, Elaine.'

Elaine felt herself tremble. A bolt of fear. *This isn't happening. It isn't.*

She thought of Bobby's jubilant return yesterday. His promises. These photos were going to be big.

'For God's sake, Clive. You had better not have.'

Then they were running, well, *she* was running, he was hobbling, all the way to Soho, to Life Corp. He wanted to get a tube or a bus, but she couldn't stay still. Her blouse was untucked, and he was carrying his jacket, and gabbling on and on and making a fool out of them.

'We can't afford a cock-up, Clive.'

But he's gone and buggered everything up.

'It was harder than I thought, I didn't realise, I thought I could learn it… I thought it would be like gutting a fish.'

'Gutting a fish!' she parroted back at him furiously. 'You didn't realise? I told you it was important. I *told you* not to get involved. What did you do?'

'I shut a door. A cupboard door.'

It sounded entirely innocuous, yet Elaine knew it couldn't be. 'And?'

'And it dried out the films inside…'

'And?'

'They're, they're… ruined.'

'How could you do this to me, how could you do this to Robert Capa? After all he went through for this! How could you!'

She pictured Bobby broken in his rooms, on the floor, crying about everything he'd seen. *At least I am telling their story,* he'd said, *at least I did something.*

'I'll tell him,' Clive said with wobbling lips. She hasn't seen him cry, not even when Mum died, but tears pooled in his eyes now. 'I'll explain what happened.'

'No, *I* will,' she said furiously. 'This is on me.'

She had let them think Bobby had recommended him. '*When Robert Capa recommends someone, we listen.*'

Dear God. What had they done?

Bobby was already in the pub with Marty.

Who were all these people? Had he slept at all?

He was laughing with Bessie, ordering drinks, complaining about them being watered down, planning a poker game tonight. He was still letting off steam. And why shouldn't he, after what he'd gone through? She said hello and waved.

'Pinky!' He sounded so delighted. 'What are you doing here?'

Marty's expression was not so delighted.

'I need to tell you something.' She tried to ignore Marty, who was sitting there like some royal courtier whispering titbits in the King's ear. He didn't get up and Bobby made no move to get up either. She would have to say it here, to them all.

'It seems a new member of staff had some issues with the development.' She addressed the floor. 'Of your photos.'

'Well, what issues?' asked Bobby, suddenly alert. 'I haven't heard anything.'

Some of the floorboards were loose. She could see the nails sticking up. She remembered when the George took a hit and helping straighten it out the next day.

'Why would they tell you, Elaine, you and not me?'

He had never talked to her like this before. He never called her Elaine.

Elaine shook her head. Now, Bobby got up.

'How do you know this? I can probably help. Where are they?'

Elaine licked her lips. She hated the people watching and listening. Hated having Marty there with his eyes glinting at her behind his jam-jar glasses. He was waiting for her to become extinct.

'I don't—'

'What's happened to my prints?' His voice. Only a few hours ago, so gentle, so caressing, now cold. Cold as the English Channel.

'They managed to save a few but—'

He squinted at her. 'Who was it then? This new member of staff?'

'It was my brother.'

'Your seventeen-year-old brother?'

'Nineteen… Clive's nineteen and he needed the money and since Larry died and—'

'I'll always give you money, Pinky. You and your brother. You only had to ask.'

They were walking now, or rather, he was frogmarching her down the road to Life Corp. He crossed them over right in front of a car, which sounded its horn, but he didn't even notice. It was little relief that Marty wasn't there. She hoped Clive wasn't hanging around. She didn't know what Bobby might do to him. She thought shamefacedly that it would be nothing she and Clive didn't deserve.

He had shot fifteen lots of film. He looked at them, pegged up in a row. Hung out to dry.

He didn't look at her when he said, 'I spent three days killing myself for these shots.'

'I know,' Elaine said quietly. She was not going to plead. She thinks, *now I will find out what kind of man Bobby is*. Is he a fighting man like her father was? Is he a Clive, or is he an Alan? Does he go outward, or does he go in? Her cheeks were aflame.

'It's the only documented evidence of what these men, these boys, went through. And you're telling me your brother destroyed them?'

'Not on purpose,' she said quietly. 'It was an accident.'

He shook his head furiously. She had never seen him like this. 'There are no accidents, Pinky.'

A crowd of Life Corp. journalists had gathered around outside the darkroom. For the first time it occurred to her how alike they all looked. Short-sighted, half of them. Keen and smart, like moles surfacing, sniffing.

'Well?'

'What happened, Robert?'

'The photos are okay, aren't they?'

Bobby ran his fingers through his hair, sighed.

'We've got nine, maybe. Ten, eleven, at a push…'

'Eleven? What the—'

'That can't be it?'

'It is,' he said flatly. There followed a hush that was worse even than the questioning.

He turned to her. 'Give me a moment to sort this, Pinky.' He touched his finger to her lips, in front of all those people, and it felt more than a standard goodbye.

'I'll wait outside,' she choked. 'Sorry.'

CHAPTER TWENTY-TWO

SPAIN

JUNE 2016, DAY FOUR

It shouldn't make any difference but what would it mean to me now, if my grandfather was someone... marvellous?

I try to play it down, play it cool, but there is something buzzing and burning inside me like a Catherine wheel. This, this is just the news I needed. Two uncles who served and a possible world-famous, derring-do grandad.

After the others went to bed, my mother repeating, 'It's Barbara, not me,' like a mantra, I looked through the Robert Capa photos on my phone. I couldn't stop myself: Agricultural workers, wounded soldiers, one with a head injury comforting an other, a battle-weary soldier petting a puppy, a woman lugging a suitcase over her head. One particularly appealed to me – a young girl milking a cow. The concentration on her pretty face is something to behold.

That is some special kind of talent, some special kind of DNA. Maybe I'm not so ordinary after all? And this, this must be why Nick lent me the camera. He thinks it too.

I texted Harry. 'You might have a famous great-grandad!'

'Cool beans,' he replied. I resist texting Paul. He's not part of my life any more and who cares?

*

You have to hand it to Mum; when she gets done up the next morning, she looks terrific. The tan, the gold jewellery, that black dress… she could be a Mafia boss's wife.

Today, they are going to a party, the wedding anniversary of some friends down the valley. I am pleased that Matthew and Alyssia are going too. This is excellent news. I've been thinking that if I don't get some time on my own soon, I might spontaneously combust.

Mum twirls and Matthew says, 'Wow, Mum, look at you!'

'It's the Hungarian in her,' I say from under my hat on the sunlounger.

She shakes her head at me, hisses, 'It's Barbara, not me.'

'Just like Zsa Zsa Gabor,' says Derek.

I take photos with Nick's camera. Mum poses – she can't help herself – but I still manage to get several nice ones. She is frighteningly photogenic, something I never inherited. She makes Matthew sit with her, and I take shots of the pair of them. I hope someone is going to ask me to join but they don't. They *do* look great together and they know it and I know that two's company and three's a crowd.

I also think someone is going to ask where the camera is from, but no one does, which I suppose is good really but also disappointing somehow.

Aunty Barbara comes out and greets Mum coolly. She has gone for her signature bohemian look and is wearing a tie-dyed skirt and a black top. It suits her. I help her tie up the cotton scarf she wants to wear. She puts her hand on my cheek gratefully.

'What would I do without you?' she says.

'Feeling better?' I ask.

'Not too bad,' she says. Leaning closer to me, she whispers, 'It's all a load of old nonsense, Jen, the Robert Capa stuff. You know that, don't you?'

'Well…' I begin. How can she be so certain? 'We don't know yet.'

'I *do* know,' she says.

'Are you going to do the DNA test?'

'Already have,' she says, surprising me. Apparently, Nick has been round early that morning, then sped off with the samples in a plastic bag.

'Very professional,' she adds approvingly.

'Why didn't anyone tell me he was here?' I ask, irritably. Mum is putting suntan lotion on Matthew's nose and they are both laughing. How do my family always manage to make me feel left out?

My aunty looks surprised. 'Sorry, love. I didn't think.'

She has bags under her eyes. I wonder if she's sleeping badly because of all this. When I ask her, though, she shakes her head, says it's just the heat. However, she admits she was on the phone for much of the evening.

'Ah… and is everything okay with Nelson?'

'Yes,' she says obliquely, 'I wasn't *only* talking to him, I was doing some detective work of my own.'

Alyssia looks very pretty in a pale blouse and skirt. There has been an argument about the skirt. I backed Alyssia, of course, as is my duty as Visiting Aunty from England. It amused me to see Matthew coming down as the heavy parent. He normally likes to see himself as Mr Liberal. I take some pictures of her too. I tell her I couldn't wish for a lovelier niece, and she smiles; the photos of her are brilliant too.

And Derek? A plain shirt, black shorts. Because it's a party, he is respectfully wearing socks with his sandals. I am reminded of Harry on his first day at big-kid school.

I can't wait for them to leave. I need some air. Once they've piled into Matthew's car, I wander around with the camera – Nick's camera – relishing my freedom. I had forgotten how enjoyable taking photographs is. There is something life-affirming about capturing a moment, a thing, and I'm determined to get a photo of the lizard, although it is too fast for me and keeps escaping into the bushes.

Listening to birdsong, I google Robert Capa some more. I read about the incredible photos he took during the Normandy invasion, how he risked his life so many times for his work, and how a development problem meant that only a few pictures survived: the Magnificent Eleven. I read about the photos he took on the American airbase that almost got him thrown out of Britain. I read about his many friends and all the girlfriends and the fact that he was a 'confirmed' bachelor (I'm not sure what they mean by confirmed here).

Nana Elaine. Mother of his children? Could it be?

After about an hour, I am so hot that I strip down to my shorts and bikini top. This is the life. I am lying on a sunbed poolside, embracing the Spanish heat, watching little sweat droplets form on my belly, when I hear a car pulling up outside.

Oh no. They can't be back already.

Nope, it's not them. It's Nick.

I am worried about all the alarms, so I talk through the fence gate. Even my voice sounds hot and sweaty.

'They're not here, Nick. They've got a… a party today.'

'I know.' He sounds shy suddenly. 'So, I thought… maybe you'd want to go out for lunch?'

I look at the three empty packets of the chirpy bear crisps I've got through since they left. But then I think of Paul swanning around Ibiza – and he did swan, Paul did, he glided around, debonair and smooth. I think of the dark hair curling on Nick's forearms. And I think of the camera he has lent me. And I think of my maybe-grandfather who, by all accounts, used to absolutely love getting himself into trouble.

'Hang on,' I say, drawing back the lock.

CHAPTER TWENTY-THREE

LONDON, JUNE 1944

Bobby was standing in front of her. That face. Those tender eyes looking into hers, more serious than she'd ever seen him.

'I've only one thing to say to you, Miss Pinky Parker.'

Guilt-riddled, wrung out. If only she had said no to Clive. Or if only she had gone along and helped him. If only she hadn't been so soft on him, but he had always had them wrapped round his finger. Mum would have been so ashamed.

'Yes?'

'Will you marry me?'

'Wha-at?'

Bobby was holding out a twisty piece of metal. His eyes were fixed on her.

Elaine stuttered. 'Aren't you furious with me?'

'You look so worried. We need some good news, baby!' He picked her up off her feet and twirled her around. 'You're all I could think about out there – I couldn't bear not saying goodbye to my sweetheart. I would have done anything to be with you… I was in the sea, when it was cold, when they were shooting at us, and…'

His voice dropped so low she had to lean in to hear him.

'Pinky, people were dying all around me, people I had shared a joke or a cigarette with just minutes before… And all I could think was: I've got to get back to my girl. She needs me and I need her.

Those peachy lips, that… bottom of yours. I told them all about you. And you? You kept me alive out there.'

'But your pictures are spoiled… the report on Normandy invasion is destroyed.'

'I'm not the only photographer in the world, am I?' he said.

She smiled weakly. 'Aren't you?'

He laughed as she continued, filled with self-loathing, 'Everything is ruined because of me.'

He shook his head incredulously. He ran the back of his hand across his forehead. 'Nothing's ruined. Nothing. As long as we're together, everything will always be fine. Say you'll marry me, sweetheart.'

Elaine didn't know what to think. All she knew was that she had this shooting sensation of unadulterated joy running through her. An almighty yes.

'Are you sure?' she whispered, watching his face, searching for signs that it wasn't true, it was a joke.

All the things he didn't know about her. The things she hadn't told him. All the people entombed during the Blitz – it should have been them. She is dirty, rotten, corrosive. A hand ripped away from hers in the street. A father who packed his shaving brush and didn't come back. Stolen goods, scavenged gloves, wirelesses, benches, you name it.

'I've never been surer of anything in my life.'

'But… but… where shall we live, what will we do?'

She waited for him to say it. His mouth curled into a lopsided smile. 'Would you… would you come with me to America?'

The big cars, the endless sidewalks, the traffic lights. The pictures.

'After the war, I mean.'

The laugh that came from her. 'You don't think the war will last for ever?'

It had been going on since she was eighteen, all her grown-up life, and she was now twenty-three. She couldn't imagine a time Britain was not fighting the Nazis.

'It won't last for ever. There'll be other wars, but not here for a while. What would you like to do, Pinky?'

Elaine hesitated. She looked to see if it was still the elation talking but Bobby seemed to be serious.

She felt silly talking about herself, her usually pointless hopes, but Bobby was looking at her earnestly, his eyebrows furrowed.

'I quite like organising. I think I'm good at making things happen rather than reviewing them *after* they've happened.'

'Then do it,' he said simply. 'Manage things. I like that.'

'I thought you liked Pinky the clerical girl?'

He pulled her towards him. 'I like it all, sweetheart. So, in America with me, you could—'

'Take care of your assignments,' she interrupted, trying not to sound *too* excited.

'You'd write my captions?'

'And keep your diary and help run the business side of things.'

'You'll manage *me*?' he asked tentatively. 'So, like a photograph agency, we could set up one maybe. We could run it together?'

He meant *that's what the plan was with Gerda Taro.* She was sure of it. But did that matter?

No.

Could she manage him? Elaine would never have been so bold as to suggest it outright. Was he laughing at her or was this genuine? She could work with him, for him, for them. They could take over the world.

But what about Alan?

Alan would be better soon: he wasn't always going to live in the asylum – that was for the really difficult ones. They'd let him out. That's what they'd suggested anyway. The doctors, the nurses, the policemen. Even Clive said Alan was only 'crying wolf'. He meant he was putting it on to avoid being sent anywhere dangerous and although Elaine hated the idea that her darling little brother was a shirker, she couldn't help hoping that maybe that was the case. It would mean he was a very good actor but…

What would her mother say about her marrying Bobby? Elaine could hardly remember her recently, never mind conjure up the advice she might have bestowed. But surely, any mother worth her salt would say to her daughter only one thing?

If that's what you want to do…

'Yes, Bobby, yes, please. And let's go to America.'

No more war. Freedom. Wide roads, big cars and marriage to the most agreeable man in London. Could you blame her?

He squeezed her tightly. 'I have been hoping for a very long time that you'd say that.'

CHAPTER TWENTY-FOUR

LONDON, JUNE 1944

Alas, Marty was not so easily placated about the pictures.

While Bobby went to have some discussions about the ones that had passed, Marty and Elaine walked back through the offices of Life Corp. Elaine hoped her newly engaged ebullience didn't show too much.

'This is… infuriating, you know, really, really infuriating,' repeated Marty. It was like he was talking in elaborate code, but Elaine didn't need a fancy machine to decipher what it meant: 'Dib, dib, dib, you're rubbish, you're really, really rubbish.' And maybe a 'Dib, dib, dib. After all I've done for you…'

'I know.'

'Are the eleven any good?'

'The what?'

'The photos, I heard there were eleven. Are there? Are they any good?'

'No – yes, eleven, yes – I think so. They're all rather out of focus. I'm sorry, Marty, really I am.'

Marty was catatonic with suppressed rage and indignation. His face was one tight over-drilled muscle. Elaine thought to herself, *Marty has the same background as you. Fiercely smart and hard-working. Everything he's got, he's had to fight for.*

'It's just such a waste. He nearly died for these pictures. Only to have some spinach screw everything.'

'Marty saved my life. Put me back on the straight and narrow.'

'I know,' she said sullenly. Was it really just a couple of days since they'd travelled down to Eastbourne together?

She had to skip to keep up with his strides. Marty wouldn't even look at her. She found this annoying. They weren't his photos, were they? *He* hadn't nearly died in a sea of blood taking them, had he?

'How could this have possibly happened, Elaine? I mean, tell me, how the hell did your brother end up working here?'

'*Bobby* seems to have got over it,' she said spitefully. *Restore the balance between them.*

Marty turned. Elaine saw suddenly that he was even angrier than she had realised.

'*Bobby* is easy come, easy go, do you hear me?'

It suddenly seemed to her that he wasn't talking about the photos at all but implying something else entirely. She suddenly remembered Justin saying, *Robert Capa has a girl in every port.* Who had told him that?

Marty pressed his glasses against his face. 'Robert told you Martha was there? In Normandy?'

'Yes, he did,' Elaine lied. *Martha? Ernest's girl was in Normandy?*

Marty didn't believe her. She could see it in his eyes. He thought he'd got one over her again.

'He's not steadfast, he's not reliable.'

Elaine wasn't having this. Not her fiancé, not any more. She raised herself up.

'Maybe that's between me and him, Marty. Do *you* get what I'm saying? We're engaged now, and that is that.'

CHAPTER TWENTY-FIVE

LONDON, JULY 1944

Ernest had decided to throw a party to celebrate their engagement. Bobby told Elaine, 'And he called you "A humdinger of a girl".'

'I thought he was supposed to be good with words,' Elaine said pointedly.

Bobby laughed. 'Actually, that's not exactly how he described you, but that's the family-friendly version.' He stroked her hair. 'You'll probably end up in one of his books.'

'Will Martha be at the party too?' she asked. Ever since Marty had said that Martha was at Normandy, it had been going round and round her head.

'Don't think so.'

'That's a shame,' she said daringly.

'Isn't it?' he said, taking her arm.

The room was done out in candles, a man in chef's clothes was playing the guitar and there were people everywhere, drinking and smoking. Ernest was sitting like a Roman emperor in his armchair, his feet stretched out on the table in front of him and his big fat cigar poisoning the room. If you requested it, he'd do a wicked Churchill imitation and apparently, he did a Hitler too, but that was only in front of a select group of friends. Ernest had an image to keep and wasn't he aware of it?

He looked her up and down like she was a succulent fig and he was about to eat her. 'Here she is: the girl who lost Robert Capa's photographs,' he shouted.

'It wasn't my fault—' protested Elaine.

'Ah, yes, it was the brother!' Ernest shouted with amusement. 'Am I right? You're too good-looking to work for the government. It's criminal that they keep you locked up in some airless office.'

Elaine laughed. 'Who should I work for then?'

'Me!' he bellowed. 'Come be my assistant. Can you type?'

'Of course she can type,' Bobby said proudly.

Ernest had snuck his arm round her. 'And do you look this pretty when you type?'

Elaine moved his hand from wandering towards her chest. 'I have to work for the government.'

'Stuff and nonsense,' he told her. And then to Bobby, 'She should be out doing something for morale! It's a travesty.'

At least someone appreciated her, thought Elaine, drinking down the punch and then coughing at its potency. God knows where Ernest had managed to get it from, but there was possibly more alcohol in that fruit bowl than she'd drunk in the last five years. And someone had got hold of a pineapple too! Everyone admired it and some of the men put it on their heads and danced around the room to Tino Rossi, one of her and Bobby's favourites. It was a fabulous party. Elaine was also pleased Martha wasn't there and that Ernest was being so gregarious. She met more of his author friends and when they asked what she did, she took a leaf out of Bobby's book and muttered that it was hush-hush, top-secret work. This they liked.

Then Ernest fell down the stairs. At first, he insisted it was all fine. 'No harm done,' and 'nothing a bit of fruit punch won't fix.' He was so heavy, no one could pick him up, and he seemed to be in so much pain that even the alcohol couldn't alleviate it.

Bobby got him under the armpits and dragged him to a taxi. Ernest was clearly in agony, but determined not to show it.

'Don't forget my cigars!' he shouted. 'And where's the girl who lost the photographs? She must come too.'

The party continued in Ernest's hospital room. Someone had even remembered to bring the punch. For the first time since she'd known him, Bobby took informal photos. It was because of Ernest probably. Ernest was dealing with the pain by ordering everyone around. When he turned away for a moment, Bobby took a photograph of his bottom protruding from the open-backed hospital gown.

'Take one of the beauty, for God's sake,' Ernest barked, 'not my flabby white arse!'

For the first time, Elaine posed for Bobby. She was laughing too much; she was all teeth: she knew the photograph wouldn't show her at her best, but once the shutter had clicked there was no escape.

Ernest blew her kisses.

'This government worker is the most adorable thing I've seen outside of Catalonia. I don't see how you can photograph anything else when she's in a room.'

'I take photos to make things come to life.' Bobby squeezed her shoulders. 'Elaine doesn't need that. Everyone who meets her can see how lovely she is.'

Some time later, Marty came in like an irate schoolmaster and shooed everyone from the hospital room.

'This party is over. And for goodness' sake, you *know* you can't smoke that in here.'

'Oh, Marty,' said Bobby. He tried slapping Marty on the back, but he was so drunk, he missed and nearly fell over. 'There's a war on. We gotta kick back sometimes. Let's wait and see what the doctors say.'

But Marty was in no mood for kicking back.

'Out,' he commanded. 'You're all such children…'

Even Ernest didn't argue with Marty in this mood. He sank back miserably into his bed, pulled up his sheet and waved them all off with a shrug.

Back in Belgravia, Elaine and Bobby slow-danced to his big band records on the gramophone, then Bobby tenderly took the pins out of Elaine's hair and brushed it.

Elaine screwed up her courage and asked him if it was true that Martha was at the Normandy landings.

'She was there, I heard,' Bobby said, pouring more drinks. 'Why do you ask?'

'I wondered if you had seen her?'

'Of course I didn't see her, Pinky. I would have mentioned it if I had.' He looked confused.

And Elaine knew suddenly and strongly that she had nothing to fear with Bobby. He loved her. She loved him. This was right. This was everything.

When you're in hell, keep on going, Churchill said. When you're in heaven, keep on going too.

Don't destroy it. Don't sabotage it.

Elaine was dreaming. She dreamed they had a big California house with an outside pool. There were bonbons on every table, pink and white sugary confections in engraved glass bowls.

He was coming towards her in pale-blue swimming trunks. Her Bobby. Putting his arm round her.

Now they are in New York. He must go here, and he must go there. Meetings with people. Photographers. And she is organising them all.

'That's Robert Capa's wife.'

'That's Pinky Capa, she's the greatest agent there is.'

'The greatest agent of all time!'

Standing outside the office block, letting Bobby hold her hand. 'The whole block. It's all ours, Pinky. You and me.'

She woke up, rolled over, and was surprised he was still there. The dream was still alive. Was he awake? She wasn't quite sure.

He stretched out his arm and patted her. 'Pinky.'

CHAPTER TWENTY-SIX

LONDON, JULY 1944

Nothing lasts for ever, as Elaine's mother used to say, and Bobby had to go away again. Of course he did. The whole world was busily occupied doing things it didn't want to do. These were the times they lived in. When everything was sliding out of control. What would make her and Bobby any different?

This time he was going to fly to Italy: he was to take a truck up into the mountains, where really bad things were happening. The commission: a photo-documentary series on the lives of the partisans.

They'd offered him six pages.

The prospect of six pages made everyone whoop. Not Elaine – Bobby was going away. She was not in the mood for whooping.

Why couldn't he cover sports or cookery? Finance or theatre? Not bloody people killing each other. Why couldn't he tell her how long he would be? One month, or two? *Who can predict, Pinky?* he said.

Whatever it is, however long it is, it's a bloody stupid idea. What's wrong with his photos of the people on the home front? Aren't we extraordinary too?

Was sending him there a death-trap, a punishment for the photo development debacle? Bobby said not, but magazine publishing was a tricky business. Elaine was learning that.

Not as tricky as being a partisan. The life expectancy for a partisan was less than two months. For goodness' sake, they might just as well fling him out of a plane without a parachute.

'Dying days of the war.'

Did he have to say 'dying'?

'You're only as good as your last picture,' Bobby said, before adding wryly, 'And your last picture is only as good as the thing right in front of you.'

Elaine couldn't tell him, couldn't tell anyone, but she was frightened for him. They would send him to the bloodiest of battles. He hadn't said it, but she'd heard it from the others. The fighting was fierce. Air fire, machine-gun fire, everywhere you went-fire. Hints from Marty. Worried talk in Life Corp.

Bobby is a lover, not a fighter.

That was what Bobby was famous for: you could rely on him for treading into fields of dead bodies. For being as near to the explosions as possible. For being in the execution zone. *If someone's getting a bullet to the head, Bobby will be next to the head. If someone's on the end of a hangman's noose, well, there's another end, don't forget it, that's where Bobby will be.*

That was Bobby's thing. That was his reputation. He got himself in the most dangerous situations. That's what they paid him to do.

In the George, some servicemen were exchanging tales of their battles in Italy. One chap said, 'We found a piano, our sergeant, clever fella, had a hankering to play a little "Moonlight Sonata", so he opened it up but the retreating Krauts had booby-trapped it. Blasted up to kingdom come he was.'

Elaine knew Bobby and she knew there was no way he would ever not open up a random piano. He would never pass up a chance for a singalong.

It would be just her luck that they would have found each other and then he would be killed. She thought about it all the time, an obscene amount of time. And it *was* like they had found one another, it was like he was the thing that was missing all her life, and it felt like she had got him back, retrieved him, discovered him, secured him.

It felt like their love was ancient – it had been across time and space – yet being with him felt brand new.

It *was* magic.

She hadn't known you could ever feel like this.

Bobby was leaving early on the Monday. On the Sunday morning, Elaine went to see Alan while Bobby slept off the poker from the night before. She and Alan walked in the grounds and it was fine. There was no headbanging, he was definitely improving, he really was – until he started to say that the squirrels were government agents. Although he was convincing, Elaine was 99 per cent certain on this one, so she argued with him. Alan grew very frustrated with her and aggrieved, so Elaine backtracked and told him a long story about Clive, the fishmongers, the things he had come home with lately, including a small umbrella and a framed photo of Churchill, and the things he was growing in the garden out the back. Then she felt terrible because what if Alan told someone and what if what Clive was growing was illegal?

But Alan wasn't listening anyway.

Sometimes Alan wanted to talk about Mum. His memories were jumbled and Elaine found it painful to listen to. She tried to change the subject.

'You remember I met someone nice?' she said. It was a relief to have something different to tell him. How very quickly you could run out of things to say. 'Nice' didn't quite describe Robert Capa, but Alan got it.

'Someone nice,' he repeated.

'That's it, do you remember I wrote about him: Robert Capa?'

'I remember,' he said, although whether he really did or not, she wasn't quite sure.

'Well, we're going to get married,' she told him. 'But I need you to get better for me first. Can you do that?'

Alan nodded.

She held his warm chunky hands. The new medication was making him put on weight. 'Wish me luck, darling.'

'Wish me luck, darling.'

She met Bobby at the Savoy at three. Elaine was beginning to think of the Savoy as 'their place'. She knew the feel of the carpet, the steps, the elevator. One side of the building had had its glass blown out during the Blitz and it hadn't yet been fixed. She knew the view from the dining room, the ash grey of the Thames ahead of them, and the exotic plants in the gardens. She liked chatting with the waiter who had lost an arm, and she had her favourite waitresses: she especially liked the sad-eyed Jewish German girl who wrote down their orders in her impeccable English.

She knew that in America there was no 'ground floor'; it was called the 'first floor' and Bobby had told her that one hotel in New York had escalators actually inside and he would take her there and they could go up and down on them for as long as her heart desired.

That day, they went straight up to the room.

Stroking her hair and nuzzling her neck, Bobby was even more expansive and loving than usual. 'I don't want to go to Italy this time.'

Elaine sat up straight. *This felt important.*

'*Tell them* then. Don't let them make you go to places you don't want to go.'

He laughed. 'I can't do that.'

'Why?'

More laughing. 'Marty would kill me.'

'Is that all? Is that the only reason you are going?'

He got up. He was wearing his white vest and his funny trousers. He looked incredible like that. Made her bite her lip with desire. He stared out the window.

She'd never seen him so pensive. Usually, he turned everything into a funny. *Don't dwell on things* was their unspoken rule.

His voice cracked slightly. 'You know, usually I don't mind going to the dark places, because the truth is: I don't care about dying.' He took his hands out of his pockets. 'I'm a fatalist – if it happens, it happens. But now, I feel desperate. I don't want to die, not now – not now I've found you. I've changed. You've changed me,' he said, and she peered at his face to check he was not accusing her of anything. He wasn't.

'What will I do while you're running around the mountains taking snaps?' She did this deliberately sometimes, pretending his work was unimportant or small. It made her feel better about the risks he was taking.

'You'll wait for me, I hope?' he said charmingly. 'Don't run off with anyone.'

'As if I would.'

He didn't look reassured.

'Clive would kill me if I did,' she teased. 'He's grown fond of you.'

'I don't *quite* trust Clive.' He laughed. Elaine's stomach dropped. Bobby knew her brother was a scoundrel, she realised, he knew. Did it change the way he felt about her?

'But you trust *me*?'

He stroked her hair. 'More than anyone else in the world, Pinky.'

That was a smart answer.

Later, they went downstairs for the Savoy's High Tea. They may be at war, but the wealthy still needed cakes. It was frightfully posh, and for once Elaine couldn't help noticing that she and Bobby looked that much younger and more dishevelled than everyone else. She thought people might be looking down on them, but they didn't, they sent over drinks.

Macaroons, pink and chocolate squidgy. Small triangle sandwiches. They'd even taken the crusts off – so used to feeding people who could afford to chuck away half the nutrition.

'Mr Capa, we wish you good luck.' Bobby went over and they talked: generals and politicians and newspapermen.

One man came over, and when he went back to his colleagues, Elaine distinctly heard: 'I've just shaken the hand of the greatest photographer of our time.' She couldn't help but smile, but when she heard the companion say, 'He'll be dead before the end of the war, mark my words,' the smile dropped off her lips and the dread feeling came back again.

And then it was back to their room; time was running out, and it was Elaine who felt overwhelmed with emotion. The worry of him, the worry of Alan and Clive. Long dreary days at work with only Annie stretched ahead of her. The letters from poor prisoners. She hated them, but the moment they stopped coming would be worse.

Waiting. Waiting.

She was never very good at being patient. Even Mum used to say she did not stick at things. Not like the middle-class girls at work with their practised hobbies and skills. They saw days as leading upwards to a sunlit world of talent. Her days were just one thing after another leading nowhere.

He kissed her neck. 'You'd better learn how to wait. This is how it is in a war. Nothing, nothing, nothing happens, then boom, everything, then nothing again.'

'I'd like to see you *out* of a war situation.'

'So would I, Pinky,' he said. 'Here's to peacetime. Not long now, I promise.'

His overcoat was hanging on the hook on the door. Elaine put her hands in his pockets, leaving a little note for him to read on the way to the plane. Fumbling around, her fingers found a box. There were condoms in his pocket! *Why was he taking those with him?*

No time for discretion. 'Bobby, what are these for?'

She held them out to him, like dirty underpants.

'You don't know?'

'No, I mean why are they in your coat?'

Bobby was not particularly interested. He was engrossed in writing a letter to his mother in New York City. Elaine hated when he did that. She knew he only wrote before the more dangerous trips.

'Bobby?' she said again, her voice shaking a little.

'The boys gave me them.'

'Why do you keep them though?'

'I'm not keeping them, I just didn't not keep them. Are you jealous, Miss Pinky?'

Yes. No. Always. 'Maybe.'

'They won't be used. Count them now. Count them when I'm home.'

He thought she was paranoid now. She *was* paranoid but she didn't want him to know that.

'They'll only be used with you.' He raised his eyebrows playfully at her. 'Until the day comes when you say otherwise.'

She pretended to hit him. 'That's not happening,' she said. She suddenly thought, *My goodness, what are we saying here?* but Bobby didn't react.

'As you wish,' he said and pulled her over for a kiss.

The next morning, they slept so late there was no time for anything. Bobby scrambled up, hastily shaved and dressed; a car was coming for him, he had to away. No time for lingering kisses. Their goodbyes weren't meant to be like this, but at least this time she had got to say goodbye.

'Any problems, Marty will look after you!' Bobby called as he got in the cab.

What kind of problems did he anticipate?

'I'll be back soon as I can.'

He blew her kisses, shouted farewell, *adios, adieu*, until the car turned left at the end of the street and she stood there feeling he and everything associated with him had vanished into thin air.

He was going into danger, danger in a war zone, into occupied Italy. And she was doing nothing but battle with the ribbons of a typewriter. She felt flat. All the air had left. When he was around, everything was so bright, colourful and big. Now it was small and uneasy. She was boring old Elaine with the sticky-out figure and the sticky-in life. Just a load of stupid dreams – marriage and running a photographic agency in California? The best one in the world? What ridiculousness was that? That stood no chance of being fulfilled.

Elaine's mood darkened as the day went on. Vera greeted her by saying she had a face that would turn milk sour. Lunch was a meat stew on her own since Annie had been asked to wait behind in the office. The canteen table was wobbly and even scrunched-up paper underneath one leg wouldn't steady it.

When Elaine came back to the office, a flushed-looking Annie was walking out with two men in uniform and Mrs Dill. Felicity and Myra were both utterly transfixed by their typewriter keys, a sure sign that something untoward was going on.

'Annie, what's happening?' Elaine imagined something awful. It had been a while since a bad news telegram had come. They were talking only the other day about how they were probably due one.

Annie was all a muddle. 'They're taking me to the you-know-where.'

Churchill's war office? The hub. The operation centre. Everything they did came from there. It was a huge honour.

'Brilliant…' Elaine managed to say.

Annie knew what Elaine was really thinking. She leaned forward guiltily. 'I'm so sorry. They were considering sending you as well, but they said…'

'What?'

'You've been too distracted lately.'

'Distracted? How?'

'I don't know...'

'You do.'

'It's probably the thing with Robert Capa and—'

'I'm not *distracted.*' Such a feeble word, designating a feeble person. 'I'm engaged. That's all. I want to work. I've never let anyone down.'

But Clive has. Is that what it's about?

Mrs Dill came over.

'You're *very* good, Elaine, and I know you're ambitious, but we needed someone brilliant and Annie just happened to be the better candidate this time.'

Candidate? She hadn't even known she was up for anything.

Was it her distress over the terrible Geoff letters? She couldn't believe it. Mrs Dill had been so kind. And it had been Mrs Dill who was the one to break down in helpless tears, not her.

'I'll see you soon then.' Annie was led away, looking anxiously at Elaine. 'Sorry,' she mouthed.

Elaine couldn't stand for her dearest friend to feel bad. Annie deserved all the good things.

'You'll be fabulous, Annie,' she managed to call out. 'Go for it!' She did the V for victory sign and Annie laughed gratefully.

'Back to your desk, please,' said Mrs Dill. 'Your work on letters is important too.'

CHAPTER TWENTY-SEVEN

SPAIN

JUNE 2016, DAY FOUR

Nick's car has all the latest mod cons. I hadn't seen myself as the kind of woman who is impressed by shiny things, but clearly, I am. A cool seat is a cool seat, let's be sensible about it. I can only imagine Harry's face if he saw this. He is a sports-car geek. I take a photo of the elaborate dashboard and text it to him while Nick laughs.

'It's a hire car. At home I drive an old banger.' He smiles sideways. 'Is that disappointing?'

'Nothing wrong with old bangers,' I say. 'Speaking as one.'

He laughs again. His laugh makes me laugh too.

'I think you look great,' he says, making me blush.

This hat is the greatest investment I have ever made in my life.

He drives us to a pretty café with bougainvillea flowers climbing the walls. Matthew would call it well-appointed or rustic.

The menu, on the blackboard, has no English, which is brilliant but nerve-wracking. Nick and I discuss our understanding of the words *alioli* and *plancha*. My Spanish, which was never more than enough to order at a restaurant, has disappeared (along with everything else) over the years. Still, spontaneity is good for me, and I feel up to the challenge in my hat, the camera still slung round my neck and my possibly new DNA coursing through me. I cradle the camera like I used to hold Harry even when he was in the baby carrier (I couldn't quite trust it was secure).

The last time I was in a restaurant this nice was with Paul when we were 'trying'. At least, I know now, *I* was trying, *he* was stringing me along. We went to a French place – appropriate because we might as well have been speaking a different language. I was all done up; I had my hair styled and had bought new shoes because black wouldn't go with a blue dress and it had to be the blue dress, because once someone said it looked nice on me. I had even prepared – yes, prepared – some stimulating conversations we might have. Paul kept looking at his phone. I couldn't bring myself to ask him to stop. I wanted him to stop by himself. I wanted him to stop because he loved me.

Stop thinking about Paul.

I smile at Nick. We order and then he says, 'I owe your family an apology, springing those ideas on them.'

'You *did* spring,' I say.

He sighs. If he wasn't tanned, I think, he would be as red as I am. 'I went about it exactly the wrong way. If I were teaching a class on family documentaries this would be a prime example of how not to go about it.'

'It was unsettling,' I say, thinking, *for some of us more than others.*

'Your mum doesn't seem too keen on the idea of being related to Robert Capa.'

'No, she isn't.'

But I am. I can't express how exciting it is. I feel like we've gone from black and white to technicolor. Everything is possible. Anything!

'I've become pretty obsessed with your family tree,' Nick says. 'Tell me if that's creepy.'

'We're a pretty creepy bunch, I reckon.'

He laughs. 'Every creepy family is creepy in its own way. Isn't that what the great Russian writer said?'

I laugh. 'Something like that.'

He asks me what I remember about my nana, but I can't tell him much that he doesn't already know. I hear myself repeating what Mum said, 'As far as I was concerned, she was kind, ordinary. To be honest, I never really thought much about her…'

He nods. 'That's quite normal, I guess.'

Nick has his folder with him. I've become fond of this perspex envelope. Harry had a similar one when he was getting tutored for high school.

'You said you wanted to see the Gerda Taro photos?'

'The… what?'

'The girlfriend before your nana.'

'Oh, yes. I do. Fabulous.'

The photos show black and white people with guitars: 1930s Spain and Paris. There is one of the two of them in a restaurant. He is gazing at her; she is all smiles, all teeth. She has an exotic face, probably less conventionally pretty than my grandmother, maybe more distinctive, compelling, I don't know.

It's clear he adored her.

I wonder how Nana Elaine felt about her predecessor. Maybe she wasn't the jealous type. Who knows? I was jealous of Paul's everything. But in a way I was right to be suspicious. Paul wasn't trustworthy in the end.

I hold the picture and try to imagine what Robert Capa was like: *was he trustworthy?*

I bet he ran off with another woman. I bet he did.

They all do.

If you squint and if you use your imagination, you can just about imagine you can see Morocco out there across the sea from Spain, that grey fuzz. Between eating, Nick and I peer and laugh and peer some more.

'Robert Capa spent longer than a year in Algeria and Morocco. Some of his most famous photos were taken in North Africa. One day, I'd like to do an "In his footsteps" thing.'

'I wonder what Elaine did while he was away all those times,' I say.

'It must have been extraordinarily tough on all the women left behind,' Nick says.

I like him, I decide, *I do*. And that's not just the champagne.

Nick asks me some more about myself. It feels like the subject of Paul is unavoidable. I tell Nick about him and about the shock of his leaving. Nick listens carefully; it feels like he's listening with every part of him.

'So hard,' he says when I've finally finished.

'Have you ever experienced a break-up like that?'

He nods. 'Not to the same extent – how long were you together?'

'Twenty-three years.' *And two months.*

'It must have been pulverising.'

I nod, because that's the word, pulverising, he's got it exactly.

'On top of it all, I feel like I've lost myself too,' I blurt out, surprising myself by being so candid. 'We were always Paul and Jenny. Ever since I was twenty-one. Paul, Jenny and Harry. Harry's mum and dad. It was clear like that. I felt safe and secure like that.'

I drink the wine fast and wipe my mouth with my sleeve, then, remembering I am in company, I dab it more daintily with my napkin.

'You're still Harry's mum.' Nick has this wistful look on his face. 'And I bet you're a brilliant parent.'

'Harry's growing up so fast, he doesn't need me.' I tilt the water jug to my glass. I worry he thinks I'm saying this to elicit sympathy. I'm not, I'm saying it because it's true. 'Now, I'm no one.'

'You're not no one, you're starting again.'

'I'm starting again…' I repeat. Such a simple phrase. A simple thought-shift. A reframing. I like that. And what a place to start again – in a restaurant with dark-eyed, gentle TV producer Nick Linfield. That's not too shabby. I look up and he is smiling at me and *is it the champagne talking, or does he have a bit of Robert Capa around the lips too?*

I blurt out, 'So do you really think my Aunty Barbara could be Robert Capa's daughter?'

Nick pauses thoughtfully. 'She's kind of the family maverick, isn't she?'

'She always has been a bit of an outsider, yeah.'

He smiles at me. He's got good teeth, which is a thing of mine.

'So, I dunno, I think – there's a chance they were *both* his children.'

YES! I want to fist-pump the air.

'Why?'

'Okay, the photo of the girls. The fact that he came back to see her. His infamous bachelor lifestyle. Her subsequent marriage. The fact that your nana and her husband didn't have any more children – perhaps they couldn't?'

'Hmm.' I like it as a theory but even so, it's not entirely convincing.

'And there's you too,' he adds shyly.

'How do you mean?'

Nick looks at his plate first, then squints at me, biting his lip. 'You're fun, feisty…' He is embarrassed, 'very attractive… and I bet you're damn good with a camera. I just think it could be, couldn't it?'

I try not to grin. I want to throw my arms up in the air – *Hallelujah!* 'It could be! But would he have just abandoned them both? Would he have just forgotten them? What kind of bastard would do that?'

'Maybe he didn't know?' offers Nick.

I look at him, grinning. That hadn't occurred to me, of course, yeah. Maybe Nana Elaine never told him they were his.

That could work.

*

As Nick drives me back, I am still glowing from his words. Fun, feisty, very attractive *and* damn good with a camera. I can't think of a way I'd rather be described. I can't stop glancing at him. This. This is exciting. The roads are narrow, and we have to wait for a van to pass. I read its number plate and it says on the side 'International Movers'. It feels like a sign. Everything's a sign. That or I am going mad in the midday sun.

'Do you have plans for tomorrow?' he says. I try not to smile too much. But tomorrow is too soon for me. I need to get my head round this, whatever *this* is.

Robert Capa could be my grandad. Nick Linfield could be my… I don't know what: boyfriend, partner, friend, lover?

'I'm free the day after?'

What's the worst that can happen?

'How about we go out for lunch again?' he asks boldly, but his profile is vulnerable. Paul is finally retreating to the far edges of my mind and it feels good. Strange, but good. I feel like I've just woken up.

I clear my throat. 'Didn't you say your hotel had the perfect restaurant?'

That lopsided smile again.

'I did.'

The new me can be bold. It's my heritage. 'How about we go there then?'

'It's a date.'

CHAPTER TWENTY-EIGHT

LONDON, AUGUST 1944

A telegram came, but not until Robert Capa had been away for four whole days, four entire days of fear of the unknown, her heart in her mouth, sleeplessness.

Bobby had got there in one piece. Excellent.

He missed his Pinky. He couldn't wait to be home.

'Well, that's nice,' said Mrs Marriot in the shop, master of understatement. Going through stacks of old *Life* magazines, she had found some Robert Capa photographs from the mid-1930s. They pored over them at the counter. There was something captivating about seeing world events come to life. Ones Elaine had never seen before. *I must remember to ask him about China.*

Elaine knew she wasn't cut out for all this waiting. The girls at work, Felicity, Myra, they all had discipline and endurance – *if you want something, you have to work at it, practise, practise, save for a rainy day* – but she didn't have those in her make-up. She was made of live for today and love the one you're with and money burning a hole in your pocket.

It felt like everything, just everything, was on hold until he was back. Yes, it felt like Christmas every time she was with him, but the rest of the time was pure Boxing Day.

Mrs Marriot knew what it was like to really wait for someone – her brother was stationed in Palestine and her nephew was on the HMS *Barfleur* – but she was a woman of great empathy and she never once said, 'It's only been a few days, my girl. How do you think the rest of us cope?'

Elaine did appreciate how patient and tolerant she was.

Instead, Mrs Marriot gave her some new books. 'Lose yourself in these, girl.'

Elaine tried, but for once, even these expert studies of romantic love weren't working for her. How could they? None of the men on the pages were like Bobby, none of them had charm whistling through them or magic in their make-up. The women weren't anything like her either. The women didn't seem to worry about food and dying and doodlebugs and criminal brothers and secret brothers in a lunatic asylum. They worried about lack of staff, their dresses, their hairdos and their pa's and sometimes their ma's.

A few days later, another telegram came from him. The plane he was supposed to be on had gone down. But he had missed the plane – because he had been daydreaming about her – and so he was safe. 'Don't worry!' it said blithely.

She remembered he had said that he was a king of the near miss. He had told her about places he'd stayed that had been hit by earthquakes, trains he'd been on that had been derailed, buildings that had collapsed just after he'd walked out their doors.

Why on earth would he tell her this? Did he think that would cheer her up?

'Don't worry'? *For goodness' sake!*

It was hot. Five o'clock on a Friday evening and the sun was a brilliant orange flame. Elaine left the government office and, at the same time, saw Marty in parallel, cautiously descending the staircase of Life Corp. She didn't know whether to say anything, decided not to, but as she was trotting down the street he called out to her.

'Oh hello, I didn't see you there,' she lied.

'Want to go for that drink?'

She wanted to say no, but what was there to lose? Sitting at home with Bettie Page? Bettie Page who had her own life, her own friends and didn't divulge any of it. Bobby had told her to speak to Marty. She was doing what he wanted.

Boy, this man can drink, she thought. He bought them a round. Bessie was behind the bar, even her powdered face was glowing. The only concession Marty made to the hot weather was an almost imperceptible loosening of his tie. He kept his jacket on.

'I miss Bobby so much,' she confided over the drinks.

'He's only been gone four weeks.'

'Four weeks and four days,' Elaine spelled out grumpily. She had optimistically sent five letters to Italy, getting only two postcards in return. One had a rude suggestion on it, the other said, 'Oh, Pinky, war is nothing but a sham,' which did nothing to ease her disquiet. Perhaps he wasn't even in Italy? Perhaps it was just like the Calais thing. Perhaps it was a con, a trick, and he was somewhere completely different.

Marty downed his drink. 'Get used to it,' he said quite crudely. He was no Mrs Marriot. 'This is war.'

'I know that. I just get lonely.'

Marty nodded. 'If you need company, I'm always here.'

Elaine shuddered. That *wasn't* what she meant.

He was very solicitous, though. Chairs pulled out, drinks fetched, ashtrays retrieved, cigarettes lit. It was not like being with Bobby, of course it wasn't. It couldn't be. But it was a second best.

Talking with the man who knew Bobby best meant the niggling doubt, that seed that had been planted there, bobbled to the surface. The contents of his pocket. The rumours. What Justin had said.

'Is Bobby faithful?' Elaine couldn't stop herself.

But this was one way in which Marty would not help. 'Talk to Robert Capa,' he said evasively. His eyes looked too big in his glasses. 'That's between you and him.'

'*You* know him though, Marty. Better than anyone.'

He shrugged.

Elaine felt 100 per cent worse.

'I had a nice evening,' he said.

'So did I.'

That moment though, it all felt faintly wrong. He stooped for her to kiss his damp cheek.

'You'll do your back in,' she said lightly.

CHAPTER TWENTY-NINE

LONDON, AUGUST 1944

Elaine didn't tell anyone where she went on Sundays. Obviously, Clive knew, but not because he had ever asked. He was possibly the least curious person in the world – he didn't ask questions because he didn't like to be asked questions. But apart from him, not a soul knew.

She told Mrs Dill, Mrs Perry and Mrs Marriot that she went to church. Mrs Dill had sniffed disdainfully but didn't say anything. Mrs Perry and Mrs Marriot were both approving; in fact, it was the first time Mrs Perry showed any signs of liking her. Elaine didn't feel as bad as she might have about the lie, because it was only a white lie, and the hospital where Alan lived was a bit like a church in a way: there was little said and it was sad; and she spent much of the time thinking, *Oh God help me*. On the train, it was mostly churchgoing families without their fathers too, children dressed in their Sunday best, playing cat's cradle or marbles.

He'll be out soon, she knew it.

The asylum was only an hour and a half away, but it felt like going into another world. It was like stepping back in time – it felt Victorian. Like something from Mrs Marriot's stories. Not the ones with romances in the ballrooms, but the ones with ghosts in the wall, skeletons and ghoulish noises. Every time she saw the bars at the window, her stomach crunched. While her mother might have been proud of Elaine, no doubt she'd have been appalled that Alan had ended up here. But what could Elaine do?

Not much, that was what.

If Alan had been good that week, they were allowed to sit out on one of the wrought-iron benches with the curly armrests. You got a good view of the allotments. There was barely a patch left in the city or the country not devoted to the war effort.

There was a woman there who carried a glass-eyed doll and she would sit on one of the other benches. Elaine learned she had lost four children in the Blitz in Walthamstow and her mind as well. The house next to the hospital had been bombed out completely too; it was just a painful carcass of a building, and this unsettled Elaine. What a reminder for the poor woman! Was there no escape? Surely they should move her somewhere less disturbing? But no one had and Elaine didn't know if she should interfere. She had a feeling the staff thought she stuck her nose in enough about Alan; sticking her nose in about another resident wouldn't exactly be welcomed.

He'll be out soon, she knew it.

Is it going to be a good day?

It was an okay day, which was, to be fair, as good as it ever got. Elaine and Alan sat out on one bench and the woman clutched her glass-eyed doll near them on another.

CHAPTER THIRTY

LONDON, SEPTEMBER 1944

Heading back to my Pinky. Meet you at Savoy.

The night Bobby came back from Italy, the band in the club were joined by Vera Lynn and it felt like she was there just for them. Sweet smile, impeccable hair, the tight dress. Didn't she look wonderful?! And didn't she sound wonderful too? No one could sing like Vera Lynn, no one. The men were clapping and smoking, they couldn't look away. Bobby didn't want to dance though; he was unusually uptight, she could sense it, and she felt frustrated. He needed to talk war and politics with Marty and his journalist friends. He needed to get it off his chest, out of his system, but she needed him, didn't he know it? She waited and waited until he nodded at her to go and dance with the other men.

'Enjoy yourself, sweetheart! I won't be long.' While she was a knotted ball of jealousy, he was as placid as a coffee cup.

She was whirling around the room, with Canadians and Americans, and they were 'yes, ma'am' and 'no, ma'am' all over the place. But even though she had their attention, it was lonely without Bobby, he was the one she was there for. So she went and sat and listened to him expound on his theories to his rapt audience and she wished they were anywhere but there.

He tapped her hand but he was preoccupied. He had a lot to say. She could have been anyone and she didn't like it.

'Sleepwalking into war, last time, this time, next time. The English are extraordinary. The kindest people – but when the rich say jump, the people ask how high?' Everyone laughed but Bobby wasn't laughing, he was being serious. 'They have the spirit of the peasant. Churchill is brilliant but these people are as susceptible to dangerous populism as much as anyone, perhaps more than most simply because they don't think they are.'

Marty, who had been nodding up to this point, suddenly stopped. He slammed his fist on the table.

'Hitler could never have happened here. We'd never fall for Nazism.'

'Rubbish,' said Bobby calmly. 'He could happen anywhere, and you know it, Marty.'

'It's a German thing!' shouted back Marty.

Elaine thought they would come to blows, but she had forgotten how good Bobby was at defusing a situation. One minute they were catching fire, the next they were lighting each other's cigarettes and Bobby was telling everyone all about his near misses and how many times he had nearly died.

Vera Lynn saved her best to the last. When she began 'We'll Meet Again', Bobby finally let Elaine haul him up to the dancefloor.

'I'll lead,' she said, laughing, and she tried, but you couldn't lead Robert Capa: he kissed her neck, and she covered less of the room with him, but he covered her heart.

When finally, *finally*, they were alone in their hotel room, Elaine felt hot fury. All the fear, impatience and distress she had eaten down for the past few weeks reared forward. All the '*don't worry!*' As if she would ever not go out of her mind with worry!

'You fool! Why do you have to put yourself in danger all the time?'

She wanted to hit him across the cheek. Both cheeks. To slap him hard; she was irrationally angry now that she knew he was safe.

'Seriously, Bobby, enough is enough. I can't put up with all this any more.'

He grabbed her wrist. 'Whoa there, Pinky. I thought of you, non-stop. You were my lucky talisman.'

He held her tight.

'It's like danger is everywhere you go.'

'I *go* to where it is dangerous, Pinky.'

'It follows you.'

'No, I follow it.'

'I hate waiting for you to come back, waiting to find out if you're dead or alive. Or if you've had another near miss,' she said, surprising herself with the venom in her voice. 'I hate it. I can't stand it.'

'Well, I'm alive now, so this is supposed to be the happy bit,' he said, taking off his shirt and unclipping his braces. How could he be so damn practical?

'And I hate having to spend time with Marty instead of you.'

At this, he looked sad.

'He's a good friend, Marty. He saved my life.'

'And you've probably saved his bacon, a hundred times over. You don't owe him anything.'

Elaine felt angry and exposed. This wasn't how she'd envisaged their reunion but she didn't know how to get it back on track.

'Okay, I don't owe him,' Bobby said, smiling wistfully at her. 'I *like* him.'

'I didn't even know your real name was Endre. Endre Friedmann.'

He laughed. 'Who is Endre? I wasn't even called that when I was a boy. I preferred my middle name, Erno. You can call me that if it is important to you.'

Elaine felt the air, the frustration, trickle away. 'It's not important to me, I just don't like secrets.'

I don't like Marty knowing more about you than I do.

Who was she to talk? she thought. *He doesn't know about Alan yet.* She'd hidden him.

'When you see those terrible things, when you take the pictures, don't you want to intervene?'

She remembered the entombment in London. The silence. The digging. Sometimes, she couldn't put the images out of her head. *Was that normal*? She wanted to ask him. Was she damaged for ever? Were both of them?

He nodded. 'Sometimes, but the best intervention is to show the world. Share it with everyone. This is what's happening. This is the first war to be photographed, sweetheart. In the Great War, they wrote poetry. That was the best they could do. Now we take photos so everybody in the future will know what happened.'

'Is it worth it though, what you do? Will it ever change anything?'

'I don't know.'

He sank onto the bed, kissing her shoulder, so slowly, so lovingly, it made her swoon. Bobby was back.

CHAPTER THIRTY-ONE

SPAIN

JUNE 2016, DAY FOUR

I have been back at the house for only about twenty minutes before they return from their party. Mum and Aunty Barbara rush to get changed out of their outfits. Derek starts up the barbecue. Matthew has a headache. He loosens his tie, pours himself a drink, then flops into the sunlounger next to me, where I am pretending that I have been all afternoon.

Matthew whispers that Mum is in a hell of a mood.

I ask why but I can guess: the theory about Robert Capa being her father has finally sunk in and she really doesn't like it.

Matthew agrees. He says that she's been going on about it all day.

'She's having a full-blown identity crisis,' he says.

'I know!' I say happily. And then because Matthew is looking at me strangely: 'Poor Mum. It must be a shock.'

She comes out in her sundress and bikini but has kept on the party baubles – the big earrings, the necklaces and the bow in her hair. She pours herself another drink and then another. She gives Matthew money for the petrol and says she'll get the plates ready for dinner soon. I don't think I need worry about anyone suspecting anything going on between me and Nick because frankly, they couldn't be less interested. Matthew and Derek run around trying to keep Mum happy while Aunty Barbara and

Alyssia go inside to play a round of Exploding Kittens, the strange card game they love.

Later that evening, when Matthew and I are about to turn in for the night, Mum demands to do karaoke again.

Aunty Barbara and Alyssia have already disappeared and Matthew looks at me wearily. I can see he doesn't want to. My mother feels differently though. She has to sing 'We'll Meet Again'. It's suddenly the thing she wants most in the world.

'Mum loved Vera Lynn,' she says stubbornly.

Matthew can't bring himself to say no. He pushes the TV screen out for us and hands us the mikes. He looks tired and I know he's missing Gisela.

'Just one song then,' I say, and Mum promises just one.

We sing it together. She is slurring slightly, but it's not too bad. I'm thinking of seeing Nick again. I wish I didn't want to tell Paul about it but the fact is, I want to rub his face in it.

And then Derek sings 'My Way,' and then Mum and Derek sing Sonny and Cher. There is no sign of them stopping.

'Matthew, Matthew,' she chants, 'we want Elvis. NOW!'

'Mum, I don't know if anyone is up for it tonight,' Matthew says mildly.

My mum is annoyed by this. It happens really quickly, and it feels unexpected, but it isn't really. It's her usual modus operandi. But instead of turning on Matthew, she turns on me.

'You're no fun, Jen.' She says it through the mike, making it squeal. 'Especially since Paul's left you.' Her voice is amplified and I imagine it echoing throughout the Spanish mountainside down to the Emerald Coast. I imagine the birds telling each other about it. 'You're so negative, honestly, it's like being under a black cloud.'

'Leave it, Mum,' says Matthew faintly.

'It's true, Matthew, even you said it. You said her spark has gone.' Mum mimes blowing out a match. 'Whoosh.'

I won't look at Matthew. I know this is what she does, she uses our words against us.

'She's no fun.'

'Sorry,' I say, getting up. I'm not sorry at all but you can't get through to Mum when she's like this. She's had these moods all her life, after a drink or two.

She rounds on me, blocking my path and speaking into the mike still. 'No fun, no fun, Jen is no fun. She wouldn't know fun if it hit her in the face.'

I stand there and take it. What else can I do? Flushed, Matthew is pretending to be deaf. Derek just looks at us, scratching his cheek, until she bursts out, 'Oh, I've had enough of the lot of you. Boring! Derek, we're going out.' She is so drunk, she is wobbling. Derek pulls out the car keys and throws them at her. 'Here you go, my love.'

She catches them. 'Let's party,' she cackles.

All credit to Matthew, he jumps in front of her then, blocks her way. 'Come on, you're not going anywhere, Mum.'

'We bloody are.'

I stare at them all. I can't believe Derek was going to let her drive in this state.

'Don't be daft,' I say. 'You're both pissed as farts!'

Mum comes up close to me so her face is in mine. She looks at me like she hates me. 'Let's go, Derek.'

She tugs at the gate, but Matthew is speaking quietly and firmly. 'You can't, Mum. No.'

'All right.' She suddenly submits and I breathe a sigh of relief. *It's over, it's over.* I help Matthew push the karaoke machine inside in silence. He can't look at me.

When I play what happened next in my head, all I can think is that it happened so fast. It did, really. One minute she had flopped back onto a sunbed, the next she and Derek were the other side of the gate, still laughing, still giggling, like small children.

'They won't…' I say firmly to Matthew. 'She wouldn't, would she?'

The laughter is more like screeching. We hear the car door slam. The car headlights flicker on. The engine roars loudly and off they go. I don't know who is driving. I know they are both drunk.

My brother and I stand frozen. Neither of us can move. What do we do now? I feel this sickness in my stomach, sickness and fury at them. Everything seems topsy-turvy. Matthew and I are the parents, Mum and Derek are the teenagers.

I don't know if Matthew is as furious as I am. I hope he is.

'They might kill themselves,' he says.

Yes, he is just as furious.

'The words tumble fast out of my mouth. 'They might actually *kill someone else*. Can you have that on your conscience?'

Matthew starts picking up the glasses. His mouth is set.

'Matthew, we have to call the police.'

He stacks the glasses on the tray. He stacks too many and they are a wobbly, stupid tower. The last thing we need now is glass everywhere.

'Matthew!' I say loudly. I can see the silhouette of Alyssia in the kitchen, raiding the cupboards.

'I'm not calling the police.' He picks up a tray and walks it indoors. I follow him. I can't get too close or that tower may come crashing down.

'Matthew!' I persist.

'If I call them, Derek will never forgive me, I could lose my job, Mum will hate me. I'll lose the house, everything.'

I get my phone. It's embarrassing – I don't know the number for the police in Spain, I don't know the number plate of Mum's car, and if I'm absolutely honest, I'm glad I don't. I don't know if I can go through with it.

'But, Matthew, it's not just about you.'

At last, he puts down the tray. His body is taut. His face is red and tired. He rubs his eyes.

'It's not about *you*, though either is it, Jen?'

'I'll call. I'll do it anonymously.'

'No, you won't. The police won't do anything anyway. And Mum will never forgive you.'

'It'll make no difference to me,' I say weakly. I know the battle has been lost. These are my last attempts. 'What's the number?'

But I let him take my phone from me. And, shamefully, painfully, we do nothing.

CHAPTER THIRTY-TWO

LONDON, SEPTEMBER 1944

Why did Elaine find it so hard to tell Bobby about Alan? A million and one reasons, none of which made sense on their own, but added up, they were everything.

Bobby was so robust. He saw men shot in front of him and he took their photographs. He drank a lot and somewhere in that stream of alcohol replacing blood, and then blood replacing alcohol, he dealt with it. Or he went to sleep and the subconscious mind dealt with it. Either way, he got over it.

He grasped life with both hands. In the mornings, he sprang awake and out of bed like a man who had never seen suffering.

Would he condemn Alan?

No, not Bobby. He didn't condemn anyone. His compassion even extended to a Nazi soldier he'd seen swinging from a streetlight.

Would he understand Alan?

No.

Elaine didn't want him in her muggy world of appointments and excuses. She liked the fresh sheets and the strawberry breakfasts at the Belgravia flat. She liked the dinners at the Savoy and Browns or dancing in the underground clubs, the games of poker and the poker faces. The bathing and the lovemaking. Robert Capa was an escape. Alan was grim reality, Alan was *her* struggle, her personal obstacle, she didn't want it to be anyone else's.

Keep Clive and Carry Al.

Alan would be out of the asylum soon anyway. She knew it. That place was for the long-term mad, like the poor lady with the doll, not the people having temporary, and in many cases quite rightful, blips.

And there were other reasons she didn't tell Bobby too. Alan was entitled to his privacy, wasn't he? He had lost bloody everything – didn't he deserve to have some peace and quiet, to have some things not made public?

And then there were the secret, darker reasons: would Bobby think the Parker madness was contagious? What would she think of him if he had a mad sister – would she still be 100 per cent sure she wanted to marry him? Honestly, no. It might well give her pause for thought.

When they are socialising, they usually begin at the George. When it's time for just the two of them, they go to the Savoy. But one time, when she walks into the saloon bar at the Savoy, she sees that Bobby is talking animatedly to a woman, a woman she's never seen before. Elaine feels threatened immediately. Tells herself not to be daft, Bobby is *her* man, but it's the way she is hard-wired. *First, condoms in his overcoat. Now a strange woman on his arm…*

For a moment, she had thought the woman was the pianist Myra Hess from the National Gallery. The woman who pressed her hand on her elbow. The trail of perfume. *He's more fragile than he looks.* Coming closer, she realised it wasn't. This woman was also dark and tidy, late sixties maybe, but she was different from Myra Hess. She was wealthy or European, it was hard to tell between them. Enough powder to make your nose twitch. Nothing for Elaine to worry about. Not in a *romantic* rival sense, anyway.

Maybe in other ways, who knew?

Bobby jumped up and greeted her with his characteristic enthusiasm.

'Sweetheart, finally, you're here! I want you to meet someone very special to me.' He couldn't have been more delighted. The more special-to-me people he could gather together in one place, the happier he was.

It was Gerda's mother. Gerda Taro, his revolutionary girlfriend.

Elaine felt faint at the sight of her. When Bobby's famous ex-girlfriend was just an idea in a box, a photo in a locket or a word in a diary, she could cope. This, though – she wasn't sure she could deal with this.

She was very dark, very beautiful, extraordinary really.

'This is my girlfriend.' Bobby smiled tentatively at her. Elaine saw, for perhaps the first time since she'd known him, that Bobby was nervous. Forget jumping out of planes or recapturing French beaches, he was more intimidated by this.

He corrects himself: 'My *fiancée*, Miss Elaine Parker.'

The woman held her hand. Rings on every finger. Probably bells on her toes. Something about her reminded Elaine of Bessie, the landlady at the George. That mixture of grace and elegance, the same aura of chill. Those appraising eyes: *what did she see?*

'Where are you from, *Hélaine*?'

Elaine didn't know whether to tell her she had no H in her name. She rather liked the H.

'From south London. I was born in Tooting Bec,' said Elaine.

'What did she say?' said Gerda's mother to Bobby.

Bobby put his arm round Elaine. 'Elaine's from here. She's London, born and bred.'

Gerda's mother nodded.

'And, *Hélaine*, what is it that you do?'

'I work for the government,' Elaine responded. Even conversations with Martha and Ernest hadn't diminished the pleasure of saying it. How she loved to announce that she was a 'clerical girl'.

The woman nodded as though she had expected it. 'You're an exceptionally pretty girl.'

Elaine didn't know what to say. 'Thank you.' She addressed her nails.

'Robert Capa always had good taste.'

Elaine could not think of a single reply.

'Most English people look like drowned rats, especially now. So dowdy. So plain. But you… you are very different. That is why I thought you were French maybe. Or Italian. You have nice things.' She eyed the coat that hid a multitude of sins. 'But more importantly, you look… satisfied.'

'I am happy,' Elaine said quietly. 'He makes me happy.'

'Robert Capa is a very good man,' agreed Gerda's mother. The way she said Robert with the rolling R was like she owned him. Like she was *his* mother too.

'Yes,' said Elaine, because what else could she say? 'It's hard not to be happy when Bobby is near.' And this was absolutely true. It *was* hard to be blue when he made everything seem bright and positive. There was hope when he was around. There was blue sky over the white cliffs of Dover. He was so positive, she said they should hire him out to the troops. Move over Vera Lynn. Forget Winnie Churchill. Put Robert Capa in charge.

'Who is Bobby?' Gerda Taro's mother asked, her eyes narrowed suddenly.

'Robert,' said Elaine hesitantly now. She had been honest with this woman and now she regretted it. She felt like saying, *he calls me Pinky too, you know.* 'It's just a nickname.'

'Rrrrobert has a responsibility to the world.'

Elaine nodded.

'It's imperative that he keeps going with his photographs. Keeps battling for humankind.'

Elaine knew where this was going. She tried to pre-empt it. 'And I'd never stop him doing his work. Never.'

'You want children?'

'I don't think so.' Elaine had never been asked directly before. She supposed it was only because Gerda's mother was foreign that she asked. And it was only because Gerda's mother was foreign that she responded.

'You don't *think*?' Gerda's mother repeated like she had tasted something nasty. 'He shouldn't have children.'

Elaine laughed, stopped quickly. Gerda's mother was not joking. 'Why ever not?'

Gerda's mother fumbled with the gold clasp on her handbag. She had pointed nails, uncoloured.

'You know this picture?'

She held up the photograph of the fallen man in a Spanish field. The man's chest thrust out, his arms either side, holding the gun. It was a photo that had shocked the world. It was the photo that made him a household name.

Elaine shivered.

It was a horrible picture. To think that the poor fella was there one moment, gone the next. It made her want to fold him into her arms. Bobby always said he hated it too. He said he handed them all in, but they had selected that one. It wasn't his best, he said, it made him feel like a bloody undertaker. He said, 'It is not easy to stand aside and do nothing but record sufferings.'

'This changed everything, you know, *Hélaine*.' Gerda's mother leaned forward and gripped Elaine by the wrists. Her rings scratched the back of Elaine's hand. 'Rrrrrobert has the secret power. It's his magic. His destiny. It's a responsibility. These are the people they want us to forget. Robert won't let us forget. My daughter had this power too. It must not be wasted.'

Elaine went through Bobby's overcoat pockets again that night, pretending to herself that she was just leaving him another note.

They were still there: the packets of three condoms that had travelled to and from Italy.

Maybe he sensed she was prying because, unusually, he called out from the bathroom: 'Pinky? Everything all right?'

'Everything's fine.'

CHAPTER THIRTY-THREE

LONDON, SEPTEMBER 1944

Government workers, journalists and men in uniforms filled the George. And Bobby, Marty, Annie and her. Annie was fed up. She said it was too crowded and she wanted to go to see *Gaslight* at the cinema.

Myra came over, weakly nudged Elaine. 'There's someone outside asking for you.'

Elaine saw the concern on Bobby's face. Sighing, thinking it would be Clive, she said, 'It'll be nothing, I'll take care of it.'

But it wasn't Clive. Peering out of the grimy window, Elaine saw that it was Justin. And he was standing in the street with three other boys in uniform. A strange barber-shop quartet of pilots. The government workers and the journalists didn't scrub up too badly, but these men were so shiny, they looked like they were from another world. They *were* from another world, where shoes and buttons and attention to detail was everything.

Elaine wiped the window so she could see better. Good grief. Justin had something in between his teeth. A red rose? Surely not!

'For goodness'… It's been *a year*,' Elaine muttered. This couldn't be happening.

Bobby put his arm round her shoulder. 'I sympathise with the poor fellow. I'd be driven into a frenzy if you dumped me too.'

Elaine smiled uneasily. 'I've no plans to.'

Now Bobby too looked out at Justin. He laughed, but he didn't look at her when he said, 'Tell me, do you have many skeletons in your closet, Pinky?'

Elaine's heart was thumping louder than ever. Was this the moment to tell him about Alan? She should have told him about Alan already. And now it was too late to tell him. She had missed her opportunity and by her omissions, she had become a liar. She was from a family of liars and once he realised, Bobby wouldn't want her.

'How do you mean, skeletons?' Elaine proceeded with caution.

'*One* crazy ex-boyfriend I can cope with, but is there anything else?'

'I don't know what you mean,' lied Elaine. 'This is just… Justin.'

'Good.' He looked at her tenderly. 'At work, things are so unpredictable that in my private life, I prefer to know in advance what I'm dealing with.'

'There will be no more surprises,' Elaine promised.

Elaine, Bobby, Marty and Annie watched from the door as Justin removed the rose from his teeth and, with arms flung out either side, launched into song.

'*I'll be seeing you-ooo-oooo…*'

'Oh no,' said Elaine. *He's not really doing this, is he?*

'Oh dear,' said Annie sympathetically into her ear. 'Crikey, I wasn't expecting that!'

'He's got quite a nice voice though,' said Myra before looking at Elaine. 'Sorry.'

A crowd had gathered around Justin. Some boys in shorts with sticks and string, men in uniform, and older women with shopping baskets. One pushed herself through the crowd, saying, 'Go on, I think it's lovely. No one will be able to resist you, fella. And a pilot as well, good grief!'

'I'll be seeing you in every lovely summer's day.'

'I'll sort it,' said Annie, brave as ever.

'No, I should go,' said Elaine.

Bobby said, 'I'm there.'

'No,' she said sharply.

'I insist.'

He thumped down his drink and picked up his coat. He rubbed his hands together.

Annie's face lit up. 'On second thoughts, this is better than the cinema, Elaine!'

Elaine watched Bobby stalk outside. She thought, *he's not long back, exhausted from war, and now I've just gone and created more battles for him…*

Within a couple of minutes, Justin and Bobby had disappeared round the corner of D'Arblay Street. Annie and Elaine waited in the pub while Elaine pictured them punching each other, the bloodstains, the very public arrests, the night in the cells. Bessie tutted them and whipped their unfinished glasses away: 'I don't want any trouble.'

Annie said diplomatically, 'No, neither do we, Mrs Larholt. Please believe us.'

It was only an hour, but it felt longer before they reappeared, not bloodied or beaten, but together. They were both drunk as lords, best friends, swearing to always be there for each other, blood brothers. Elaine was reminded of the comic interlude in a Shakespearean play.

'I'm no spinach,' Justin was declaring, thumping his chest. His hair was dishevelled and up close, he looked less shiny and far more like someone who had been grappling in the gutter.

'No one would dream you were, sir, no one,' Bobby was saying in his too-loud drinking voice.

Elaine cautiously approached. They were so closely entwined, so engaged, it was almost as though she were interrupting a pair of newlyweds.

'Here she is.'

Elaine regretted her impatience immediately, but Justin jumped to attention. 'Good luck, dearest girl!' he shouted, then gave her the biggest and most huggiest hug he had ever given her, almost knocking her down in the process, before whispering in her ear: 'Now that I've met him, I don't blame you for a single moment. He is UTTERLY MAGNIFICENT.'

CHAPTER THIRTY-FOUR

LONDON, OCTOBER 1944

A few nights later, Elaine was boiling some mutton that they'd been keeping in the cold box when Clive came home, even more puce-coloured than usual. He went to the cupboard over the sink, poured himself a glass of rum, then rolled himself a cigarette. Elaine saw that his hands were shaking.

'What happened? Was there a doodlebug?'

'No,' he said. 'What is that goddam smell?'

It was the mutton. Grey and fatty, it was probably off, but Elaine had hoped she might somehow boil it back to life. Eating at the Savoy with Bobby took the edge off her hunger, but Clive had no such escape.

With a flourish, he pulled out a sausage from his coat.

'Can we have this instead?'

'Where did you get it?'

He tapped his nose. 'Ask no questions, tell no lies, I saw a German doing up his flies.'

He could have stolen it from some hungry children, but what could Elaine say? She who day by day was looking plumper and rosier than ever.

Green and shaking, Clive sat himself down.

'I need to tell you something.'

Elaine waited. She felt angry with herself. She should have known something was going on with Clive. He had been avoiding her, but she had assumed it was because of the botched photographs. Who wouldn't be ashamed? Clearly, though, there was more to it than that.

'Hang on.' Elaine fished the mutton out of the boiling water, wrapped it up in newspaper, then took it outside. This was terrible wastefulness. Mrs Perry would be horrified. Lovely Mrs Marriot would be heartbroken. But rather that than poison them all.

When she got back, Clive stood up abruptly, causing the chair to scrape against the floor. 'I'm having a baby.'

'You?'

He snorted at that. 'Well, not me. I'm going to be a dad.'

Clive was going to be a father. He was going to be a parent. Clive the scoundrel, the petty criminal, the destroyer of photographs, a father. Elaine tried to think of her brother's good points: well, he could get you almost anything you wanted, he had helped women into the underground when the sirens went off and he did make a policy of never stealing from people in wheelchairs or the elderly.

'That's... amazing news.'

'Yeah,' he said. 'Why do you look like that then?'

Elaine rearranged her expression quickly. 'I just didn't expect it. It's come out of nowhere...'

What would Mum have said?

She wouldn't have said much, she'd have just got on with it. That's what their mother did. That's what Elaine would try to do too. Be more Mrs Marriot than Mrs Perry. More Annie than Vera. Anyway, Elaine liked Maisie – always had. A hard-working, sunny girl, she had lost her small brother in the crush at Aldwych tube station, a nasty event that no one liked to talk about. Elaine talked about it with her sometimes though.

Clive might not be good at much, but he had impeccable taste in women – and that was a life skill much underestimated.

Marty will have some advice, she thought suddenly, surprising herself. It was strangely a relief to have a troubleshooter on your team. A Mr Practicality or a fixer on your side. She and Marty had developed an understanding recently. They were not threatened by each other any more, but seemed now to exist in mutual harmony, both circling Bobby protectively.

They could have their wedding party at the George. Bessie would do it for them, she was sure. This would be the start of Clive's new respectability and if he needed a bit of a leg-up to get him going, well, wasn't that normal?

Sullenly, Clive sat on the kitchen chair, still as a fish after a struggle. Elaine stared at him, noticing how he had acquired a load of dark hair on his upper lip, almost but not quite a moustache. He looked like a soldier in every way, except he wasn't a soldier – the only battles he fought were his own. She felt a tenderness towards him suddenly. A pride. Her little brother was growing up. A baby was on its way. A baby – a blessing. She put her hand on his shoulder.

'So how is Maisie feeling? Tired, I expect.'

'It's not Maisie,' he said suddenly. The words just erupted from his mouth.

'What?'

'It's not Maisie's baby.'

Elaine felt like she was falling. 'Whose baby is it then?'

'You don't know her.'

Elaine couldn't find her words. Sweet-faced Maisie May, often on the verge of tears, with her apron and her stale cakes. The long blonde hairs she left around the place like a shedding cat. It wasn't hers?

'Does Maisie know?' Elaine asked miserably. Poor Maisie. First her brother, now this.

'Yeah,' he said. He hid his hands deep into his pockets. He couldn't have looked more guilty if he had tried.

'And?'

'Well, she's not thrilled,' he said. 'Obviously.'

'Dear God, Clive, what on earth have you been doing?'

'Same as you do every weekend and half the week at the Savoy,' Clive said, tipping the ash into the saucer.

'But...'

'Oh, don't come all high and mighty with me, Elaine,' he said venomously. 'You've hardly been acting like a nun. Lord Justin Snootypants, then Robert the Mighty, it's hardly like you keep your legs shut.'

Elaine stared at him in shock. Where had this come from? 'I... I wasn't saying that... Clive, I just...'

'There's a war on, you know. We could be dead next week.'

'But, but... poor Maisie – she thought you were going to marry her,' Elaine said, thinking, *I thought you were going to marry her.* 'She loved you, I know she did.'

Clive said nothing now, he just stubbed out his cigarette and then lit up another. He wasn't happy, that was obvious. Elaine tried to be sympathetic. She wanted to be on his side.

'You'll marry this other woman then?'

He stubbed out the cigarette. 'Looks like it.'

'What's she like?'

Clive considered. 'She's stubborn.'

Stubborn? thought Elaine. *What kind of description is that?*

'She works in munitions,' he added. And Elaine thought, *ah well, she can't be that bad, if she's doing her bit for the country, can she?*

'How far gone is she then?'

'A month.'

'So, it's early days.' Elaine thought of miscarriages she had heard about. It wasn't as easy as you'd think to carry a baby to term. Maybe this young woman wouldn't even want to go through with it? She knew that, if needed, Marty could help arrange that. Perhaps it could all go away.

'One month *to go*,' Clive clarified grimly. 'Yeah, so any help you could give would be... nice.'

Elaine couldn't help it. She knew it that night and she knew it as she woke up the next morning: America was sliding out of focus. She just couldn't picture her and Bobby there any more. She couldn't conjure up the image of it; it came back only in the way the Normandy prints had done, blurry or shaken or downright wrong. It wasn't happening. The more she tried to keep it solid in her mind, the more it felt like she was cupping water with her fingers. She couldn't bring enough to her parched mouth.

She'd have to tell Bobby. She *had* to.

He was making all these plans. 'Our agency this', 'Our agency that'. Did she know Henri Cartier-Bresson? No. Well, look at these, Pinky, they will knock you out! He wanted to be an unemployed war photographer, he joked. Then, when he was being serious, he would say dryly that unfortunately, war photographers are rarely unemployed.

Over dinner at the Savoy the next evening, she resolved to tell him. Her salmon. His beef stew. He said food like this reminded him of his mother. He talked about his mother a lot lately. He was pontificating, gesturing, talking about going there, just as soon as the war was done: their honeymoon, and then the big ship, sailing until New York, New York. Elaine remembered that her mother had always said that when she met her father he had wanted to go to New York but she had told him she got seasick so they never got there. She used to think it was strange how something as small as a little nausea could redirect the whole of your life.

Bobby was pontificating. 'Once you see the Statue of Liberty, I mean, you just know that this is the new world. They don't call it Liberty for nothing.' He was rhapsodising. '"Give me your tired, your poor, your huddled masses, yearning to breathe free". It's a place you can start all over again.'

Start all over again.

Bobby looked up at her, met her eyes. 'Together, we'll start this thing together.'

Elaine took a deep breath. This wasn't just seasickness. This was everything.

'I have something important to tell you.'

'You can tell me anything.'

'You might not be happy.'

Bobby's face fell. He paled. Alerted by this rapid change in demeanour, a waiter came over.

'Can I get you anything, sir?'

'I don't know,' he said. He gestured helplessly at Elaine. She stared at him. Could this be real? He gulped down some water. His eyes never left her face.

'Bobby, the thing is, I don't think I want to leave London.'

I can't leave Alan. I can't leave Clive now, Clive and the baby, but mostly, I can't leave Alan. I can't abandon him in that dreadful place. Family first.

'Why not?' Always to the point, that was Bobby.

She had two things she could tell him. She chose one: 'Clive is having a baby.'

'Clive is? Clive's only a baby himself.' Bobby was laughing. He was laughing into his napkin. He couldn't stop it. He was almost choking. The waiter came back, his expression alarmed, but Bobby waved him away.

Finally, he said: 'That's it, that's all?'

'Well, it's quite a big deal, isn't it?' Elaine sniffed. 'I know how much you want to go to America and for us to make our new lives there. I did too, Bobby, I really did. But…' She took a deep breath and went on bravely. 'I'm sorry, I can't. I don't feel I can go so far away.'

His face. His voice. Very, very softly, he placed down his knife and fork on the plate on top of each other like someone who'd just learned how.

'No, it isn't a big deal. Not compared to what I thought it was.'

Elaine flushed.

'What on earth did you think I was going to say?'

'I thought maybe that Justin had wooed you back.'

'Never,' said Elaine vehemently. 'I promise you this has nothing to do with him.'

'And then I thought you didn't love me any more.' He looked so upset that she couldn't help but come round to his side of the table, and there she clutched his face to her chest, and kissed his dark, dark hair, so dark it was darker than black. Such a relief it was. Such a relief. They would still be together. Their love was strong enough.

'Don't leave me, sweetheart,' he whispered.

How could she ever doubt it?

'I'll never leave you, Bobby, never.'

CHAPTER THIRTY-FIVE

LONDON, OCTOBER 1944

Marty and Annie were playing a sweaty game of gin rummy with a group from Life Corp. Annie looked happier than Elaine had ever seen her. She had styled her hair in the big roll that suited her, and she said she loved her new job at the War Office. Everything was going her way. She even won the game, getting first to 501 by a long chalk.

After Bobby told them the news, Marty was almost seething with rage. 'You're not going to California? You're kidding me. You've *always* wanted to be based in California.'

'I can work from anywhere in the world!' Bobby said. 'We're still going to open an agency, aren't we, sweetheart, but it will be in London instead.'

Elaine nodded, averting her eyes from Marty.

'We'll be the best in Europe. With my photos and her…' He smiled at Elaine adoringly. 'Multitude of skills.'

Marty snorted. Elaine's reaction was not dissimilar.

Still, Bobby went on. 'We'll be unstoppable.'

'What about your mother?'

Bobby laughed at that. 'My mother is in New York, Marty. It's the same distance from here! Nearly.'

'Hardly… Anyway, she's waiting for you there.'

'My mother will love Pinky,' Bobby said evasively.

'That's not the point.'

'Pinky looks a bit like her too,' Bobby added.

Elaine stared at him in astonishment. He had never said that before.

Annie scowled. 'You two! When will you make up your minds?'

'Hang on, we've only changed our minds once,' said Elaine mutinously. When did Annie get to be the make-up-your-mind police?

'This is what I want,' Bobby said expansively. 'This is what *we* want. We want to live the London life. We want to knuckle down here.'

'Settle down,' corrected Elaine quietly.

'Whatever down.' Bobby clinked his glass against hers.

Goodness, Elaine thought, she adored him. She really did. Even if they had to live in Timbuktu, as long as they were together it would be fine. He made the world come alive. He made it clear she had a place in the world, even if sometimes her mutinous heart told her she didn't.

'Can you even get a visa to stay here though?' asked Annie, practical as ever. 'I thought last time, after the incident with the pilots and the visas, it was all a bit hairy.'

Elaine swallowed. She had forgotten the visa thing. The bane of their lives.

'Sure, sure.' He got his wallet out and pulled out a note. 'Another round? Visa, schmisa! You'll help sort it, won't you, Marty?'

'Each time you go in and out of the country?'

'Er, yeah.'

'What if I don't want to?' Marty snapped. He tugged at his tie. Elaine found she disliked him again. Every time she softened towards him, something happened and she was back to square one. No, they *weren't* on the same side. Who was he to put such a downer on everything? Who was he to say they should leave? But Bobby didn't seem to mind at all. Bobby thought this moaning, this grumpiness, was fine.

'You will help,' Bobby said happily. 'Because you love me and you love Elaine. And this way, my Pinky gets to be with her family, and if she's happy, I'm happy.'

Marty was staring at Elaine with narrowed eyes. He took the note from Bobby's wallet and strutted to the counter, where Bessie was warmly interrogating two American soldiers. Annie was smiling. 'Well, it's good news for me that I get to keep you.' She leaned closer to Elaine. 'Can I still be your maid of honour?'

Elaine lowered her face. 'No one else gets a look-in.'

They drank, danced and partied. At the casino, Bobby was confident – all on black, five times.

The croupier complimented him. 'I'm lucky in love too.' He winked. Elaine felt like purring.

They would live and work in London. All they had to do now was hope and pray the war ended soon and they both made it out alive. It didn't seem too much to ask, after all.

They went back to his rooms in Belgravia. Just him and her alone was Elaine's favourite part of the day. Although she loved Annie, the journalists, the editors, Peter who played the piano – and Marty was all right – she and Bobby were always better without the others, without the photos, without the camera, just two lost souls, two babes in the wood.

She hoped he didn't mind staying here in England. Was it a huge sacrifice? Was she ruining his life? She knew Marty thought she was. Did she need to spend her whole life being grateful that he was staying? He'd given up something for her – what might she have to give up for him? *Even if everything has changed*, Elaine decided, *this is exactly what I want*. And this was exactly what he wanted too. Like a picture, it was all there. You just had to take it.

CHAPTER THIRTY-SIX

LONDON, NOVEMBER 1944

Clive didn't want to go to the hospital by himself. He didn't say it in so many words, but Elaine knew it. He had a thing about the smell of disinfectant and the starchy aprons of the nurses and their winged hats.

The baby was in with all the other babies born that week. Fifteen or more of them – in one week! How could they know which was which? Elaine and Clive leaned against the window to their room and she willed the glass away. Here they all were. What a triumphant sight! Each baby a symbol of hope. Each baby was a two fingers up to the war, an up-yours to Mr Hitler. Each baby was a sign the peace would come, *had* to come, soon.

All the babies in their little incubator homes, lying in them like hairless pups. Her heart went out to each of them. Well, wouldn't you just want to go in and stroke their downy cheeks?

'Oh, Clive.'

How proud he looked, how jittery and nervous.

'There she is.' He pointed to the one in the corner, second row back, a little scrunched-up thing, pink and red, tiny, eyes clenched shut. Name tiny, squint-worthy: Baby Parker. 'That's her. That's my girl.'

And Elaine felt such a rush of emotion she had to cover her mouth with her hand, because here it was: her little brother was growing up. The brother they said was bad was now father to a daughter.

New life. Something good and tiny, a beautiful curling flower, was growing in the dirt. Mum would have been so proud.

Now to meet the girlfriend. Clive staggered ahead to let her know they were there.

'She might not want visitors,' Elaine had offered, hopefully, but Clive had muttered that she did, she would, of course she would, why not?

Elaine approached nervously, wishing her shoes weren't so loud on the tiled floor. There were a hundred reasons this new mother might not want to see her right now. She couldn't help but wish it was sweet, simple Maisie May ahead of her and not some stranger. A stubborn stranger. She kept her eyes away from all the other new mothers in their beds, many of whom were asleep, and followed Clive's shirted back and braces as he sped lopsidedly towards Bed Five.

The girl was wan and exhausted, as you'd expect, but with long, dark, curly hair and grey eyes, which Elaine certainly hadn't expected. She didn't look Clive's *type* at all. And she must have been several years older than him too. She wasn't a girl, she was a woman. She looked at least thirty. Clive whispered something and she jerked her head upwards to look up at Elaine. Her dark eyebrows moved rapidly and in an incredulous voice, she said, 'You? You're not really his sister?'

Both Clive and Elaine laughed because they looked so similar, they always had. It was a good icebreaker if nothing else.

'Yeah, she is,' said Clive. 'Why not?'

'Are you going to introduce us properly?' Elaine prompted Clive.

'Nora, this is my sister Elaine. Elaine, this is Nora.' It was like the words had to be fished out of his mouth.

'Did you bring anything?' she said.

'I brought my sister,' Clive said.

'I can't dress the baby in that,' she retorted.

Clive sat himself down on the wooden stool next to the bed and drummed his fingers impatiently on the bedside table. He wasn't comfortable with Nora, Elaine realised instantly, not like he was with Maisie May. He was slightly afraid of her. Elaine decided to stand behind him, she too out of hitting distance.

'You look far too sophisticated to be related to *him*,' Nora said flatly. The words may have been complimentary, but the tone was not.

'I've come straight from work,' explained Elaine. She immediately felt she didn't like this woman, but she knew she needed to give her a chance. Under the circumstances… This situation wasn't entirely her fault either. 'The baby is sweet,' she added quickly. She didn't want Nora to think she was as hoity-toity as she looked. 'Congratulations. You must be so pleased, Nora.'

Nora pulled a face that Elaine couldn't decipher.

Elaine unloaded her straw bag. She had brought a tiny cardigan and a hat for the baby. She expected they wouldn't fit. The baby was quite a bit bigger than she thought she would be. And they were all yellow. Yellow wool was all there was available, apparently. Myra had had her mother knit something. Unpicking old things and turning them into something new. She had planned to say, 'There's a community out there who already care about you and the baby,' but she couldn't find the words. She wasn't sure how this Nora would react but she anticipated she wouldn't react well.

She didn't know if Nora was a reader, but she had an assortment of books that she had selected with Mrs Marriot. She had taken a risk and put in a paperback on baby-rearing. She didn't want to cause offence; she didn't want to suggest that Nora might not know what she was doing, but she had flicked through and couldn't resist. It had some excellent labour-saving suggestions such as putting the baby out in the garden during the day so it got some fresh air – if you had a garden, of course – and how a thimble of whisky could help with sleeplessness.

Elaine had bought several books for the baby too. Well, for when the baby was older. That couldn't possibly cause an upset, could it?

She wasn't sure. There was a Ladybird book of nursery rhymes – might that look as though Elaine thought Nora didn't know her nursery rhymes? She hoped not. There was a book about two children, Janet and John, and there was one about different breeds of dogs. (Maisie May had loved dogs.)

Neither of the new parents spoke. Elaine thought she should have got Bobby in. Why hadn't she? He was so good at things like this. He would have won Nora over with his agreeableness. He could at least have taken photos of them or something, anything, to warm the atmosphere. She thought of the last time she had visited someone in hospital: prancing around with Ernest, pulling at the strings of his hospital gown – the contrast in mood couldn't have been greater.

A blonde nurse came by and looked at the clipboard at the end of Nora's bed. Clive didn't take his eyes off her, and Elaine wished he would because Nora wouldn't like that. Another nurse delivered a water jug to the bedside table. Elaine felt embarrassed when neither Nora nor Clive managed to produce a thank-you.

'What are you going to call her then?' Elaine asked.

'I've got a name I like, but he doesn't like it,' Nora said flatly. She rolled back the starchy blanket from her chest. Elaine felt anxious that she was going to see more than she would like to see, but Nora was only rearranging herself.

'I wanted Shirley,' Clive said. 'After Mum.'

Elaine's heart leapt. *Of course, of course.*

'I don't like that,' Nora said. 'What if people call her Shirl?'

Elaine wondered what would be so terrible about that, but she realised she must try not to get Clive into further trouble. His fingertip drumming was becoming faster and faster. It must have been annoying for Nora too, or had she trained herself to tolerate such things?

'I want Barbara.'

'All right,' said Clive, irritation in his voice. His eyes followed the smiling nurse around the ward. 'Have Barbara.'

He raised his eyebrows at Elaine as if to say, 'See what I'm dealing with here?'

Elaine pulled on her coat. Nora immediately clocked that it was expensive.

'Very nice,' she said in a voice that said it wasn't nice at all. 'You've got a famous boyfriend, Clive said.'

'That's Clive's opinion,' said Elaine hesitantly. She didn't know where this was heading, but she didn't like it.

'He's foreign, yeah?'

'Hungarian,' muttered Elaine.

'You should get out of London. I would if I could.'

'I'd miss you and my baby niece though now, wouldn't I?' said Elaine. She was surprised to see Nora's face light up. For a moment, she looked quite sweet. And then she frowned and the moment passed.

CHAPTER THIRTY-SEVEN

LONDON, NOVEMBER 1944

'*Life* want to do a story on you,' said Bobby, quite casually, as they were drinking watery cognac in the George after work.

Elaine jumped. 'What? Me? Why?'

'The war photographer's girlfriend.' He grinned at her. 'Pardon me, *fiancée*. They want to do a feature on the human face of the witnesses to war.'

'You have a human face?' said Annie sarcastically, while Elaine stared between them. *A story on her?*

'No,' she said. 'I don't want to.'

'Don't blame you,' said Bobby. He got up, hitched up his trousers. His braces were too loose. 'Drink, anyone?'

'It's not a big deal, Elaine,' said Marty coldly. He took a long slurp of his pale-yellow drink. 'You should do it. It will be good for Robert's reputation.'

Elaine shook her head. They were not going to make a story out of her, of Clive, Alan, or Nora or the baby. They would have a blooming field day!

'She doesn't want to, Marty,' called out Bobby as he made his way to the bar.

Elaine wondered if this was more serious than Bobby was making out. When she got him alone later, she asked him, but he repeated, 'Honestly, sweetheart, it's fine. Marty's just being overprotective as usual.'

*

Bobby was sent back to France. This time his mission was to track villages and cities as they were taken back into French hands, the retreat of the German troops and the public response. Whereas he had been reluctant to go overseas last time, this time he was unapologetically excited.

'It is going to be brilliant!' she heard him say to his journalist friends on the steps at Life Corp.

'You lucky bastard,' they said. 'This is the story you've been waiting for.'

Elaine swung her head round. She hadn't known that.

Meanwhile, Elaine's mission was to hold tight and stay focused. It wasn't too hard. Everything felt different now. She kept reminding herself how far she had come. She had a steady job, an engagement ring on her finger, her and Bobby's shared plan for a bigger, brighter future. The agency would start small – it would focus on him while they built up their reputation and then, in due course, they would take on more photographers. Elaine was improving at writing captions; she enjoyed parties, charming people. And what she didn't know about the business she could learn with Bobby by her side.

She was a girl going places. Once the war was over, that was.

At night though, she sometimes startled herself awake, thinking, *this is too good to be true*. She didn't wake up when she was asleep next to him at his rooms in Belgravia or in their room at the Savoy. It was only when she was at home, in her flat opposite the station.

At work, she missed her laughing lunches with Annie, but Myra and Felicity sometimes sat with her, and at least they didn't try to scavenge food from her plate. Felicity was planning her wedding to Rupert and Myra dreamed of escaping her mother. At her desk, Elaine transcribed her letters earnestly and quickly, never forgetting to look for strange phrasing. At five o'clock most days she bypassed the work drinks and hurried home.

Nora had moved into Clive's room. Elaine wanted to be a good sister-in-law and a good aunty to Barbara, but Nora was not the easiest person to be around. She just never seemed happy. Elaine had thought she might be more cheerful now she had left her much-hated munitions job. Not so. Nora confided in Elaine that she was bored staying at home all day. She still wanted to help the country. She felt lazy, she felt like she was letting people down, and she hated that. Elaine sympathised, but she didn't like the way Nora expressed herself so… so angrily. Nora had also revealed that she didn't trust Clive. In one way, Elaine felt she was right: Clive was duplicitous and secretive; but in another, Elaine felt obliged to defend him – he was her brother. Elaine didn't know what to say when Nora said that. What was she expected to say? She settled on 'But he loves Barbara,' or 'I think he's changed,' which seemed to be the fairest comment both to Nora and to herself.

Bettie Page was unimpressed with Nora too and came home even less. Elaine suspected that her cat was sharing her time with everyone in the building.

She boiled Barbara's nappies for Nora and hung them out to dry. Something quite satisfying about seeing them all lined up and bright, flapping in the wind. Barbara fed such a lot and Nora complained she was stuck in the armchair for so many hours at a time that it was exactly like being locked up in prison. Elaine didn't like to ask how she knew.

Elaine offered to get her more books from downstairs, but it turned out Nora wasn't much of a reader. She complained that the girls in the stories had rip-roaringly good times and happy endings with lords and dukes that just highlighted how dull her life was.

Elaine thought she may have had a point.

Elaine read to the baby though. Barbara cooed along to Janet and John and the *Ladybird Book of Nursery Rhymes* and Elaine did her best to 'rock her cradle in a tree top and swoosh down will come baby cradle and all'. She did 'round and round the garden like a teddy bear' on her plump palms and 'this little piggy' on her toes.

The dog book went *whoosh* over her head, but Barbara did listen attentively to the parenting tips – until Nora decided to use that one to steady the table the wireless was on.

Although Elaine loved spending time with the little bean, she was always glad to hand her back to Nora afterwards. Babies weren't for her; she felt that more strongly than ever now, and a few hours were more than enough, thank you. She was impressed with how tolerant Nora was with her daughter though. Far more than she'd expected. So that was pleasing. Nora hardly ever shouted, even when Barbara fussed early in the mornings – even at two, three and a quarter to four. Nora just called her a hungry bug, a crybaby, and that was that.

Elaine made soup and her special Woolton pie for Nora. It would be fair to say the pie was not received half as well by Nora as it had been by Bobby, but then Elaine understood Nora was not an effusive person.

One Sunday morning, when Elaine got up early to visit Alan, she found Nora already fixed in place in her armchair in the kitchen, Barbara lying stretched across her like an ocean liner. Clive was already dressed and seemed just about to go out, although he wouldn't say where. He never said where.

'You're not going out as well, are you, Elaine?' asked Nora desperately.

'I always go out on a Sunday morning,' she said lightly.

'Where do you go?' Nora said. Barbara let out a little cry and Nora switched her efficiently to the other side. 'She was up at three, four and five.'

Elaine had forgotten whether that was an improvement or not. 'Ah,' she said. 'Make sure you rest today.'

Elaine looked at Clive as he flapped around in the kitchen pretending to be helpful. He hadn't told Nora about Alan then.

'I must go to church…'

She felt bad lying and because she hated Clive for being so secretive with Nora – and here, wasn't she just doing the same thing?

For some reason, Clive took this as a cue to laugh at her. 'Didn't you realise, Nora, my sister is a God-botherer?'

Nora's grey eyes were fixed on Elaine's.

'I'll come with you next time.'

'Um.' Elaine swallowed. 'That would be… nice.'

'We need to get this one baptised, don't we, Clive?' she went on.

'If you say so.' Clive smirked over at Elaine. 'I bet Elaine knows someone who'd do it. She's very in with that crowd.'

Elaine shook her head. Clive *knew* where she was going. Why would he do this? She pulled him into the hallway. 'Tell her where I'm really going then.'

He came up close to her and then laughed, right in her face. 'Tell Nora that her baby's uncle is a raving lunatic? That's hardly going to go down well, now is it?'

It would have been nicer to go to church, Elaine thought. She felt increasingly that the asylum was a heinous, heinous place. How hadn't she realised that at first? How had she let him go there? Not that she had had a choice, but… If Alan hadn't been mad when he'd been taken in there, Elaine felt certain he would be by now. To get to see him, you walked along the corridor, which reverberated with screams and howls like something in a ghost story – there was no other way of putting it.

If a monster or a ghoul or giant man-eating spiders turned up, it wouldn't have been much of a surprise.

She always looked out for the woman with the glass-eyed doll to say hello to her, or to hold her white trembling hand for a while, but today she couldn't find her. She asked one of the less brusque nurses and the less brusque nurse explained she wasn't allowed to leave her room any more. She wouldn't tell her what had happened for the poor woman to be subjected to such a punishment and, in a way, Elaine didn't want to know. She held onto Alan's puffy, speckled hands tighter.

The windows on the train back were so smeary, it was worse than having no windows. The carriage was empty when she got on, but then two soldiers came in and threw their backpacks on the shelf over her, their gas masks hanging off. They were a sight, whisky on their breath, black teeth – guffawing at each other. They had little picture cigarette cards and were drooling over them. She thought that they were very young. They were pushing each other to say something to her and finally, the scrawnier, frecklier one squeaked – his voice could hardly have broken –

'I'm on leave, miss. How much?'

'Pardon?' she said, gripping her handbag closer. She knew she could punch Freckly, but the stocky one could probably overpower her. Stocky one got up. His boots were muddy. He had so many pockets. He could have all sorts of weapons in there. But Elaine remembered the penknife she always carried in her bag. She was a Parker, after all.

He leaned right over her. Spam breath, tilted cap, arrogance of it.

'You'll do it for free, won't you, girlie?'

'Get away from her.' And, out of nowhere, it was Marty. Marty was looming over them all. 'I'll report you,' he said. He didn't seem nervous or agitated. He sat down on the bench next to Elaine, took a cigarette from his pocket and lit up.

'No offence meant, fella,' Freckly said. The stocky one was also apologetic. 'Didn't realise she was with you.'

They walked down the aisle and out of view. Elaine breathed out. She was relieved, but also annoyed. She probably could have handled it. And if anyone had to rescue her, why did it have to be Marty?

'Are you all right?' he said. He sat next to her, offered her a cigarette. She took one, irritated at the situation. Those horrible men had gone off thinking she was with Marty. They only left because they thought she was the property of someone else. She almost wanted to go and give them what-for again.

'Yes, thank you. What are you doing here?' she asked, then corrected herself. 'I mean, where have you been?'

'I have an aged aunt who lives out this way.' He pointed at the grimy windows. You didn't know which way was which.

She didn't believe him. Hadn't Bobby said he was alone in the world? And who said 'aged aunt' any more? It sounded like something from Mrs Marriot's books.

'What's your aunt's name?'

'Cressida,' he said without missing a beat.

'I thought that was something you put in your sandwiches.'

He laughed, far more than the joke merited.

Could it be true? Was it a lie?

'So where have *you* been, Miss Parker?'

Is he teasing? He is pretending to be like a police officer. It's not funny, it's strange.

'Church,' she said. 'Those windows could do with a clean.'

'I never suspected that of you.' He gave her his cross-eyed smile. She wanted to take him up on that, *why shouldn't she go to church?* But she knew she mustn't. She needed to move the conversation on, on and away.

'It *is* Sunday,' she added. Her big, her only, alibi.

'Course it is.' She didn't know what he meant again, but hoped he'd leave it there. *Let's discuss the weather, the trains, Hitler's bloody invasion plans: anything but church.*

Trust Marty – he didn't leave it there. He couldn't leave anything anywhere.

'Which one do you go to then?'

'What's it to you, Marty?'

'I just…' His palms were uplifted. 'Polite conversation, that's all, Miss Parker. Small talk, have you never heard of it?'

Elaine relented. She sat back in the worn bench chair. The edge was scratchy. She looked down at her pretty shoes. Bobby loved these shoes. He said her slender ankles could bring down empires.

'The Church of Our Lady?' She thought of the last sausage roll waiting for her in the cold box, if Clive or Nora hadn't got to it first.

'Catholic?'

'I… yes.' Everything looked muted or impressionistic. A good thing maybe, for it meant you couldn't see the damage of a thousand bombs in the land out there.

'The Church of Our Lady in Stepney?'

'That's the one…' Elaine smiled winningly. Now she looked at her nails, she looked at the unhelpful window, she looked anywhere rather than at Marty's intense and gleaming face.

'It was bombed to smithereens during the Blitz. Flattened. I know because I used to go there.'

Elaine faltered. She had a sudden untimely flashback of Bobby pushing back her blouse collar and kissing her on the collarbone. God, she would have done anything to be with him now.

She proceeded laboriously. 'It's not that one… It's the other one.'

Marty laughed. 'Why are you lying to me?'

'Why are you following me?'

He leaned back in his seat, his voice low and quiet. 'Don't overestimate yourself, Elaine.'

She persisted. 'Did Bobby send you?'

'He doesn't *send* me anywhere.' Annoyance twitched in Marty's cheek. Elaine realised belatedly that she had insulted him.

'I mean… did he ask you to follow me?'

This time he laughed. 'No, Robert Capa trusts easily.'

'Unlike you?'

'Unlike me,' he agreed. His eyes were fixed on hers. *What did he want?*

'So?' Elaine shook her head.

'Look, Elaine, Pinky or whatever it is you like to be called. Robert Capa and I are like this.' Marty crossed the fingers of his right hand elaborately in front of her. The middle and the index. Elaine wanted to snort. Like she was going to be impressed by that!

'He's probably told you I'm his fixer. I'm more than that. I am the gatekeeper. I am the kingmaker. Look, he has a lot of fans, and they're not all as benign as you and Annie. I always need to know exactly who or what we're dealing with.'

Elaine remembered Bobby telling her about him and Marty. How Marty saved his life. She forced open the train window and, at last, the outside came in. The rush of air. She breathed it in. And began to tell Marty the truth about Alan.

'So you see why,' she said, when she had finished, 'I don't like to tell many people.'

Marty nodded thoughtfully. He pressed his glasses onto the bridge of his nose.

'Thank you for telling me, Elaine. I mean it. You've done the right thing today.'

'And you won't tell Bobby?'

'That's for you to decide.'

'Do *you* think I should tell him about Alan?'

Marty hesitated for just a fraction too long. 'Maybe not.'

CHAPTER THIRTY-EIGHT

LONDON, NOVEMBER 1944

One of the POW letters just didn't make sense. Something didn't ring true. It sounded forced. It was like the words were shoehorned into letter shape but they didn't add up to 'letter'.

Always Mum, it began. *Tell me, how are you?* Elaine read it again and again.

She shouldn't take it down to the canteen, but she did. *Get closer*, she thought.

It was perhaps only the fact that she had been reading letters every day for the last two years and a half that gave her the experience needed to spot something amiss. It was the flow, the rhythm of it, the order of the words on the page. It was what wasn't said as much as what was. Plenty of men wrote badly, but it wasn't that this was badly written, it was just… Something.

Strange phrasing. Strange.

Elaine peered at it, she started again and again. She folded and unfolded it. She stroked it and flapped it. She would have eaten it all up if she could have.

Suddenly, she had an idea. The first word of every line, like a poem she was once taught. Acrostic poetry. She remembered one at school about a peacock. *Proud. Earnest. Able*. Etc.

You were meant to raise your hand if you found something and Mrs Dill was supposed to come to you, a bit like being in a schoolroom. In all the time she'd been there, she'd never seen that happen. They were so close to each other, even whispers wouldn't escape Mrs Dill. Instead of raising her hand, Elaine got up and walked over to Mrs Dill's desk, self-importance coursing through her. This was something, wasn't it? She wasn't mistaken, was she? How embarrassing would it be to be mistaken? To be the person who set off a false alarm or the boy who cried wolf.

'Mrs Dill,' she said timidly.

Mrs Dill put down her pen and smiled. 'Yes?'

'I think... maybe. There's something here. In this letter.'

The room fell silent. Felicity said, 'What? Really, Elaine?' Myra didn't move a muscle but her typewriter let out a sudden ding. But then the clatter of keys stopped. All eyes were on Elaine. Mrs Dill's smile slid off her face. She squinted into Elaine's face.

'What on earth is it?'

Elaine pointed to the crumpled note in front of her that had travelled so many miles with its small hopeful prayer inside. With her pencil, she softly outlined the words she had found.

Atck Camp K 23 Dec Pls help

Two days later, the Major who had visited their office once before came in, accompanied by his beaver teeth. Elaine was transcribing a letter from James to his mother. All seemed normal again.

'Was it you?'

'The letter?' said Elaine uncertainly.

'Yes. Very well done,' he said. 'Strictly confidential, yes?'

'Yes.'

And they never talked about it again. It was forgotten. Elaine didn't even tell Bobby or Annie, although Mrs Dill must have told Joyce something, because she got the biggest dollop of crumble ever that lunchtime.

She had underestimated her boys. She had always thought of them fondly, she had always worried about them but she hadn't realised that there could be more. That there was more than love. There was duty, passion for one's country, there was obligation, there was something bigger. It did her good to remember that.

And over the next few weeks, she would remind herself, she was not a nothing, she was a something. She had made a difference; tiny it was, but still it was there. It was the most incredible feeling. She wouldn't tell Bobby, but somehow their path seemed less impeded than ever before. She was his equal, she had worth.

CHAPTER THIRTY-NINE

LONDON, NOVEMBER 1944

Bobby was filthy and exhausted when he came back from France. He stank of cigarettes and apologetic body odour. As he took his bath in the Savoy, gin in hand, praising life to the heavens, Elaine sat on the ceramic side, knocking back the vodka. They were both getting silly and amorous and it wasn't long before she had pulled off her tweedy skirt and good blouse to climb in with him. So good to be in her darling's arms again – even if the water wasn't as hot as she would have liked.

Although Bobby always tried to be positive with her, Elaine felt this time that something really was different. Bobby really did feel the war would be over, and soon. The Allies were getting somewhere now. He had followed the American advance through France, taking photos of villages and small towns as they were recaptured from the Nazis. He told about a bewildered farmer greeting them there, two children welcoming them, one holding a guinea pig that the soldiers joked about roasting and eating.

'They do in some parts of the world.'

'Well, we're not in those parts yet!'

He described a colonel giving a rousing talk to the troops, a plaster across his nose: that strange human detail, providing a distraction. Every soldier there was spellbound by that small rectangle over his schnozz.

People not knowing whether they were coming or going. People crying. People stealing.

'It's nearly over, Elaine. We'll soon be able to get on with our lives. You and me in peacetime.'

'I hope so.'

He talked about how some of the French were jeering at first, but most – when they realised what was happening – were weeping with happiness. '*Les Américains sont arrivés!*' They gratefully lined the streets to give out presents to the triumphant army. One soldier was disappointed with his ball of cheese as he thought it was something sweet. A fight had nearly broken out between him and the insulted cheese-giver. And children; forgotten children were emerging from everywhere, pale and dressed in clothes too small for them, legs sticking out of the shortest of shorts or creased skirts, some of them even a little wobbly on their feet like baby calves because of their ill-fitting shoes. One of them offered a hug and an American soldier gave one little girl a piece of gum, which she swallowed straight away, eyes wide.

'Ay, ay, ay, you're meant to chew it first!' he called.

They were awake much of the night, talking about it. Elaine wouldn't let herself go to sleep. She listened as hard as she could. It was her mission to listen to Bobby, her patriotic duty. He needed to talk, and she understood the importance of getting it out. Otherwise, it would be like toxicity clogging up the rivers of their love for the rest of their lives. And, in truth, it was refreshing to be with someone who did talk, who was upfront. It made her yearn to be the same. *Why had she had no practice at this?*

There was often a dark story at the heart of Bobby's exuberant adventures though, and although this trip was essentially a tale of triumph and the prospect of the coming peace, it was no exception.

Elaine knew the signs. His voice lowered and he gripped her closer. They were in bed, curtains open because he wanted to see the moon, and she could feel him shake slightly as he spoke.

'Some of the women… they had been hurt. They offered themselves to the soldiers. That's how desperate they were. Some of them had had their hair shaved, and there was this one woman, only sixteen, seventeen maybe… when she came out into the street the villagers all yelled at her or spat at her, or they threw old shoes at her face.'

'What had she done?'

'Collaborators. Sex with the Germans. Babies with them sometimes.'

He was squeezing Elaine and, uncomfortable as it was, she didn't want to break the spell of him talking.

'I hated her, and yet I sympathised with her. I thought about you and what you would have done.'

'I wouldn't have gone with a Nazi, Bobby!' Elaine said, momentarily stunned. She wriggled from his arms. 'What are you trying to say?'

'I don't mean you would have,' he said. 'That's not what I'm saying. I mean, it's about survival, isn't it? She had to do what she had to do. We all would. The human condition. I couldn't judge her for it, I wouldn't judge anyone for it.'

Elaine had planned to tell Bobby about Alan that night but she found she couldn't. She just couldn't. Bobby was so full of story, she just wanted to make everything all right for him. Once again, there were too many other things going on. She decided to tell him when she next saw him.

He was waiting for her outside work the next day, yet she wasn't ready to tell him then either. He wanted her to see his work. Together, they walked up to Life Corp. He had a great big umbrella, which he pretended was a weapon. She hurried up the stairs alongside him. She liked this. How quickly she had grown used to the kudos of being the war photographer's girlfriend.

'You'll love my new stuff, Pinky.'

'That was a quick turnaround.'

'Yeah, well, I didn't have Clive buggering them up this time.'

'Ha ha.'

Up they went to the darkroom, where Elaine surveyed the prints slowly. She didn't need to speak. He was right again. The war was nearly over, it must be. The contentment on the face of that Frenchman with no teeth. The cheering children waving little flags. There she was, the woman he had told her about – the one with the grimace, shaved head and her mother weeping over her. *For shame.*

'These are brilliant.' She remembered Gerda Taro's mother. 'They're perfect. You know… this is your destiny, Bobby.'

She felt tearful for a moment, they were that good. And to think: he had been there, he had seen all this first hand.

He swept his hand through his hair. 'I can't wait for it to be over and done with. I can't wait to be free of all this… turmoil. I will never take another war photograph again.'

Elaine stared at him uncertainly. *What about their agency plans?*

'Don't look so worried, sweetheart. I will always take beautiful photos. But I will be a peace photographer. The very best in the world.'

And then before she could tell him about her brother Alan, as she had planned, he gave her a big sloppy kiss and even though it was nine o'clock in the morning, he went off to play poker with Marty and the guys.

After work, Elaine spent a quiet evening at Annie's place, leafing through old magazines and drinking black coffee. Elaine told Annie all about baby Barbara and how she was a good girl, hardly made a fuss at all. She didn't tell her about Clive and his gloomy attitude, nor her struggles with Nora, but Annie kind of guessed anyway, and she sympathised.

'You broody at all?' she asked.

'Not really,' admitted Elaine. It was easier to say 'not really' than 'no', which sounded altogether too abrupt or too final and therefore too nasty. 'There are so many things I want to do after the war. You?'

Annie suffered no such qualms. 'Never,' she said cheerfully. She puffed herself up. 'If there's one thing this war has shown me, it's that I'm a career woman through and through.'

A few evenings later and Elaine and Bobby had been dancing, drinking and playing cards. She still hadn't brought up Alan – or, come to that, told him that Nora and the baby had moved in – but everything was sweet between them, things couldn't have been sweeter. They were both alive, weren't they? And in wartime this was a big deal! *And* they were both together. For ever.

As he nuzzled her collar bone, he murmured, 'One more trip, Pinky,' and Elaine felt her happiness tilt.

'So soon?'

He was going back to North Africa. 'Not yet. Don't worry.' She searched his face for emotion. He was matter-of-fact about this one. 'The war is nearly over, Pinky. I'm not going to die now.'

Elaine had a bad feeling about this trip though. A really bad feeling.

CHAPTER FORTY

LONDON, JANUARY 1945

The easterly wind was so harsh that for the first time, Elaine actually considered trousers for work. It was the coldest January on record. Bobby had been home for Christmas and it was everything she had ever hoped for. He had plied her with presents – goodness knows where he had got them all – and they spent every free moment together, laughing, dancing, or in the bath or in bed. The Savoy had a big Christmas tree and a band of carol singers. And although it wasn't technically a Christmas present, Elaine's favourite thing had been the second-hand typewriter Bobby had given her, for when they set up the agency business. Things were becoming real. It was really happening. They just needed the war to end.

Now, though, it was January and he was in Morocco or was it Tunisia, and all her hopes were tiny and useless again like things that belonged in a doll's house. Elaine worked, she came home, she played with her baby niece, but her heart was racing all the time and when she couldn't sleep, she didn't count sheep but repeated, 'Come back, Bobby,' for hours on end.

One night, Nora was pacing the flat. Clive had said he'd be home for her, and he wasn't. She'd gone and made him a sandwich for tea too. Nora was agitated. She had already upset Mrs Marriot with some off-the-cuff remark about her books, and she had annoyed Mrs Perry too. She wouldn't eat. She just wanted Clive. Clive never came home early. He sometimes came back with peace offerings – *did*

Nora realise they were stolen? – but he never came home early. Nora said she didn't want things, she just wanted Clive there – but she couldn't help herself, she had a magpie's eye for a trinket.

'If I'd known what he was like, I'd never have got involved,' she told Elaine. And 'I'd never have got involved with him in normal times. I lost my mind with this bloody war.'

Nora wouldn't settle in the armchair. It was a full moon, and outside, it was bright and cold. Barbara wailed as though catching her mother's tension. Elaine wondered what the book about parenting would have to say on this.

'Try and relax. Clive will be back later.'

'You take her,' Nora said firmly. 'I need a breather.'

Nora put down baby Barbara in the drawer-cot. She grabbed a scarf and stalked out, slamming the door behind her.

Elaine put on the kettle.

Two minutes later, there was an almighty explosion. It was so bad the house shook and Elaine nearly fell down. Bettie Page screeched and ran out from behind the curtains. The drawer where Barbara slept had wriggled right to the very edge of the table – she let out a shocked howl too. Elaine scooped her up, swearing to herself. She didn't know what to do. She couldn't leave the baby alone. She raced downstairs two at a time, Barbara in her arms.

Mrs Marriot was at the door, her hands at her mouth. 'That must have been very close.'

'Please look after the baby.' Elaine pushed Barbara into her neighbour's arms, then ran out to look for Nora, *damn Nora. Why couldn't she have stayed at home?* The shop seemed to be okay. Books had crashed to the floor but nothing major had been damaged. But in the street, it was impossible to see but it felt like everything had disappeared. Silent choking white dust and blinding smoke. It was like the worst nights of the Blitz all over again.

Elaine called out, 'Nora, Nora!', but there was nothing, just the distant wail of approaching sirens. She tried to move to where she thought the explosion might have happened but it was too hard to make anything out. It was rubble and dust and bricks and fear.

In a dizzy haze, she ran back to Mrs Marriot's, where Mrs Marriot was giving Barbara some warm milk from a teaspoon. Elaine saw that despite her calm manner, her hands too were shaking. Barbara spluttered and gurgled. Mrs Marriot said she was happy to keep the baby for now, but Elaine didn't know what to do. *Should she go back out, should she stay in?* She stood quite frozen. A certain knowledge was setting in. Mrs Marriot was trying to soothe her – 'Stay here, girl, the police will be along in a jiffy' – but Elaine couldn't quite work out what she was saying. She watched Mrs Marriot put on the kettle and realised her own hands were covered in dust.

They waited and waited and waited but Elaine knew, she could feel it in her bones.

The baby mostly slept and when she did wake, Elaine and Mrs Marriot managed to rock her back to sleep. A few hours of this and Mrs Marriot was exhausted with it, so Elaine told her there was nothing they could do and best to go to bed; she would take the baby up and come down tomorrow to see about tidying the bookshop.

It must have been about three o'clock in the morning when the doorbell went. Elaine answered the door with Barbara, still sleeping, in her arms. There was Clive, looking wrecked. He also wasn't wearing his boot or a coat. He wouldn't look at her or the baby. A policeman was standing closely behind him.

'Is this your brother, miss?'

'Yes… Clive! Have you found Nora?'

The policeman was very sorry. Nora had indeed been found and it wasn't good news. He said he would send someone round in the morning. There would be arrangements to be made.

At first Elaine could not speak, but then, thinking of her own mother, she found herself, wobbly-voiced, offering tea.

The policeman did not accept. He said, 'This young man's in shock, miss.' He put his hand on Clive's shoulder and propelled him into the room. 'A terrible thing, sir. Rest assured, it was so quick, she wouldn't have known a thing.'

As soon as the police officer had left, Clive went into his room, grabbed a bag, then came out looking for something.

'What happened, then?' whispered Elaine.

'It must have had her name on it.'

'She's definitely gone? Are you sure it was her?'

He looked up. 'What are you saying?'

'I don't know,' Elaine admitted. 'I just can't believe it.'

Everything was broken now. *Poor Nora.*

Bobby, she thought, *why do you have to be away? Why do you always have to be away when I need you most?* She felt herself aching for him to be there, as if he could make it all right.

Clive continued throwing things into the bag. A breadknife. Some spoons. A tin cup. Some soap. His ration book. Handkerchiefs. His toothbrush.

'What… wait, where are you going?'

'Away. Anywhere away from here.'

Elaine laughed; she couldn't help it. *He's in shock*, she reminded herself, just as the police officer had said. She'd seen it before. She'd make him some tea. Carefully, praying the baby didn't wake, she placed Barbara back in her drawer and got up. Barbara did open her little eyes and sleepily surveyed the room but for just a second – she must have decided there was nothing to bother with, for she shut them again. Filling up the kettle, such a mundane task, made Elaine feel calmer and when she spoke, she surprised herself at how measured she sounded.

'You can't leave, Clive. Not now.'

'I can do what I like.'

'No, you can't. What about Barbara?'

'I didn't want this,' he said gruffly, gesturing around the room, which had been taken over by baby cardigans, hats and nappies. 'It's not me.'

Elaine looked at the poor sleeping baby and could hardly believe what she was hearing. 'That's not her fault…'

'It's not my fault either.'

'It isn't anyone's fault,' said Elaine, realising she wasn't going to win the argument this way. 'But she *is* your responsibility.'

'I don't want her. She's probably mad.'

'Wha-at?'

'Oh, you must have guessed it, Elaine. It's hereditary.'

'No, it isn't.'

Elaine felt her insides folding. No, it wasn't. Clive was mad himself to say it. They both looked at Barbara, her lips obliviously puckered, her cheeks obliviously rosy.

'You'll look after her for me, won't you, Elaine?'

'Don't be daft, Clive!'

'I'm going.'

For a moment Elaine was too incredulous to speak. *This couldn't be happening.* It was too much to take in. First, Nora, poor stubborn Nora, now this. *No. No way. She would not let it happen again.*

'You can't go, Clive. You can't leave her. You always hated Dad for abandoning us. Don't turn into him!'

He looked at her with an expression of immense pain or fury, it was hard to tell. Then he shook his head, grabbed his bag and slammed the door behind him. The flat shook. He had left them.

Barbara started to cry.

CHAPTER FORTY-ONE

LONDON, JANUARY 1945

Mrs Perry said looking after Barbara was no bother at all. She enjoyed having her in the flat of a morning. She had taken her to meet her friends at church. Barbara was such a good girl, everyone knew that.

'The customers like her,' agreed Mrs Marriot, who had her the rest of the day in the shop. 'And she's too young to miss her mama.' Elaine felt certain this wasn't true, but nothing would be gained from arguing this. *Poor darling*: it would be the defining feature of her life, it would be her burden, her albatross, her cross to bear. Elaine, realising she was thinking about herself, shook herself. Maybe Barbara *wouldn't* feel it so keenly. You never knew. Maybe they could, you know, glide over it.

Anyway, Mrs Perry didn't know the half of it yet – the other half.

'Dadda will be home soon, little one,' she cooed repeatedly into Barbara's placid face. 'Da-da-da. Go on, *you* say it.'

'Oh, didn't I say? Clive has had to do more…' Elaine was annoyed at herself for not thinking up a better – or at least more realistic – excuse. 'Training.'

She was playing for time. What to do, what to do?

'Training?' Mrs Perry didn't like that one bit. 'With a dead wife and a tiny babby to look after?! What is it with these fishmongers? Have they no sympathy, no compassion?'

*

Marty had a message for Elaine. Since Mrs Marriot and Mrs Perry had had Barbara while Elaine went to work all week, it seemed wrong to ask on a Saturday, so Elaine brought Barbara along with her to the George. Pushing her along, she realised she had never known how hard it was to push a bloody pram over cobblestones. And the craters in the ground. You never think of things like that until you're doing it.

'Who on earth is that?' Marty asked irritably.

'She's my brother's baby. My niece, Barbara,' Elaine said. *What a way of talking he had!*

'Why have you got it?'

'Her. I've got *her* until my brother Clive gets back.'

If she didn't tell anyone he'd gone, maybe he hadn't?

'Where's he gone?'

'I don't know.'

'How long has he gone for?'

'I don't know.'

Marty sighed a big end-of-the-world sigh. (As if it had anything to do with him.)

'Robert Capa *needs* to be overseas.'

'I know that, Marty.'

'It's not about the money with him. It's not *only* about the money,' he went on.

'And I'd never stop him…'

'He's got a duty, you know. A vocation.'

The baby had started to wail. Maybe she was fed up with being talked about as a burden all the time. Elaine picked her up and patted her fat cloth nappy the way she had seen Mrs Marriot do. Barbara nuzzled into her neck. It was quite sweet, really. You couldn't help but enjoy it despite yourself.

'He shouldn't marry you. Not just for his sake, for yours too.'

'It's got nothing to do with you what Bobby does.'

'I suppose your brother has done a disappearing act,' Marty continued. What a bad mood he was in. Just because of a baby, a little baby.

How Elaine wished she could say no. How she wished she could laugh and say, 'Don't be ridiculous, Marty, you've got the wrong end of the stick.' But she couldn't because he knew the truth about Clive. She knew it.

Marty's voice softened. 'That baby is going to need someone steady. Constant. Safe.'

Elaine's shoulders slumped. *Not this again*. The way people talked! Like she was Bobby's jailer. Like she was his keeper. No one *kept* Robert Capa. She understood that. Why didn't anyone else?

She bounced Barbara on her knee and ignored both Marty and the small ladder that had formed in her stocking. Little stoical Barbara. With her oversized cheeks – or did all babies have these? Elaine wasn't sure. Barbara also had eyes that seemed to watch and know everything. Was that quite normal? They gazed at her intently now. It was like she was expecting Elaine to communicate something profound. Elaine looked away. Didn't have much chance, did she, poor Barbara? Abandoned like an old sock.

She remembered something. 'What was the message? You said there was a message?'

'Robert Capa is the best photographer in the world right now.'

Elaine pulled a face. 'I know that. What did you want to tell me?'

'He gets back next Saturday and there's an award ceremony in the evening. Make sure he goes. He won't want to, he never does, but he should go. It's good for him.'

CHAPTER FORTY-TWO

LONDON, FEBRUARY 1945

Of course Bobby didn't want to go to a stupid awards ceremony. He'd much rather have a cosy night at the George with his sweetheart. Elaine protested over the telephone, several times in fact, and wholeheartedly too, but he insisted. 'I need to see my Pinky now!' He went on and on about it, until she agreed to meet him that evening.

Mrs Marriot was delighted to have Barbara overnight. 'She's good company,' she said. 'And don't rush back. I know you want to see your young man. It's natural.'

Elaine and Bobby met at the George. Hugging her excitedly, Bobby told her she was more beautiful than ever, that he adored her, even in trousers, and he was never happier than when he was with her.

Elaine told him that she had missed him, and missed him, and had she told him she'd missed him?

He got their drinks. When he put hers in front of her, he asked what she'd been doing, and she admitted that most evenings she'd been looking after poor baby Barbara. She had written to him about Nora's terrible death and he had been very sympathetic and sent pink flowers.

'She's a sweet little thing,' she added.

'I'll bet,' Bobby said, wiping his mouth. A few men in uniform came over, interrupting them and asking to shake his hand.

'Still alive then?' one of them said.

'Just about.' Bobby laughed. After they'd gone he put his arm round Elaine and squeezed her.

'So how is Clive coping without Nora?'

This, she hadn't told him. That one brother had abandoned his whole life, one brother had abandoned his child.

'He had to go and do some stuff. He'll be back soon though.' She kept her fingers crossed. It wasn't a complete lie: maybe Clive would eventually see sense. You couldn't rule that out. And she and Bobby were having such a lovely evening too. Why spoil it?

'He's missing out,' Bobby said. Elaine nodded absently. 'Pinky, you'd tell me if something was wrong?'

'Course I would,' Elaine said. *Wrong*, she thought, a word that was open to interpretation.

The George filled up with the usual lively crowd, and Peter played 'Knees Up Mother Brown' on the piano. The men in uniform had lots of anecdotes as usual: villages captured, Nazis defeated, the tide was definitely turning. Bobby was entertaining everyone with his stories too. Elaine rested into her fiancé's chest, his arm round her. Together at last. This was how it should always be. Her woes did disappear when he was there. He was a magician in that way.

They had been back together for about an hour or so when Marty stomped in. Elaine saw immediately that he was shaking with rage. All dressed up in a tuxedo and smelling of aftershave, he marched right over to them. 'What the hell?'

'Hey, Marty,' said Bobby, as relaxed as ever. 'What can I get—'

'It's not just your career on the line, it's all the people who are counting on you! Everyone at *Life*. Everyone at *Time*.'

Bobby stretched out his arms. 'It's not important, Marty.'

Marty clenched his teeth. 'You think you're a free agent, but you have to toe the line, play the game. You won't get work if you don't get the jobs, get the visas, keep friends… It's not just about you.'

Bobby continued to slowly sip his beer.

Marty shot Elaine an anguished look. Peter at the piano started on a lusty rendition of 'It's a Long Way to Tipperary'. Some young women pushed towards the bar, all dressed up for a party. The men in uniform looked pleased to see them.

Marty stalked away without a backward glance. 'Don't say I didn't warn you!' He barged into one of the men, who growled, 'Hey!', but Marty just bulldozed on.

Elaine knew this had to be settled. 'Go,' she told Bobby. She could see he was in two minds. He hated upsetting Marty. 'Honestly, it's fine. It's just one night. We can see each other tomorrow.'

'I want to be with you,' he said mutinously, his face like a young boy.

'We have all the nights in the world,' she said. 'You don't want to miss this.'

'I do.'

'Please go, Bobby. It'll make me feel better if you go.'

She knew he'd give in eventually, but even so she was surprised at how quickly he did. He necked his drink then jumped up, pulling on his leather jacket. He gave her a fulsome kiss on the lips, slapped her bottom, then with a 'You're the absolute best, Pinky,' he chased out after Marty.

CHAPTER FORTY-THREE

SPAIN

JUNE 2016, DAY FIVE AND SIX

Mum is playing chicken with us. She didn't call in the night to let us know they'd got home. She doesn't answer Matthew's calls the next day. Poor Matthew is in a state.

'Do they do this a lot?' I ask, but I'm worried too.

He shrugs. 'Sometimes.'

During the night, I thought about leaving, of flying back to England in a fit of rage, *that'll teach 'em,* but now that morning is here I don't want to. I want to stay. I want to find out about my family history, and I want to see what is going to develop between Nick and me. Nevertheless, it's a quiet and subdued day by the pool without Mum and Derek. Matthew spends most of the time in his study; I don't know if he's working or moping. I've moved from anger to worry to anger again. I was taunted by her expression, her mockery, the things she said. 'No fun, no fun, even Matthew says...'

Okay, she was drunk. People act badly when they're drunk. But still...

'She'll turn up here as if nothing's happened,' I tell Matthew when we reconvene at midday in the kitchen.

'Probably,' he says, but his expression is pained. My brother tries so hard. He isn't angry though, he is hurt.

'We'll have to do karaoke when she comes back,' he says. 'I wish we'd done it yesterday, could have avoided all this fuss.'

I roll my eyes.

I write Harry a postcard. It's probably daft and it is *definitely* premature but I can't help imagining Nick and Harry meeting. I think, I *hope*, they would get on. A few months ago, I said I couldn't imagine ever being with someone else but now I'm getting to know Nick, I'm beginning to think I can.

In the evening, I'm in the kitchen scrolling through still more of Robert Capa's photos – *this guy really was prolific!* – when Alyssia runs in, crying. My first thought is that something has happened to Mum and for a moment I can't speak, but it isn't that. Alyssia finally gets the words out – it's her phone. She dropped it in the pool. I think it's finished, but I put it in a bowl of rice to soak up the water anyway. Alyssia is furious with herself. I hug her, tell her we should add chicken and prawns, turn it into a paella, *a phonella, get it?*

She sighs. As we wait, though, she cheers up, telling me more about her school and funny stories about her friends. Then Aunty Barbara comes in and tells us about Nelson's job – he works for a phone company – and their last holiday, to Tunisia. 'Did you know Robert Capa took some photographs there too?' I tell her, and she gives me a stern look and says, 'I really don't think we were related, Jen.' But with my aunty we can laugh about it, and we do. I just wish I got on with everyone the way I do with her and Alyssia.

Matthew has been trying to persuade me to go out cycling with him since I arrived. The next morning, I decide to go out on Gisela's bike. Matthew says he will stay back this time. He is awkward about it; says he's expecting some calls. I think it means he is still waiting for communication from our mother.

I am happy to go on my own though because once again, I have woken up full of resolution. I am now the kind of woman who cycles around the mountains of Spain. *I am my grandfather's granddaughter!* Today, I have a date with Nick Linfield!

Matthew explains which roads to stick to, the ones that are the best for unfit beginners like me, and I set off. The scenery is fantastic, and I am glad that I have managed to break away from the poolside. To think I nearly missed these wonderful sights: the lush plants, a donkey, hillside views, the rich palette of colours. After about half an hour, I stop and take photos on Nick's camera, looking forward to showing them to him later. I think about the old days when there was such a long gap between the taking of the photo and the development – and how you just had to trust in the process. Now the camera does it all for you. I wonder what Robert Capa would have made of it all.

I am on my way back when I see something down the valley. A car – from here it looks tiny, like the Matchbox cars that Matthew used to play with. Light blue, tumbled, smashed. Just like Mum's car. Embedded into nature, a foreign body, an object out of place, an upside-down vehicle.

'Oh, Jesus!' I cry, hopping off the bike.

It couldn't be, could it? It couldn't.

Running down through the overgrowth, grateful for my sensible footwear, my sturdy legs, which spring me there faster. I slip and fall down. I'm picturing the scene – bodies hung upside down – I'm pushing past reeds and weeds and it's getting closer and bigger, it's more silver than I thought, but it's in worse condition than I thought, and I start yelling, 'Hello?' and a little whiny sound comes from my throat, 'Mum! MUMMM!'

Let them be okay, let it not be her. If it's not her, I'll never say another mean word against her in my life.

It's not my mum's car. Thank goodness. I clock that when I'm about halfway to it.

But it is someone else. *Someone might be in trouble.*

I'm on a mud track, dirt everywhere. The car is empty. I lean against it and pull away as it wobbles, catch my breath. There's nobody here.

There's a note on the windscreen in Spanish. I presume it's 'police aware' or something. I catch my breath and start the long walk up to the road and my bike. I feel both grateful and foolish.

As soon as I am back on my bike, I am thinking more fondly of my mum than I have for ages. Mum has not been killed in a road traffic accident and, well, how brilliant is that? I don't think I will tell her how relieved I am – she will simply think it's a dig about her driving – but I will tell Matthew. I know he'll understand.

It only takes two or three pedals to realise that the front tyre of the bicycle is flat. This trip is a disaster. It wouldn't have happened like this to Robert Capa. I will have to push it, and it's going to be slow. I'm going to be late for my date. I'm going to balls up my first proper shot at something for twenty-seven years. I don't want Nick to see me all puffy and sweaty like this either. Nor do I want him to leave without waiting for me, but that's one thing I feel pretty confident of – he won't just give up on me. He is a patient man.

And then I realise I have my phone. *We have mobiles these days!* I text him and ask to meet an hour later than we'd originally planned. That's all I need to do.

'I'm running late,' I type with trembling fingers. *Please let this work, please.*

'Sure.' The response comes quickly. What a joy to communicate without drama. It was a revelation! 'See you then x.'

That *is* a kiss. A definite kiss. I haven't had a kiss on the end of a text in years!

In the end, it takes me about two hours to get back and as I approach, I can hear them talking around the pool. Mum and Derek have returned. Barbara is explaining crystal therapy or something. And then I hear a voice, dear God, even more familiar than all of them.

Matthew comes out to open the garage door. He sees me pushing the bike.

'What have you done?'

'Is Paul here?' My voice sounds as hysterical as I feel.

I am a mixture of horrified and delighted. Mostly horrified. *Paul. Is. Here.*

Matthew sucks in air like he's about to give me an estimate for my plumbing. He takes the bike from me and leads it inside.

'Mum and Derek are here too. Is it a puncture?'

'Uh? Matthew?'

He calls back over his shoulder, screws up his lips. 'Gisela said I should have warned you about that road.'

'Is Paul actually here?'

'Yeah, he's out by the pool.'

'What the hell is he doing here?'

Matthew leans closer to me. I can smell the spray he puts in his hair, the garlic mayonnaise he had for lunch.

'I might be wrong, but I've a feeling he wants you back.'

The wheels are still spinning.

Here Paul is. Just as I'd dreamed. Trim beard, apologetic smile. Here's Mum in her kaftan and sunglasses, wafting around, looking every inch the proud mother-in-law, all upset forgotten. There's Derek, at the controls of the barbecue like some superstar DJ. Steak and garlic bread. And there is Paul, motorboating in the bosom of my family and he couldn't look more at home. Mum is resting her acrylics on his arm. She steers him to the loungers. I watch him plonk himself down, gangly legs, somewhere over my favourite lizard. Mum's telling him to take care of his skin. She knows how sensitive he is. *Lovely.*

'Even when it's cloudy, that's when it gets you, Paul, you know that.'

'I know it,' Paul says. He looks up and finally sees me, but he doesn't like to interrupt my mum in full flow. No one does.

'Most people look better with a tan, but not you, Paul. Pale and interesting, that's you.' Mum sees me and covers her mouth, 'Oh goodness, darling! You're all sweaty!'

'Thanks, Mum. That's… that's pushing a bike up a mountain for you.'

She pats Paul's arm. 'You'll never catch me on a bike.'

'You're more of a drink-and-drive kind of woman, aren't you?' I say icily.

Her smile vanishes.

Paul gets up, walks over to me, his face wreathed in a self-conscious grin. He is wearing green trunks with blue sharks on them. *Some kind of warning?*

'Paul?'

He holds out his arms, helplessly.

'Bet I'm the last person you were expecting to see!' As I stand staring at him, he says, 'Do you want a hug, or do you want to go and wash first?'

I shake my head. Matthew comes out with long thin glasses of gin and tonic on a tray. He's got the tiny pink paper umbrellas out too: this is an occasion.

'Get that down you, mate,' he says. They smile adoringly at each other.

'Oh, mate, it's good to be here,' says Paul.

'Any time, mate, any time,' says my treacherous brother.

Paul swigs his gin back. *Cheers, everybody*. The glasses clink together. Mine doesn't clink. Mine stays on Matthew's tray. A lonesome glass and an unwanted umbrella.

The insects buzz, furiously busy. A tiny tinny noise from Alyssia's phone in the armchair on the pool. She's listening to the Backstreet Boys. She loves her 'retro' stuff.

'Cheers!' says my mum fruitily. 'We've got so much to tell you, haven't we, Jen? We've been finding out about our family tree, Paul.'

'I heard!' says Paul. 'Genealogy.' He says it again, and again, like the long word is going to impress us.

Unfortunately, Aunty Barbara smiles at him, clearly impressed. 'That's it, Paul, genealogy!'

'Matthew told me all about it.'

I scowl at Matthew. I didn't know they'd been talking.

Derek chortles. 'They're all bloody Hungarians apparently!'

'That's weird because you never could do the Rubik's cube, could you?' quips Paul.

Rubik's cube? I blink at him.

'Everyone's got skeletons in the cupboard,' Mum says in a sing-songy voice. She won't look at me. She is still annoyed at me. *How dare she be annoyed at me?* All my sentimentality towards her after seeing that crashed car has vanished.

'You've got a whole graveyard, Shirl,' says Derek, making Matthew and Paul guffaw loudly.

I clear my throat. 'I think Paul's got a bit of explaining to do first, before we dig around the family closet, no?'

And then Nick is walking in. He is smiling and then, as he takes us in, our happy family tableau, his smile fades. It's painful to see him try to adjust to the new situation.

Matthew wanders over. 'Mate, I didn't know we were filming today.'

Nick stares straight at me. I make a desperate expression back that I hope says something like: *I had no idea this was happening, and I would never have dreamed of putting you in this awkward position, but please go away before we make it any worse,* but it probably just looks like I need the loo.

'We're not,' he says. He glances at me again. 'I just… I was passing by and—'

'Of course, you want your camera back,' I interrupt. 'Hang on.'

I run into my bedroom. My heart is beating madly. *What is going on? What am I going to do?* I want to stop, look in the mirror, stay and hide in here, but I can't.

I dash out. I must look crazed. The camera is still outside on the table, where I left it. Ye gads! I *am* a numpty.

'Here, thank you!' I don't know why but I place the strap over his head, like I'm a Hawaiian giving out a garland. *Aloha!*

'Sorry,' Nick says, in a low voice.

'No,' I say. 'It's me. I'm sorry.'

The sound of his car crawling away on the gravel makes my heart drop, but worse is the feeling when the sound disappears altogether. Something of me has gone away with it.

'That's the documentary guy?' says Paul, vaping. Yes, he is a vaper since six months back; he takes great pleasure in all the flavours and the names of the flavours. 'I had imagined something different.'

'How do you mean?'

'He doesn't look like he'd be able to direct traffic, never mind a documentary.'

And breathe. Paul is back. He's come back.

He puts his arm round me. 'I've got so much to tell you.'

'Yeah.' I shrug his arm off for now. 'You really do.'

This is what I wanted for so many months. And here it is. Served up on a platter.

We sit at the table at the far end of the garden where no one usually goes. Paul has brought his ukulele in its little black case. He is wearing designer trainers. His hair is lighter. All these additions to his life, once he was liberated from the gaol of matrimony with me. I wonder if he's learned any songs. Harry jokingly calls him a 'poor man's Tommy Steele'.

We watch Barbara get in the pool in her burkini outfit. She waves over. She's wearing a swimming hat today too, with bulging flowers on it.

'God, I love your family,' says Paul emphatically after Matthew has equipped him with gin number three.

'What are you doing here?'

'Can't you guess, Jen?' he says, half-shyly, half-cockily, if that's possible.

'No.' I *can* guess but I refuse to guess. He's going to have to spell it out. That's the least he can do.

'I want a second chance.'

'Paul,' I say. 'Forgive me, but haven't you just been to Ibiza with your…' I think of the word 'mistress' and decide it's too old-fashioned, or too dark, for this situation '…girlfriend?'

'Eva and I have decided we're better off as friends.' He pauses as though to allow that to sink in for me, and a window of opportunity to express my inevitable relief. I deliberately say nothing. I am relieved, it is true. I had grown to hate Eva, a woman I'd never met in my life, and this made me hate myself too because I like to lift up women, not imagine awful humiliating scenarios for them. And it isn't her fault that she shares a name with Hitler's girlfriend either. But Paul doesn't need to know I'm glad she's out of the picture.

'You're the one I want.'

You're the one I want? I can't help thinking of that moment in *Grease* where John Travolta becomes 'square' and Olivia Newton-John becomes 'rebellious'. Is he thinking of that too? Is this the kind of transformation we require? Paul's hands are on my legs and are tentatively stroking my thighs. *Presumptuous*, I think. *Familiar*, I also think.

Poor Nick. Sent away with a flea in his ear.

'Think about Harry – he's not had the best year because of us.'

Us?

'He'll be made up if we stick together.'

Paul doesn't know the slightest thing about Harry's state of mind. He doesn't know about the bunking off school or the visit to the doctor or the plunging grades.

'And so will Pushkin,' he says, as though he can win me over with an endearing mention of the cat he had abandoned without so much as a backwards tickle.

He has a tattoo on his ankle. Another new thing. It's a musical note, a bass clef. He has been leading a whole new life without me. He sees me looking at it.

'We could get matching ones?'

I can't take my eyes off it as he goes into his speech.

'I love your mum and Derek – even Aunty Barbara although she's mad as a box of frogs—'

'She isn't,' I interrupt.

He raises his hands for me to be silent. He has a monologue to perform. *Who does he think he is? Bloody Hamlet?*

'Let's move forward as a family.'

And here is my mother wobbling out towards us in her heels, shaking a bottle of champagne.

CHAPTER FORTY-FOUR

LONDON, FEBRUARY 1945

The sports journalist from *Life* magazine had come down with the flu and Bobby had offered to take the photographs of a football game for him. He was excited. 'Balls makes a change from bullets,' he said. 'Although you're going to have to explain the rules to me.' Marty and Annie were invited too, only Annie was working and couldn't come. Elaine didn't much want to go without her, but Bobby pleaded. 'You might enjoy it, Pinky,' he said. 'Give soccer a chance.'

The stadium was full their end although virtually empty the other side. Elaine looked around, wondering if among the people here was her brother, her weaselly runaway brother. The crowds jostled against her and she was pushed into Marty. Tall and brooding and holding a cigarette, he looked like he should be at the opera.

'How is your brother, Clive?' he asked. 'Has he come back yet?' It was as though he was reading her mind.

Elaine kept her eyes on the referee as he galloped down the pitch. He was a sprightly fellow considering he must have been over sixty. Lots of the team were in their forties or fifties since the younger men were mostly away fighting. 'Not yet.'

Marty sighed. He found them a seat on a wooden bench. Everyone shoved up for them. The bench trembled and shook at every movement.

'And Alan? How is he?'

'Not too good,' she admitted. 'I'm not sure that place is doing much for him.'

'Try a different place.'

Elaine laughed. *As if it was that easy.*

Marty turned round to face her. His collar was up. He looked ridiculously and deliberately out of place.

'You can't afford it?'

She nodded.

He looked at his feet. 'I'll sort something for you.'

Elaine watched the men in shorts on the pitch chasing around the ball which, she had explained to a disbelieving Bobby, was made from a pig's bladder. She wasn't sure he believed her. The players were all so earnest, spitting into the mud, scowling. What a distraction this was – but then she supposed it all was: poker games, dancing, lovemaking; pick your poison. Bobby described it as bread and roses. A distraction from the fact that they were killing us, *we* were killing each other.

Marty was still waiting for her to speak.

'I don't know what to do.'

Marty stared at her. 'You *do* know what to do, Elaine. Deep down, you know.'

She was baggage. She would ruin Bobby's life. A brother in the asylum and now a baby. Too much. She didn't want to do what Nora had done to Clive. She didn't want to tie bricks to his feet. And she knew Marty was saying she should let him go.

'I can't…'

And he was always away. Away when she needed him most. Marty had said she needed someone to pull her through, to steer her, and he wasn't wrong. She had been strong all the time, and it was exhausting by herself. Really, she should have stuck with Justin. Instead, she always had to twist. Twist until bust.

'You have options, Elaine,' said Marty quietly. 'You've always had options.'

'I don't.'

'Robert Capa *says* he hates it – he hates the travel, being away, the awards, the dinners – but he loves it. You know he does. He'll never stop.'

She knew he wouldn't. He'd be nothing without his camera. That's what he was. Some people just did a job. He *was* his job – even if he didn't know it about himself, she knew it about him. It ran through his blood. The George wasn't his first love, nor was she, nor even Marty. It was his camera. Always his camera. No, it wasn't the camera – it was the photographs. It was the act of showing, the act of remembering the forgotten ones, the act of acknowledging them. If he couldn't do that, he would be nothing. But she didn't want him to stop, did she?

'But the war will be over soon,' she said quietly.

'There will always be wars for Bobby,' Marty said.

He was breathing faster over her. There was whisky on his breath and this felt strange and rare. Had he got drunk to come to the football today? Why?

His voice was unusually low when he asked, 'It's not too late, is it?'

Elaine looked up at him, bewildered. 'How do you mean?'

'You're not… pregnant, are you?' He said the word 'pregnant' like it was a terminal disease.

Elaine laughed. She and Bobby were so careful. But in a way, that just showed, didn't it? Like her, he didn't want children or to settle down. But unlike her, photography was his destiny. His responsibility. *It must not be wasted.*

She shook her head at Marty, no.

Marty said, 'That means there is one less thing to worry about. Listen to me carefully. There are people who will look after Alan, who would love to take on the baby – who would love to build a family with you, who will stay with you, right now. *Now.* What's her name? Barbara, is it? It's a nice name.'

She would not cry. This would not be her final straw. Her hump would not be broken.

She looked up at the endless man folding his arms beside her. The only man who knew about Alan. And the only man who knew about Clive.

There must have been a reason she hadn't told everything to Robert Capa. There must have been a reason she didn't get closer.

'Who?' Her voice came out croaky. She knew the answer, of course, but she wanted to hear it aloud.

He readjusted the glasses on his nose. He breathed out slowly. Somehow, she knew he had been waiting for this moment for a very long time.

'Me.'

The crowd went wild. She had missed it. A goal. First goal of the match. She searched for Bobby, found him. He was clicking like mad, immersed in his photographs, and then he was waving at them both from down by the wire fence, smiling his big agreeable smile. Five seconds later, he bounded up the concrete aisle, pushing through the people, taking the steps two at a time, his lust for life written all over him. He edged his way along the benches, all the way along, to reach them, and although there was no room, he found room, he picked up Elaine and twirled her around again and again.

'I like this game!' He was laughing with his big white teeth. 'I'm even beginning to understand the rules.'

CHAPTER FORTY-FIVE

LONDON, FEBRUARY 1945

The weariness and woe on Alan's face. The pathos of his hair. Someone combed it over for him every morning. It was not the natural way his hair sat, and over the hour Elaine spent with him, it worked its way back.

'Eisenhower told me where they are going to attack. You must tell someone.'

'But how did he tell you, Alan?'

'The squirrels.'

He looked so tired Elaine thought he mightn't believe it himself. Maybe he was saying it out of, she didn't know, a misguided sense of duty. But then he sat himself upright again: 'They leave them in tiny notes in the acorns.'

'Okay. Alan, we're moving you. This place is doing you no good. I'm going to try and find you somewhere better.'

'Nice man?' he said.

'Very.'

Where had they all gone wrong? Her, Clive and Alan. What was it about the Parker siblings? She'd tried, she'd tried so hard to lift up, to take off. She remembered the nights she had spent timing herself typing. She'd wrapped a blindfold over her eyes, and Clive had read to her to get her dictation up to speed. She remembered one time, looking at the typed paper, when she knew it was as near perfect as it would ever be: not a comma out of place anywhere, not a capital letter missed, and she knew she had arrived. She had done it. She would be a clerical girl if it killed her. Yet here she was, here they were, stumbling around in the mud again.

She thinks of the condoms in Bobby's coat pocket. The girls and the pink gin. The French whores who'd go with anyone. The coincidence of Martha being in Normandy. Merry and Faye in the office. His enduring affection for Gerda Taro and her mother. She couldn't bear it any longer. She loved him too much, she knew this. It wasn't right.

Elaine met Annie on a small bench near work. She had missed Annie at her desk. There had been no replacement, just the forlorn sight of her chair, her ashtray, her typewriter every day. She had missed her in the canteen, pontificating, fork in the air, under the posters or arguing with Felicity over some question of etiquette. But Annie was angling to see *Lady in the Dark* at the cinema. They hadn't been to see a film together for ages. Heart in her stomach, Elaine asked, 'Would you mind?', explained there was something she wanted to talk about. And Annie, always a friend indeed, put away her yearning to see how Ginger Rogers got on with Ray Milland and pretended she didn't mind at all.

Slowly, Elaine outlined the situation, and as she did so, she realised how desperately she needed Annie to be on her side. For Annie to take her hand and say, 'I see, Elaine, and yes, good point. Well done.'

No one else did that.

Elaine was giving up work to look after the baby. Work didn't mind. There were fewer and fewer letters – and anyway, care of a small child was more important. Annie nodded along gravely. She could see that was for the best, she nodded. *Poor Barbara*. She took Elaine's hand. 'You're doing the right thing.'

And here, Elaine took a deep breath: she was also giving up something else: Bobby.

'He needs someone better than me.'

But here, Annie took her hand away and she didn't say kind words or 'good point' at all; now she was shocked and Annie was never someone who was easy to shock.

'Who could possibly be better than you, my dear girl?'

'Someone, anyone free.'

'Oh, Elaine! He doesn't want *free*. You must know that.'

Annie was like the other side of her conscience. If Marty was a cherub encouraging her to do the right thing, Annie was a little devil sitting on her shoulder, pitchfork at the ready. And what she said was convincing too. As convincing as the doubts in Elaine's head were, as convincing as Marty.

'Don't you know Robert Capa at all? He wants *you*. He adores you.'

Elaine thought of all the women Bobby had told her about or introduced her to over the last year. Martha Gellhorn who he was alone with at Normandy (and God only knows what happened between them). Gerda Taro who flung herself into oncoming trucks, Gerda's mother who had escaped from Nazis across the Pyrenees, Bessie the landlady of the George, who came from nowhere to build a pub empire, Myra Hess who sang in a war zone, all of them… great women all of them.

Not her. Nothing like her. She didn't have baggage. She *was* baggage.

The only thing she'd ever done of note was a touch of code-deciphering and no one would ever know about that. She was entirely forgettable.

'I'm a nothing.'

'How can you say that? A lovely girl who looks after the shop when Mrs Marriot can't, who takes care of her brothers, who takes care of her brother's child, who worked so hard for the country during the Blitz and for the prisoners of war after and… Oh Elaine, how can you possibly say you're a nothing?'

But Elaine thought only of those awful stolen gloves of which she had been so proud, the tap on the shoulder that never came in the office, even when she'd found those clues in the letter, the brothers who had, in all honesty, contributed next to nothing to the country… Good grief. If the most agreeable man in London could do no better than her then something was seriously, seriously wrong.

Elaine got up.

'I'm not enough for him. I'll never be enough.'

This was a painful truth. Some people never learned it and spent their whole lives thinking they were destined for greatness. At least she knew. She knew defeat when she saw it.

But Annie gripped her wrist. The devil prodded her in the heart. 'Why don't you just tell Bobby about Alan and the baby?'

'I just can't. We never had that kind of a relationship.'

Whenever she thought of Bobby, it was light, it was dancing, it was making love, it was taking baths together, it was the moon at the window, it was pink flowers on her desk, chocolates on her tongue.

It was a dream, an escape.

It was a wartime romance and the war was nearly over.

'You could try. You should try.'

Why was Annie getting so upset? Annie who initially had warned her off him. Fly-by-night. A playboy. Her words, not Elaine's.

'He's a good man. He's perfect for you.'

'But I'm not perfect for him.'

'You're more than—'

'I couldn't do it to him, Annie. Believe me.'

She might as well break his beautiful legs and cripple him. She might as well pull off his wings. She might as well take his photos and burn them. This wasn't Bobby. This wasn't Robert Capa. This wasn't Endre Erno Friedmann. Whoever he was, he deserved all the best in the world.

CHAPTER FORTY-SIX

LONDON, MARCH 1945

Saying goodbye to Bobby was one of the hardest things Elaine ever did. No. It was *the* hardest thing. The conversation started in the street outside the government offices, Mrs Dill just thirty yards away, feeding pigeons. For a moment, Elaine wondered if the woman was spying on her, but that was ridiculous. Why would Mrs Dill want to know the ins and outs of Elaine's sorry love life?

Bobby wanted to take her to the Savoy, where they could discuss it further. Or he wanted to talk about it back in his rooms.

'Let's get a cab to Belgravia,' he tried.

He didn't understand. There was nothing to discuss.

'You're *not* winning me back, Bobby,' she told him, eyes fixed to the ground.

But everything she said, everything he did, seemed to make him think he was.

He was incredulous; he was a man who had never lost with the ladies. That arrogance might have incensed her, *should have* incensed her, but mostly it endeared him to her even more. She tried not to look at him, but she couldn't resist: This was the face she loved more than any other in the world. She knew then with a sinking feeling that she always would. It was written in her heart.

He was tired though, too. He rubbed his eyes like he did after a poor night's sleep. He cupped his cheekbones in that way he had.

'Let's just go to bed together now and talk about all this tomorrow, darling.'

As if bed would work! As if they could resolve anything there. Typical of him, to want to just make-love it away.

'There's nothing more to talk about.'

'A hot bath?'

'We've over, Bobby.'

'Or the restaurant at the Savoy. We can see if they have any of your pork medallions.'

Even the way he said 'medallions' was adorable. He mustn't be adorable at this time, he mustn't. It was just a ruse to put her off what had to be done. Adore him less, that was her task and she wouldn't be swayed.

'For goodness' sake, Bobby.' Now she hesitated over the word 'Bobby'. Their private word. She should go back to calling him Robert Capa from now on, like everyone else did. Oh God, but that felt too painful a step; the words wouldn't come out of her mouth, they felt like something that didn't fit.

'But I'd do anything for you, Pink— Elaine.'

A part of him must have understood where this was going though, because he never usually called her Elaine.

'I don't want you to. I don't need you to.'

'Is this about Christmas? Last Christmas was wonderful. I understand how much it means to you now. I will try to always—'

'It's not about bloody Christmas.' Elaine nearly laughed in spite of her grief. This was so Bobby. She couldn't do this, though. She wanted nothing more than to have him embrace her, but it was too late, decisions had been made, she couldn't go back and forth, she couldn't. Indecision would only prolong the agony. Hold firm.

Self-denial is how the war will be won.

Please, Bobby. She wished he would just evaporate and take all her memories with him. Wipe out the last two years and she would be just fine. It would be better if he'd never existed.

'What is it then? P— Elaine? I deserve an answer.'

He did too. But he would know none of them made sense on their own. It was all the answers piled together that made it right.

He was staring at her and she could see he was floundering and she had a horrible image of him trying to stay alive off the coast of Normandy, thinking of her, his Pinky, among the five-foot waves and bodies, and gunfire, and everything that was trying to pull him down. *You kept me alive out there…*

She tied the belt of her coat and started to walk, but he followed her, he kept up with her, was next to her, dismay fierce in his eyes. She stopped outside Life Corp. and wished he would just let her be and go away inside. Merry and Faye would look after him, everyone would.

'I'll stay with you in London, sweetheart. Or we can move to the countryside.' Scratching his forehead, he was looking for solutions. 'You know, we don't have to open an agency. We don't have to do any of that. We'll go wherever you want to go. You can be whatever you want to be. I'll give up photography. I'll find something else. There's lots of things I can do.'

She shook her head. Suddenly, his tone changed. He narrowed his eyes at her.

'It's not Justin, is it?'

'No, it's not Justin.'

Something about the way she responded must have given him a whiff of something though, the scent of a trail. He always could sniff out a good story before anyone else: that was what made him so brilliant at his job. The intuition that there was more here than met the eye.

She paused. It was like he had trained his lens on her, like she was encircled, he was ready to shoot. She had been captured. *Oh, Bobby.*

Bobby recoiled suddenly. His expression hardened. 'It's not Justin, but it *is* someone else, am I right?'

'No…'

'*Who* is it?' He grew angry now.

'No one. There's no one else.'

She couldn't tell him, she couldn't. Marty would have to do it. She couldn't.

And he looked incredulous, shell-shocked, all over again. If it weren't so painful, she would have laughed at that expression. She thought he probably looked the way she did when Alan was coming out with one of his squirrel theories.

'Why, though? Why won't you stay with me? What has he got that I haven't? Pinky, sweetheart, tell me. I love you. What do you need me to do?'

With his pumped-up pigeon chest, his receding hairline, his bewildered expression, she felt she could have destroyed him then: *you strutting little emperor, you peacock, you goose, you really do think you're better than everyone else, don't you? Well, you're not, you're not, you're not.* But Elaine loved him then, loved him more in his befuddlement, in his loss, than she'd ever loved him before.

She loved Robert Capa. She loved him more than she loved Clive, Barbara or Alan, and *that's why* she had to say no. She was family-first. He was photos-first. It was as simple as that.

He had to go.

CHAPTER FORTY-SEVEN

SPAIN

JUNE 2016, DAY SEVEN

Paul knocks on the bedroom door and comes in with a black coffee for me, which is pleasant if a little disorientating. He sits on the end of my bed and smiles expectantly at me. This is *very* disorientating. I made him sleep in one of the many spare rooms last night. Thank goodness there are spare rooms here.

Paul is buttering me up because he wants to be back in my bed tonight. *Not yet.* My head is still all over the place. He's already been for a swim – says he had to avoid Barbara, who won't stick to her lane – and now he and Matthew are going for a bike ride. He is very courteous; he asks if I mind. This is a new Paul. Active, energetic, considerate.

I say I don't. It's fine. Great.

We are taking it easy and seeing where this thing goes, and trying again – no, not trying again, just letting it run its course. Paul has a lot still to give me, apparently, and I find myself saying I don't give up easily. Our language is of perseverance, persistence. *We are not snowflakes, Derek. We are sticklers. We are black ice.*

Paul says he is willing to offer me complete transparency. I stare at him, unsure what this means. I wonder if Sophie the counsellor is behind this. Of all the things we promised each other – love, honour, respect – transparency was never one of them. For some reason, I think of Nick's plastic folder with its easy love letters inside.

Looking puzzled, Paul tells me it means I can look at his phone any time. *Of course*. He places the phone down on my bedside table. 'There.'

I think to myself, *I'm not sure if I want to*. I think to myself, *he's been reading up on this*.

He says, 'You can have complete faith in me. I won't let you down.'

He asks me if I want to know his password. 'That's fine,' I say. It feels like I'm doing this all wrong.

Paul comes back from his bike ride sweaty and less careful than before. He bowls into my room without knocking, and asks if I want a sniff of his groin. Somehow I manage to resist this alluring invitation. I'm going to have to bite that particular bullet some time, but not here, not yet, and no.

I can't bring myself to think about that.

Idling by the pool, I let the sun at my body. I try not to think about Paul and my body, because every time I do, Eva is there. She has no wrinkles; she has no C-section apron tummy and I imagine she is up for it all the time. I can't think about the many times Paul lied to me: yes, the cliché, late-work/gym excuses, and the many times I fell for them. *It's nothing. It's only texts. I haven't met her. We're only friends. We only kissed.* Textbook stuff. There are a billion other painful things, but certainly he must win a prize for assholeness for the way he ridiculously brought home Pushkin without consulting me, then left me to take care of him. It's only a small thing, I know, but it feels illustrative. It feels symbolic. Maybe it is a big thing?

I can't think about it all though because I won't forgive him if I do, and I do want to forgive him. If I were a lizard, I'd forgive him. I'd probably just jump on him and live for the moment. That's the thing with lizards. I bet they've got shorter memories than goldfish.

I look at my phone and google Robert Capa again. I steam through the photos and stories. He is my hero. He had seen and done such a lot. A life well lived. Looking at his photos makes me want to take more of my own and I wish I hadn't returned Nick's camera. I'd love to take more pictures of Alyssia in the pool. One day, I decide, I will do an underwater shoot; I dream about underwater cameras and photographing legs kicking and dancers dancing in costumes. Maybe next year, I think. If I convince Gisela, Matthew wouldn't mind.

I am pleading with the gods of genetics. *Make it so, make Robert Capa my grandad.* It's not like I ask for much, I just could do with some good news. I need a sprinkling of special in my life, now more than ever.

When I go in the kitchen, Mum, Paul and Matthew suddenly hush, so I know they were talking about me – or at least talking about something they don't want me to know.

Mum quickly says, 'Isn't this fantastic?' about the boiling water tap. Matthew says, 'Oh, everyone's got one now. They're two a penny.'

'I haven't got one,' says Mum, smiling, like it's a big laugh. 'Have you, Paul?'

They are all still giggling though and it's not about the tap.

'What's going on?'

'You might as well tell her what you told me,' Matthew says to Paul.

'No!' says Mum coyly. 'Jen won't like it.'

'What?' I ask, predictably. We have played this game a million times before, and I am never the winner. 'What won't I like?'

Matthew sighs. He makes tea with the water from the hot tap. I stare at it distrustfully. Can it really be boiling at all times?

Then he says, 'Paul was thinking—'

'And you were thinking, Matthew,' says Mum quickly. She adjusts her sarong even though it needs no adjusting.

Matthew continues, 'We were *all* thinking… If Robert Capa really was Mum or Aunty Barbara's dad… well, then there's likely to be a claim.'

'A claim?'

Paul shakes his head at him, exasperated that he hasn't explained it properly.

'On his estate. He must have been a wealthy man when he died. And he didn't have any other children, so what happened to all the money?'

I stare at them both.

'Nick would have said if—'

'Nick doesn't know everything,' says Matthew cockily. 'Gisela thinks—'

'Gisela thinks what now?'

'I'm saying, it's just… he was a legend, for Christ's sake. He would have been super-rich. This could be life-changing. For all of us.'

I think, *how many hot taps does he need?*

'You can investigate,' I say, 'but I doubt anything will come of it. Plus, we don't know if they were his daughters yet, do we?'

I don't want anyone to know how important this has become to me.

'And I don't think I am,' Mum adds as though she is on my side.

'All I'm saying,' Matthew says, patting her elbow, 'is that it doesn't have to be such terrible news if you are, all right, Mum?'

'All right, darling.' She submits.

'It could be really good,' he goes on. 'For all of us.'

Mum nods slowly. 'I suppose so. And thank you, Paul. You've always been good at cheering me up too.'

Paul winks at me. And the wink very clearly says, *See, your mother still likes me even if you don't.*

CHAPTER FORTY-EIGHT

LONDON, MARCH 1945

A small bare room, the kind of room you walk into and know immediately there's something wrong with the design or look of it, but you're not entirely sure what it is. Its windows too small maybe or its lighting too fierce. The wallpaper too flocked, the carpet too sticky; but it's a place, a good place, and who worries about place, really, not really, during a war? You're too busy being pleased you're alive. Anything else is ungrateful.

There was a mahogany desk with an ink pad, the kind Elaine might once have thought was incredibly posh, a grandfather clock with a noisy tick backed into a corner and, on the registrar's table, there was a temporary ring in a cardboard box in tissue while Marty's mother's one – the one Elaine should wear for the rest of her life – was 'resized', which was a pleasant way of saying it wasn't big enough for Elaine's fat fingers.

If Annie wasn't pleased with Elaine's choice of groom, she was even less pleased at her choice of venue: Marylebone Town Hall.

'It's like a sausage factory there, Elaine. What's wrong with a pretty church?'

'We're neither of us religious,' explained Elaine patiently. 'As you know.'

'I thought you went to church?' Mrs Perry had persisted when she was told the news. 'Every Sunday. That's what you said.'

'Ah,' said Elaine, biting her lip. What could she say? 'It's Marty, you see. Marty is not religious.'

Annie wouldn't drop it either. 'Don't you want to do it somewhere a bit more out of the ordinary?'

But Elaine didn't. She just wanted it done. The paperwork was the thing, the commitment was the reason, not the song and dance around it all. What was wrong with ordinary?

She had in fact half-heartedly invited Alan to come and he was all set to, apparently, but at the last minute, someone from the asylum called to say he had a head cold and it would be too distressing for him to travel. Elaine couldn't say that she wasn't relieved. It would have been tricky getting him there, making sure he was happy, getting him home, and that was even with 'the fixer' at her side.

There was still no news from Clive. Elaine hadn't expected any; it was as though he had evaporated into the London smog, but she had hoped.

Mrs Marriot could have come but Elaine had decided she didn't want little Barbara there, and someone needed to take care of her. Mrs Marriot didn't mind – Barbara didn't make a fuss. Whatever Annie said, it was too weird to have a child at her own parents' wedding. And that's what Barbara was now – her daughter – and that's who they were now, above all else, her and Marty, they were Barbara's parents. And this was her marriage for richer, for poorer, for taking care of everyone, for having Marty take care of her. His wallet was deep, and his fingers, like the rest of him, were long.

Marty had brought another man from Life Corp. with him, Elaine vaguely recognised him as Nate Cooper, a sports editor. An American. He had fits, which was why he wasn't doing national service, but no one had ever seen them. He was going to be Marty's best man. When Marty told her, Elaine couldn't bring herself to reply.

Best man? Someone he'd known only ten minutes instead of his best friend of years and years?

How the registrar's assistant could talk! *Somebody gag this woman, please*, thought Elaine, as she fiddled with her hair. Annie had taken her to a hairdresser that morning and the girl had stuck in a thousand pins. Elaine felt sure pins would rain down on her for the next few months.

'It's non-stop,' the registrar's assistant continued. Very proud she was of her elevated status. 'Run off our feet. Everyone thinks they're about to drop dead and they want to get formalised, get their ends tied up.'

Annie nudged Elaine. 'Everyone wants to get their ends away, more like.'

The registrar's assistant laughed. 'I say we're like an emergency service here… The urgency! People don't understand that they have to post the banns before the wedding. Between you and me, I believe there are more than a few shotguns… if you understand my meaning.'

Everyone gazed at the fraying carpet, although just looking at it made Elaine's eyes itch. Elaine thought longingly of little Barbara tucked in her nook at the back of WHSmith bookstore, innocently kicking her toes or biting off her socks, while Mrs Marriot served up the day's news.

'Beg your pardon?' said Nate Cooper.

The woman flushed scarlet.

'Oh, I didn't mean… I'm not saying *this is* a shotgun wedding, of course. I'm sure *you're* not the type, Miss Parker…' Her voice trailed away.

But she had to dig again. 'And even if you were in trouble, it would be none of my business…'

'That's the first sensible thing you've said all day,' Annie said haughtily, reminding Elaine of the time she had seen Justin off in the rain. A small part of her wondered if Annie wouldn't see Marty off too.

*

Elaine stood at the sink in the Ladies gazing at her reflection over the shiny Armitage Shanks taps. She seemed to have aged exponentially in the last two weeks – was that possible? Tips of silver were sticking through the pinky blonde. Grey at twenty-two, what a thing! She wasn't 'in trouble', not in that way anyway.

She remembered Gerda Taro's mother saying, 'You are an exceptionally pretty girl,' and she had suggested it was because Elaine was so satisfied.

Well, she looked sick as a dog now, so what did that say?

A button shirt with lace detail, a tweed skirt she wore for work. Bobby used to admire the way it stretched across her bottom. *Don't think about Bobby.* Best shoes – Clive got them once from God knows where, probably stole them off some unlucky corpse, but those days were over now. Marty would see to that.

She could have been on her way to the office. She didn't want to wear the gloves Bobby had given her, so she had borrowed Annie's. Annie wanted to buy a new pair with her coupons, but Elaine had refused.

'What does it matter?' she had said hopelessly, and Annie had looked at her, concerned.

'That's not like you, Elaine.'

She didn't want to dirty Robert Capa's name. She didn't want to sully the man, saddle him with all of them, the misshapen, rubbish Parkers. And if Annie or any others, or her own conscience, sometimes said, 'No, treat him like an adult, give him the choice, he'll understand,' that was because they didn't know the half of it. Not a quarter.

She wasn't going to do that to the world-famous war photographer. Prize-winning photographer. A little baggage, fine. This was too much baggage. A lunatic brother, a colicky baby and a good-for-nothing girlfriend.

Elaine imagined a doodlebug falling on the bathroom of Marylebone Town Hall, finishing them all off. The noise, the silence, the smell. *Over. Make it over.*

*

When Elaine came out, they were all still gathered in the same spot in the hallway. They tried not to look as though they were waiting for her, but they were. The assistant registrar, Annie, Nate Cooper and the husband-to-be were all looking at their wristwatches. Was it possible that Marty seemed to want to be there even less than she did?

He smiled at her ruefully and said, 'Oh, I gave Mrs Marriot some extra milk coupons for the baby.'

Why are you telling me this now? she thought.

'Thank you.'

'What about photos?' the assistant registrar asked, more nervous since Annie had had her words.

Marty and Elaine looked at each other. Even the word 'photos' set off something uncomfortable inside her. *Robert Capa – war photographer.*

'I don't mind,' Marty said. He pulled at his watch strap.

'We're fine,' Elaine said, which meant, *no, no photos please*, and Marty smiled weakly into the old-cigarette-smoke air. She pretended that there was something about the bother of photos and not the fact that she knew she didn't want to be reminded of this moment now, never mind in five years' time.

Something about the place made her think of Myra Hess playing at the National Gallery and the queues there. She imagined Bobby storming in on the 'any reason these should not wed'. That's what often happened five pages from the end in Mrs Marriot's novels. That's what happened in the Hollywood films. The day was always saved. The phoenix would rise from the flames. Victory snatched from the jaws of defeat. Or was it defeat from the jaws of victory?

But that just wasn't Bobby. *You look like a woman who knows her own mind.*

Behind the noise, behind the label 'greatest war photographer of all time', Bobby had been a loving partner, a sensitive man, and Elaine knew she had hurt him very deeply.

*

If Elaine's voice was trembling throughout the vows, Marty's was even worse. Elaine couldn't help but wince each time he stuttered. She stared at his Adam's apple and dreaded what was to come. At the end, the registrar smiled, as relieved as anyone. 'I now pronounce you man and wife.' And it felt like a dream. It felt like it was happening to someone else and she was not really there.

She knew, just knew, that Annie would be pondering the words 'man and wife' – why not *man and woman* or *husband and wife* – and she determined not to meet her best friends' eyes, even though Annie was the only one she wanted to smile at.

'You may kiss the bride.'

Elaine could hear Annie whooping, but quietly, like a celebration in a library. It felt like it came from a long way away, another country, a country at peace maybe, even though Annie was only six steps from her at most. Then Marty kissed Elaine uncertainly, awkwardly – a bit how you'd expect strangers to kiss – and then he shook her hand. *Bank manager to new client.* It was their first kiss on the lips, she registered. It wasn't as bad as she had feared; she supposed that it was neutral. *It was Switzerland; and wasn't it true that they kept bank accounts for Nazis there?*

Then Annie and Nate Cooper were congratulating them and having to sign the book. And Annie dropped the pen and the pen rolled, and while she was still flapping under the desk, she explained she'd gone and booked the Savoy for afternoon tea, no ifs or buts.

'Not the Savoy!' Elaine was aghast. This was her and Bobby's place, for goodness' sake.

'It's all right, you're Mrs Marty Harding now,' said Annie, misunderstanding. She whispered, 'No one will know that you used to—'

Marty and Nate Cooper clearly thought it was a splendid idea too.

There were more surprises in store for her there. Myra, Felicity, Leon and Mrs Dill were waiting for them, all dressed up and lovely, and they had brought a two-tiered wedding cake. Elaine and Marty pretended to cut it, one hand each on the knife, but when Elaine suggested actually sharing it out – 'who's hungry?' – Myra explained sheepishly, 'Mum made it from cardboard, Elaine, sorry, but most of them are these days.'

Marty had booked a room for them upstairs so, that evening, they could drink and dance to their hearts' content. Elaine did the first dance not with Marty but with Nate Cooper, who was a keen mover, although Elaine worried that he might have one of his legendary fits. Not long after, the *Life* crowd did turn up after all. There were Faye and Merry with their knowing eyes, and kind picture editor, Mr Bell, and all the weasel-like journalists who knew about Clive and the photographs. She had thought she was blacklisted but she had forgotten how everyone loved a party and especially a black-market drink or two. And some of them were shy with her at first, like maybe being married had changed her from the girl they all joked with in the George to someone serious and stern. Or maybe it was because of who she had married. Marty – executive fixer at Life Corp. Who had a bad leg, rumoured to be his trophy from Passchendaele.

She knew they didn't approve of her behaviour. The dumping of Bobby was the elephant in the room. She knew they would all be gossiping about it, asking each other why.

Dancing to jazz and dancing to this and that.

'In the Mood', that's what he told me.

She could feel Marty, her husband, watching her.

'In the Mood', and when he told me.

There was a bowl of sweets on the counter. Elaine took another handful, and thought, *I must stop eating them or I am going to get very fat,* but that did not seem a bad idea. And anyway, the wedding cake had been made of cardboard. And that made her want to cry because it seemed to sum up the whole thing.

'In the Mood', my heart was skipping.

At just after midnight, Marty told Elaine it was time for them to go. She followed him upstairs; she deliberately didn't tell him about the lift where she and Bobby had kissed and kissed some more, because taking the stairs was fine, taking the four flights was delaying the inevitable. She was hoping and praying it wasn't a room she had been to with Bobby, and as Marty walked three steps in front of her, she took in his long, thin frame, and she thought, *well, so here I am, he is here, I will be safe here. These are safe hands, adult hands, and this is what I need, what we all need.*

The thought of little Barbara nearly made tears come to her eyes. And Alan. She scolded herself for a moment of forgetting him. From now on, Alan would be fine.

Afterwards, she didn't remember much about that first night at all. Marty took off his glasses and rested them on the bedside table. Each move he made seemed very deliberate and unnecessarily slow. She had a silly urge to grab them, to try them on and do the Groucho Marx impression that used to make Bobby roar with laughter. Marty didn't fold his clothes like she expected him to, he kind of wrangled his way out of them and somehow arrived with just his underpants on, next to her in bed. They had a lot to learn about each other, that was a given.

He liked her to say his name over and over again.

When he thought she was asleep, he stroked her hair and said, 'I can't believe you're mine.'

CHAPTER FORTY-NINE

SPAIN

JUNE 2016, DAY EIGHT

Nick and Stella arrive the next day as planned. I can see Nick would rather be anywhere but here. If I could have been anywhere but here I would have, but when I suggested going out for a bike ride, everyone was in uproar.

'You can't miss today!'

'It's the last bit of filming.'

'And the DNA results will be back today!'

We will find out if we are what some of us are hoping we are. And what some of us are hoping we are not.

As they arrive, I can see Paul trying to catch Matthew's eye and I would wager good money it is about how gorgeous Stella is.

All right, Paul, I think. *We get it.*

Nick kisses me on both cheeks and as he does so, he murmurs, 'I'm really pleased for you,' I think he's being sincere. 'I know how much you wanted this.'

'Umm,' I say. 'Thank you. That's very kind.'

We all gather round in the garden. Paul and Matthew are cracking funnies again. Mum is shaking her head indulgently. She says she has a headache and my disapproving gene says it's because she's hungover again. Derek speculates it's because she didn't eat much at lunch – it was undercooked pork chops – and maybe she's hungry.

And Paul says, 'Maybe you're a little *hungary* too.' Derek, Paul and Matthew roar with laughter. I get the feeling these jokes have been rehashed several times. Paul keeps putting his arm round me, and looking at me for approval, which is something he hasn't done for years.

Nick puts on his glasses and says, 'So I imagine you want your answers…'

Paul keeps moving his hand lower and lower down my back like he's searching for an on switch.

Matthew jumps up. 'You all go ahead,' he says, flapping, and I think, *why are you pretending to be disinterested now?*

Stella begins with her impressive posh accent. It's one of those voices designed to suppress opposition. She could claim the world was flat and you wouldn't think to question her. She pulls out a document.

'So, Barbara first…'

We wait.

'The test shows that you are not related to Robert Capa.'

My Aunty Barbara lets out a breath. 'That's right,' she says. 'That's what I expected.'

Matthew comes out with a cafetière and places it heavily in the centre of the glass table.

'What did I miss?' he asks.

'And the test is 100 per cent accurate?' asks my mother, shaking her head.

'Pretty much.'

'So, Elaine had the two of them on the go at the same time!' Derek shouts out from behind the barbecue, where he is flipping burgers already. *Who doesn't fancy a burger at 11 a.m.?* 'I knew it. Dirty stop-out.'

'Der-ek!' says Mum in a voice more severe than she usually uses with him. 'That's not nice.'

Alyssia looks up. 'Don't try and slut-shame Great-Grandma.'

Paul snorts. Matthew laughs. 'So, that rules out Aunty Barbara. But what about Mum?'

I don't know how long I've been holding my breath for. Nick looks up at me and I meet his eyes. I don't want to look away.

'Well...' Nick begins. 'That's not all—' He glances at my aunt.

Barbara nods at him. 'It's okay, Nick, I guessed it.'

'Wha-at?' I ask impatiently. 'What's going on?'

Barbara nods at me, then begins haltingly. 'Deep down, I knew that Mum didn't really want me. She wasn't that interested, you know. It was always Shirley this, Shirley that. Shirley is beautiful, Shirley is creative, Shirley is charming.'

Mum half-heartedly tries to protest 'Oh Bar—' but Barbara continues, gathering strength as she rolls on. 'I was just *Barbara, don't make a fuss.* I heard that so many times, I thought it was my actual surname.' She laughs, then looks at all of us seriously and repeats it: 'Barbara Don't-make-a-Fuss.'

'But still...' I say, confused.

'Jen,' she says, 'that's the thing. I don't think Robert Capa was my father and I don't think Elaine was my mother.'

Barbara explains that she had heard that one of Elaine's brothers had disappeared just a few weeks after she was born – so she dug a little deeper.

'Disappeared?' Mum says tightly, rubbing suncream into her arm. Priorities. 'You mean Missing in Action?'

Derek nods sympathetically. 'Did I tell you about my uncle who died in Malta?'

'It doesn't look like either of them saw much action, Shirley,' Barbara says slowly. 'I think one was mentally ill.'

'Mentally ill? From the war, you mean? Like shell shock?'

'Not quite. It was some kind of psychosis, I think – and the other was exempt from service because of a disability. He's the one who ran away.'

Nick and Stella exchange a look.

'Who told you all this?'

Barbara isn't one for being the centre of attention, but she doesn't hate it either. She fiddles with her bangles and waits until we are all listening carefully before she continues.

'Mum had a friend, Annie, who she stayed in touch with. She died a few years ago, but her husband, who was quite a bit a younger than her, is still around and he talked to me.'

She takes a deep breath. 'I think I was Mum's brother's child, but Mum took me on.'

No one says anything for a moment. My little lizard friend scuttles across the floor on some scratchy mission or another.

Nick unknots his hands. He rubs his forearms. He catches me looking, so I look away. Paul squeezes my thigh.

Finally, Nick says, 'I think you may be right, Barbara.'

For a while, we all just sit there in the sunshine, drinking in the information. My aunty refuses the offer of a handkerchief, a burger and a white wine spritzer. She says she is fine, okay, it isn't a shock, but it is something to hear it in black and white, as it were. After a few excruciating minutes have passed, I lean forward to Stella and nervously say, 'That only explains Aunty Barbara, what about Mum… Shirley?'

Stella looks around awkwardly. 'I was coming to that.'

Mum cranks her neck from side to side as if she doesn't care, but it only illustrates to me that she does. Matthew and Paul are listening intently again. I think of the pound signs in their minds. It occurs to me suddenly what a coincidence this timing was. Had Paul resurfaced just as I might inherit?

Paul runs his fingers down my spine, nuzzles my neck.

Surely not.

Before Stella can speak, Nick says quietly, 'What do you think, Barbara?'

'I think…' She looks over at me gently, and I feel embarrassed because *when did this become about me?* But I am desperate for it to be true.

No, not for the money.

But for me.

'…It's *highly* unlikely. Not unless your mum was incredibly overdue – he'd already left the country by early March, you see. So, Shirley was born late December and I'm virtually certain there was no crossover – he came back in June but that wouldn't – I mean, once she married Dad, Robert Capa left the country and as far as anyone knows, there was no further interaction between them at all… well, for several years anyway.'

Nick nods his head slowly. He addresses Mum.

'The test shows that you are not related to Robert Capa.'

Damn.

Nick looks me right in the eyes. Behind the glasses, his eyes are sympathetic.

'I'm sorry, Jen.'

'I see,' I say. My mum high-fives Derek and looks over at me, her eyes gleaming. 'There you go!' she says triumphantly. 'I'm as English as you! Probably more!' Matthew and Paul are laughing. I hear Matthew say, 'That's a tenner you owe me, Paul.'

'Shit,' Paul says, 'I really thought you were in with a chance.'

I nod. I will not show anyone how disappointed I am. I will not show that I suddenly feel like I've slid all the way down to the bottom of the snake. But then I have another thought: 'None of this explains *why* they split up – Nana and Robert Capa. What do you think happened there?'

Nick and Aunty Barbara look at each other. Again, he nods at her to go ahead.

Aunty Barbara says, 'I think he lost interest in her once she had to look after me.'

'That wasn't very nice,' I say. I suddenly feel tearful at the idea that Robert Capa lost interest in my nana just because she was looking after her brother's abandoned daughter. *What. A. Bastard.*

Nick is more hesitant. 'We don't know that for sure. *Personally*, I'd be surprised. For one, I don't think he even knew about her brother in the asylum. You've got to remember it was… it was a really bad thing in those days. And for another, I don't think she told him, certainly at first, that she was taking on Barbara. I think she kept a lot of secrets.'

Paul ignores him. 'Yeah, but by the sounds of it, Robert Capa could have had any woman in the world.'

'Well—'

'Why on earth would he hang around for her then?'

I stand up. I feel deflated. It's ridiculous but I had put a lot of hopes on this, ridiculous, stupid hopes. I wanted to feel important after several months of feeling like something on the bottom of a shoe, and now it wasn't to be. I know I shouldn't be this gutted, but I am, I am.

Matthew notices. He gets up, throws his arm round me, squeezes. 'Would have been nice, though, Jen, wouldn't it?'

Paul laughs. 'So, it was all a big fuss about nothing?'

'Well,' says Nick slowly, 'I think it was probably pretty amazing while it lasted.'

I think of the lunch Nick and I had together. Four hours – no, five in total. That afternoon I had felt happy and optimistic for the first time in months. I had felt special then. Was that just because I felt like Robert Capa's granddaughter?

'Yeah, but…' Paul is like a dog with a bone. 'It didn't last.'

'I think he loved her,' Nick says shortly. I can tell Nick doesn't like Paul. He picks up his perspex folder, where the copies of the love notes sit spilling their secrets here and there. *Transparency.*

'I think she broke it off with him. I think she didn't believe someone like him could love someone like her.'

Paul shrugs. 'She didn't trust him enough to tell him her truth then. She blew it.'

Nick looks weary.

'That doesn't detract from the fact that what Elaine and Robert Capa had was extraordinary; it really was quite a love story.'

Paul laughs. 'But it didn't last.' He repeats it again, chuckling to himself, but no one else is laughing.

CHAPTER FIFTY

LONDON, MAY 1945

Everyone was celebrating the end of the war, everyone except Annie.

Annie was in a rage about it.

'You can go back to looking after your family now,' she had been told by the kindly pen-pusher at the war office. 'The demobbed soldiers will come first. I'll give you six more months, then you're out.'

As Annie relayed this to Elaine, her voice was high and jolly, but she looked bereft.

'So, what *are* you going to do?'

'Look for another job, I expect,' she said. 'I'll be lucky to find a position. We were the reserve team, weren't we, all us women? However well we did, they want their bloody A-team back.'

'Not everyone will—'

'Oh, Elaine, I know it, you know it, men look after the men. Jobs for boys. You know that.'

One day, Annie asked if Elaine really was going to church every Sunday. Elaine told her about Alan. Annie went quiet. She couldn't understand why Elaine hadn't told her, so Elaine explained.

'To have one difficult brother may be regarded as a misfortune, to have two…'

Annie laughed. 'We've all got scandals and rogues in our families.'

'I bet Felicity, Myra or Mrs Dill don't.'

'They do, they just cover them up, same as you. They have just as difficult lives as you do – just in nicer surroundings.'

Elaine laughed, but Annie was suddenly serious.

'I do wish you'd told me. As if it would change how I feel about you.'

Elaine found this a huge comfort. She couldn't say anything, she would cry if she did.

'Was this… was this why you broke it off with Robert Capa? Was it part of the reason anyway?'

Elaine nodded and Annie squeezed her hand.

You couldn't avoid Bobby's celebration photographs. They were everywhere: on the seats on the train, the tables of the canteen and the George, even the bench where she and Annie used to go before the cinema. He must have done a deal with all the newspapers. He no longer worked only for *Life* magazine. Instead, he seemed to work for every media outlet in the country.

Mrs Marriot shouted the headlines out from the shop: 'Victory in Europe!'

There was something beautiful about them. Even if you had a grudge against the man – which Elaine didn't, how could she? Okay, even if you were trying to put him out of your head when he was there constantly, you would have to admit these were perfect: people grabbing each other in the streets. The relief, the glee on their faces. Children, who had only ever known war, larking around, now experiencing peace.

These would become world-famous photos. He would become not only the greatest war photographer but the greatest victory photographer of all time. Elaine knew it.

What a time! He made it look beautiful. Perhaps it really was. *He must be happy*, she thought. What a scoop! The whole paper rack at WHSmiths was through his eyes. Heck, the whole war was seen through his eyes. She remembered he'd told her once there were other photographers. You wouldn't believe it.

Tall, beautiful girls waving flags. One of them kissing into the camera, her eyes gazing provocatively towards the onlooker. A shock going through Elaine: *I bet he's sleeping with her.*

White-uniformed sailors clutched each other, soldiers with grins wider than their mouths. There were photos of politicians, there was Churchill waggling his cigar. *I told you so.* There were generals, there was a hospital director, there was a chief of staff. There was, *goodness me, was it really him?* the major whom Elaine had met in the office, the one with the beaver teeth.

The best ones, though, were of the ordinary people, the ones usually forgotten about: a boy delighted at his puppy, a woman shyly but delightedly waiting for her man to come home, a girl skipping through a field of corn. Robert Capa was a master at showing what freedom was.

'He came in,' said Annie the next time she saw Elaine.

'In?' She knew it was Bobby without asking. She just wasn't sure where.

'The War Rooms.' *Everyone* went to visit the War Rooms now.

'And… how did he seem?'

'Exuberant, elated, everything he ever is.'

No change there then.

'Did he ask after me?'

'Of course he did,' Annie said, but she didn't offer what he'd said and somehow Elaine felt it was no longer appropriate to ask. She put her hands on her stomach. She was growing bigger and bigger. Marty kept asking her if it was normal to get that fat.

Marty had been to tell Bobby soon after they were married. He refused to elaborate on what had happened between them, but his black eyes and smashed glasses spoke for themselves.

They were temporarily renting rooms in Clapham, in south London. It was a ghost land, half standing, half ruined. Marty wanted to get her and Barbara out of London as soon as possible; she wasn't sure why – hadn't she got through the Blitz? But Marty said just because. Elaine felt so tired recently she found herself agreeing to most things he said.

She took Alan the newspapers to show him the victory pictures and the triumphant headlines.

'We are a nation at peace,' she read aloud to him on a bench in the garden. 'After six years...'

He trembled and told her, 'It's not over yet, not by a long wrong.'

'It's long *run*,' she corrected him. 'And it is, Alan.'

'Don't believe it, Elaine,' he warned her darkly. 'Dark clouds are gathering.'

Alan was no happier in the private house they found for him than he had been at the institution. And it was deathly expensive. He was unsettled, he wet the bed, he cried. He missed his old bench, he said. Elaine returned him there, back to Dartford, one cold June afternoon, where they cuddled outside.

Which kind of blew apart some of Elaine's reasoning for this whole shebang. But still...

Marty had exactly the same routine every morning – a clockwork cuckoo, she called him. He leaned down, tickled Barbra's cheek, then tickled hers. 'Have a good day, girls.'

And now, a new baby waiting to be born. A little boy, Elaine hoped. She couldn't say why, but somehow she thought that having a little boy would be less painful. Not physically, but life-wise. She felt if she had a boy, they would just get on. It would be an uncomplicated kind of love. Boys love their mothers without question and she could do without questions.

One morning not long after the war had ended, when Elaine and Marty had been living together only two months or so, she didn't hear the door click shut, and she realised her clockwork cuckoo hadn't left the house.

She got up, frantically pulling her dressing gown cord over the growing bump, wondering, *what is it, what is it, is it bad news?* and saw him by the front door, staring down at a postcard that must have just that minute grazed the mat. She hadn't heard a thing. The baby was kicking nineteen to the dozen though, the baby must have felt something going on.

It was a picture of a flower. It was a black and white photo, but she knew the flower was pink.

Elaine didn't hesitate. She picked it up hungrily and turned it over. For those seconds, Marty wasn't there, the babies didn't exist, she was a million miles away. She would have recognised that writing anywhere. The slope to the right, the fat curve of the y.

All it said was:

There is absolutely no reason to get up in the mornings any more.

Marty took the card out of her fingers like she was feeble-minded or something, like she was Alan in Dartford. A brief glance and he knew all he needed to know. He screwed it up and dumped it in the kitchen bin with the chicken carcass and yesterday's dinner. Then he put the bins out for the rubbish collection, even though it wasn't until later that week, just in case.

CHAPTER FIFTY-ONE

SPAIN

JUNE 2016, DAY NINE

We have got to the gardens of the Alhambra, in Granada, finally. That place on Aunty Barbara's bucket list sandwiched between 'Watch the Northern Lights' and 'Sunrise at Machu Picchu'. Matthew drove us down to the station and between us, with our remedial Spanish, we managed to book tickets.

We don't have time to see the inside of the palace, but the outside is more than enough for us; it is overwhelmingly beautiful. Aunty Barbara wanders around in a kind of ecstatic daze, glorious old hippy that she is. She says she doesn't mind me going off to take some photos because she can 'feel it better on her own'.

I kneel down and take photos of flowers on my phone. I rearrange and fiddle with the light options and this leaf here, and that one there.

'If your pictures aren't good enough, it's because you aren't close enough.'

I take some photos of tourists too: I like doing studies of people; that group following the leader with the yellow umbrella, that one waving the handkerchief and everyone wearing earpieces. There are some teenagers too, from England, backpackers full of energy, and they make me miss Harry. We've never been apart as long as this. One day, I'd love to come here with him.

Aunty Barbara and I find a seat and spread ourselves out. We are perfectly satisfied with our lot and enjoying that buzz of experiencing *a successful day out.*

'I do remember meeting Robert Capa once actually…' Barbara says to me.

'That time he took the photo?'

She nods.

'Just fragments really, it's hard to know if it's real or imagined now, but yes, he was a very nice man. Warm. Fun. I remember he let me hold his camera and he ruffled my hair. He called Mum "Pinky" and she got all embarrassed and told him not to. She smiled a lot when he was there. I had never seen her so animated. She didn't call him Robert Capa though, you see, she called him Bobby.'

We stretch out our legs, with our matching sandals – and matching blisters.

'Dad…' She looks at me – 'I mean, Martin, was all right,' she says. 'He was decent enough. He was generous with us all, and very patient. I wrote him a poem once, "Dear Daddy", and was thrilled when he put it in a frame in his office. He was very respectful of Mum, especially in their later years. He wouldn't hear a word against her. I would have loved to have met Clive though… and Nora, of course. What a terrible shame.'

I am reminded that it is my dear aunty who has had the biggest shock this week. She is the one whose world has been swept away from her, whose history has been rewritten, but strangely, she is the one who seems the most level-headed about it.

'Are you really okay about it all?' I ask. The question is too small, but it's a start. I want her to know I care.

'Never better,' she says. 'I always felt I was the outsider in the family, but I sometimes felt a bit stupid for feeling that. Now I know I really was. It wasn't me being paranoid.' She smiles at me, my lovely thoughtful aunt. 'I feel so sad for my…' She pauses. 'Birth mother – and for my father too, but it is what it is. It was a terrible time, Jen, people forget how terrible it was. They romanticise those days but people didn't have choices, especially poorer people. Things are so much better now. Mum – Elaine – did the best she could, and she and Dad did love me very much in their way.'

She takes my hand and I squeeze hers, here in the sunshine.

'I've got Nelson now. And you and Matthew. And your mum. You are all very important to me. You know, I've got a family, and that's fine.'

Before our day out at the gardens, Paul had been pestering me. 'We have to have sex again,' he kept saying. 'Reconciliation,' he called it, only half-jokingly. 'Forgive and forget.'

Actually, I agreed with him. You have to forgive and forget, or you can't move on. This was obvious, this was fact. If you want to heal divisions, then you have to ignore that one of you wanted the division, and the other, well, the other one didn't. If you keep harping on about that, then you're stuck in a loop and that's no good for anyone. Grudges kill relationships, not quickly, but eventually. Grudges could be worse for a relationship than the initial wrong.

That was all very well in theory, I thought, but my body was crying out no. Worse, my disobedient mind kept referring me back to Nick's forearms and his shy, kind eyes, the long lunch we had together, the way he listened when I told him about my life and the way he encouraged me.

I knew that probably, just a few days previously, I would have leapt at the chance to have Paul by my side, *on* my side again. But he had hurt me and betrayed me, and I found I couldn't forgive him.

A better person might have done. But I wasn't a better person. And actually, I was realising, it *wasn't* about being better. I was slowly starting to understand that staying with Paul could be the most damaging decision of my life. (And it wasn't like there weren't plenty of damaging decisions to choose from.)

After Nick and Stella left on that afternoon of revelations, Paul kept crowing about my nana and Robert Capa. It was almost like he was gloating.

'All this fuss over nothing,' he kept saying, 'they didn't get married, they didn't have children…' and then, when we were in the bedroom that evening, and he was begging for 'reconciliation', he said something else that made me shudder.

'You thought there was going to be money in it, didn't you, Jen?'

I was shocked. 'No,' I said. 'It honestly didn't occur to me until you said so.'

He shrugged. 'Matthew did. He thought so all along. He told me on the phone before I came out here.'

'Did he? And is that why you came?'

He laughed. He was lying on my bed, his arms behind his head, confident in his shark trunks. 'Every little bit helps.'

I just blew up. I was a hot tap of rage. And an understanding seemed to come over me all at once, like a downpour, clouds opening, or perhaps the way some people have a spiritual awakening: this – Paul – was not what I wanted, and really, didn't *I* get to have a say here? In my own life story? Was that too much to ask?

And I suddenly knew that it was lack of confidence that was leaving me here, letting this man into my bedroom. And I should know better than that. My poor Nana Elaine didn't have confidence. She was beautiful and brave, but she didn't know it, she didn't think it, so when she found love with Robert Capa, she never could quite believe it. She felt she didn't deserve it. She didn't understand her own worth. Instead, she married another man because she felt that she wasn't the equal of the man she adored and who adored her.

This made sense to me, and I knew there was a lot I could learn from that, and the number one thing was that I wasn't going to make the same mistake.

*

When I told Paul to go, now, get out, he thought I was joking at first. He resisted, naturally. He said I was being over the top, melodramatic, hysterical, ridiculous. He refused to leave me alone. He tried being seductive. If I would only have sex with him, everything would be all right, I would fall back in love with him again. That's what I *needed*, see? He tried being sad. He tried being angry.

I stormed off. I went to look for Matthew first but I couldn't find him and instead came across Derek cleaning the barbecue.

'Please help me get rid of Paul. *Now.*' Derek was spurred into action immediately and told Paul, if somewhat apologetically, that he wasn't welcome in the house any more. (This was brilliant of Derek and something I would be grateful about for a long time.)

Unfortunately, both Derek and my mother were half-tanked as usual, so although they offered to take Paul somewhere, anywhere, I rapidly had to back down and insist they couldn't. I wasn't having *that* on my conscience again. In the confusion, Paul thought I had changed my mind about everything and that I did want him to stay. Derek had to spell it out to him again.

'She doesn't want you, mate. Get it?'

Matthew eventually returned, wet and sticky from a bike ride, and was recruited to drive Paul to the airport.

'You don't mind?' I whispered.

'If that's what you want, Jen, that's what we're doing,' he said, squeezing my hand.

Paul was furious. He didn't see why he had to go tonight. 'What's the hurry, babe? Harry will be upset!'

At the mention of Harry I wavered and almost gave in, but this time Matthew held the line. He grabbed Paul's bag. 'Stop messing my sister around, yeah? She deserves better than that.'

Of course, Mum had to give Paul a huge hug at the door: 'If you ever need anything, *anything*, you must get in touch. You'll always be family,' but we don't need to talk about that.

*

Now Barbara wants to take cuttings of some of the plants in the Alhambra gardens. I think Mum's right on one thing: sometimes Aunty Barbara really does have strange ideas. She has smuggled in some shiny scissors in her bag. I tell her *no, no way*! 'Are you joking, Aunty Barbara?' She makes a harrumphing noise.

We sit, admiring the plants and watching the people admiring the plants.

I take more photos on my phone. Aunty Barbara doesn't mind me photographing her. I take one in profile and one of her standing from behind, and I hold my breath because she looks so beautiful. You can somehow see the little girl in the photograph in her even now. It's in the rod straightness of her back, or the way she holds her neck, or *something*.

The camera on my phone is not like Nick's fabulous camera, of course, but the pictures aren't bad. I get some beautiful ones of the plants and trees. Still-life isn't my natural province, but these are too good to be true. I take close-ups of the flowers: *get closer*, I remember. It feels a little impolite to the flowers, which are of course beautiful, however you look at them, but I do love how the closer you get, the more they look like something else entirely.

I take some shots of a speckled butterfly and one of a wasp on a leaf. *When I get back to Matthew's*, I decide, *I'll get down on my knees and finally get those shots of my lizard friend*. I wander back over to Barbara, who has made friends with a man and his daughter from Germany and a woman from Japan. Barbara loves talking to people and they love talking to her.

When they've finally gone, in a flurry of exchanging of numbers and email addresses, and we're talking about the next few days, I admit, 'I struggle with Mum sometimes.'

Aunty Barbara nods. She knows. 'You should talk to her.'

'What can I say?' I'm thinking, *what can she say?* I doubt *anything* she ever says will do me any good.

'You've got to understand that's the way we were brought up. Nana did the best she could for us, but sometimes she didn't get it right. And it's the same with your mum.'

I resolve to try to speak to Mum alone as soon as possible. I don't know if she's trying not to be alone on purpose, but Derek is certainly sticking to her like flies to sticky paper. If she's not sunning herself on the loungers, she's 'cooling off' with Derek in her room.

'La la la,' as Matthew would say.

Too much information.

CHAPTER FIFTY-TWO

LONDON, DECEMBER 1945–AUGUST 1947

Annie was living in marital bliss with a man she met at the George on VE Day. His name was George – a fact Elaine and Annie would never not find funny. Of all the names in the world! Fancy meeting a George in the George! A serious man with a bit of gorilla about him, George seemed much older than he was – maybe that was the fault of the war. Elaine was shocked when she found out he was only twenty-seven, a whole ten years Annie's junior. Although she knew couples with large age gaps – she and Marty, for example – she didn't know any that were *that* way round.

Shirley and Barbara were good babies, and so alike that no one knew – or at least no one said they knew – about their parentage. Shirley's eyes and eyebrows were a little blonder than Barbara's and her temperament was a strange mix of both recklessness and docility. She got on with almost everyone.

And Shirley turned out to be a daddy's girl, whereas Barbara never much took to Marty. It was a private funny that, because no one knew they had different fathers. Annie once asked about Shirley, after the baby came early. Elaine was sitting in the hospital ward, smoking, and Annie came in with a baby sleepsuit and a cardigan.

'She's got Bobby's smile.' It was a question without a question mark.

'I wish,' Elaine responded softly. And Annie looked at her with such sympathy – if Elaine were anyone else she knew she would have cried.

But it was good she didn't because Marty came in then, tray in hand, playing the attentive new father. These days, he never left Annie and Elaine alone for long if he could help it. Maybe he thought Annie was a bad influence. He'd got Elaine some honey, blagged it from the ward sister – swapped it for some cigarettes.

'Oh, Elaine,' said Annie. 'No more. You'll lose your teeth.'

Elaine wouldn't normally let anyone talk to her like that, but this was her best friend.

She shrugged. *Teeth, schmeeth.*

She had been alive, truly alive, for two years. She figured it was far more than most people get.

On Sundays, Elaine still took the train to see Alan, without fail. Packed lunch. Spam in a tin. Plum in a handkerchief. Warm days, they'd let them sit out in the garden. It was nice to get away from the staff. Alan wasn't over-keen on any of them. Elaine wondered if they should try yet another place.

'He thinks we're all Nazis,' the nurse told Elaine in her South African accent – which, Elaine privately thought, probably didn't help one bit.

'Alan was in the army,' Elaine said. And to labour the point, she took out a photo she had of Private Parker looking younger, slimmer and almost handsome in uniform. Sometimes she wanted to pin his early letters, including his sweet postcards, onto the end of the bed just so the cynical doctors and nurses knew what they were dealing with. This wasn't a commonplace lunatic – this was a loved brother, a loved son lunatic.

Be gentle with him, she begged the efficient nurses with her eyes. But she knew she was less pretty than she used to be, and her wide eyes no longer worked so efficiently. *He's my brother, he's very dear to me.*

To be honest, the best thing about the visits was the time spent away from Marty and the girls. That and the occasional boiled sweets she allowed herself on the way home.

*

Marty came home from work one evening and for once his good mood filled the whole of downstairs. He hummed show tunes and threw the girls up in the air until they squealed, and Elaine insisted he had to stop. Why did he have to wind them up just before bedtime? He pronounced her kipper supper the best fish he'd tasted all year. He pressed his glasses to the bridge of his nose and beamed around him. She couldn't work out what it was. *A promotion? A mistress?*

He managed to keep it to himself all evening, although he must have been bursting with it. He told her as she was applying cold cream to her face in the dressing table mirror.

'Everyone's talking about Robert Capa at work.'

Elaine drew in her breath. Moisture slip-sliding on her nose and cheeks. Circle, circle. The magazines said always use an upwards motion or you drag your face down (and you cannot be having that).

'What's he done?'

Don't let him be dead. Don't let him be…

'He's only going out with a film star.'

Gulp. 'Who is she?'

'Ingrid Bergman.'

'I don't know her,' Elaine lied. Of course she did, *everyone* knew her. She was beautiful, with that sensuous Swedish face. Those sultry lips. And that exotic accent. She and Annie had watched her in *Gaslight*. Clive had had a crush on her; almost everyone did.

'Typical Capa, eh? He always loved foreign tail and the high life.'

Elaine was sitting in the cinema when she should have been doing housework. She felt like she was playing truant with Clive and Alan down by the common, flicking sticks at each other, like they had when they were children. Marty wouldn't have liked this. He didn't like her taking time off. He didn't do the allotment or golf, so why should she? Anyway, who needed hobbies when one could spend one's time disapproving of basically everything she did? That was the groove they found themselves in and it was hard to change. In bed, Marty was more passionate than she had expected, driven and concerned that she 'enjoyed herself'. Only once did he say, 'Did you do that with Robert Capa too?' but before she answered – *was she really going to answer?* – he had pushed his fists into his eyes and said, 'No, don't tell me, don't.'

Elaine parcelled lumps of sugar candy into her mouth like there was no tomorrow. It helped keep the complicated things inside her down. *Push them to the bottom.* It was like keeping the monster in there happy, imprisoning it. Feeding it. *Don't let it out, don't let it up. Keep on pressing it away.*

She and Bobby had only been to the cinema once in all their days together: *Destination Tokyo* starred Cary Grant and she had been more into Bobby than the film. Bobby was always too much of a glorious distraction. Who would concentrate on anything else when he was there? Hands everywhere, whispering in the darkness; the flickering of the screen was like an aphrodisiac.

It was painful to watch Ingrid Bergman now. *Notorious* also starred Cary Grant, but this time Elaine had eyes only for Bergman. She was at ease, effortlessly in control, irresistible. *Did she look at Bobby like that too?*

Bobby wouldn't have been happy with suburban, domestic little her, would he? Visiting one brother every Sunday, bringing up another brother's child every single day. It was too much baggage for a free-spirited man like him. A man whose vocation – no, mission – was to reveal to the world what was going on. Whose faith was to show the dark underbelly of life. While she, she brought nothing to the picnic: crumbling teeth, chubby, no money, no education. All she was good at was typing fast and keeping on smiling through it.

He deserved revolutionaries in white breeches or the glamour and glitz of award-winning actresses, not a girl from south London with an unwanted baby, a lunatic brother and a runaway father.

The sweets were delicious and no, she didn't care any more about her figure or her teeth.

She had done one right thing at least. A good thing. He was her gift to mankind. She might not have done anything herself, but at least she hadn't trapped him. She had let him go. And as long as he kept on taking his photographs, as long as he provided a face for those forgotten or suffering, and a window for the privileged, then she had made the right decision.

As soon as the lights were down, she hurried home to Shirley and Barbara. When she had time away from them, she found herself craving to get back to them. It was quite the oddest sensation.

About one year later, another message – this time from the new state of Israel. A spanking white envelope with strange biblical stamp.

This time, Elaine was wise to the wicked. She snatched up the envelope before Marty could see it, would ever see it, and stuffed it in her dressing gown pocket – *send thanks to the god of big pockets* – and waited until he left for work.

It was a photo of her alongside Ernest's bottom. She is tugging at his hospital gown and laughing fit to burst. It was taken the night of Ernest's party when they were messing around in his hospital room, drunkards, the lot of them. She remembered Marty came in and told them all off. She remembered vividly the expression on his face. 'You're all children…' he had said, leading them out. She remembered looking at him and thinking, 'toad.' How she had resisted leaving poor Ernest there, and how Bobby had calmed her down: 'Don't take it out on old Marty. He only wants the best for us.'

She examined the print in her hands. Hard not to laugh. Hard not to cry. Only two years had passed since it was taken, yet she hardly recognised herself. In the picture, she was silly and obnoxious. That was the night Ernest had been paying her all those compliments. They'd probably gone to her head. Bright-eyed and bushy-tailed. It was black and white, of course, but you could see she was golden. She was a woman who was going places and who knew it too.

She was, without knowing it, having the time of her life.

It was one of the very few pictures Bobby ever took of her. She hadn't noticed it at the time, but now she wished he had taken more – and she wondered why he hadn't. He said it was because photography was his work and she was his pleasure, he said it was because he would never forget her face, but even so… Why was there so little evidence of their time together? Maybe it was deliberate. Maybe he knew it wasn't going to last all along…

This time, there were no words.

Marty had his heart set on Basildon new town in Essex, thirty miles outside of London, and three years after the war, the four of them moved into a nice semi-detached house in the Pitsea area. It was a good location; it was only two trains to visit Alan. It was awkward for Marty's work, but he didn't mind travelling to town, he said, and he could always stay up there if it got too late or if the trains weren't running.

Elaine had her own washing machine and for their housewarming, Marty got her a toaster. He was very conscientious about presents. That was another one of his peculiarities. Whatever the issue, he made it up to her with white goods.

One difficult thing: in Pitsea, their next-door neighbours were snobs. Elaine knew it instantly. Could see it in their faces, those tight nostrils, and in the lace curtains. Goodness knows what they thought made them so special. They made Mrs Perry look affectionate. Mr and Mrs Oldham were their names; car-washing and disapproval were their hobbies. Elaine tried her best with them, but there was only so far you could go. It made her chuckle to think how disapproving Mr and Mrs Oldham would be if they knew the truth about Barbara's parentage.

Marty was arranging and organising here, there and everywhere. Taking care of this, sorting out that. He was untouchable, unknowable. Every evening when he came home, leather briefcase in hand, she stretched to the very tips of her toes to kiss his cool, flat cheek. She joked that she could have done with a stepladder and then blushed. They got on better than she had imagined. She didn't mind him coming home most days, although it was a good evening when he stayed up in town for work. She even missed him when he was away for long periods.

Every evening, he took himself and his briefcase upstairs – in all the years they would spend together, she would never get to see inside that briefcase and its contents would attain almost mythological mystery. Then he lay in the bath. He needed an hour or two on his own to unwind. That's what happens when you're tall – there's a lot of you to unwind.

CHAPTER FIFTY-THREE

SPAIN

JUNE 2016, DAY TEN

Late Thursday afternoon, Derek has taken too much sun and trundles off for a lie-down. He tells Mum she doesn't need to come inside. He'll be dandy. Barbara is reading the paper in her favourite spot in the corner of the garden and Alyssia is watching TV. Matthew is in his study, probably calling Gisela. For the first time, I have a chance to get Mum on her own and I grab the opportunity with both hands. My heart is beating fast. I feel like I'm on a plane with turbulence again, only this is worse. I plunge in.

'Mum, I was so hurt that you didn't come to see me in England when Paul first left me.'

Straight away, my mum is on the defensive. I can't see what her eyes are doing behind the big black frames of her sunglasses – I don't even know if she's paying attention to me.

'Were you?' she says. She twists her wedding ring round her finger. Her shades face anywhere but me.

I give her time to say more, but she doesn't. The sun has mooched off over the hills for the night, leaving the sky patchy pink and purple. My goosepimples are up. Matthew comes out and starts to deflate Alyssia's chair the other side of the pool. It slowly flops into a new shape. From here its armrests look like tentacles.

Funny how just a bit of air was powerful enough to keep it afloat.

'Why didn't you?'

'I suppose…'

'Yes?'

'I suppose I didn't think I could help very much. I'm not good at emotional stuff.'

'You are good, you're my mum.'

'And Derek and Matthew didn't want me to go, so…'

'Okay.'

Blame someone else.

But what I want to say is that it wasn't just about that one time with Paul – it's always been like that – it's always putting Matthew first, always serving his needs, always putting me in second place. But I can't find the words. Mum's twisting is getting faster and faster. It's as though she's trying to shut me up with all that twisting, keeping the lid on.

The other side of the pool, Matthew has got out the long pool-cleaning net. Elaborately, he tries to reach the beach balls on the water, but they bob away from him like they are having a joke at his expense.

Mum yells out, 'Don't fall in, darling,' to him. Even though he's nowhere near the edge, she is still worried about him. Even though I'm here, begging for reassurance, she is not looking at me.

He laughs, shakes his head. Raises his eyebrows at me.

He wields the net around.

The evening is quiet without Derek and although it's probably wrong to wish someone away, I must admit I do. Things would have been so much easier between us without Derek. It's not that he's a bad man, it's just he changed the dynamic between us for the worse and I think even Mum knows that.

Mum taps my knee with her fan. 'Take it,' she says.

'No, thanks.'

'It's yours.' She presses it into my hands before adding, 'It's not worth much, but I want you to have it.'

I try again. 'I feel like everything is swept under the carpet with us…'

Mum takes off her sunglasses, places them on the floor and stares directly at me. She has very blue eyes, swimming-pool blue, and she makes me nervous.

'What do you want to do with the dirt? Get up and sing to it?'

I feel tired and regretful that I've started this – *she will never understand* – but I have started it now. I can't turn back. 'Just… it would be good to acknowledge we have issues.'

'I do acknowledge them,' she says tightly. 'Who says I don't?'

I feel profoundly unsatisfied. I feel… *How can you even argue with someone if they don't know what you feel?* If they don't *want* to know. I feel like she's just slapped a 'police aware' sign on the wreck of our relationship. Well, she's going to have to deal with it now.

'I'm annoyed that you've always put Matthew first.'

She doesn't respond. She lies back in her chair with her eyes closed and I'm not sure if she even heard.

I separate the fan's ends and the dancer opens out in front of me, her arms and legs outstretched. Perfectly content – dancing through life, taking every opportunity that comes her way. *Que sera, sera.*

Suddenly Mum grabs my hand. 'I didn't know how to love you like you want me to. You were always so strong. Independent. Fierce even.'

I swallow. I wonder if she is criticising me again but she doesn't seem to be.

'And then Derek needed me so much and Matthew, and it was easier to just do things for them, I suppose. Matthew would ask me outright, tell me what to do – with you, it was always…' Her voice trails away. I'm swallowing back her words like a fine wine.

She can't stop there.

'I'm always what, Mum?'

'You look like a fisherman there, Matthew!' she calls out gaily.

'I am, Captain Birdseye!' he laughs back.

She coughs. I'm desperate for her to go on. It's like the words have to be squeezed out of her. 'I don't know, I just have always struggled with getting it right with you. You've always been so self-contained.'

I feel choked with tears. 'It's because I've had to be.'

'Guarded, I suppose. That's the word. Defensive.' I let her go on even though it hurts. 'Matthew was just so easy, whereas you were so capable.' She pauses. 'You so remind me of my mum.'

'Really?'

'Oh yes. Even Nana Elaine thought so. She used to say you were a chip off the old block.'

I smile. 'Did she?' It's the first time I've been told that I take after my nana. It feels good.

'And you were the responsible one. You just got on with things. Maybe I stopped trying hard enough with you. I should have tried more, Jen. I'm so proud of you. I'm sorry I let you down, Jen. Really I am.'

And it is like a spell. Her words are the aftersun I need. Her awkwardly netted apology means the world to me. I feel acknowledged even if I know this conversation will never be on the table again. I will always have this, whatever it is.

Tears prickle my eyes.

'Now, now,' she says. 'I didn't want to make you cry. We're better than that, Jen.'

I think of all the times she has, without knowing it, made me cry, but I don't say that. I think if Derek knew I was crying, he would mock me or snowflake me, or tell me what a let-down my generation were. But my mum isn't mocking me. She is being kind now and this is what I need. We both stare over to where Matthew has unfastened the beach balls and is squeezing them flat, a great look of satisfaction on his face.

'Thank you, Mum. I love you.'

I know she's doing her best. She looks surprised but for the first time in a very long while, she manages to get the words out: 'I love you too, Jennifer. Really I do. I should show it more, shouldn't I?'

CHAPTER FIFTY-FOUR

NORFOLK, APRIL 1950

'We'll stay with Annie in Norfolk.' Elaine went over the plan three, four times with Marty. 'She's been asking us to stay for ages.'

It was not a complete lie. Annie *was* living in Norfolk. Her George worked as a caretaker at a local school. Annie was working in the National Health Service. She was the only woman in her department, and she liked that.

And Annie *had* been asking them to stay for ages.

But Marty narrowed his eyes at Elaine. He was always alert and suspicious. He always knew who was twitching the nets the other side of the road.

'Why now, though?'

'It's the holidays, Marty. It'll be good for the kids – change of scene...'

Change of scene. Change of cast.

They took the train to London, then one to Norwich and then another. The girls played gin rummy with a pack of cards that was missing a four, they counted cows and sheep out the window and Shirley combed her hair. Barbara's was too long and she wouldn't get it cut. Elaine thought of Alan and the way his hair now gave him three or four extra inches. Once, when she didn't realise Elaine was in the room, a nurse there called him a nickname: Professor Einstein, and she wasn't far wrong.

Shirley wanted to adopt a cat and she set to persuading Elaine of the viability of keeping one as a pet.

'It's not happening,' said Elaine. She remembered Bettie Page and how, just after she had married Marty, she had disappeared. Elaine stuck up notices on trees and lamp-posts. 'Please look in your sheds,' they had said. 'Much-loved cat missing.' Not a single person replied. It was probably a car accident. Or worse, she was trapped somewhere, waiting for Elaine to rescue her, wondering what on earth she'd done wrong.

Elaine shivered.

'I'll do anything, Mumma, please.'

Now Elaine scowled. The conversation wasn't funny. The child was exasperating. The last thing she needed was another responsibility. *Did she look like she needed more mouths to feed, to get up for in the morning, to clothe, to house?*

Okay, so you don't have to clothe a cat but still.

She found Shirley's repeated requests – not just for a cat, for things, for *all* the things – annoying. She seemed to move from one want to another. *Why aren't we enough for you?* Elaine wanted to say. *You are MORE than enough for me.*

Barbara was less trouble overtly, but she could be sneaky and worse, she could be sly. You had to watch her. Especially in shops. She'd go up to the counter at WHSmith with her pennies in her outstretched hand for her and Shirley's *Beano* magazine, innocent as you like. Then, two streets later, Elaine would find a brand-new Enid Blyton storybook stuffed in the bottom of her bag.

'I told you, we go to the library for books!'

Barbara would have to return it, shamefaced, scarlet hot, but that didn't stop her trying again and again.

One time, Elaine whacked Barbara about the legs with *The Mystery of the Burnt Cottage*. Her calves did go red, but it couldn't have hurt that much, and of course Barbara had to shriek like she was being murdered, and Shirley had to join in too, because she must have felt left out or something.

Barbara wailed, 'But I wanted it, Mummy!'

In her fury, 'You're just like your bloody father!' had popped out of Elaine's mouth and she had regretted that and got even more angry with Barbara for making her say such nasty things.

'I just want something nice,' howled Barbara as Elaine dragged her along the street back to the humiliation of the bookshop counter. 'Something of my own.'

Barbara was good at school though. She once wrote a poem called 'My Mummy' and Elaine talked to the other mums about it. Was it something they had all been told to do at school?

No, they hadn't.

Shirley liked art and making things. She took everything very literally. You only had to say: 'There's a thing with your name on it,' to her and she thought she owned everything.

The girls weren't interested in the war; why would they be? But as they grew older, and once Marty got them the TV, they watched the black and white films and Elaine told them of the bravery of the soldiers. She didn't *exactly* tell them that her brothers were soldiers, but she may have suggested it, yes. Just for something positive for them to tell the children at school. Everyone else had heroic uncles and grandparents, so why shouldn't they?

Elaine didn't tell them about the Blitz, the near misses or the deprivation, or the doodlebugs, or any of the horrors she experienced. But then she also didn't tell them about her work with smuggled letters, the sadness of it or her one successful find. Even Marty didn't know about that, and Marty made it his bloomin' business to know about everything.

No one talked much about the dead. What good would it do? Everyone talked about the ones who came home with the medals, and the ones who came home didn't talk at all.

The war she told her girls about was intended to make them feel very proud and warm inside. It was a morality tale: the good guys won because they were right. They were persistent and they worked hard with team spirit. Here lay life lessons better than the Bible – which, after all, could get it so wrong sometimes. And it worked on her children. They both behaved well. Barbara took it upon herself to learn the dates of the major battles, which Marty encouraged and found endearing. Shirley liked waving her collection of flags – she was always more interested in learning about empire. When a little dark-skinned boy moved in three doors up (*can you imagine how much the curtains twitched?*), Shirley helpfully told him that, if he liked, they could play slaves and owners.

When she heard about that, Elaine had visited the boy's parents and explained that Shirley had got the wrong end of the stick. She thought of Robert Capa then. Him talking about fascism and hate. She felt tired when she thought of him though, tired and lost, like when you've been on a long journey then find out you've been going in the wrong direction the whole time.

Did she manage to smooth it over with the dark-skinned boy's family? Probably not, although she did come home clutching a tandoori chicken, a plate of dhal and two naans hot from their oven.

The teachers said that Barbara might try for the grammar school. This didn't seem fair on Shirley, who 'showed no signs of aptitude,' so to avoid the trouble, Elaine didn't let Barbara sit the test. She thought they would both be good at typing though. Perhaps they might get jobs at a local branch of the bank?

On their way to Norfolk, they walked up and down to the buffet car. She let them have black coffee. She and Marty were always arguing about coffee. She and Marty could argue about anything. They played a game where you draw a head, fold the paper, pass it along, draw a torso, do the same and then the feet.

What misshapen figures they produced. What horrors with mermaid tails, wings and trunks! But sometimes the things that shouldn't go together looked wonderful too. Sometimes, between them, they created something unexpectedly beautiful. The girls howled with laughter and Elaine couldn't stop smiling. Sometimes they could be so sweet.

Annie lived in a ramshackle house backing onto the canals, which Elaine found amusing because Annie had never shown the slightest inclination towards the countryside before and had seemed a London woman through and through; but Annie said that Elaine had always appeared that way too. And look at her now!

Yes, look at her now.

Annie made a lovely cup of tea and she was good with the children – Elaine decided she was a far superior mother figure to Elaine herself, for she was more patient and more interested in them – or at least, her voice sounded as though it was. When Elaine told her this, Annie laughed, said she only had to feign interest for a couple of hours every year or so – how hard could that be? – while Elaine had to do it every single day for the rest of her days.

'Thanks, Annie.' Elaine pretended to find it funny too.

The girls were happy though and Annie got on the floor and joined in with their gin rummy game. They had different rules, which created a row – they all asked Elaine to adjudicate –and they forgot to tell Annie about the missing four of spades.

Then they ate crumpets with Annie's home-made jam, which they agreed was delicious, and Elaine was pleased that neither mentioned how lumpy it was. Shirley put on her coy and simpering voice and asked Annie some, admittedly, quite sensible questions about the area.

'She's good, isn't she?' said Annie, charmed.

Barbara squinted and coughed and stared around the house, and Elaine couldn't help but fear for some of Annie's more precious ornaments. The teddy bears were right up Barbara's street. *I must check the bags before I go*. She would have liked to make a joke about Barbara's proclivities – if anyone would find it funny, she knew Annie would – but she didn't want to give her oldest daughter a reputation before she'd even started out on life. She'd grow out of it, wouldn't she? Like the eczema she used to get on the backs of her legs.

They sat in the garden and watched the boats go by, and the girls complained they were so slow, it was almost like they weren't moving at all. Annie said, *do you know the story of the tortoise and the hare?* The children did, and Annie smiled and said, 'I always wonder where the other animals fit in, you know, the ones who are neither fast nor slow.' And Elaine thought, *you always were the clever one, weren't you? Things like that just never occur to me.*

When Annie asked, 'So, did you manage to arrange to see *him*?' Elaine couldn't say 'shush' any more, because the girls were tree-climbing and out of hearing distance (even if their ears seemed to go on stalks at any sign of 'adult conversation').

'Tomorrow,' she admitted. 'That's the idea, anyway.'

If he even turns up.

'Excellent,' said Annie.

'Is it?' said Elaine. Annie shrugged. They smoked cigarettes and blew smoke at the sunset like they had fifteen years ago, waiting for the bombers to obliterate London.

The tranquillity didn't last long. Shirley caught her skirt in a branch and then wailed that she couldn't get down. They had to go and catch her. Barbara was watching the rescue, waiting in the high branches like a know-it-all owl.

'For heaven's sake, Barbara. Why did you let her go up so far?' Elaine muttered.

'It wasn't her fault,' Annie said, a curious expression on her face. 'How could she stop her?'

Elaine ignored her and got on with the job at hand. That's what she did. Other people could deal with the emotional side of things.

She would just make do. She collected a chair from Annie's kitchen, brought it outside, stood on it and reached skyward.

'Don't look down.'

Annie seemed very happy with George. She said she couldn't believe how lucky she'd got. She had always anticipated ending up with a grumpy old man, and look, she'd only gone and got herself a grumpy young man. She laughed loudly. In a lower voice, she said George would have loved children, but it hadn't happened so… Elaine stared; she thought she couldn't stand the guilt, but Annie didn't seem to feel guilty about it at all.

'He's not exactly James Cagney,' she said happily, 'but I like him!'

'And he does have a bit of Johnny Weissmuller about him,' lied Elaine.

Annie nodded contentedly. 'He does, doesn't he?'

There was spam pie for dinner. Elaine smiled to herself. What else would Annie cook?

They talked about the work they used to do for the government. They had signed the Official Secrets Act – although Elaine didn't think anyone would ever be interested – and sometimes it was nice to talk with someone who knew. Annie didn't know about the letter Elaine had cracked the code for at work – she had already left for the War Rooms by then – but that was okay.

'Boy, you were fast. The fastest typist in town,' Annie said.

'For all the good it did me.' Elaine remembered painfully how she hadn't been promoted and almost everyone else had.

'You haven't done too badly,' said Annie gently. 'Two fantastic daughters.'

'Uh-huh,' said Elaine, because she couldn't say anything else, not even to Annie. Annie was sympathetic and modern and all that was good, yet Elaine knew she wouldn't want to know about Elaine's struggles with being a mother – she just wouldn't wish to hear it.

And Annie had been in touch with all the girls – Annie had never *lost* touch with them, unlike Elaine. Felicity and Rupert had married and had a little girl who they reckoned was already, at two years and three months, an expert map-reader. Myra and her mother had moved to Basingstoke, where Myra was managing a shoe shop and her mother continued to knit. Mrs Dill had been reunited with Captain Dill, recipient of the Victoria Cross, and the children from Wales. Dolly and Joyce had opened a bed and breakfast in Southampton and Vera was still menacing visitors from a secret government location. Elaine listened to the stories of her old friends, but she felt no desire to see them again. She felt they would only be disappointed with her.

They tossed a coin and 'heads' – Shirley, who always said 'heads' – won, so it was Shirley wriggling next to her in the bed, kicking her knees and telling off wizards. Barbara was quiet as a criminal on the floor.

The next morning, the sun streaming through the window woke Elaine, but she couldn't move without waking the girls, so she lay as still as she could. She didn't want them up yet. They took away her space to contemplate. They didn't mean to, but that's what they did. It wasn't personal, Elaine thought, any child would be the same, it just was. She wished she could have explained that to Annie.

She counted the hours and minutes until the meeting time at twelve. She counted the minutes until she should get up. She heard Annie and George's low voices in the kitchen. Then she heard the front door click, which must have been them leaving for work. Not long after that, Shirley and Barbara roused themselves – within seconds of each other as usual –and jumped up full of restored beans.

There was a note on the kitchen table telling them to help themselves – Shirley wanted porridge, but Elaine didn't want to cook and scrub a pan, so they stuck with the bread and Annie's jam. That morning, the girls both mentioned how lumpy it was.

*

She told them it was time to meet Mummy's friend.

'We're meeting Annie?'

'No. Yes – Annie's friend.'

Palpitations, sweats, checking her hair.

'Shirley, can you not swing on my arm, please? Barbara, you didn't take anything from the house? No, of course you didn't. I wasn't saying that. What's that sticking out of your… oh, okay, that's fine. Do these shoes look all right? Do I look all right? A princess? Thank you, Shirley, I don't think so. A queen, that's too kind, that's too much. Shhhh, give me some space, let me think, run ahead – no, stay in sight, we're nearly there. You will behave, won't you, won't you? And by behave, I mean don't speak unless you're spoken to, use your please and thank yous and no…' Elaine finally paused for breath. 'Don't let me down. Are we clear? Try and be… normal. Please. Just for once. Just today.'

He was walking down the towpath, the same gait, the same camera – or maybe it wasn't? – slung from his shoulders. Still hanging on gamely to his hair, still smiling despite all the horrors. Still long eyelashes. Still – Lord, Elaine hated herself – the person she most wanted to see in the world.

'Pinky!'

The children looked up at her and she wished more than anything they weren't there. For goodness' sake, how did she not arrange a sitter for this? But she had no one, and she could not bring herself to beg Annie to take a day off from work just so she could see him properly.

'Who is Pinky?' Barbara's question.

'It's an old nickname. It's nothing.' She would have to tell him to stop that. The girls might tell Marty. *Unlikely, they don't small talk with Marty – but you never know with kids. They've a sixth sense for words that they shouldn't know.*

Their hands met – and she was transported back all those years to the George and that first night.

'Bobby,' she whispered.

Gather yourself, self-control, pull yourself together, remember where you are. Loose talk costs lives.

'Children, this is an old friend of Annie's…'

'I got fat,' she said ruefully. She remembered how uninhibited they had once been with each other. How they used to bathe together, in that en suite bathroom at the Savoy. She'd never been anywhere like it, before or since: bubbled water; he would massage her calves and then her thighs. Those towels. They probably spent more time together with their clothes off than with them on.

That was wartime, she told herself. Everything was heightened. Emotions. Love. You thought you might die the next day.

'You always look incredible to me,' he said. He said it like he meant it, but then he always did.

She was afraid of that.

Thank goodness, the children's good moods stayed in place. Which was more than you could say for their hairdos and cardigans. They were less argumentative, less whiny than usual. It was as though they knew where the end of the tether was for once and they didn't want to go there. They often were better in company, she'd noticed. More amenable.

The girls walked ahead of them until they came to a beautiful twist in the canal. For once, they were holding hands.

'Wait.' He pulled out his camera. Took the shot.

'I need something to remember you all by.'

She was standing next to him. Arms folded. Hair curled. Hesitant smile. Wondering if he'd want to take one of her. As usual, he didn't.

Shirley told him some jokes about penguins and polar bears, but mostly she had forgotten the punchlines. It was desperate and funny at the same time.

'Who are you again?' Barbara asked when they'd stopped laughing.

Bobby hesitated, laughed. 'Who am I?'

They mustn't tell Marty about him. He will go mad.

'He's Aunty Annie's friend, that's who,' Elaine said. She couldn't meet his eyes.

'We'll have the girls this evening,' said Annie. 'Won't we, George?'

George, who was reading his newspaper in his slippers – a sixty-year-old man in a twenty-five-year-old body – grunted his assent.

'We'll do some painting, right, girls?'

'Nudes!' shrieked Barbara, who had more interest in the human body than was seemly in a girl her age.

'I was thinking still-life,' said Annie, laughing. 'What do you think, Shirley?'

In those days Shirley was still in full-time people-pleasing mode. She folded her hands primly into her lap. 'I would like to draw your pretty face, Aunty Annie! Something to remember you by.'

Annie laughed. She nodded at Elaine and when the girls got up to take their plates to the sink, she whispered, 'You could probably do with some time alone with him.'

Elaine grasped Annie's lovely warm hands. 'Thank you,' she whispered.

CHAPTER FIFTY-FIVE

SPAIN

JUNE 2016, DAY ELEVEN

I am lying out on the sunbed. The Mediterranean sun is gleaming into my face and I feel so much better after having talked to Mum. If only we'd talked more all these years. I know that Matthew will always be the apple of her eye, but I feel fine with that. There are certainly downsides to being the apple of someone's eye too: I saw that the night she got drunk.

And so what if I'm not her apple, but a tangerine or a pear? That is okay too. I have freedom that the apple doesn't have. I know that now.

Derek is warming up the barbecue already. I am in such better temper, I almost feel affectionate towards him: in his dealing with Paul so firmly the other day, in his always being there, in his undercooking the meat.

I am going home in three days' time and I am already looking forward to the cool and the change of clothes. I am dreaming about covering up my arms and legs, of not smelling of oil, and getting going on some of my ideas.

Yesterday, when Aunty Barbara and I sat out, she told me a story.

She said, 'Did I tell you Mum never cried? She prided herself on it. Made of stone, she said.'

'I guessed that,' I said quietly.

Aunty Barbara paused. 'One time though, just before she died, she was sitting in her armchair, you know the one, holding that photo, the photo of me and your mum, and she was weeping, and she was saying, "I'm sorry," over and over again.'

There is a kerfuffle behind me. A dread pushes forward: *It's not Paul trying again, is it?* I spin my head back to see Mum and Aunty Barbara racing towards the front of the house, where Matthew is parking up, making tracks in the gravel. I didn't even know he'd gone out.

It's Harry, my boy, long and lean – my son – long shorts, his hair always bedhead, his smile the best smile in the world. He's embarrassed at being the centre of attention. He rubs his forehead with it. My child, my son.

I hug him. I am aware I am too much skin in my vest and shorts, and he pats me on the back like I'm an elderly great-aunt. He's awkward; then Mum grabs him and Aunty Barbara. Alyssia paddles over in her chair to the edge of the pool nearest us.

'Hello, cousin.'

'Hello, sailor.'

'What are you doing here?' I say, although I don't actually care. I just want to say *thank you, thank you.* I throw my arm back round his waist again. My boy! If I have done nothing else right in my life, at least I have sent this wonderful being out into the universe.

'Uncle Matthew paid for the flight.'

I look at my sweet brother, the family apple.

'I'll pay you back, Matthew.'

Matthew blushes. '*De nada.* It was Gisela's idea. You should all have come months ago.'

I feel infused with happiness and then, remembering, shriek, 'But what about Pushkin?'

'No worries, Ma. I arranged something with the neighbours. It's sorted.'

'You're a good boy!'

Harry is hastily stripping off his Metallica T-shirt. He can't get out of it quick enough. I remember the year he would only wear his all-in-one Spider-Man suit. Everywhere he went, he was in that suit: playschool, supermarket, playground. Nothing would get him out of it. No threats, no promises carried any sway. In the end, Paul and I just left him to it.

He has real muscles instead of those padded-suit ones now, and a smattering of blond chest hair. *How did this happen so fast? When did he grow up?*

And I'm glad he's an only child because it's stupid, but I don't think I could have ever loved another child as much as I love him.

'We getting in, then?'

And suddenly everyone is dropping their clothes to the ground – although Mum folds hers and then picks up Derek's and folds his before glamorously sashaying her way over to the pool.

'Mum?' says Harry, grinning at me.

'I didn't bring a swimsuit,' I apologise.

'You've got underwear on, haven't you?' Matthew says, matter of fact. 'What's the problem? We're all family here.'

Harry runs to the pool, then throws himself in with a screech, his body crunched into a clenched fist, a power salute. I watch him swim over to his cousin. His strokes are firm and strong – a tribute to many chilly mornings spent being shouted at by Mrs Woodward in the school pool. Made me proud to be his mother on the edge then and now.

Aunty Barbara takes to the steps, stately and determined as ever. Small and gangly, legs of a deer on land, but graceful, weightless, when floating. Those goggles fit in place like a tiara. Derek rearranges the barbecue tongs and then does a frightful bomb. Everyone cheers. The splashback he makes almost reaches the house.

I'm down to my bra and knickers and suddenly I don't care. Mum looks at me – she is surprised, and not altogether approving, there's that head-tilt again – but I won't let that annoy me, I won't. We stand next to each other, toes peeping over the side. I count loudly, 'One, two, three', and on 'two' she has grabbed my hand, and on 'three' we jump, me and my mum.

I'm in the pool! I'm down, down, down, cold, it's super-cold, and then I'm up, my bra popping all over the place, and I'm laughing with the exhilaration and so is Mum.

Matthew has come out from the kitchen. He has wrapped a bright white towel round his waist. I think how happy my brother looks. A man in his prime surveying his kingdom. He's beaming from ear to ear. Suddenly he says, 'Ah, sod it,' and then he strips off down to his trunks and gets in the pool. He takes the route Barbara decorously took, the metal ladder, but he does so more quickly, almost like he's sliding down a pole. It's the first time in for him this week. As I watch him, he keeps his head held high, his salt and pepper bouffant out at all times, and I remember what Nick told me about Robert Capa and water. And it makes me laugh. Matthew invents a catching game with the beach ball and for a moment nothing and no one outside this cool blue rectangle exists. As my mum says delightedly, 'We could be absolutely anywhere.'

We carry on splashing playfully. I ride on the dolphin, then Mum takes over Queen Alyssia's throne and Derek and I do our best at capsizing her. Then it's my turn and they do the same to me. Getting underneath the seat and making me go upside down, inside out, legs in the water. I used to do handstands, and I do one now. Aunty Barbara is the only one who sees my sloppy attempt, but always the encourager, she whoops and claps for me.

I throw the beach ball at Harry and he heads it, a perfect arch onto the sunlounger.

We are in Spain and it's lovely, the people I love most are here, and the water buffets me and caresses me and holds me better than any man. Everything is going to be all right. The birds sing it and I know it. What a privilege this is, to be alive at this exact moment in time and in this beautiful place. And how lucky are we, to have our peace and to have our freedom. And I think about all the people who went before us and I splash harder in loving gratitude.

CHAPTER FIFTY-SIX

BASILDON, JANUARY–MARCH 1954

Vietnam. The French. The Americans. The domino theory. The communists. The tunnels. Elaine delivered the children to school, warned them to drink their milk. *Yes, I know it's warm, Barbara, but it's hardly the worst thing in the world.* Then she took her usual chair in the library and read everything she could get her mitts on about Vietnam.

By pure chance, the beardy librarian was interested in Vietnam too. He brought over magazines for her, plumped them down triumphantly, the way Bettie Page used to bring in dead birds.

'This is *Life* magazine. Their coverage is really good. Best in the world, probably.'

'I know it.' Elaine smiled at his plain, earnest face. You didn't get many men like him in Essex.

'Not many people care about the Vietnamese people,' he said admiringly. 'I suppose for most people, it seems too far away – alien even. I love Asian cultures though.'

'Exactly,' Elaine said. She tried not to think about the Japanese officers who made the lives and deaths of Geoff and Derek and William so damn miserable. War was war and people were people and who knew what you'd do if you'd been brainwashed too? Plus, thanks to the maps in *Life* magazine, she knew Japan and Vietnam were as close as, say, Britain and Turkey.

The beardy librarian was staring at her expectantly. His breath smelled of cabbage.

'Poor people,' she said. '*There but for the grace of God go I*,' she added, remembering this, a favourite phrase of Mrs Perry that she thought might be quite suitable.

'You're not wrong.' He put his hand over hers. 'Don't be afraid to ask me anything,' he said. 'About this or... anything at all.'

Why would she be interested in an almost war the other side of the world?

There was a reason, a good reason.

Marty had said it, just casually, on his way out the front door one morning. He had yolk on his tie, a detail that would be forever linked with Vietnam in her head. 'Oh, Robert Capa is over in Saigon now. They were talking about it at work.'

This was how much she knew: she had thought Saigon was in China at first. She must have confused it with Shanghai. And then she thought since it was French, maybe it was in North Africa – she got it confused with Algeria. Then, after she consulted a map, she was more confused because hadn't there just been a war in quite nearby Korea? How did that one end? She never did find out, but however it ended, it didn't seem to have put anyone off having a go again. They were communists, she learned, like the Russians. She knew about Russian communists from Bobby; she knew about Stalin, Lenin and even Karl Marx. She knew they were friends with the UK during the war but only because of the war and deep down, they hated each other. It looked like the hate was popping up again. But what were Stalin and Lenin and even Karl Marx doing in Asia? Then she realised they were all still fighting.

Domino theory was about dominos – not when you play by joining up numbers but when you line them upright and then watch them tumble down, one after another. Or another way, like when you get chicken pox – like Alan did when he was about six – and you actually watch the spots come out bit by bit.

Cambodia was Vietnam's neighbour and there was also a lot of talk about a Laos that wasn't an insect. Ho Chi Minh was a bad joke and Hanoi sounded like a new dance or hairstyle. 'I'll have a Hanoi, please.' Or, 'He was doing the Hanoi all last night. No wonder he's got a sore back!'

Elaine didn't know how bad it was at first. No one did. Or perhaps some people did, but it's easy to dismiss other people's fears as hysterical or fearful, isn't it? Pessimists are easily silenced, optimists less so. It's the nature of the beast.

She waited for the photos to be published with his credit underneath them. *They'll come soon*, she knew it. The humanity in the people, all the people, whether they were the Cong (*was that really what they were called?*) or the other ones, would be unearthed by Bobby. It didn't matter if they were the good ones or the bad ones, the right ones or the wrong ones; he would find their compassion, he would find their suffering. The photos would be cabled to magazine offices around the world. Journalists, editors, management teams would say, 'Well, I'll be blowed, he's done it again…' There'd be no amateurs allowed in the darkrooms this time. No mistakes. The prints would endure. His photo stories would change the course of history. If anyone's could, his would.

Viet-nam. Viet-nam. A word she didn't know six weeks ago was now on her teeth when she woke up, and in her hair when she went to bed. She said it with a soft B, *biet* – and with a long A, *naam*. Others said it differently. She chose the same way as the beardy librarian because it sprang off his lips. Confidence is the thing.

'Is it dangerous out there, in *Biet-naam*?' she asked Marty a few weeks later, so casually, so disinterestedly, she might as well have been telling him that Barbara had won a writing prize at school.

Marty's eyes were very large behind his new glasses. He looked more like a beetle than ever.

'No more dangerous than anywhere else at war,' he said, but he knew what she was really asking, for in a tighter voice he added, 'Robert Capa goes where the danger is. That's what they pay him all that money for, after all.'

When they first moved to Pitsea, Elaine had taken a part-time job as a secretary in Worthing Estate Agents. Worthing Senior and Junior had interviewed her. Her typing speed had bowled them over. 'She's not even looking at her hands!' they kept saying to each other. They timed her, just for the hell of it.

Stanley Worthing was an ambitious young man; he'd recently taken over the business from his dad, who'd had to retire suddenly for health reasons. At the interview, both chatted companionably over each other until Worthing Senior sighed, 'My son has a very different vision of the future to mine.'

'I think that's often the case with parents and children,' Elaine had said gently and they both beamed at her as though she'd chosen their side.

Worthing Junior told her that he knew the future of the estate agency and could she guess what it was?

Elaine could not guess.

'Photos,' he said loudly.

As soon as he said that, she thought of Bobby. What would he say about that? His beloved art form, the way to make people *understand*, used to sell houses in Pitsea?

He wouldn't mind. He wasn't a snob.

'I'll photograph the houses and then more people will be able to see them. People in London. Manchester. Scotland.'

'Scotland!' repeated his father as though that was the most ludicrous thing.

'Won't that be really expensive?' Elaine asked quietly.

He shrugged. 'Not as expensive as not selling houses.'

She had only done a week in the office when Worthing Senior died, which was both sad and terribly awkward. She had only met him once, after all, but Worthing Junior insisted that he wanted her to come to the funeral. She went and supported him throughout the day. Very quickly that seemed to cement a bond between them; more than employer and employee, they became great friends.

Stanley Worthing Junior was very kind to her, always checking that her chair was comfortable, the lights weren't too bright, that she had time off for her trips to the dentist, or that she had enough work. Although there were five years between them, and she wouldn't have thought it was possible, over the next few months she got that weird yet familiar feeling, a gulp in the throat, that he was falling a bit in love with her.

She arrived in the morning and he would call out, 'Kettle's on!', like they were living together and at home. He insisted on making her tea even though she protested, it should be the other way round. He asked shy questions about Marty sometimes and one time – although he later apologised – when she said she had put on weight and should walk more, he answered: 'You're perfect just the way you are.'

She decided to leave Worthing Estate Agents before things grew 'complicated'. The hours were brilliant and the tasks were not onerous, but she was a married woman and so their proximity and intimacy were unfair. He was a nice single man and he needed to get himself a nice single woman. It was a sad decision because the girls were needing her less and less at home and she felt she needed to be out more rather than less. Nevertheless, Elaine felt she might try for another clerical role, perhaps at a bank or at a local solicitor's office? It had been good to get her brain back, and her typing fingers. She wasn't as useless as she told herself she was.

Marty laughed when she told him the reason. 'Sometimes you really think you're it, don't you, Elaine?'

'I don't… I'm just… I don't want to upset anyone.'

'If you don't want to work, you don't have to, you know. You don't need to make daft excuses.'

CHAPTER FIFTY-SEVEN

BASILDON, MAY 1954

It was only a few weeks after Elaine left Worthing Estate Agents when she found the story upstairs in his study. Marty shouldn't really have had the study. It was meant to be Shirley's room, but the girls – who argued all day long – bizarrely preferred to sleep in the same room together, so step by step, Marty had taken over Shirley's room.

Hard to know if he wanted her to see the magazines or not. She went up there to dust and vacuum, but not every day. There they were, in a pile on his desk, on top of *How to Win Friends and Influence People* by Dale Carnegie. It was several copies of *Life* and yesterday's *Sun* – a newspaper he professed to hate. Not everything Marty did was deliberate, was it? He might just have forgotten he left them there. But he wasn't usually so careless, was he?

First casualty of a journalist working for an American press agency. *Of course Robert Capa always had to be the first at everything.*

Camera in one hand – he had wandered off the beaten track. Landed on a mine. Thrown up in the air and then *down, down, down.*

The cover page was him, laughing with his cigar up, hair full of Brylcreem, face full of life and love. Passion and drama. Her Bobby. Gone.

He wanted to be a peace photographer, you stupid warmongering bastards.

*

Elaine took the magazine to her bedroom and got into bed with it. Even standing was too difficult at that moment. She felt suddenly aware of her own stolid body and its horrible human frailty. She felt undeniably heavy and old. Pulling back the grey sheets, lying on the mattress, where she and Marty lay in their compartments of silence, she imagined there was a mine beneath her that would go off in two minutes. *Boom*, a silent bomb putting her out of her misery. She could join her Bobby at last in death. The love of her life was now dead. She had let him go. She had sent him to another war.

Everything was null and void.

She read the article again and again. Next to the main obituary, there were lists. Lists were the type of journalism he and Marty used to sneer at. Lists of all the wars and the not-quite-wars he'd covered. She remembered Annie talking about him and laughing about Tarzan. There were his photos and lists of his most famous pictures. There were some of her favourites: girl milking cow, puppies, American pilots – none of his favourites. There was the man dying in the Spanish field. Paragraphs were devoted to the 'mess-up', as they called it, in the darkroom, and his bravery at the Normandy landings. There was his advice, 'Get closer,' to the photography students he met. 'The pictures are there, and you just take them.' And 'For a war correspondent to miss an invasion is like refusing a date with Lana Turner.' Did he say that? Did he? There was a eulogy written by his younger brother, Cornell. There was a column on the many women he had loved. *Many?* Gerda Taro. Martha Gellhorn. *Martha? How did she get in there?* There was a large photo of the gorgeous Ingrid Bergman.

They'd missed her out. They'd neglected to put her in. She, Elaine Parker, the one he had loved in London. His darling Pinky. Nowhere to be seen.

Tears prickled her eyes. No. She wouldn't be sad, she would be angry. She had been engaged to him for goodness' sake. Why would they miss her out? Just because she hadn't done anything of note? What the hell was that about?

Scornfully, she threw the magazine down. They didn't capture him, they couldn't even begin to capture him with their foolish, easy lists. There was also a 'Guide to Robert Capa' – like he was a medieval street. Fools and dolts. 'It's not enough to have talent, you also have to be Hungarian.' What did they know of his dreams, his fears? The way he loved her hot-pink thighs and how she danced. The way he stood up for her and sat down for her.

Poor Bobby. She found she couldn't be angry, and she couldn't be sad. She felt swamped in a kind of underground of despair. It seemed she was stuck in a dreadful truth. *This is it. This is bloody it.*

She took out her teeth and put them in the glass on the bedside table. Old water in the bottom quarter had turned it cloudy. She needed to change it but couldn't bring herself to get up. She hated Marty or the girls to see her without her teeth, but right then she didn't care who saw. If she hadn't given up her job at Worthing's, she might have had something to get up for, but she had, and she didn't. Dark in and out of sleep, like getting lost in a maze: the entombment of those people in the Blitz. All those innocents. Mummy and the car that knocked her down. Whipped her hand right out of hers. Frozen shock. How different things would have turned out if her mum had been there alongside her all along. Maybe she would have had the courage to stay with him then. Maybe it wouldn't have even needed courage.

Shirley and Barbara got themselves home from school. She heard them arguing over the best way to slice the bread, then the best way to grill it. They didn't know she was home. She called out to them, and after several shouts, they heard. She told them she wasn't well. 'Don't come up.'

But Shirley came up anyway, a plate balanced wibbly wobbly on one hand. The bread was now black.

Barbara stood to attention just behind her, holding a kitchen knife that looked far too big, obscenely big in her hands, and a pot of Annie's lumpy strawberry jam. She stayed in the doorway while Shirley walked in. If Mummy had told them not to come up, she wasn't keen on coming up.

'What's the matter, Mummy?' persisted Shirley.

'Turn away.'

This they did obediently. They didn't want to see her as much as – maybe more than – she didn't want to be seen. Elaine shovelled her falsies into her mouth, shoved at them, then made a face at her daughters, even though the teeth hadn't settled down and they twitched uncomfortably on her gums like a pillow that was too big for its case. They stared at her uncertainly. She tried to smile reassuringly but they still seemed stiff and frightened. *I am old and finished*, she told herself. *What does it matter now?*

They eyed the magazine still on the carpet where she'd thrown it. She followed their gazes and saw Bobby's big beautiful face smiling up at them again. He was alive when that photo was taken. And now he was dead. *Deep breaths. Breathe.*

'Isn't that…' Shirley, who had quite the gift for names and faces, said hesitantly, 'Annie's friend?'

Barbara said nothing, but Elaine knew from the straightness of her back, the fold of her arms, that she thought it was too. She just wasn't giving anything away.

'Don't be silly, girls,' she said.

Barbara relaxed. Shirley moved over to the dressing table, silent predator, and had her fingers in Elaine's pot of moisturiser before Elaine could say, 'Don't you have any homework?'

'No.' Shirley now had Oil of Olay on the end of her nose. 'Can I use your talc?'

It made no difference whatever Elaine said. Shirley had already upended the tin and a little white dust cloud appeared around the mirror and the girls' eyes peered out of little cartoon ghost faces.

'Muuum,' said Barbara, coughing. 'Look what Shirley did!'

'Just go downstairs,' said Elaine, exhausted by the inane interactions already. Did they have to be so needy? It was like having two little shadows following her everywhere, suffocating her at every turn.

'And take that down with you.' She pointed at Bobby's face on the floor. 'Go now.'

And they did. Shirley stormed off, but sometimes with Shirley, it was as though she just liked storming. Barbara hovered at the door. 'Hope you feel better soon, Mummy.'

'Don't fuss, Barbara.' She could be very kind, that girl. 'Thank you.'

Teeth out. More sleep. Later, she saw that a lipstick was missing from her dressing table, a very pale one from Yves St Laurent that she had bought with her last wages from Worthing's. *Never mind, for hadn't Bobby always preferred the bright red?*

Later still, she found the magazine on the floor next to the toilet. That would be Barbara, always had her nose in a book, even when she was doing you-know-what. They had decorated Robert Capa with felt-tip: he had been blessed with a thick, Stalin-like moustache, rectangular glasses, and – the funniest thing – they'd topped his head with a jewelled crown. They didn't normally do things like that. They weren't demolishers. They must have sensed something about this particular magazine, this particular cover, she supposed.

They'd made him into a king, a funny one, but a king nevertheless.

Her first reaction was that it was sacrilegious and heinous. They had desecrated him, mocked him, vandalised him, and she was set to punish them, but something twanged at her. Bobby would have laughed at this. He had managed to laugh when Clive wrecked his career-best photos. He laughed when he found out about those ridiculous stolen gloves. He laughed when poor old Justin had come to woo her back.

He would say, 'I think I need a beard, no?' Or 'Where are my earrings?'

*

Marty gave Elaine four days, then five. Then, on the sixth, after she had still failed to rise for any substantial amount of time, he said it was about time she got up, she had to bloody get on with it 'like everyone else has to'. He stripped the itchy blanket from over her and pulled the marital sheets from under her, formed them into a fat Dick Whittington bundle and marched downstairs with them, tsking all the way. She heard him say 'wallowing' to the children, three, four times, and Barbara, who was probably at the kitchen table, crayoning in houses or sea monsters, asked, 'What's wallowing?' and he snapped back, 'What your mother's doing right now.'

She would have ignored him, but it was Sunday, so she did have to get up anyway. She dressed in her old office clothes, before pulling on the coat that Clive had stolen for her so many years before, when she was just about to start work for the government. It had grown shabby and the stains down the front were almost admirable in their persistence, but somehow it still managed to have that air of quality that she had once loved so much about it. It was a coat that had earned her many compliments. But really, who cared about all that any more?

She remembered the posters on the wall of her office in the government building, the place she had been so happy, the clattering of the typewriter keys.

Marty looked up and Elaine could see the relief on his face, quickly replaced by fear.

'What are you doing now?'

'Going to see Alan.'

She was already keenly anticipating the walk to the station. And the liquorice she would buy and the book she would read – *Falling for the Veterinary Surgeon* – on the train.

The children cuddled her uncertainly round her waist and she patted them back. She had made them anxious and they didn't deserve that, her forgotten girls. She smoothed Barbara's cloud of hair and tweaked Shirley's pretty nose. Over their heads, Marty was also looking at her uncertainly. He squinted, then moved his lips, like he was about to say something but couldn't. He didn't know what she was up to, and he didn't know how to ask.

'I'll be back the same time as usual,' she told him.

'Good,' he said. He sounded so nervous.

'Good,' she repeated.

'I'm upset too, you know, Elaine. He was my friend.'

'Yes.' Elaine went over to Marty. She kissed his damp cheek and the children squealed with pleasure at this unfamiliar display of affection.

Marty caught her hand in his. His long fingers lay on hers. 'Are we all right?'

'We will be, darling,' she told him. 'I promise.'

CHAPTER FIFTY-EIGHT

LONDON, AUGUST 2016

Nothing has changed on the outside. But everything has changed on the inside. I feel excited all of a sudden. Everything looks like a possibility. My family are not going to be who I want them to be, and I'm not the daughter/sister/niece/aunty/mother they probably would like me to be either. And that's okay. I'm over it now. Life is for living, not for lamenting other people's choices.

I have surprisingly vivid dreams about lizards and car crashes, karaoke tunes and Nick's wrists and his feet in Roman sandals. I don't know what Sophie the counsellor would have made of me.

Harry is working in a fast-food restaurant for the summer. He has burns up both his arms from the chicken fryer, and he has decided to become a vegetarian. Secretly, I'm pleased, but I hide this because if he knows I'm pleased, he will probably switch back. That is the way of the teenager *and* the adult. Anyway, we get along fine, especially now he's learned how to use the dishwasher and where the cat food is kept.

My photography portfolio is looking none too shabby now: I've got the plants in the Alhambra, I've got great shots of Pushkin rolling around like a pre-Raphaelite model, I've got the glories of the Olympic-sized pool. I've got some gorgeous pictures of Alyssia too. She's told me that she never thought she looked like that, and all her school friends say she is *guapa*. It's a start. I haven't quite settled into myself yet – am I a portrait photographer, or do I want to take pictures for magazines and art shows? But I have the confidence to know that will come. I just have to keep on keeping on.

I feel like mercury is running through me again. Pictures and shutters, new stories to be told. And old ones to be remembered.

Harry is helping me design my website and business cards. When I say helping, I mean I am paying him. These are not mates' rates; offspring rates are exorbitant.

I survey the screen ruefully. 'Robert Capa would be spinning in his grave if he saw this.'

'I don't think he would,' Harry says quietly, click-clicking and changing font size and colours. Apparently Comic Sans is out, unless I want to look like a noob. I don't know what a noob is, but I can guess looking like one is not a good look. I consider everything I knew about Robert Capa the man, my grandmother's lover. Not a nasty man, not a cruel man. 'Maybe not.'

It took me ages to come up with a name. It had to be memorable, it had to be relevant, it had to be appealing, but also it had to be *me*. I knew it was a big ask. I doubted I would find anything right. But then I woke up with something in the middle of the night, wrote it in my phone and was still delighted with it the next morning. It's silly, but it felt like it landed on me from above. It felt like it was parachuted in.

Pinky's Photography Service.

In honour of my overlooked nana, the forgotten Elaine Parker.

The tagline is: 'The pictures are there. I just take them.'

Even Harry said he liked it.

Pushkin has graciously forgiven me for my absence, although he punished me at first; he now walks the length of my body on the bed and rubs his face on mine in the morning. I don't mind if it's after 6 a.m., but he's under very strict instructions never to try anything earlier yet he still does.

The humiliation of being knocked back in front of my entire family is like water off a duck's back to Paul. He just doesn't give a damn. It's like it never happened – *we* never happened. He's started seeing someone else, a young woman from Poland. When I say 'seeing', I mean he isn't quite seeing her yet, but it's all going terrifically well. Which is nice. I suspect he had her lined up long before he visited me in Spain.

I am nervous about contacting Nick Linfield. I treated him shoddily, after all. Matthew promises he'll let me know if he hears from him, but he calls every week and never mentions him. I guess the documentary hasn't yet got off the ground. Nick had mentioned there were funding questions, but he never made it seem a big deal. Mum calls me and says, 'Just get in touch with him, for goodness' sake,' and 'I want to know if I'm going to be a TV celebrity.'

'And if you are?'

'I'll do the celebrity circuit for a couple of years: *Bake Off, Strictly Come Dancing...*'

So, she'll come back to England for those (priorities, Jen!).

It takes several more weeks before I can bring myself to get in touch with Nick. I am busy setting up Pinky's, packing up the last of Paul's boxes (*well, not exactly packing, more like tossing*). But I don't think it is busyness exactly that holds me back.

Half of me doesn't want to speak to Nick Linfield because I'm afraid I will be rejected. Paul might be able to seamlessly glide over getting dumped, I couldn't. I wouldn't. My skin is far thinner now. My emotions nearer the surface. Is it any surprise? They say it's better to have loved and lost than never to have loved at all, but I'm not sure. Can I have the evidence for that, please?

On the other hand, part of me feels instinctively that if I get in touch with him it is going to be the start of something bigger, something serious, maybe even something life-changing, and I need just a little more time to ready myself for that.

I ask Harry his opinion. Shrugging, he says, 'Dad's moved on. Why shouldn't you?'

From the mouths of babes.

'Hello, Nick,' I text finally. It is the second week of August.

> *I hope you're well. I'd love to hear the latest on the Robert Capa documentary – and I've got some explaining to do. When you're next in England, do you fancy meeting up sometime?*

There. I send it before I've time to change my mind.

His text comes back within minutes.

> *I'm back in England now. Yes, of course you can explain as much as you like and I'll tell you all the Robert Capa news.*

We go for tapas, naturally. Nick is wearing a pale blue shirt, which looks good with his tan and his eyes, and he rolls up his sleeves, which looks good, full stop. After we order the tiny plates of everything – which seems to me a good philosophy of life – Nick tells me the good news and the bad news: the film *is* still being made but the producers made him cut most of the Elaine section.

'You're just about still in it,' he says, 'laughing, in your cute hat.'

'Oh no!' I say, but actually I am glad I have not been entirely erased.

Matthew did not make the final cut, Nick says, which I think is a shame but kind of amusing. It's mostly Mum, apparently, leafing through the pictures and narrating.

Mum and Derek are coming back to England in October, apparently. It is an idea that fills me with both delight and terror. I decide I'll save this news until then. It'll put her in a good mood, which hopefully will set the tone for the whole trip.

Barbara is briefly in the film too, swimming in her strange wetsuit, and Alyssia is in the background, floating. But between us all, we are in the film for just under five minutes out of a total of 110 minutes.

It seems our part in the film has turned us into a small plate at the tapas restaurant; we are not the main course that we had all envisaged.

Nick says he is annoyed about the decision and I can see that he's being genuine. He explains, 'They wanted to focus on the more famous women that Robert Capa knew.'

So instead of Nana Elaine, the film focuses on Gerda Taro, it focuses on Ingrid Bergman, and also – this *is a bit left-field,* I think – it focuses on Hemingway's wife, Martha Gellhorn.

'Really, he had a thing with her too?'

Nick rolls his eyes. 'Well, *I* don't believe it, but they seem to want to think it, so…'

He says he kept finding out more and more about Elaine Parker. 'She wasn't *just* a typist,' he tells me. 'Did you know she was nominated for an OBE?'

I didn't know. 'She didn't get it?'

'None of the women did, but…' he says, 'she must have done something pretty incredible even to be nominated. But that aside, she *was* a remarkable woman – looking after her brothers and then the baby.'

'It's a shame we couldn't tell her story.'

He wrinkles up his nose. 'There may have been opportunities for her to tell it. I think maybe she chose not to. Perhaps she didn't like the limelight. So possibly, it's for the best.'

He continues to say what a brilliant woman Nana Elaine must have been and I nod, because yes, *finally*, I can see that now. She was part of that silent army of people, mostly women and girls, carrying on and coping during that terrible time. Taking care of each other, the little ones, the elderly ones, the vulnerable ones. But where is the kudos in that? We clink our glasses together: 'To Elaine Parker, forgotten hero.' As his glass clinks against mine, I feel a shiver run through me. Something is happening here, I know it, and then I blush; he'd better not be reading my mind.

Nick and I don't only talk about my nana. We eat, drink and we order more *patatas bravas*, the bravest of all the potatoes, and more garlic mushrooms and fried squid, and when we've stopped talking about the film, I take a deep breath and make my explanation and my sincere apologies for standing him up that day, which he accepts most graciously.

And then I tell him that Paul and I did not get back together and could we… perhaps… give it a whirl. Yes, I say 'whirl', and 'gosh, sorry'. This is ridiculous and mortifying. I am the timidest potato of all time.

He doesn't leave me to agonise over my announcement for too long. He says yes, he would like us to spend time together to… *umm, see how we get on?* But he admits he is nervous, and *would it be just a rebound thing for me?* I tell him no, absolutely not.

We kiss across the tiny plates, and the waitress, a smooth-skinned nineteen-year-old, says, 'Oh bless!' at the sight of our burgeoning decrepit love. We carry on kissing in the street, and in his car – a glorious old banger, as promised – and we also make arrangements to meet the following evening.

And the photograph? That beautiful photo of two little cherubs looking across the water in 1950, the one my mum gave to Matthew? The one in the dirty gold frame.

Three months after my visit to Spain, Matthew calls to tell me that it has gone missing. He's searched high and low but has absolutely no idea where it is. I can't work it out. Neither can he. Even all-knowing

Gisela – fresh and enlightened from her latest retreat – can't explain it. And she is very annoyed with him for losing it.

'So, you're in the downward doghouse?'

'Yes, she's not giving me the morning salutations any more.'

'La la la. Too much information.'

Later that day, though, Matthew calls back. Mystery solved. He is laughing so much, he can hardly get the words out. 'You're not going to believe this, Jen,' he says, 'but Alyssia is sure she saw Aunty Barbara slip it into her handbag…'

There is another special photograph now. On my bedside table, next to an adorable drawing of Harry as a baby, I have a print in a solid silver frame that Nick gave me on my forty-fifth birthday. It's that picture of a man from behind and a young woman laughing and pulling at the strings of his hospital robe. Hemmingway's buttocks and Elaine 'Pinky' Parker as photographed by her boyfriend, Robert Capa. I love it.

My lovely nana, remembered.

A LETTER FROM LIZZIE

Hello,

I hope you have enjoyed *The Forgotten Girls*. A huge, huge thank you for getting this far. *The Forgotten Girls* has been an absolute labour of love for me from start to finish.

If you want to keep up to date with my latest releases, just sign up at the following link. I can promise that your email address will never be shared and you can unsubscribe at any time.

www.bookouture.com/lizzie-page

I first became aware of Robert Capa when I found the *Life Book of Photographs* on a shelf at home as a small child. I became quite obsessed. I loved learning about the world through those photographs. It opened my eyes to different cultures and terrible conflicts. For years, I wanted to be a war correspondent. The film *The Killing Fields* only made me more certain.

This ambition didn't take into account several things: I had no eye for photography, no idea about technical things; worse, I had no interest in technical things. I was also very shy. Too shy to ask people to pose for me, too embarrassed to take people's photos without them knowing. And mostly, I've not much liked the idea of getting in dangerous situations. At all. I've always been a scaredy-cat but as I've got older, I've got worse.

At university, I studied politics and international studies, and – like Paul – I did have a photo taken by Robert Capa as a poster in my room, next to one of Che Guevara. I still loved and romanticised the lives of the war correspondents. They did and have done an incredible job. But it wasn't for me.

When more recently, I found out Robert Capa had a relationship with an English woman in London during the war years, I was thrilled. I knew straight away that this was a story I had to explore!

As some of you may know, my favourite thing is to write about the women behind the scenes, the lesser-known ones. *The War Nurses*, *Daughters of War*, *When I Was Yours* were all inspired by the experiences of real-life women and, I hope, are a celebration of them. For a long time, women have been written out of history. This is my effort to restore them to their rightful place. The title *The Forgotten Girls* could quite well be applied to all my novels because this is what I like to do: Remember those – usually women – who have been forgotten.

I chose a dual narrative in *The Forgotten Girls* for several reasons. It's the connections and legacies that interest me, rather than one moment in time. I love exploring how things are passed on. How we are affected by our grandparents' history. I wanted to explore a complicated, but I think fairly typical, modern British family. For many of us, families are our own personal war zones! It might not be life and death that's at stake, but it often is our sense of self.

Why did I choose to set the modern part mostly in Spain? I find the British ex-pat experience in Spain interesting. How does it feel to move away, and how does it feel to those left behind? The potential for drama is greater when we are forced together and since my World War Two characters were gallivanting and disappearing off all over the place, it was quite nice to keep my modern-day characters trapped in one place, in a villa with a pool, where I could keep my eye on them. ☺

It's always fabulous to hear from my readers – please feel free to get in touch directly on my Facebook page, or through Twitter, Goodreads or my website. If you have a moment, and if you enjoyed

The Forgotten Girls, a review would be very much appreciated. I'd dearly love to hear what you thought, and positive reviews help to get our stories out to more people.

I'm currently working on my fifth book with Bookouture. Twenty thousand young Jewish women left Austria and Germany in the 1930s and came to England to work as domestic servants, and I am exploring one such story. Look out for more drama, more family conflicts, more awesome bravery against the backdrop of the coming war, in a story where women will, once again, take centre stage.

Thank you so much for your time,
Lizzie Page

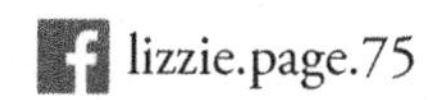

AUTHOR'S NOTE

Robert Capa's book *Slightly Out of Focus* beautifully demonstrates the spirit of the man. It is an account of his time in London and is full of vim, vigour and *joie de vivre*. Robert Capa is widely known to have been extraordinarily brave and devoted to his photography; less well-known is the fact that he was also wickedly funny.

I have taken great liberties with the character of Elaine Parker. She was not working-class, nor – so far as I know – did she have two complex brothers. There are some photographs of Elaine – unsurprisingly, she was gorgeous! She and Justin, who in real life was no spinach, were already married when she and Robert Capa met. If you want to know more about this love affair, do read Robert Capa's book.

I was very fortunate to see the eleven surviving photographs from Robert Capa's Normandy landings at the Imperial War Museum, London, in their 2019 exhibition. The rest were spoiled, but they were not spoiled by Elaine's brother.

It seems that Elaine did go off with Robert Capa's close friend – who in his book is called Chuck – and she married him.

The section about Myra Hess playing lunchtime concerts at the National Gallery is true. I couldn't resist mentioning these events that pulled Londoners together during their darkest days. The brilliant book *Wartime Britain* by Juliet Gardiner was once again invaluable on this.

As for the George and its stalwart landlady, Bessie Larholt, this was based on my great-aunt. She came from Poland in the 1910s, married a wealthy man who was a gambler, and yes, she kept a super autograph book. She was terrific. I couldn't leave her out!

ACKNOWLEDGEMENTS

All the thank yous to my editor, Kathryn Taussig, my agent Therese Coen at Hardman and Swainson and my publishers Bookouture. I struck gold with them – I'm a very lucky writer.

To all the Book Bloggers and book readers – we are nothing without you.

To my friends, you're all brilliant. Thank you.

To my family, you guys certainly keep me grounded. ☺

Made in the USA
Monee, IL
29 August 2020